Where Hope Begins

Center Point
Large Print

Also by Catherine West and available from
Center Point Large Print:

The Memory of You

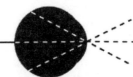

Where Hope Begins

Catherine West

CENTER POINT LARGE PRINT
THORNDIKE, MAINE

ISBN: 978-1-68324-848-4

Library of Congress Cataloging-in-Publication Data

Names: West, Catherine (Catherine J.), author.
Title: Where hope begins / Catherine West.
Description: Center Point Large Print edition. | Thorndike, Maine : Center Point Large Print, 2018.
Identifiers: LCCN 2018012816 | ISBN 9781683248484 (hardcover : alk. paper)
Subjects: LCSH: Married people—Fiction. | Adultery—Fiction. | Large print books. | GSAFD: Christian fiction. | Love stories.
Classification: LCC PR9680.B43 W479 2018b | DDC 813/.6—dc23
LC record available at https://lccn.loc.gov/2018012816

For my brave friends who have been through
the fire and come out the other side.
Not unscathed, not unchanged, but refined,
stronger, and even more beautiful.
You are so, so loved.

For I am confident of this very thing, that
He who began a good work in you will
perfect it until the day of Christ Jesus.
Philippians 1:6

Chapter 1

"The heart will break, but broken live on."
—LORD BYRON

My husband is leaving me.

The thought, the reality, presses against my throat as I stand outside and take in the view from the back patio of our home. Beyond the copse of Scotch pines that stand sentry at the boundary of the perfectly manicured lush green lawn, a patchwork of fields stretches north. Frost-covered fields that will soon be white with snow. Clean. Pure. Unblemished.

Beyond the horizon line I imagine another world. A world far from the Boston brownstones and skyscrapers less than an hour away. A world of warmth and sunshine, golden sands and sparkling oceans and second chances.

I imagine standing with one foot here, on this hard, cold, and unforgiving ground, the other hovering over an invisible marker that separates winter's edge and what lies beyond. And I wonder . . .

The back door slams. His boots clomp down the wooden steps, hit the stone deck, and thud into silence a few feet behind me.

I cannot bring myself to turn around.

7

Tears warm my cold cheeks and I raise a trembling hand to swipe them away. Breathe. In and out. Forced effort. A sudden wind whips up and makes me shiver.

"Savannah . . ." His sigh is heavy, but not quite reluctant. "I'm going now."

I nod and slowly turn to face the truth written on his face.

Our bedroom was barren last night when I arrived home from dinner with friends. Only my clothes remain. Naked hangers swing in silent accusation. He took most of his things then and hauled the remainder out the front door moments ago. His hands are empty.

I inhale again and find my voice. "Did you leave the keys?"

"The keys?" He sounds surprised. I can't for the life of me imagine why.

"For the house." I shiver again. "You won't need them."

"I should have one for emergencies." He clears his throat and his eyes narrow. "Don't you think?"

Emergencies.

Yes. Of course.

Sirens wailing, screaming through the silence.

Anxious faces peering, stricken, speechless.

Bathroom tile cold against my cheek. Warm liquid pooling around my wrists.

Those kinds of emergencies.

I lock eyes with this man, this man I have known

8

for twenty-four years, lived with for twenty, and promised to love forever. This man who gripped my hand while I cursed him through contractions. Three times. This man I have laughed and cried with, shared silly jokes with, and given all of myself to. This man who stood beside me, trembling and broken, as we watched a tiny casket being lowered into the ground.

This man I don't know at all anymore.

"Do what you want, Kevin." You always do.

"I think it's best. I won't . . ." He looks away. His normally vibrant blue eyes seem oddly dull and his jaw quivers just a bit. "Look, Savannah—"

"Don't." I hold up a hand. The wind picks up speed and rustles through his dark hair.

At forty-two, Kevin is aging well. Not aging at all, actually. Runs for miles, eats what he wants, and doesn't put on a pound. I have just turned forty and find it hard to look in the mirror. Lines that were not there yesterday appear today. Gray hairs grow overnight. Weight does not come off as easily as it used to.

"I might go away." The thought slips out and startles me.

"What? Where?" He cannot contain his astonishment. His eyes shift, uneasy under my stare, and I know what he's thinking. I have not taken a trip alone in years. Have not been alone in years. How will I survive?

"I don't know where." I grip my elbows and

9

watch a few flakes of early snow descend from the sky. They rest on Kevin's head, as if a silent blessing from above. I give no such blessing. At this moment I abhor him.

"Let me know." He sounds tired. Looks tired. I don't know where he's been the past month, although I can imagine. No. That's not entirely true. I do know. He has not been in our bed. My bed. Even when he was there, I know now his mind was elsewhere.

"I'll tell Zoe." I fiddle with the zipper of my green down jacket and survey the lonely patio. Empty gray clay urns and neglected flower baskets testify to my horticultural failures. Snow bounces on the black tarp covering the pool. "We're supposed to get two inches tonight. Crazy, huh?"

"You want to discuss the weather?" He's incredulous, perplexed. "Zoe isn't talking to me." Now he's annoyed.

"Isn't she?" What a shocker.

Our daughter, our eldest, but not our firstborn, is stalwart and loyal to a fault. She hates him now, but I hope for both their sakes she will forgive him. Eventually.

I don't know if I will do the same.

I stiffen as I stare at him, stuffing down the overwhelming need to end this conversation. This miserable moment. Instead, it feels freeze-framed. Forever cemented in memory—this one defining moment in my life when I realize all I've done, everything I've poured myself into, has been for naught.

Memories meld together in a mosaic of children's activities, women's luncheons, and boring business dinners. Car pools and car washes and carnivals to raise money for whatever charity the school or church picked that year. A life now divided into three compartments: Zoe in college, Adam away at school, and me here. Where I've always been. With my other half about to step into his shiny black Mercedes-Benz and drive away.

"I'll text you then," I offer. "If you insist on knowing where I am."

"You don't text." One side of his mouth lifts in a half smile that fades too soon. I can't remember the last time I saw my husband really smile.

"Maybe I'll learn." I step aside to give him room. He won't go back through the house. Not with Adam there. And I don't want him to. "Well." I need to let him go. "Mustn't keep her waiting." She has apparently been waiting for this day for quite some time. And I never had a clue.

Kevin runs a hand down his face, lifts his shoulders under the heavy cashmere coat he wears. A soft plaid scarf hangs around his neck. It's new. I notice he no longer wears his wedding band. Three weeks ago, when I last saw him, he still did.

"I'll need to get in touch, Savannah. There'll be papers to sign at some point."

"Christmas." Visions of a decorated tree and

stockings strung along the mantel skip across my mind. "What will we do for Christmas? Thanksgiving?" Why am I asking these things?

Kevin shrugs again. "Adam has his ski trip over Thanksgiving. Christmas . . . I don't know." His phone vibrates from a pocket in his coat. "They're not little kids anymore."

No. They are not. But they are still kids.

Our kids. And he has broken their hearts.

Not to mention mine.

"Good-bye, Kevin." It's all I can say now. As much as I'd like to tell him how I really feel about what he's done, as many times as I've thought of telling him where to go, today the words won't come. Besides, I am already there.

In hell.

It is not big enough for us both.

And some days I still believe I deserve this agonizing pain even more than he does.

Adam sits at the kitchen table, his sixteen-year-old lanky frame huddled over a half-eaten bowl of Cheerios. I lock the back door and try not to flinch at the sound of Kevin's expensive car engine revving. Tires peel off in a soul-shattering screech.

He can't get away fast enough.

Adam lifts the end of his spoon and lets it clatter against the bowl.

Over and over again, until I want to snap at him to stop. But I don't.

I shrug out of my coat, hang it up, and notice the array of shoes along the rack by the door has diminished in size. I kick off my loafers and forget where I put my slippers, so I walk across cold travertine tiles and return to the sink. Kevin arrived as I was doing the pile of dishes I'd ignored all week.

The water has gone cold.

I grab the plug, yank it upward, and watch reluctant soapy suds swirl toward the eager drain. As I pick up a glass to load in the dishwasher, it slips, shattering against the white ceramic sink.

"Why do you need a sink that looks like a bathtub?" My mother's first question once her inspection of our newly built home was complete.

"It's called a farmhouse sink, Mom. I like them. Plenty of room for large pots."

Who knew ten years ago, when we built our dream home, that this day would come? Who knew my husband would turn his attentions elsewhere? That he would decide it was no longer worth the effort to keep a marriage together after tragedy.

That he would declare *we* were no longer worth the effort.

If someone had told me then what I know now, I would have called them a raving lunatic.

My fingers curl around the splintered shards too

tightly. A stinging sensation shoots up my arm as red drops drip and streak the smooth white stone, and my sink is no longer sacred.

A word I seldom use escapes before I can think.

"Mom. Here." Adam is beside me with a wad of paper towels. He watches through worried eyes as I squeeze them around my fingers.

"Just a scrape. I'll be fine." Someday perhaps this will be true. But today it is a lie.

"Dad is such a jerk."

"Adam." I blink wetness. Tears still come too quick, too often. I suppose there are other things my son could have said. Other words he wanted to use. I think I've thought them all.

He lifts a brow, and suddenly he is not the little boy I remember. He is a man ready to go to war, whichever one calls first. Ready to take on the world and win. But I don't want him to. I want him to remain a child, to keep him here at home, safe, protected. Yet I know I can't. I have failed both my children in this regard.

Failed all of them.

I pour coffee and sit, clutching my hand, willing my heart to slow down. Adam slumps into the chair opposite me and flicks his finger against a couple of crisp green bills taking up space on the table.

"Two hundred bucks." He snorts. "That's what he left me. I told him I didn't want his stupid money, but he left it." His cheeks blotch and his eyes fill.

14

"I'm sorry." I reach across the table and he slips his hand in mine and we sit, silent.

"I don't have to go back to school." He sets his jaw, so like his father. Pulls back his hand and rakes long fingers through his dark hair. Another mannerism I recognize.

"Of course you do." I hope my smile is brave. "You'll be home for Christmas. And I . . . I thought I might take a trip." The idea still surprises me. I'll have to find a fill-in for my Meals on Wheels days. And let the library know I won't be around to help out. Maybe this isn't such a good idea. But I don't think I can bear many more nights alone in this house.

"Yeah?" Adam tips his chair back and grins. "Going to Aunt Peg's?"

The suggestion sends a shudder through me and we laugh. I cannot dream up a greater punishment than a visit to my horsey sister's Kentucky ranch, alive with cats and dogs and rabid barnyard animals and her four unruly children.

"That wasn't what I had in mind, no."

"She called. Aunt Peg." He picks up a crinkled note and winds it around his finger. "While you were outside with Dad. And then Uncle Paul called. And then Grandma."

We're going down the line. They all watching, waiting, holding their breath. I tuck my hair behind my ears and smile. "Well, you've been busy."

"Wanna know what Aunt Peg said?" His blue eyes are too gleeful and I shake my head.

"Something you shouldn't be repeating, I'm sure." My sister uses minimal discretion when it comes to airing her true feelings over what Kevin has done. While I appreciate her support, I should probably ask her to tone it down a tad around the kids.

But Zoe has said it all already. With such venom that she frightens me. I don't want her to hate Kevin. I don't want to hate Kevin. And I don't, always. Just most of the time.

Adam . . . I worry about Adam. He seems to be sitting on the fence, shell-shocked, wondering when and where the next grenade will fall. He insisted on being here this weekend. Thought it would be easier on me, I suppose.

But not on him. I doubt he thought of that. I should have been firm. I told Zoe to stay away; I knew she would make a scene. I should have said the same to Adam. Stay at school where you don't have to witness the unraveling of a marriage that was meant to last. Where you don't have to watch the life you knew and counted on crumble into broken pieces that cannot be put back together.

But I haven't played this game before. I don't know the rules.

"Uncle Paul said to tell you he loves you. You don't have to call him back, but you can if you want."

My older brother does not mince words, but he is kind. Always kind.

When I called to tell him the news two months ago, I sat through unnerving silence on the other end for quite some time. And then my Baptist preacher brother uttered sentiments he certainly was not taught in seminary. Words I'm sure he had not said since high school. I miss Paul. Oregon is too far.

It's funny how we all went in different directions. Paul out west, me on the East Coast, and Peg, as usual, somewhere in between. My retired parents spend most months in Florida.

Tomorrow, when I put Adam on the bus and he heads back to school in upstate New York, for the first time in longer than I can remember, I will be alone.

Pathetically, unwittingly, yet utterly alone.

I have absolutely no idea what to do with that.

Chapter 2

"In three words I can sum up everything
I've learned about life: it goes on."
—ROBERT FROST

I wake slowly Sunday morning, and the world is somehow still spinning.

In the kitchen, armed with coffee, I sit at the table and open my laptop. I didn't have the energy last night. But now I'm ready to give my furious feelings freedom. Blogging was something I kind of fell into years ago, after Shelby died. One of my many counselors suggested journaling. Writing down all the emotions I couldn't yet voice. A friend suggested taking it a step further and starting a blog. "You could really help people, Savannah. You know, deal with their grief."

Because I'm not the only parent who has lost a child. She didn't say it. But back then, that's how it felt. Like I was the only one. Little did I know, the blog I began for cathartic reasons would turn into a popular community of soul survivors. None of whom know my real name.

"Mornin', Mom." Adam is already dressed, khakis and a white button-down, clean and pressed. His hair is damp and combed off his face. It still makes me grin to see the kid who would only wear jeans and a red T-shirt to school until he was about ten dressed like a grown-up.

I twist the rings on my left hand and try on a smile. Part of me will be relieved when he's back at school. Putting on a brave face has worn me down. "How'd you sleep?" I won't ask if he's packed, ready to go. He will be. He is as thorough and organized as his father.

I hate this. Sending him away to school was not my idea, yet he seems happy enough there and he's doing well. Still. Good-byes are always the worst. And this weekend I've had my fill.

"I slept okay. You didn't, huh?" He shoots me a grin.

"Is it that obvious?" I pull my robe tight and wonder what I must look like after playing tug-of-war with the bedcovers all night. My hair feels like forest creatures have made their home in it. My head hurts. And I ache like I've run a marathon. Not that I have, ever, but I imagine a body the day after might feel this way.

"Want to come to church?" He forages the fridge.

"I'll make eggs." I push my chair back, but he shakes his head.

"I can do it." He grabs the carton and heads for the cooktop on the island. His search for the frying pan is noisy. "So, church?"

Laughter gets stuck in my throat. "Um . . . you

19

see me, right?" Church is not on my list of things to do this morning. Hasn't been on my list of things to do for quite some time.

We've always been involved, both Kevin and me. Raised in Christian homes, we inherited our faith and passed it along nicely. We took the kids to Sunday school, youth group, attended Bible studies . . . I took my relationship with God very seriously for a lot of years. I was what they call a "woman of faith" once. And now?

Now I'm just broken.

We wanted a miracle. Asked for one. Maybe even expected one. And when it didn't happen, when God didn't come through, my faith faltered.

Badly.

And yes, I know how shallow that sounds.

After the service, I hover behind a potted palm in one corner of the modern sanctuary's sprawling foyer and pretend to study the bulletin. There is nothing worse than standing in a crowded room feeling completely alone. I remember now why I haven't been to church in a while.

People cast cautious glances my way. A few smile and nod as they pass, saying things like, "So nice to see you, Savannah," but I know what they're saying behind their hands. The widened eyes, the whispers, the wondering. Bad news travels fast along the prayer chain.

As I watch the people around me, people I used to spend time with, women I shared life with, studied Scripture and prayed with, I realize I can't be here anymore. I don't belong. What am I supposed to do, sign up for the singles group and hang out with twenty-year-olds? I'm not widowed or a senior. Far as I know, our church does not have a life group for divorcées.

Kevin has taken this from me too.

The ability to connect with other like-minded individuals. I have crossed the line, been shoved over it really, yet somehow I feel *I* am at fault.

"Don't hide back here." Beth finds me, slips her arm through mine, and gives me a reassuring smile. I roll my eyes and squeeze my best friend's hand. When we talked last night, I told her I wouldn't be here today.

"Adam wanted to come. Wanted me to come." The explanation isn't necessary. I'm glad I came. At least, I was ten minutes ago. But I wonder how red my eyes are.

There are too many questions God hasn't answered. Too many prayers he's simply ignored. It's not that I don't believe anymore. I do. But there's too much I don't understand. And Kevin? Who knows what Kevin believes now. The faith he once had seemed to slip out the door days after Shelby's death.

But I tried to hold on. Tried to have faith, tried to pretend one day we'd be normal again.

It didn't happen, and I don't know what to do with this anger.

And nobody here knows what to do with me.

"Come for supper tonight," Beth insists. "After you drop Adam off."

"Thanks." My breathing is shaky. The last thing I want to do is fall apart. Not here. Not with everyone watching. Beth pulls me into a hug, and I struggle to compose myself.

"Sorry to interrupt . . . Savannah, sweetie . . ."

We pull back at the familiar voice. Tracey Fitzhugh stands before us, sympathy stamped across her flawless face. I wipe my eyes. Beth grabs my hand and hangs on.

"I'm so sorry," Tracey purrs. "You know . . . when I heard . . . well." She pats down platinum-blond hair and pinches her lips. "I've been praying for you and Kevin. I think you'll come through this just fine." Her smile is dazzling, disarming.

"Do you? Did God tell you that, Tracey?" I clear my throat and toss her a smile of my own. We were better friends when the kids were small. But I've seen and heard too much, and now it seems I'm on the receiving end of Tracey's pious platitudes.

She's unfazed. "I know you're angry, Savannah. Heaven knows, I'd be livid. Actually, I'd be mortified." She titters. "But Brad would never . . . Anyway. You'll work it out. You're going to counseling, right?"

22

"Counseling?" We've been in and out of counseling for the past ten years. Christian counseling. Psychiatric counseling. Family and couples counseling. I can quote books verbatim on how to put a family back together after loss, how to grieve, how to pray for your husband. I must have missed the one on how to keep him at home.

"Adam is looking for you." Beth pulls me away before I open my mouth and say something horrible, shooting Tracey a scathing look as we pass. I want to laugh but I can't. The numbness floods through me again. Novocain. That's exactly what this feels like. The stuff the dentist injects into your mouth before a procedure.

My entire being is filled with it.

❧❧❧

"You should go to the lake house."

"Uh-huh." I curl my toes under the thick duvet in my now-too-big king-size bed and listen to my mother's voice. She's been talking awhile. Since I came home from Beth's an hour ago, discovered four more voice mails from her, and finally called her back.

"I've been thinking about that. About getting away." Going to the lake house had not occurred to me. I'm not sure I can go there.

Our family summer home on Lake Garfield in the Berkshires is where Kevin and I met so many years ago. It'll be cold up there this time of year. But warm inside. Mom has had the house modernized, renovated, and redecorated more times than I can count over the years they've owned it. The sprawling white-clapboard home still maintains its original historic outward appearance, but the interior resembles something out of *Better Homes & Gardens* or *Architectural Digest.*

"I can have the house opened and all ready for you, just say the word," Mom says.

Sure, Mom. Can you get rid of the memories before I get there?

"Savannah? Are you still there?"

"Yes. Just thinking."

She's helpless down there in Florida. If she were here, my house would be spotless, my fridge filled with food, and my faith in humanity somehow restored. My mother is not always tactful, but she possesses the remarkable talent of knowing exactly how to make me feel better, sometimes without words. "Well." She sighs. "I would say come here, but, you know . . ."

"I know." I can't stop a smile. If I'm forced to face my father's blustering berating of Kevin once more, I'll probably lose it completely.

"Ellie, don't forget to ask her!" Dad's booming voice is loud enough for me to hear even though I know he's probably stretched out in his favorite chair in front of the television and Mom is no doubt on the other side of the great room with its

24

long glass windows, perched in the window seat where she can watch the stars.

My mother sighs again and I feel her frustration. "Your father wants to know if you've talked to Walter Kline yet."

"You have rights, Savannah!" Dad yells. "Don't give that belly-crawling snake an inch. Call Walter!"

"Sug-ah, hush!" I imagine her turning toward him with a frown, one perfectly pink manicured finger pressed to her lips.

My parents are quintessential polar opposites. Indisputable proof that completely contradictory personalities do indeed attract. Together they are the perfect blend of southern charm and Bostonian brawn.

My father did not come from money. Michael McCleary is third-generation Irish American and portentously proud of it. He put himself through college by earning scholarships and working three jobs between semesters, plus construction all summer.

Mother had quite a different upbringing. Her parents were bred from well-known Georgia families. Plantation owners originally, slave owners most likely—a fact that horrifies my children—but my grandparents never talked about that unpleasant part of the past.

When my father appeared on the scene, they were not so impressed. Grandmother softened first. Granddaddy Hale accepted Daddy over time, partly because of his Harvard education, which hinted he was going places, but mostly because of his gumption and take-no-prisoners attitude. Daddy proved him right. When I was five, my father threw caution to the wind and formed his own insurance company. Our family has lacked for nothing since.

I will call Walter, the man of many hats: my father's best friend, my godfather, and our family's lawyer.

But not yet.

"Sweetheart, Zoe phoned." Mom is talking again. "She's terribly upset."

"I know she is." Zoe clung to the misguided belief that her father and I would work things out until two months ago, when he declared he wanted a separation. Followed by the more recent announcement that he was moving out. Permanently.

My daughter texts me every hour on the hour. I don't attempt to return her texts. I email and message her on Facebook, and this seems to suffice. One of these days I will get my thumbs coordinated enough to text. But then there's that noxious autocorrect that turns seemingly innocent statements into steamy suggestions. Not worth it, really.

"Zoe would be far better equipped to handle crises if she'd gone to Harvard!" Daddy yells again. Laughter tickles my throat. The feeling is almost foreign. I can't remember when I last really laughed about anything.

Zoe's decision to accept Princeton's offer over Harvard's was a mortal blow to my father, or so he says. I think he is secretly amused. He likes women who assert their independence. Of course, he blames Kevin for Zoe's desertion. I can't help wondering if my father and Kevin would have a better relationship if Kevin hadn't been a Princeton grad. Not that it matters now.

"Savannah, darling? What do you think about going north? Shall I call and make arrangements?"

I pull my fingers through my tangle of too-long curls and decide. "Actually, Mom, the lake house sounds wonderful. Is Tuesday too soon?"

We make plans and hang up. I go downstairs for some water. It's ten o'clock, but I can't bring myself to return to that empty bed. The big house is strangely silent. The antique grandfather clock ticks out the hours in the hall. Its gong sounds a bit like a cow in labor now, and it's about thirty minutes slow. Kevin promised to have it fixed but he never did. Kevin promised to do a lot of things.

I don't like being alone in this house.

It's not that I'm afraid, really. Well, maybe a little. It's just that it's so . . . quiet.

Perhaps I should get a dog. We never had pets. Kevin is allergic. There was that time when Zoe was six and brought home a puppy she found wandering in the park. But the puppy was claimed the next day, and Zoe's little heart was broken.

In the living room the pictures on the mantel pull me toward them with a force I can never ignore. The kids' school portraits at various ages—Zoe all seriousness, with dark hair and startlingly blue eyes, Adam with similar coloring to his sister, but with Kevin's hard jaw and nose, and a hint of humor in his smile.

And Shelby . . . she looked like me. Blond curls and dimples and a goofy grin I could never get enough of. Dust sits along the top of her fourth-grade photograph. The last one we have of her. I take a tissue from the pocket of my bathrobe, wipe it clean, and put the picture back in place.

The built-in bookcases on the far side of the room beckon. I check the shelves for any gaps, thinking Kevin might have taken some of his favorites. But all the old books we've collected over the years sit in place. We've amassed quite a collection. Scouring surrounding towns' book-shops for antiquated copies of well-loved stories was a shared hobby.

My eyes smart a little as I glance at the long black cross on the hardcover spine of Chaucer's *Canterbury Tales*. I probably paid more than I should have for the 1934 first edition, signed by the illustrator, but it was Kevin's fortieth birthday and I wanted to surprise him. Kevin loves Chaucer. We have books by Dickens, the Brontë sisters, poems by Emily Dickinson and John Donne, Whitman and Emerson. Some books are leather-bound, others have well-worn hard covers, all with delicate pages and illustrations to delight the eye. Next to the fraying copy of *Winnie-the-Pooh* that we read to the kids over and over again should sit our treasured copy of *Alice's Adventures in Wonderland*. It went missing shortly after Shelby died. We turned the house upside down looking. I thought perhaps Adam or Zoe had stashed it away someplace, but we never did find it.

The carefully color-coordinated room with its expensive furnishings, beige tones, and black baby grand that nobody plays in the alcove by the large bay window sags with loneliness tonight. I never imagined it would be this way. It wasn't supposed to be this way.

Kevin found the land. He came home late one night in August, years ago. The kids were racing around the kitchen of our overpopulated bungalow. The window air-conditioning unit had up and quit that morning, and the lazy stand-up fan only blew hot air across the room. I was desperate to get dinner on the table.

"Shelby, stop singing and help me out here!" At nine, she's old enough to corral Zoe and Adam. The past few days, though, she's been obsessed

with the latest boy band, and I'm about to lose my last nerve.

Adam, four and all boy, has captured a stinkbug, brought it inside, and is chasing Zoe around the house with it. Seven-year-old Zoe is not fond of bugs, and her shrieks let the entire neighborhood know it.

Kevin bangs through the back door, his face split in a handsome grin that even after almost ten years of marriage still makes my stomach flip.

"Welcome to bedlam, Mr. Barrington." I burn my hand on the lid of the pot and mutter a word that makes him smile wider. He ignores the shrieking, dodges flying legs, and sneaks up behind me.

"Hey, gorgeous." His low growl makes me laugh. He smells like summer. Wrapped in his strong arms, it's easy to forget the chaos. Easy to forget we have three children who need to be fed, bathed, and put to bed. He lifts my hair off my sweaty neck and plants a kiss. There. And there. That spot . . . Oh, he is wicked.

"Kevin." I sigh and lean against him. "The kids. Dinner—"

"Can wait. Actually . . ." He spins me around, his eyes shining with secrets. "We'll go out. Who wants to go out to eat?"

All three of them immediately stop the rampage and jump around us instead.

"McDonald's!"

"Chuck E. Cheese!"

"Denny's!"

I catch his eye and raise a brow. Words aren't necessary at this point. He knows what he's done.

But he just grins. "We can eat whatever you made tomorrow. Cover it. I'll clean up when we get back"—he snakes a hand around my head and pulls me in for a long kiss—"from looking at the plot of land we're going to build our new home on."

That last year we had together, all five of us, was magical.

Three months after moving into this home we planned to raise our family in, everything changed. In one split second, when I wasn't looking, Shelby was taken from us.

I'm not sure she ever saw the oncoming car that swerved across the road to avoid a cat and sent her and her pink pedal bike flying through the air.

I didn't.

But I should have.

I shut down the thoughts before they suck me in.

It's not something you ever get over, losing a child. But it is something you have to learn to live with.

Years later, I still don't know how.

Chapter 3

"Every man has his secret sorrows which
the world knows not; and oftentimes we
call a man cold when he is only sad."
—HENRY WADSWORTH LONGFELLOW

Today will be about survival.

I scan my to-do list on Monday morning. I've already made calls, arranged for others to take up the slack during my absence. I apologized for not knowing when I'll return. I'm going to miss taking meals to the seniors who have become friends over the years. I will also miss the quiet sanctuary of the library, where I sorted and stacked and sought refuge surrounded by stories of other worlds, other lives. Spending my days doing things for other people helps me feel less useless.

After we lost Shelby, I did anything I could to get out of the house until the kids came home from school. Pilates, yoga, tennis, volunteering at church and school. Anything that would put me to work, keep me busy. These days, when I return home at the end of a long day, the silence unsettles me. Will it be like this the rest of my life?

Getting away now feels necessary. For my sanity, if nothing else.

I take the highway exit and head for the entrance to Stop & Shop. Beth's kids are going to come in and feed Adam's fish and water the plants while I'm gone. I want to make sure there's enough fish food, and I'll get a few groceries so I don't have to stop before I reach the Berkshires tomorrow.

I brake for the car in front of me while I make a mental list of things I need. The car moves forward, and subconsciously I see it's Kevin's car. But Kevin wouldn't be shopping on a Monday morning. He'd be in the city, at work. I suck in a breath and look closer. There's a woman behind the wheel. Not Kevin's car. But it is.

The Princeton decal Zoe proudly placed there her first weekend home tells me it is.

Awesome.

My heart thunders as I debate my next move. Ramming the back of the spotless black Mercedes that is only two years old is a tempting option, but I don't have time to deal with the ramifications of that impulsive urge. The sensible thing to do would be to back up and find someplace else to shop.

Since when have I been sensible?

My stomach churns as I pull into a parking space a row behind her.

Her name is Alison. Kramer. Alison the home-wrecker Kramer. I've met her on several occasions. She and Kevin were business colleagues at my father's company. They were both let go shortly after news of the affair broke.

Kevin has a new position with another insurance company in Boston, and Alison . . . apparently spends her days driving my husband's car.

Next thing I know, I'm trailing her into the store. I grab a cart and follow at a distance. She's not as stunning as I remember her being. But she's tall. And thin. And ten years younger than me. Silky dark hair hangs to the middle of her back. Of course she's wearing yoga pants. Skinny women who can pull that off make me even more aware of the extra pounds I've put on. Although at last glance, the bathroom scale said stress has shaved off several of them. One good thing has come from this fiasco.

Alison is not a fast shopper. She ponders, compares labels. Reaches for healthy options, checks her iPhone every few seconds. She's probably got a list on there. I'm more of a "grab and go and get out" kind of consumer and she's boring me. Two months ago, had I been in this position, I might have marched right up to her and slapped her hard across the face. I still want to but don't have the energy. How pathetic is this? I'm stalking my husband's lover. In Stop & Shop. I have stooped to new lows.

What was I planning to do, accost her? Demand she take her hands off my husband and return him to his rightful place immediately? The truth is, he was gone long before she came along.

I'm not doing this.

I spin my cart around, find the fish food and the few other items I need, and hightail it out of there.

≫≪

The cursor on the laptop screen blinks as I ponder how best to answer the outpouring of irate responses on my blog after my last missive describing my new state of abandonment. The things these women are saying about Kevin—well, not that they know it's Kevin. I've never used our real names in all the years I've been writing, and tonight I'm grateful for that. There is venom and an almost unhinged hatred here, flat-out man-bashing.

An uncomfortable knot tightens my stomach. Perhaps I shouldn't have let it get this far. This isn't what I intended when I first started the blog. Back then we consoled each other, shared stories of lost loved ones, and I found the outlet provided some relief. But this . . . this I don't like. I sigh and click away from the site. I need more time to think.

The doorbell rings as I'm lugging my suitcase down the stairs before I go to bed. I want to get an early start in the morning. The clock in the hall says it's around nine fifteen, which means it's closer to ten. My pulse picks up as the doorbell chimes echo through the house a second time. I can't imagine who's out there at this hour. Unless Beth forgot to grab the extra key I put out for her this afternoon. This is why I need a dog.

Peeking through the curtains out the sidelight window, I exhale. Disarm the security system. Open the door and stand there, a bit out of breath and more than a little wary.

"Kevin. It's kind of late." And you scared the crap out of me.

He stands on the front porch, staring at me, snow in his hair. The white stuff is falling in a frenetic dance around the streetlights at the bottom of our winding drive. I hope I'll be able to leave tomorrow.

"I didn't check the time." He's in casual mode, jeans and sneakers and his favorite Boston Red Sox sweatshirt under an unzipped leather jacket. He looks me up and down, taking in the shabby sweater I'm wearing over a pair of gray sweat-pants. "Can I come in? It's cold out here."

I cross my arms, move aside, and he enters the warm house, stamps his feet on the mat, and nails me with an anguished expression I don't understand. His normally neat hair is windblown and dark shadows underline his eyes. If he hasn't been sleeping well, I can't say I'm surprised. Or sorry.

"Adam says you're going to the lake house. Tomorrow?" He shoves his hands in his pockets and rocks backward.

"Leaving first thing." I indicate the suitcase that sits beside him and bite back a "Duh." "Weather permitting."

"And you weren't going to tell me?"

"I said I'd text you."

Ripples run across his forehead. "Is that supposed to be funny?"

"What do you want, Kevin?" I don't have time to stand here and argue with him. Actually, I do. I'm just not in the mood.

"I'd like to know where you're going to be," he says in a quiet voice that is slightly unnerving. "Just because we're not together doesn't mean I don't need to know where—"

"Oh, it doesn't?" I shake my head and move toward the hallway on the other side of the stairs. "I think that's exactly what it means. You moved out. You want a divorce. You don't get to know what I do and don't do on a daily basis anymore."

"That's not how it works."

"It's not?" I turn to face him and tear trembling fingers through my hair. He's unbelievable. "Well, clearly I don't know how it works. They don't have a how-to guide for this one. On second thought, I think they do. *Divorce for Dummies*. Maybe you can get me a copy for Christmas."

"God, Savannah."

"God? You want to bring him into this now? It's a little late, don't you think?" My chest is so tight I can't stand to look at him.

He follows me down the hall, stalks across the spacious kitchen, gets a glass from the cupboard, and fills it at the tap. Stands with his back to me as he drains the glass and sets it in the sink.

"Why are you here, Kevin?" I shouldn't have let him in.

He makes a measured turn and sighs. "I wanted to ask if you . . . will you tell Zoe I'd really like to hear from her? Ask her to call me?"

He looks bereft, and I suddenly want to hug him. No idea where that came from. "I can ask her, but I can't promise she will."

"Okay." He nods, strolls along the counter, and picks up a prescription bottle. Glances at it, then at me. His mouth turns downward. A familiar fear fills his eyes. "You're taking meds again?"

He needs to go, needs to stop tormenting me with his presence. "Dr. Clarke thought it would be a good idea. As a preventative measure. He thought that finding out my husband has been having an affair and wants to divorce me might send me sailing toward another nervous break-down."

Kevin swears again, puts the small orange bottle back where he found it, and takes a step toward me. But that's it. One step. It's not enough, yet in the same breath it is too much.

"Did you get the snow tires put on the Escalade?"

"I forgot." The luxury SUV probably doesn't

need winter tires. But Kevin has always insisted we change tires seasonally on every car we've ever owned.

"Are they in the garage?" He's already taking off his jacket.

"No, I hauled them out into the garden. Thought they'd make cool lawn ornaments. Picked up some gnomes too. Look, you don't have to—"

"Savannah, give it a rest. For once, just . . . stop. Please." He sends me a despairing look and yanks open the back door to the garage.

"Knock yourself out," I mutter. The walls close in and I flounder for things to do. Put the kettle on. Sort through unpaid bills. Make sure my cell phone, laptop, and iPad are charged. Make a feeble attempt at texting Zoe.

Yur father heree. Be in a pan in thee . . .

I give up. How is anybody supposed to type with their thumbs? It's unnatural. I erase the message before I succumb to childishness, manage to text that I'll call her before I leave tomorrow instead, and hit Send. I think it actually goes. I'll talk to her about calling Kevin when we speak. Maybe. About five seconds later my phone buzzes with a

Cool. Love you.

It's the little victories that count. So I smile.

An hour later Kevin stomps back into the kitchen, disheveled, a dirt smear on his face. He's breathing like he just ran the Boston Marathon. Which he does. Every year. A wicked part of me

39

wants to ask if I need to go make sure he really tightened the lug nuts. Remorse pricks. Kevin may be an adulterer, but he's not a killer.

"What's so funny?" He dries his hands after washing them, staring at me through cool eyes.

Guess that giggle snuck out of me unawares. "Nothing. Thanks for doing that." I manage a smile and indicate the kettle. "Want tea? Water's still hot."

"No." He reaches for his coat, pauses, his brows arching downward in a perplexed frown. "Were you . . . at Stop & Shop this morning?"

Shoot. She saw me. "I was." No point in lying.

Kevin pulls on his jacket and sighs. "Alison thinks you're stalking her."

"For crying out loud, Kevin! It's a grocery store. I was not . . ." I widen my eyes at the sight of his grin. He actually thinks this is amusing. I should tell him where to take his warped sense of humor and what to do with it when he gets there. But that grin . . .

An unwanted tug pulls my stomach inward. I inhale and fight the feeling. "Are we done here, because I'd like to get some sleep tonight. At least try to."

He gets serious and clears his throat a couple of times. "Can I run upstairs? I forgot something the other day."

My husband is asking permission to go upstairs. This is new. And sad.

Terribly, tragically sad.

I shrug and let him go.

This has been the strangest day and I'm so ready for it to end. I wait by the front door and he jogs back down a few minutes later, a wooden box under one arm. It's about the size of a large jewelry box and looks old but well made. Mahogany maybe. I don't recognize it.

"Running off with the family fortune, Kev?" It's a joke, but his look tells me it's a crass one. Still, I want to know what's in that box. "Seriously. What is that?"

For a minute I think he's going to storm past me, slam the door in my face. Then he shrugs, holds out the box, and flips the lid.

Pictures of Shelby scream through the silence.

There are colorful, childish drawings of houses and horses and happy families. Father's Day cards, birthday cards, and report cards. And the delicate silver cross we picked out together and gave her the day she was baptized.

My breath hitches and the images blur.

I . . . can't . . .

The room starts to spin.

Ten years disintegrate in ten seconds and we're standing in a stark hospital room, holding our daughter's hand, watching life slip away from her. Absolutely powerless to do a thing about it. Parents are supposed to protect their children. Not watch them die.

I shut the lid and push the box back toward him. Our eyes meet. I can almost hear our hearts pounding together in steady staccato. And somehow we connect in a way that hasn't happened in months, maybe years.

Kevin's eyes glisten. "You know how they said we should have a memory box . . ." The words choke him. "Something to keep things in, things that were important . . ." He bites his lower lip and swallows whatever he was about to say next. "I shouldn't have shown you. You're upset."

"It's okay." I wipe tears and try to smile. But there is nothing to smile about in this moment. Nothing remotely pleasant in uncovering yet another layer to the man you thought you knew everything about. "You never cease to amaze me, Kevin." My words sound cold. Like the icy wind that blows around the house this evening. Bitter as the lemon I dunked in my tea earlier. And I have to say what I've been thinking all day. "I don't want her here when I'm gone. Alison. Not in our house. My house."

I've startled him. Stunned seems more like it. He narrows his eyes and slowly lets out his breath. "I wouldn't do that."

"No? Well, I don't know what you would or wouldn't do anymore."

"Can we not do this?"

The exhaustion he wears like a second skin tells me he's had enough. Enough of me. Entering this house is like entering a war zone, and he's tired of dodging bullets. I'm tired of firing them, but I can't come up with another line of defense. And I have plenty of ammunition left.

"I guess it's getting old, huh?" I twist the rings on my left hand and wonder why I still wear them. Maybe I should slide them off now, throw them at him, wave the white flag in final surrender. Somehow I think that's exactly what he wants. So I refuse.

He's composed himself again, but he wraps a hand around my wrist. "Please call me or email me when you get there. Okay?"

Tears trickle out despite my best efforts to make them stay. I don't want to call him. I don't want to email him. I don't want to think he still cares. I don't want him to care. Knowing that he might makes it even more difficult to let him go.

It's like we're standing graveside again under a darkening sky as huge drops start to splatter the ground and bounce off the gleaming black flower-covered casket.

Tonight I am grieving another kind of death.

The death of a marriage.

"I don't know how to do this." The admission pushes out a sob and I fold my arms against it, ball my fists at my rib cage, and hate myself for not being strong enough.

And then he puts that stupid box on the floor,

moves into my space, wraps his arms around me, and just holds me. Tight. And he's crying too.

I inhale the familiar scent of him, aftershave and the cologne he's always worn, and can't help wishing for the impossible.

Can I stand back now and look him in the eyes and tell him I forgive him? Would he want me to, even if I could?

Kevin releases me with a shuddering sigh. Rests a hand against my wet cheek and simply shakes his head. While I am no longer privy to my husband's intimate thoughts, I wonder if he, too, cannot believe it has all come down to this one final, catastrophic moment.

"I'm sorry, Savannah."

He's said this before. Too many times.

He has apologized, but he has never asked for my forgiveness. He told me once he doesn't deserve it.

I don't believe that. Not really.

But I am not God.

I don't know how to forgive this sin, this appalling act of complete abandonment. Don't know if I'm capable of it. And right now I don't want to forgive him, even though I know I should.

I nod and let him leave without another word.

Then I rush to the kitchen, open my laptop, and click over to my blog, where I know I will be comforted by women across the country whom

I've never met, but whom I have come to count on to talk me through this unbearable heartache.

It's easy to share your deepest sorrows and secrets when nobody knows who you are.

Chapter 4

"There are dark shadows on the earth, but its lights are stronger in the contrast."
—CHARLES DICKENS

Today I will try to begin again.

The first morning in new surroundings always startles me. That moment you wake, just cresting consciousness, and realize you are not at home creates a shift that takes some getting used to. My eyes flutter open and I register the white-paneled walls, botanical prints, light-green floral curtains that match the pillows on the armchair by the window, family photographs on the dresser across the room, and I sink back into fluffy feather pillows. In a way, I am home. Yet not.

My yawn is loud and forces me to stretch. Exhaustion has weighed me down so long I wonder if it will ever desist. Sleep is something I play with each night. It hides and teases me in fits and starts, allowing a few hours here and there, but then retreats to leave me alone in the blackness with thoughts I cannot abide. Thoughts that often push me out of bed and send me elsewhere.

I breathe deeply and stare at the ceiling. It's cold this morning. I can see my breath. Yesterday afternoon when I arrived, the house was warm enough. I didn't bother to adjust the thermostat. Sunlight peeks through half-closed California blinds. I don't know where I left my phone. I flip onto my side and reach to move the digital clock to face me. 9 a.m. That can't be. I can't have slept from midnight all the way through . . . Worry niggles at me now. Maybe I'm losing it again.

Once I find my phone, I see the time is right and I have actually slept. I want to do a happy dance. Instead, I opt for a hot shower, then pull on jeans and my warmest sweater and venture downstairs to get the coffee going. Zoe calls as I'm sitting down with my second cup and two slices of whole wheat toast, scanning the news headlines.

"How is it up there?" she wants to know. "Is there snow?"

"A bit." I munch and wander out of the long country-style kitchen into the warm living room. Logs sit in a neat pile beside the large stone fireplace and someone has already laid wood for a fire. "Still kind of early for it. It's cold, though. But very pretty."

"We should come for Thanksgiving, me and Tim. Or will you be back home?" There's a lot of background noise, and I figure she's probably hightailing it across campus to get to her next class in time. I scan the mantel for matches.

Thanksgiving is just a month away. Will I be

home? "I'll probably still be here." No point in going back to an empty house. "But you're going to Chicago, to Tim's parents'. Your tickets are booked." Tim and Zoe have been dating a few months. We like him.

"I know, and Adam's going to be in Killington. Which means . . ."

I will be alone.

"What are you going to do up there all by yourself?"

"Zoe, I'll be fine, sweetie. I'll hunker down by the fire with a good book. Don't worry about me." She does. She always has. But being alone is something I'm going to have to get used to. My new normal.

I cradle the phone between my ear and shoulder and fumble with the matches. Soon small flames flicker and fill the room with the scent of burning balsam. I stand back, pleased with the small accomplishment. "I'm going to relax, Zo. Maybe I'll take up crocheting or knitting. Get a couple of those coloring books. Adopt a few cats."

"Ma." She's giggling, but I'm pretty sure her eyes are worried. "Seriously." She sighs and I recognize the sadness returning. "Why is this happening?"

Oh. She has asked me this before . . .

"I don't know, sweetie." I smooth down Zoe's dark curls and wipe away her tears. Since we came

48

home from the hospital without Shelby, Zoe has been waking each night, crying. How do we explain death to an eight-year-old? She'll turn nine in two weeks, and her sister won't be with us. She doesn't understand that sometimes children die. That sometimes horrible accidents happen and there isn't anything we can do to stop them. She doesn't understand why God allows tragedy.

Neither do we.

Zoe wants her big sister back.

So do we.

"Hey, princess." Kevin stands in the doorway of her room, rubbing sleep from his eyes. "Bad dream?"

She nods, her little body convulsing with another sob. He joins us in her bed and takes her into his lap, letting her cry it out. "I . . . want . . . Shel . . . beeee." Her wails are too much for me and I turn away. Kevin puts a hand on my shoulder and I shudder, stifling my own sob. Adam will be awake soon if she doesn't stop. And then his questions will start. I don't have answers for him either.

I don't have answers for anyone.

All I do know is that this hideous nightmare my family has been thrust into is entirely my fault . . .

"Mom, will you tell Dad to stop calling me?" Zoe's voice drags me back to reality and I take a long gulp of coffee. Outside, the world is

49

peacefully white. Perhaps later I'll pull on my boots and go for a walk.

"Call him back, Zo."

"What?"

"Come on, Zoe, no need for drama." My grin catches me unawares. "I'm trying to be mature, so maybe you can too."

Silence stretches like the long arms of sunshine that clear the clouds and bounce off the sparkling snow on the front lawn. If it stays cold like this, the lake might be frozen by the time Thanksgiving rolls around. I won't miss the cooking and cleaning up this year. I will miss the family, but not the celebration itself. I'm not convinced I have a whole lot to be thankful for right now. Which sounds pretty callous, but that's how I feel.

"I really can't believe he would do this," she whispers, sniffling. She doesn't have to say more. Kevin was her hero. Mine too, once upon a time. But even heroes fail.

"He's still your father and he loves you." My hands start to tremble and I walk back to the kitchen, fumble in my purse, and find my pills. I forgot to take one last night and now my nerves are shot. "Call him."

"And say what? How's Alison?" She comes by her sarcasm honestly, and I can't stop a smile.

"Sweetie, the longer you put it off, the harder it'll be when you finally do talk. He knows you're not going to be around for Thanksgiving, but then there's Christmas. He's going to want to see you then."

"What are we supposed to do? Split our time between you guys? What's Adam going to do over the summer, spend half his vacation with you and half with Dad? This sucks, Mom."

That it does. I pop a pill and swallow more coffee. Knowing her schedule, I need to get her off the phone. "You're going to be late for class, sweetie. I'll talk to you tonight, okay?"

She hangs up reluctantly. I love talking to Zoe, but she can be exhausting.

I clean up my breakfast things, fill my mug with more coffee, wait for the fire to die down, then find my coat and boots and venture out the front door. If it's not windy I might sit by the lake.

Outside, the world is white and draws a smile as the scene reminds me of a favorite quote from *Alice's Adventures in Wonderland.* I pull my phone from my pocket to look it up.

"I wonder if the snow loves the trees and fields, that it kisses them so gently? And then it covers them up snug, you know, with a white quilt; and perhaps it says, 'Go to sleep, darlings, till the summer comes again.' "

The moment I glance up, I see her.
A little girl skipping up the path to the house,

51

wearing a pink winter coat with a fur-lined hood, blue jeans, and bright-red boots that demand attention. Blond curls bounce as she waves and comes closer.

Shelby.

"Hi!" She's almost at the steps now and I see it isn't Shelby, of course, but the mug has already slipped from my hands, shattered on the wooden porch, and coffee pools around my boots.

"Ah . . ." I struggle for words, stare at her and the mess, then I notice a man come up behind her.

"Did I scare you?" Her blue eyes are wide.

Blue eyes.

Shelby's eyes were hazel. Like mine.

My heart thumps against my chest and I try to find a reassuring smile. "No, I'm just very clumsy."

"Mrs. Barrington?" The man places gloved hands on the little girl's shoulders and she looks up at him with adoration. "Sorry, ma'am. Maybe we should have called. I'm Brock Chandler, Clarice's nephew. We live next door to y'all here. I've been keeping an eye on the place for your folks."

"Oh." Fog fills my brain and I try to clear it. "Right. Joe used to . . . How is he?" I remember an older gentleman who repaired broken windows, kept the gardens neat, and locked up after us each summer.

"Uncle Joe passed on some time ago, so I imagine he's doing just fine." Brock Chandler is all straight white teeth and sparkling eyes and smiles like a movie star. And his voice sounds like Matthew McConaughey's. Suddenly I can't find mine.

"I'm sorry to hear that," I squeak, self-conscious of my rumpled appearance. Did Mom mention Joe Chandler dying? I can't remember. I sidestep the brown puddles and what used to be a coffee mug and fold my arms against a cool breeze creeping up from the lake. "You're not from around here."

"No, ma'am. Atlanta born and raised. But we've been up north a few years now." He pushes thick hair a few shades darker than the child's off his forehead, indigo eyes shining in the sunlight. "This is my daughter, Maysie."

"Hello, Maysie." She skips forward as I come down the steps. "I'm Savannah."

"Miss Savannah," her father interjects, making her grin.

I crouch a bit, reach for her mitten-clad hands and study her face. So like Shelby, yet not. "Maysie. What a pretty name."

"Yours is pretty too," she says. "I'm sorry for scaring you." Curious eyes look back at me while her face puckers with the earnestness of a child her age.

"That's okay, sweetie. You just . . . you look a

bit like someone I wasn't expecting to see." Ever again.

"You made a big mess. Was that your favorite mug?" She frowns at the broken pieces of painted china. Not my favorite but probably my mother's.

"Let me grab the mop and bucket." Her father scoots past me before I can stop him.

In no time at all he's picking up the broken bits and mopping up spilled coffee while Maysie happily builds a snowman by the old oak tree. He shoos me off when I try to help, so I sit on a white Adirondack chair and watch him work. And I'm dragged backward once more . . .

Headlights flash across the darkened kitchen. A moment later a car door slams and I hear his footsteps. The back door opens and Kevin enters the room, flicks on the light, and jumps a little when he sees me standing there, waiting for him.

I take my best shot.

He ducks. The glass I hurled at him shatters against the door, remnants of red wine splattering across the kitchen tile and onto Kevin's expensive Italian leather shoes. Only a few splats, but enough to stain the tile if I don't get to it in time. I don't care about his shoes.

"What the—Really mature, Savannah!" Kevin glares. "You missed, by the way."

"Go back out. I'll get another glass and try again." I sway toward him, but he puts up a hand.

"Don't move. You're barefoot." He exhales and pushes both hands over his hair. *"And drunk. Aren't you?"*

Am I? I don't remember. Probably. I don't know what time it is either, but I know Kevin's so-called business dinner lasted longer than usual.

And I know where he's really been.

I haven't had this much to drink in years, but tonight . . .

He goes for a broom and throws down some paper towels. Sweeps up the glass, slips out of his shoes, and sponges them off. I'm a little dizzy so I slump into a bar chair at the counter and place my palms on the cold granite.

"Beth saw you." I don't know if I'm whispering or yelling or even talking out loud until he snaps his head up.

"What?"

I sit back and nod, tears sliding down my cheeks. "She happened to be in the city today. She saw you. In a restaurant. Holding hands with . . . that . . . woman."

He stands in slow motion.

Finishes cleaning up, washes his hands, and turns, his eyes hard. "Knowing Beth, I suppose she has the picture to prove it."

"She does." If she didn't, I don't know if I would have believed her. Except she's my best friend and I know she'd never lie to me. And I've had my suspicions for a while. Still . . . I don't

want it to be true. But the look on his face tells me it is.

"You won't deny it?" Even now I want him to make something up. Tell me she's just a good friend. Her mother died and he was comforting her. Reading her palm. Anything. I'm drunk enough to believe it.

"No." He bends over his knees for a long moment. Straightens and takes slow steps toward me. His expression is haggard. Beaten. "We should talk."

"Talk?" He wants to talk? I want to grab another glass, and this time I won't miss.

"I can't do this anymore, Savannah." The bitter words burn like acid and eat away my last thread of hope. "I don't want to be here anymore. With you. I . . . can't."

"You . . . can't?" My stomach lurches and I have to give in to the violent urge to vomit. I'm half tempted to stay where I am, let him clean that mess up too, but instead I race for the bathroom and lock the door behind me.

Four months ago.

That's when I confronted him. That's when he moved out of our bedroom to the guest room down the hall. At first we tried to work through things, but she won in the end. I can't believe it's been that long because the memory of that mid-summer night still feels raw.

Betrayal bites hard, then leaves gaping wounds

that will not heal no matter how much salve you slather over them.

"Are you all right, Mrs. Barrington?" The man, Brock Chandler, has put away the bucket, erased my mess, and stands in front of me with a skewed expression. Like he knows me. Knows what I'm thinking. Feeling.

I shake my head and push out of the chair. "That was awfully nice of you. You really didn't have to. And call me Savannah." I extend my hand and he grasps it, gently, just for a moment, the barest of smiles gone in a flash.

"Savannah, then." He clears his throat. "My aunt wants to invite y'all to come for tea. Tomorrow afternoon. If that suits?"

I do believe I could listen to that southern drawl all day. My cheeks actually heat. "Well, it's just me. Tomorrow afternoon would be lovely." Lovely? Since when do I say *lovely?*

Maysie has finished her snowman and joins us on the porch. "Are you coming for tea with Aunt Clarice?" She jumps up and down at my side, chipmunk cheeks glowing with cold and excitement.

"Tomorrow," I tell her. Something about her smile creates an ache that scares me. Once Zoe and Adam reached high school, I went out of my way to avoid small children. Raising the two of them was hard enough. I can't bear to be around anyone who reminds me of Shelby.

Yet here I am, smiling back at her almost mirror image. "What time should I come over?" I ask her father.

"Teatime, I guess." He gives a quick lopsided grin partnered with a shrug.

"It's four o'clock, Daddy. That's teatime, you know."

"Yeah?" He rolls his eyes, tweaks her nose, and gives a chuckle that warms me and chases away my fear. "You think you're pretty smart, don'tcha, Miss Maysie?"

"I am smart," she declares, hands on hips. "You tell me so all the time."

"I do indeed. You're the smartest six-year-old I've ever met." He pulls her against him and she wraps her little arms around his waist and my heart twists.

"You hafta be on time." Maysie turns to face me and pats my hand, looking very serious about it. "Aunt Clarice is British and she does not abide tar . . . tarda . . ." She looks up at Brock. "What is it?"

"Tardiness." His proud father's grin is wide.

Maysie nods and looks back at me. "Tardiness. It means don't be late. Aunt Clarice said."

This is nothing to joke about, apparently.

"Well then, I shall be right on time." I nod and try to hold back a grin of my own.

I don't remember Clarice. When I was Maysie's age, a German couple owned the house next door. He was a botanist, and the greenhouse was full of tropical plants and bright-colored flowers that could just be seen behind the steamy glass windows. The Schwartzes were not the friendly sort, despite my mother's best efforts to be neighborly. I never did get an invitation to visit their greenhouse, but my imagination as a young girl said it must be the most beautiful place on earth.

The Chandlers bought the house a few years ago. My mother said Dr. Schwartz only sold it to them because Joseph Chandler was also an avid gardener with an interest in botany. Kevin and I stopped coming up here before that.

Brock pulls Maysie's hood over her head. "You know where we are, right?" His eyes land on me again, like he's infiltrating all my secret thoughts, sifting through them, sorting which to keep and which to deem completely cracked. Which is how I'm feeling at this moment. Completely. Cracked.

"Um. Yes." I walk to the edge of the porch, shade my eyes against the sun, and point. "You're the large house with the green shutters. That way. I can walk through the garden to get there."

"And we have a greenhouse too!" Maysie's eyes shine with this news. From my vantage point I can just make out the glass structure that looks like a long finger stretching toward the lake. When I was last here, a brief visit with my parents over a holiday weekend last summer, it lay derelict. I remember my mother remarking on it as we walked past the house. *"Terribly sad,"* she said, with her usual dramatic flourish.

"Well, it's not much of anything anymore." Brock sounds as bereft as my mother. "Since my uncle passed, Clarice can't bring herself to go inside the place. Most everything's dead by now, I reckon."

"C'mon, Daddy. Let's go home now." Maysie is already skipping down the steps. "I'll see ya tomorrow!"

"Thank you for stopping by." I cough and force a smile. "And for cleaning up my mess." This man unnerves me. Not in a creepy way . . . but . . . "We haven't met before, have we, Brock?"

"Can't say that we have." Something flashes in his eyes and I think whatever it is, I'm better off not knowing. "Oh, there's extra firewood in the shed out back. You should have enough in the house for the next few days. When you need more, give a holler."

"That's very kind of you." I sound too formal and I have no idea why. But the man does not seem the overly talkative type. Nice enough, yes. Good looking, definitely yes, but not chatty. Which is fine by me. I think.

"See ya, Miss Savannah!" Maysie calls. Brock simply nods, takes the steps two at a time, and jogs to catch up with her.

I blow air through my mouth as I watch him leave.

Okay. So that was interesting. My racing pulse and dry throat inform me I'm not quite the dried-up old bat my husband seems to think I am. Take that, Kevin.

I'm actually a little stunned. Finding a man that attractive . . . not that I'm looking, or even in a position to do anything about it. At least I still have morals.

I need to speak to Beth. She will talk some sense into me. I'll call her.

Immediately.

Chapter 5

"Life is never fair, and perhaps it is a
good thing for most of us that it is not."
—OSCAR WILDE

Survival.

To say he was obsessed with the task of late
would be an understatement.

"Did you meet her?"

"How did I know that would be the first question out of your mouth?" Brock shrugged off his
coat and sat at the kitchen table, fumbling with
the laces of his boots. Even with gloves on, the
cold found its way in, and now he felt like an
icebox. Maysie hung up her jacket and scarf,
peeled off her mittens, left them on the floor,
and skipped down the hall. Brock sat back and
uttered a groan that seemed to dredge up all the
feelings he couldn't yet put into words.

Why was this happening?

Why did he feel like his life was spiraling out
of control? Why did it seem like he was suddenly
all out of options? And why, why, *why* was his
aunt always infernally right?

"Well?" Clarice moved lithely across the
kitchen and picked up Maysie's mittens, shoved
them in the pockets of the pink coat. For an

eighty-year-old woman, she had far more energy than he did these days. Another unwanted reminder of what was to come.

"I met her." Brock wrapped his hands around the mug of cocoa she offered and met his great-aunt's eyes as she sat across from him. "She's a nut job." An extremely attractive one, he wouldn't deny that, but a nut job just the same.

"Oh, pishposh!" Clarice's lined face crinkled in a smile as she wagged a finger. "What a horrible thing to say, Brock Chandler. You should be ashamed."

He rolled his eyes. "She took one look at Maysie and practically lost it. Dropped her coffee, broke the mug, the stuff went everywhere . . . She didn't really say more than two words to me, and her hands didn't stop shaking the whole time we were there. Nut job."

"Wounded soul."

"Really?" Brock sipped and let the hot liquid slide down his throat. "I suppose you're going to tell me the two of us are going to get along well on that account."

"Perhaps." Clarice presented him with that smug smile she used when she wanted to say she was right but refrained because she was too much of a lady. "I did tell you this day would come."

He gave a muted sigh. "You did, but I pretty much ignore you when you yammer on about your premonitions, Aunt Clarice."

Her sharp eyes lit with humor. "You should pay attention, Brock. Remember what's at stake here."

Like he could forget? His temples began to throb and he went to the cupboard for Tylenol. "I think you're way off on this one. You'll see. She's coming tomorrow for tea, like you asked."

"Ah, lovely." Her beaming smile pulled a chuckle from him as he sat down again.

Lovely. Who says that? Oh, right . . . the crackpot next door.

And his semi-senile great-aunt.

"Maysie told her about the greenhouse."

"I expected she would." Clarice waved a withered hand as she looked across the kitchen to the long glass structure beyond the closed door separating it from the rest of the house. "That's perfectly all right."

"You're planning to show it to her, aren't you?" He knew she was. He could see the glint of excitement in her old eyes.

"Perhaps. If God tells me she's the one."

Brock cleared his throat and hid a smile with his hand. He should probably take her with him next time he went to see his doctor. "The family never comes up in winter anymore. Why is Savannah Barrington here this time of year anyway?"

"Why, indeed?" Clarice sipped her tea. "I presume she has come here to seek refuge. Her husband has left her."

Brock put down his mug. A strange and unexpected sense of foreboding slithered down his spine. The haunted look on Savannah Barrington's face made much more sense now. "I suppose God told you that too?"

"Oh, don't be a ninny, Brock." Clarice's small frame shook with laughter. "Her mother did. When she rang to say Savannah was coming."

"Ah." He didn't hide his smile this time. "Well, I've got a headache. I need to lie down for a bit. I'll leave you to your plotting, Aunt Clarice."

"Dear boy." She nodded, sorrow flooding her face. "I will keep an eye on Maysie. You rest."

He rose, put his mug in the sink, and rounded the table.

She grabbed him firmly by the wrist as he passed and skewered him with a look that demanded his full attention. "You will be here tomorrow afternoon, Brock. For tea."

A growl stuck in his throat and he sucked back his first thought. It wouldn't do any good to argue anyway. It never did. "Yes, ma'am. I will be here."

❧❦

"You should totally sleep with him."

"What? Beth!" I press the phone to my ear and fall against the cushions of the couch. "I cannot believe you just said that!"

"I'm kidding, Savannah!" Beth dissolves into

65

laughter, and I can't help joining in once the horror dissipates. The thought of actually being intimate with anyone other than my husband is too terrifying to contemplate. It is indeed laughable.

"You did say he was hot, though, right?" She's incorrigible.

"No, I don't think I said that at all. You don't have to worry, Beth. I'm not getting involved with anyone. Kevin can go off and do what he likes, but I'll be just as happy to never lay eyes on another man again."

"Oh, sweetie." She sobers and her breath catches. "I read your blog this morning." Beth is the only one who knows about it. "You're still so angry."

"Am I?" Of course I am.

"Do you really think . . . Do you think you'll get divorced?"

"It's what he wants, Beth. He's found someone else. He doesn't want me." Not anymore.

"And is it what you want?"

"No." It's not? I ponder that, studying my mother's collection of photographs on the wall of the living room. Years upon years framed into lifelong memories. The last thing I ever wanted, ever expected, was a divorce. "What I want doesn't seem to matter. We've exhausted every avenue possible for reconciliation. You know that. Kevin's given up. Moved out. Moved on."

"It's just so wrong. So sad."

"You don't have to tell me. I hear it from Zoe ten times a day. And my mother. And Adam . . . everyone. Everyone is painfully aware of how sad this all is. Everyone except Kevin, it seems."

"He's running away."

"Oh, he's running all right, away from me and right into Alison Kramer's bed. He emailed me last night, said he wanted to make sure I got here, then asked if I'd started the process, filed for divorce. Nice, huh? I'm not about to beg him to come back. I'll just accept the new status quo and get on with filing the papers." I sigh and shudder at the thought. "Daddy wants me to call Walter. You know his reputation as a divorce attorney, and he'll go all overprotective with the goddaughter angle too. It'll be a bloodbath. I'm not ready for that."

Beth sighs. "I think you can take your time. Make Kevin wait. Don't file until you're absolutely certain . . ."

"Beth?" I hesitate, fiddle with the rings I still can't remove, and close my eyes a minute. "I love you, but I'm going to hang up now. Okay?"

"Sleep well. I'll call you tomorrow."

"I know. Good night." I smile as I put down the phone, but my eyes burn. Beth still believes in our marriage. Still prays for us. Prays for Kevin.

I don't pray for Kevin.

Huh.

The thought grips me and I bring my knees to my chest. But really, when was the last time I truly prayed for my husband? My sporadic prayers of late have been bitter. Filled with contempt and outrage. Part of me wants to ask God to smite him with some horrible plague, maybe something to disfigure him. In even darker moments I see him standing in the way of an oncoming tractor trailer.

In that time-stopping moment, when I knew for certain what he'd done, I ceased praying.

For our marriage.

For him.

I gave up too.

I rest my forehead on my knees, close my eyes, and try to summon words that won't make me sound like a witch. Before I can get one out, my phone belts out an old Beatles tune.

"All You Need Is Love."

The irony in Kevin's ringtone is not lost on me.

"Hello, Kevin." I stretch out again and try to sound friendly.

"I gather you made it there in one piece. You didn't answer my email." His words are clipped and cold. My prayers change to ones that plead for patience.

"No. Didn't you get my text?" The one I never attempted to send.

I am a horrible person.

"Why'd you call Walter, Savannah? Do you have any idea what kind of damage that pit bull will

68

do to me? I'm willing to be fair, but I'm not made of money, you know. Your terms are outrageous. What the—" He pauses, draws a breath. "What on earth are you thinking?"

Truly, at this moment, I have not a single coherent thought. "When . . . did you hear from Walter?"

"This afternoon."

"Well." It takes me a minute to realize what has happened. "You did ask me to file."

Okay, that was snotty.

"I can't believe you would do this!" He's raging.

I shake my head. "I'm glad you can't believe it, Kevin, because I didn't do it."

"You what? You didn't call Walter?"

"Nope."

Silence. Then . . . "Your father."

"That would be my guess." I watch the sun dip toward the towering pines and realize I never made it down to the lake today. Seeing that little girl, thinking about Shelby . . . My eyes start to puddle again. I am so tired of crying. So tired of this hatred, this anger. I want it all to end.

I've felt this way before.

"Savannah? Are you still there?"

I grab a gaily patterned cushion, hug it to my chest, and hold tight.

Hang on, hang on, hang on.

My breath leaves me in a slow heave. "Look, I probably don't even need a lawyer. I know you'll take care of the kids, and I certainly don't need your money. I just . . . need this to be over."

There is another long silence. "Okay." He's tapping his fingers against his phone.

"I'm not going to fight it. If this is what you want, let's get it over with."

I hear him blow air through the phone. "You need a lawyer. Keep Walter, since he's apparently already started the process, but tell him to back off. Like I said, I will be fair. I want to do this amicably."

"Amicably?" How I hate that word. "Then you might want to start by apologizing for snapping my head off a minute ago."

I should be used to the silences by now, yet I still find them unnerving.

"I think you're probably a little sick of hearing me say I'm sorry."

"I think you're probably right, Kev. Don't bother." I wonder if my father has that nice California cabernet I enjoy. I'll open a bottle. Or a case.

The thought is tempting, but I know I can't do it. More than a glass and I'll turn into a raging lunatic. Too dangerous. I'm teetering on the cliff's edge tonight as it is.

"Savannah, are you all right?"

My eyes widen. When did he become a mind reader?

"Am I all right?" Sure. Dandy. And if I tell him I thought I saw Shelby this morning, he'll be on the phone to my shrink and have me back in the psych ward before the week is out. "Like you care." Brilliant. Very mature.

Kevin makes a noise like he's got a rock stuck in his throat. I'll bet he's squeezing the last bit of stuffing out of his stress ball. "I care. I will always care about you, Savannah."

"You've got an awfully warped way of showing it."

He sighs again. "How long are you going to stay up there?"

"I haven't thought about it. I just got here. I don't have anything to go home for, do I?"

"I suppose not."

"Right. By the way, I told Zoe to call you. You're welcome." And I hang up.

Anger and sorrow duke it out against the wall of my stomach and I glare at the photographs on the wall. I don't know when this will get easier. When I'll be able to talk to Kevin without wanting to hurl obscenities at him. Frankly, I'm getting tired of it.

After I gather my racing thoughts, I call my parents. My father picks up almost at once, like he was expecting it. "Savannah, honey."

"Hi, Daddy."

"Everything okay up north, hon?"

I roll my eyes. "Yes. Everything's fine here. Is Mom there?"

"Sure. Let me just—"

71

"No. Put the phone on speaker. I want a witness."

He does. "Ellie, it's Savannah. On speaker. She wants a witness." The look of chagrin he's probably wearing clues my mother in at once.

"Oh, sug-ah. You didn't." I hear my mother's sigh of disappointment and almost smile.

"Yes, yes, he did, Mom. Daddy, are you there?"

"No, I'm in Monte Carlo." He's gruff now.

"Well, listen up because I'm only going to say this once. I love you. But call off Walter. I'll talk to him, but on my terms. When I'm ready. And you . . . stay out of it."

Chapter 6

"Hope is a waking dream."
—ARISTOTLE

Stepping back into the past.

That's how I feel as I approach the old house next door.

Like I've been here before.

As if somehow it knows me and has been waiting for this day.

Clarice Chandler is five feet nothing and looks about a hundred years old, but she is the most intimidating woman I have ever met. Her hair is not gray but almost white, like her finely lined paper-thin complexion, and she wears it pulled back in a neat bun. Her clothes seem to match her personality. A navy dress covers her knees, and a colorful silk pashmina is draped around her small shoulders.

It's the fuzzy pink house slippers that throw me off.

Although she leans on a walking stick, she possesses the self-assurance of a woman who knows who she is, where she has been, and where she is going. She studies me through deep lake-blue eyes that seem to hold a thousand secrets. And when she takes my cold, trembling hand in hers as I stand on the threshold of her historic home, I almost want to cry.

"Savannah." Her firm grip is warm and sends a little strength into me.

"Yes, ma'am." I have not said *ma'am* in years. Suddenly I am Maysie's age and ready to do whatever this ethereal sprite tells me. She links our arms and leads me down a dark paneled hall into a cozy sitting room where a fire is burning.

While this house was probably built in the early 1920s, around the same time as my family's, there do not appear to be any modern upgrades in Clarice's home. It's like walking through a museum. Chintz wallpaper, black-and-white pictures on the walls, a gleaming copper hood over the fireplace, and a gramophone on a high table by the window. Floor-length, floral-patterned curtains faded with age lay heavy along-side the windows, tied back with twisted blue-and-gold brocade. A gilded birdcage sits in one corner of the room. A blue-and-yellow parrot of impressive size blinks black beady eyes at me, tips his head, and croaks, "Hallo."

The air sings with scents of potpourri, wood polish, and the musty books that sit on shelves along the far wall.

I truly feel as though I've stepped back in time. I like it.

"Won't you sit down?" Clarice waves me into a chair, settles into its twin, and taps her rather formidable wooden walking stick—complete with ivory bird-head handle—on the floor in three sharp, successive beats. The parrot squawks. Clarice swivels to face him.

"Oh, Martin, do be quiet."

A moment later Maysie skips into the room. Clearly the child does not know how to walk. She's wearing a pretty velvet dress today. Deep purple, with a white-lace collar. Blond curls bob at her neck as she bounces in black, patent leather Mary Janes. She also looks as though she could have lived a hundred years ago.

"You're here!" She lands at my feet with a wide grin.

"Well, don't you look nice, Maysie." I place a hand over the stain on my jeans and wish I'd worn slacks instead. At least my hair is washed and brushed.

"We always dress up for tea parties," Maysie is pleased to inform me. Then she jumps up and does a little twirl.

I didn't get the memo.

"Good afternoon." Brock Chandler's brooding presence suddenly fills the room. He's pushing a cart that carries a silver tea service and a three-tiered cake plate filled with delectable goodies I can't wait to sample. I'm relieved to see he's also wearing jeans and a rumpled plaid shirt that isn't tucked in. Clarice peers at him over her bifocals, disapproval sparking in her eyes.

Guess he didn't get the memo either.

He maneuvers the tray until it is within Clarice's reach, and she begins to pour steaming dark liquid into gold-rimmed china cups. "It's Darjeeling. How do you take your tea, dear?" She raises a thin brow and smiles at me.

"Just a little milk, please." There'll be enough sugar in those macaroons I'm eyeing. If coming over here for tea becomes a habit, I'll have to break into Mom's stash of workout videos. My sixty-five-year-old mother is in much better shape than I am. In fact, I'm pretty sure she has Jillian Michaels on speed dial.

Brock presents me with the most beautiful china cup and saucer I've ever seen. Royal blue, patterned with gold overlay. Has to be vintage and probably worth more than a few dollars. I'm almost afraid to take it from him, afraid I'll send it clattering to the ground. The smirk he's wearing under a day's worth of blond scruff tells me he's thinking the same.

But I manage to hold steady and sip the slightly spicy tea with some degree of decorum. Maysie gets a pretty cup too and sits in a small wooden chair not far from me. She soon jumps up to offer around the mouthwatering treats. I set my cup and saucer on the mahogany wine table beside the wingback chair I'm sitting in, accept a delicate plate from her tiny hand, and muster great restraint, taking one finger sandwich—chopped egg, my favorite—and two macaroons. And then a chocolate biscuit. Why not?

"You can have more if you want." Her eyes get bigger, like she can't believe that's all I'm having.

"Oh, no thank you, Maysie. This is just lovely." I think Brock Chandler just snorted.

He doesn't take tea but grabs a few cookies and sprawls on the floor, long denim-clad legs stretched out in front of him as he wiggles his gray-socked feet by the fire. There is a hole in one and his big toe sticks out of it. I allow my gaze to wander as nonchalantly as possible toward his left hand. No ring. Interesting. Why am I curious about that?

"Brock, for heaven's sake, can't you use a chair like a civilized gentleman?" Clarice puckers and peers at him over the rim of a red-and-gold china cup.

"For heaven's sake!" Martin the parrot echoes.

Brock scowls at the bird and munches on shortbread. "If I were a civilized gentleman, Aunt Clarice, I'm sure I could use a chair. But your chairs are over a hundred years old, and they hurt my bu—back."

Maysie giggles and the two share a smile.

My heart clenches without permission.

"I'm quite civilized, aren't I, Daddy?" Maysie crosses her legs and lifts her cup, sticking out her pinkie finger.

"No thanks to me, darlin', but yes, you are a proper young lady."

Clarice looks at me and sets down her cup. "Savannah, you have children, don't you? Remind me again. How old are they?"

I nod and return her smile. "I have two. My daughter, Zoe, will be twenty in a couple of months. She's studying at Princeton. Adam is sixteen, and he's away at school, upstate New York." And Shelby would be twenty-one.

"So you are all alone." She angles her head, already knowing the answer, I'm sure.

"Quite." My smile falters and I lower my eyes, but not before I catch Brock Chandler staring at me.

"That's sad." Maysie reaches out and pats my knee. "It's not good to be alone. Don't you have a husband?"

"Maysie." Brock clears his throat, uncomfortable. Clarice opens her mouth to say something but shuts it again.

They know.

Courage. What was that line from *Macbeth*? "But screw your courage to the sticking place, / And we'll not fail." Oh, but we have.

Failed.

And failed miserably.

"It's all right." My voice sounds as though it could use a good dousing of WD-40. "Maysie, my husband and I aren't living together right now.

78

Sometimes grown-ups don't get along anymore and that happens." But not to me. At least, I never thought it would.

She nods, full of understanding. "My friend Felicia's parents got a DE-vorce last year. Are you getting a DE-vorce, Miss Savannah?"

"Maysie, dear, do have another cookie." Clarice leans over and taps the child on the shoulder. Maysie smiles and chows down, her questions forgotten.

Brock slides his legs up, hugs his knees, and gives me a tight smile. "Sorry. She's just curious."

"It's fine, really. I remember when mine were that age." I squirm in my seat, my heart hammering. He's right. These chairs are not comfortable.

"So, Savannah." Clarice's warm smile is calming. "What is it you do? Have you a profession?"

"Uh . . ." Wow. Did I sign up for this game? "Not exactly. I was a stay-at-home mom. The kids kept me busy. These days I volunteer with Meals on Wheels two days a week. And I help out at our local library, take books to seniors, shut-ins."

"Sounds like you spend your time doing a lot of things for other people," Brock says. "What do you do for yourself?" He seems sincerely interested.

"Oh. Well." I smile and wonder how much to

share. "I play a little tennis. Yoga, sometimes, and I like to walk. I enjoy writing. I love reading. And we . . . I . . . collect old books. It's something my husband and I started years ago. I love reading the inscriptions inside, thinking about the people who owned them over the years. It's fascinating when you think about it, how many hands have held this one copy . . ." I'm talking too much, but there's a gleam in his eye.

"You're an antiquarian." His smile broadens.

"I suppose so. I mean, not professionally or anything, but . . ." My cheeks begin to prickle.

"Have you checked out the bookstore in town? You've probably been there before, but Sol has a few new acquisitions you might be interested in."

"I haven't been yet. I'll do that." I eat the last macaroon on my plate and study the handsome man on the floor. He could be around my age, but since he says we haven't met before, I can't figure out why he feels so familiar. "What do you do for a living, Brock?"

"My daddy's famous!" Maysie gets up, puts her plate, cup, and saucer on the cart, and hangs over his broad shoulders.

"Oh?" I clasp my hands together, suddenly nervous. "Should I know who you are? Are you a movie star or a singer or something?" He's probably a household name and when he tells me who he is I will look even stupider than I feel.

"Oh my heavens!" Clarice's cup clatters against

the saucer and she sets it down. She's highly amused by my assumptions.

"Nothing that glamorous, I'm afraid." The man has turned beet red, which somehow makes him all the more attractive. He takes his daughter into his lap, snuggles her close, and kisses the top of her head. "I write books."

The lights come on inside my head. He's *that* Brock Chandler. B. J. Chandler. One of my favorite authors.

No wonder he seemed familiar.

I'm pretty sure my smile is wider than the Grand Canyon. "Wow. You're B. J. Chandler! I think I've read every one of your books. My husband . . . Kevin . . . loves your books. We both do. We fight over them, actually. Well, used to. *Mountains of Morn*, *Willow Road* . . . oh . . . and your last release is my favorite, *Charity's Box*. And you have a new one coming out soon, right?" I put a hand to my mouth and realize I'm gushing.

And he's grinning.

Clarice claps her hands like a child. "Brock, dear. You have a fan."

"So it would seem." His smile dips as he leans over and whispers something in Maysie's ear. She jumps up and runs from the room at once. "Our dog is expecting puppies," Brock explains. "Any day now. Maysie's off to check on her."

"Puppies. Really?" I lean forward. There is

definite excitement in my voice. I don't even attempt to mask it. "What breed?"

"Willow's a yellow lab. Bred to a chocolate, so we'll see what we get."

"I wouldn't say *bred*." Clarice sniffs her disdain. "The brute burst into our backyard one night and forced himself on poor Willow while she was out having a wee." Her disgust is quite comical.

Brock's shoulders shake with subdued laughter, but he tries to compose himself. I'm laughing before I can help it and that sets him off again and soon we're both in fits.

Clarice straightens and taps her ancient stick on the floor as though we are schoolchildren. "You won't find it so amusing when you have a handful of puppies to look after, Brock Chandler. Have you made any inquiries as to finding homes for them as I asked?"

"Yes, ma'am. Sort of." He sobers and coughs. "But you promised one to Maysie."

"I know very well what I promised, but the vet said it looked as though there were at least five in there."

"I'll take one." The words are out of my mouth before I can think.

"You will?" They speak in unison. Brock sounds shocked, while his aunt has that hint of veiled amusement about her again.

"Well, why not?" I nod, convincing myself this is indeed the best idea I've ever had. "I was just thinking the other night that I should get a dog. It's horrible being alone."

"I hear that," Brock says quietly. His expression crosses the border of nonchalance to interest and lands on compassion.

"It's settled then. You must have a puppy," Clarice proclaims, beaming. "You'll get pick of the litter. And we won't even charge you."

"We won't?" Brock's eyebrows shoot skyward.

"It wouldn't be neighborly," his aunt decrees. She ejects from her chair like a gymnast and stands before me. "It's not terribly cold out today. Shall we stroll the grounds, Savannah? I believe Brock has cleared the pathway." I notice the wary glance she throws him, followed by a positively mischievous smile. "I'd like to show you my greenhouse too."

※※

Brock and Maysie disappear and it is just Clarice and I who walk the path down to the lake, bundled in coats and scarves and gloves. The land around us rests in the serene silence of early winter. Tall pines tower over us and conifers cover the perimeter of the vast body of water, broken bits of ice bobbing by the shoreline, a hint of what is to come. One good freeze and the lake will be covered.

A few wisps of smoke rise above the white-capped trees, houses hidden from view. We stand and stare in silence. A lone snowmobile zips across the trail on the other side of the lake until it rounds the corner and is swallowed out of sight. It's so quiet down here I'm almost afraid to speak.

Clarice places a gloved hand on my arm, but she doesn't look at me. "Why did you tell us you only have two children?"

The ground shifts beneath my feet. "I . . . I'm not sure."

"You mustn't be afraid to talk about her, my dear. To talk about Shelby."

"How . . ." I whip my head around and stare into kind, luminous eyes. I don't need to ask how she knows. She just does.

"Joseph and I lost a son. Our firstborn. His name was Mark. He was sickly from birth and didn't make it past his first birthday. I thought the grief would kill me." She holds tight to my arm as we continue on the path, back toward the house. "At first, Joe couldn't bear it. He wouldn't enter the nursery, wouldn't speak his name. Wouldn't visit the grave with me. He stopped coming to church. Stopped talking to me like he used to. In a way, part of him died right along with my sweet boy."

My throat constricts and it's hard to breathe.

Kevin.

Oh, God. Why is she telling me this?

"How did you get through it?" I have to know. I have to know if they survived it, have to know they didn't stay together out of duty.

We arrive at the end of the long glass and white wood structure, and Clarice pauses. "How?" She turns to look at me through watery eyes, yet she is smiling. "I began to pray. And not prayers I normally prayed either. Oh no. But that's for another day, dear."

No, not another day. I want to know now! But I can't say that because we've just met and I feel off-kilter around her as it is. So I nod instead and hold my breath as she hands me her stick, lifts a slim gold chain from around her neck, and slides a small key into the lock on the door.

Old wood creaks against the intrusion as Clarice gives the door a push. It shudders open and air that should not be warm kisses my face in welcome.

"Come, Savannah," she says, stepping over the cement threshold and disappearing inside the greenhouse that I have longed to enter since I was a child.

Chapter 7

There is strange magic here.

And it is just as I imagined.

The entire structure, at least twenty feet in length, is filled with lush, green growth. Some trees hold delicate flowers painted in pinks and reds and purples. Jasmine, lavender, and sage permeate the air with their heady perfume. Tropical plants squat with shining leaves that drip with moisture. A gurgling waterfall sits at the far end, and water runs down the cement in thin rivulets along pathways that wind through the deciduous growth. Exotic orchids of every description and color hang from wooden slat boxes and baskets along poles near the top of the building.

Everyone has a different perception of heaven.

This comes close to mine.

Crisp white gravel crunches under my feet as I step forward, inhale the sweet scents on the warm air that is making me a little light-headed, and then I blink.

I hear myself gasp as I move backward, unbelieving.

Oh . . .

Dead and half-dead plants sway in the cold wind that whistles through cracked panes of glass. The top of my boot hits a pile of broken clay pots. Rubble is everywhere. Overturned benches, brown shriveled vines . . . gray roots litter the worn path, having given up the will to live a lifetime ago.

This is a war zone. Some wayward missile has landed, left its calling card.

There is no beauty here.

Only desolation and death and the dregs of what this place once was.

What did I see a moment ago? Chills race through me as confusion dries up my throat. I shut my eyes and open them again, just to be sure.

How? How is what I saw even remotely possible?

I did see it, didn't I? Of course I did. The faintest scent of jasmine still lingers in the air. I breathe deeply and almost smile.

Then I clutch my elbows and feel the world tilt again.

I need to call Dr. Clarke.

I've really lost it this time.

Clarice moves to stand beside me. Her sad sigh sings over the wind. She places her hand on my arm and simply stands there. Then, finally, she speaks. "Sometimes we are allowed to glimpse the beauty within the brokenness, Savannah."

My breath comes in shaky fits and starts and I turn to face her. "But I . . . saw . . ." How to begin?

Her knowing smile says there is no need. "This place was my Joe's refuge. He could spend hours in here, puttering away, talking to his plants, caring for them. Of course, he never had to do much, as magnificent as it was when we moved in. But he kept it going, until he got too sick. I've never been much of a horticulturist myself, and once he died, I couldn't come in here at all. So I'm afraid it's gone to rack and ruin." She shuffles forward, bends to pick up a stray pot, and turns. "But there is hope." Out of the dry dirt, one tiny, stubborn shoot appears and Clarice nods her approval. "There is always hope."

I reach for the sliver of green and slide my finger along the cold plant. "Must be a bulb of some sort." How it has survived is beyond me.

"Do you garden, Savannah?" Her eyes light with interest.

I shrug and kick aside a few shards of terra-cotta. "I used to. These days I only seem to kill things." Friendships. Marriages. Children.

Clarice places the pot on a shelf that has not fallen down, brushes dirt off her hands, and smiles. "Brock can get the electricity back up and running in no time. He's quite handy when he wants to be. Once we get some heat in here . . .

and water . . . repair the windows, it could be lovely again. What do you think?"

I don't know what to think. The old greenhouse is a heap of rubbish waiting to be thrown away. "It would be a massive undertaking. Besides, it's winter. Nothing will grow now."

"Don't be so sure." She pulls her coat tight. "I think you'd be surprised what can happen when you work for something you really want."

I shove my hands in the pockets of my coat and study her. I'm not so sure we're talking about the greenhouse anymore. "Some things aren't repairable, Clarice," I say softly. "Sometimes it's better to let go rather than linger, wishing for the impossible."

"My dear." She rests her hands on my arms and looks up at me. Through me. Straight into my soul. "Nothing is impossible if you have enough faith. You know that, don't you?"

I did. Once. I'm not so sure I do now.

"And when our faith seems to fail?"

She shakes her head and lets me go. "You pray for more." Clarice clasps her hands together and gives me a smile that almost makes me believe in miracles. "Will you work in my greenhouse with me, Savannah? I'd like to see what can be made of this mess. It's time."

And before I know it, I am nodding. And smiling.

I have a new friend. A new purpose.

And maybe a reason to get up in the morning.
Perhaps Clarice is right.
Perhaps it is time.

※※

A week later I'm startled from slumber by some-one banging on the front door. I'm fully awake in seconds and glance at the clock as I pull on my robe. It's 9:00 a.m. Why am I sleeping so well here? Must be the fresh air. And maybe the fact that I'm not in my own half-empty bed where the scent of Kevin's cologne still lingers and screams my sorry situation each time I enter the room.

The knocking grows more insistent.

"Coming!" I pad down the hall, smother a yawn, and fling open the door. "Maysie."

She's beaming, jumping up and down like her red boots are pogo sticks. "Willow had her puppies!" she squeaks, her eyes bright as she relays the information. "There's six! You have to come pick yours, Miss Savannah!" She grabs my hand and pulls. "Come now!"

"Whoa, sweetie, slow down." I look down the path, across the lawn. Snow is falling lightly around us, landing on her hair and coat and nose. "Did you walk over here all by yourself?" Scratch that. She ran. Her flushed cheeks say so.

"Uh-huh." She nods and blows out a big breath. "Aunt Clarice doesn't mind, 'cause I've got my guardian angel."

"Your . . . what now?" I rub my eyes. Maybe I'm still asleep. Still dreaming.

"My guardian angel, silly." Delightful childish laughter fills the air as she points to the path. "She's right there." Maysie takes a long look at me and her mouth turns downward. "You can't see her, can you?"

I shrug. How am I supposed to answer that? But she's smiling again, so maybe I don't have to.

"It's okay. Daddy doesn't see her either. Just Aunt Clarice and me." She jumps up and down impatiently. "Are ya coming?"

And I haven't even had my coffee.

Maysie waits in the kitchen while I take a quick shower, dress, and grab a bagel. I also call over to the Chandlers to make sure they know she's here, which of course they do, and Clarice tells me that it's quite all right indeed.

The little girl practically drags me all the way back to her house through ankle-deep snow. By the time I enter the kitchen, I'm pretty sure there's about a foot of the white stuff in my boots. I shake them off at the door and wipe down my socks and jeans as best I can. Maysie has already scampered away in the direction of the laundry room, where she tells me Willow and the puppies are resting.

I find a hook to hang my coat on, turn, and almost barrel into Brock.

He arches a brow, steps back, and holds a steaming mug toward me. "Coffee. Can I trust you with it?" His voice is thick with sleep, he's bleary-eyed, his hair is mussed, and the sight of him steals my breath.

I really need to stop fangirling over the fact that I'm living next door to a bestselling author. "Tha-thank you." My stammered words are nothing short of embarrassing. And why can't the man be ugly?

"Welcome," he mumbles and heads back to the coffeepot for his own cup.

The aroma is tantalizing and I breathe it in. "Guess you didn't get much sleep last night?"

"Nope." He takes a gulp from a turquoise ceramic mug that says *Daddie*, obviously made by Maysie, and gives a tired grin. "But Willow's fine and all the puppies look sound and healthy."

"That's good. You do this often? Have puppies?"

"Uh, no." His smile brings out a dimple in his left cheek. "It's my first time."

I just asked the man if he has puppies. Often. Somebody slap me.

"I meant . . . has Willow . . ." I give up because he's laughing at me.

So not nice.

"You ready?" He nods toward the door at the end of the kitchen. "Maysie'll start yelling soon if we don't get in there. You remember that age, right?"

"Very well. My girls were just as persistent."
I realize too late what I've said. He shoots me
a sidelong glance but makes no comment, and I
follow him through the door.

The puppies are gorgeous. There are four boys,
one yellow and three black, and two girls, one
black and one yellow.

"Chocolate's the dominant gene," Brock explains
with a hint of self-satisfaction. "I looked it up."

I choose one of the girls, the black one, and
Brock ties a soft-pink ribbon around her little
neck. I watch his careful hands and memories
plunder my mind again. How sweet it was in
those early days after we brought Shelby home
from the hospital . . .

*I'm barely twenty years old, sore, sleep-deprived,
and scared out of my mind.*

*Kevin carries the car seat into our one-bedroom
apartment like he's carrying a crystal chandelier,
puts her down in the middle of the living room
floor, stands back, and crouches in front of our
sleeping infant. "Hey, sweet pea," he says in a
singsong voice just above a whisper. "You're
home now. Mommy's going to go lie down and
you and Daddy can hang out awhile, what do you
say?"*

*We've been married barely six months and he's
never talked to me like that. Like I'm the most
important person in the world.*

Huh.

I take off my spring coat and slowly make my way across the room to them. He glances up at me and we share a smile, as though we still can't believe what we've done. Shelby's perfect little face is puckered in slumber, oblivious to anything around her. My eyes smart when I look at her. She is two days old and has already become my world. Our world.

Kevin stands and slides his hands around my face. He stares at me for the longest time, not saying a word. And then he kisses me.

And I know I have not lost him. Not really.

"I have the most beautiful wife in the entire universe," he whispers, leaving a trail of soft kisses along my neck. "And together we make the most beautiful children."

"I only see one, Kev." I smile and weave my fingers through his hair. "And she wasn't exactly planned, if you recall."

"Not by us, maybe." He kisses me again, with a gentleness that makes me ache. "But we'll do right by her, Savannah. I'll be the best father, the best husband I know how to be. I swear it."

"I know you will." My emotions are spinning like a smoothie in a blender and tears crest my cheeks. "You already are."

"Miss Savannah?" Maysie tugs on my sleeve. "You have to name her."

I blink and catch Brock's cautious gaze. He's probably wondering why I'm sitting here on the floor of the warm laundry room surrounded by the smell of detergent and dogs, with tears swimming in my eyes.

"You with us, Savannah?" His soft voice sears me, and somehow says maybe, just maybe, things might work out. And that whatever way they do, I will survive. "What will you call her?"

I reach a tentative hand toward the soft bundle of fur and touch a finger to the puppy's velvet head.

"Hope." I meet his eyes again. "I'm going to call her Hope."

"That's a beautiful name. She'll like that very much," Maysie declares, snuggles next to me, and wraps her arms around my waist. I stiffen slightly because it's been so long since I've felt this kind of affection: the unconditional love of a child who has no ulterior motive, only wants to give of herself.

My throat is too thick for words, so I just lean in and hug her back.

"Hope." Brock rolls the word on his tongue, thoughtful as he processes it, but then he smiles too. "Well chosen."

Chapter 8

"Friendship is certainly the finest balm
for the pangs of disappointed love."
—JANE AUSTEN

I feel I'm finally finding peace.

This dilapidated old greenhouse is the last place I expected to find it.

Brock has been tasked with fixing the electricity, and he's also taken it upon himself to rebuild the shelves. The smell of sawdust still fills the air and I set out a row of pots on a shelf he's repaired in record time. I'm impressed, but I keep that to myself. There is still so much work to do. But each time I set foot in here, the warm and mysteriously fragrant air winds its way into my soul and whispers that all may not be lost.

As I add to the pile of broken terra-cotta, I do have doubts.

Even with the heat on, how will anything grow, let alone bloom again?

Despite what I saw or think I saw that first day, I'm not convinced this place can be resurrected.

Even so, a sweet fragrance filters through the air every now and then, and I swear when I close my eyes I hear the sound of that gurgling stream.

It's hard to believe I've been in the Berkshires almost a month. My heart doesn't hurt as much, and I smile when I wake in the morning. In between hauling away dead things from the greenhouse, I've spent some time scouring the surrounding towns, venturing into every bookstore I can find and all the small knickknack shops that are still open. I've been searching for the perfect gift for Clarice. She's been so kind to me. Eventually I settle on an orchid that I find in a whimsical store that seems to be a cornucopia of sundries, plants, and handcrafted furniture. It's in bloom, a deep pink with a faint vanilla perfume. I think she'll like it.

The happy smile on her face as I present it to her that afternoon, along with a loaf of banana bread I baked last night, proves me right.

"I wanted to thank you. For being so welcoming, for inviting me into your home." She has done so numerous times now. Tea. Lunch. Morning walks and talks as we work together in the greenhouse. "It's so nice to know you're just next door here. I don't feel quite so alone."

"Oh, my dear." She laughs and beckons me in. Once I shed my coat and boots, Clarice leads me through the house, her fuzzy slippers slapping the wood floors. "You're never alone, you must know that by now. Ah. I've got the perfect place for this beauty." She stops outside a door I've not noticed before, clicks the handle, and pushes it open. "The library."

She's not kidding.

It is indeed a library.

An absolutely amazing room, and one I immediately long to get lost in.

It's like something you'd see on Pinterest or in the movies. And I suddenly feel like Belle from *Beauty and the Beast*.

Books are everywhere, from floor to ceiling. There's even one of those cool stepladders you can slide from shelf to shelf to reach the high places. Two long windows let in the light and show off the lake. A fire burns in the far corner, framed in marble and sheltered by a thick wood mantel that holds a myriad of photographs I wouldn't mind examining. But it's the books that demand my attention.

The entire room hums with the energy of story. Ancient leather bindings in reds and browns beckon and fill the air with anticipation and I wonder what their gilt pages might offer— adventures and romance and poetry and long-ago odysseys—worlds beyond my imaginings.

"Magnificent." I almost feel the need to whisper.

"Isn't it? Brock had the room remodeled when he moved in." Clarice marches across a patterned rug and places the orchid on an empty, ornate wooden plant stand by the window. "There. We were waiting for you, my beauty. Now you settle in, and I'll get you some water in a little while."

She talks to her plants. Somehow I'm not surprised.

"Would you like to stay and look around?" Clarice is positively beaming. "Brock works over there." She nods toward a massive desk that holds a computer surrounded by piles of papers and notebooks. "Don't touch anything. I tried to tidy once and never heard the end of it."

I can imagine. "Thank you. I won't venture that far. I'll just look at the books. Is it all right to touch them?" I'm afraid to ask. Some of them look so old. This collection is far more impressive than ours, and I'm in awe.

"Of course you may touch them. Books are written to be read and enjoyed, dear. Don't you agree?"

Sounds simple enough, I suppose.

She watches me wander around awhile, until heavy footsteps and the sound of someone clearing his throat interrupt the sacred silence.

Brock strolls into the room, iPhone in hand. "Mitchell wants to say hello." He holds it out to Clarice, whose face lights like a Fourth of July firecracker.

She shoots me a look of apology. "Excuse me, Savannah." She scurries out of the room and Brock lets loose a low chuckle.

"My brother. He calls once a week. They'll talk for a good hour. Lord only knows about what." He moves toward one of the long bookcases and an almost wistful sigh leaves his chest. "I see you've found my sanctuary. I've been meaning to bring you in here, but Clarice has beaten me to it." He runs a finger along a row of old books and I watch his smile. "This is my favorite room in the house."

"I can see why. It's amazing." I return to the shelf I'd been studying and reach for a leather-bound copy of *Pride and Prejudice*. "Oh my goodness." I'm seriously thrilled as I turn to the first page. "This is one of my all-time favorite books."

" 'I declare after all there is no enjoyment like reading! How much sooner one tires of any thing than of a book!—When I have a house of my own, I shall be miserable if I have not an excellent library.' " Brock's voice startles me and I glance his way.

"You . . . memorized that?"

He taps his head and grins. "Photographic memory. Comes in handy at times."

"I'll bet." I clutch the book to my chest. "I've read this so often. I wish I could quote from it. But I'm not great at memorization." Save for the few Alice quotes that have somehow stuck, I have to look up everything else.

"Maybe you just need to take more time. Some things are easily attainable if we want them bad enough." He leans forward a bit, his eyes dancing. " 'The power of doing any thing with quickness is always much prized by the possessor, and often without any attention to the imperfection of the performance.' "

I can't stop a smile. "You do suit Darcy."

The corner of his mouth lifts ever so slightly to tease that dimple out of hiding. "I don't know whether that's a compliment or an astute observation." His eyes catch the glow of the ornate Tiffany lights that hang from the ceiling and turn an even deeper shade of blue.

My stomach does a traitorous flip all on its own.

There is something inherently attractive about a man who quotes Jane Austen.

"Where does your brother live?" I ask, thinking it probably wise at this point to direct the conversation elsewhere.

Brock's half smile says he sees right through the diversion. "Back in Atlanta, when he's not traveling. Mitch is a pretty high-profile attorney, specializes in international law. He's a few years younger than me, single, rich as sin, and not in the least bit ashamed of it."

"Should he be?"

"Oh, I don't know. When you spend your time jetting around the world, chasing skirts and the next big adventure with little care, save what five-star hotel you'll be sleeping in that night, life seems good, I guess."

"You don't get along?"

"We get along fine. When we're not together."

"I see." I reach to put the book back in place.

"Take it home if you like," Brock offers. "If you want to read it again."

Because I wasn't flustered enough. "Oh, I couldn't . . ." What if I spilled something on it?

He laughs, rounds his desk, and starts to sort through the piles. "As long as you don't attempt to hold a cup of coffee at the same time, I trust it will be safe enough."

My face flames and I look away. "I'll look after it. I promise."

"It's not a first edition. Those are over there, in the glass case."

They are.

I peer through the Windex-clean glass at the titles. "You have an amazing collection." Austen, Chaucer, Dickens, Shakespeare, Robert Frost, T. S. Eliot. Kevin would be in his element. I walk the length of the room. On a middle shelf I see a row of books I recognize. Brock's. They are all here. And I remember reading every one of them. We called him a cross between Nicholas Sparks and James Patterson; enough romance and intrigue to keep us both hooked.

"Did you always want to be a writer?" I turn to face him and find him already looking my way.

"Not always." He grins slow, eyes shining. "First I wanted to be a fireman. Then a pro basketball player. Thought about being an astronaut . . ."

"Okay, okay." Laughter feels good. I'm not sure when I last had anything to laugh about. I sink into a soft leather chair by the fire, uninvited, yet feeling perfectly at home. "My sister, Peg, and I have that kind of relationship. Like you and your brother. We get along great when we're not together."

"But you keep trying." He leans back in his chair and puts his hands behind his head. "Don't you?"

"It seems wrong not to." I sigh and study the orange flames. "She means well. She just doesn't always understand me. But I know she'd do anything for me in a heartbeat. I have a closer relationship with my older brother, Paul. He's four years older than me, Peg is two. My family has always been pretty tight-knit, though, despite our differences and the distances between us. I'm lucky I guess. They've all been super supportive through this whole mess with Kevin."

He nods, his eyes serious. "Family is family. I suspect Mitchell will wake up to that fact at some point."

"And your parents? Where do they live?"

Brock powers up his computer and I hear the ping of his inbox. He scans the screen and then his eyes meet mine again. "Our mother died a few years ago. Our father is in Atlanta. In a nursing home. He has Alzheimer's."

"Oh, I'm sorry." I almost feel bad for asking, and a little guilty that I have two perfectly healthy parents.

"Don't be. Life is what it is. Sometimes it's hard." His furrowed brow testifies to that. I wonder what secrets hide within those vibrant blue eyes I find myself so drawn to. Wonder where his wife is and why he's here in the Berkshires with his great-aunt, raising his daughter alone. I suppose the answers to my questions can be found on the Internet, but somehow I'd rather hear them from him.

But not today.

He's studying the computer again and I push out of my chair. "I'll let you get on with your work. I can show myself out. Please tell Clarice I said good-bye."

"Sorry." He shoots me a smile. "I would be more hospitable, but I have an important call scheduled in about ten minutes." Brock rises and walks me out anyway, proving southern charm and chivalry are not dead. "As I suspect my aunt has told you, you're welcome here anytime, Savannah." He opens the front door after helping me with my coat. "I may be a little rough around the edges, but truth is, company is nice."

I try not to look too surprised. "If you're sure. I don't want to intrude."

"You're not. Aunt Clarice enjoys spending time with you." He pushes his fingers through his hair and takes a step back. "I'm beginning to see why."

Well then.

I'm not sure how to respond to that, and I think I should leave. Immediately.

"Good-bye, Brock. Happy writing." I slip through the door and skitter down the steps, Brock Chandler's chuckle ringing in my ears as I walk as quickly as possible down the path toward home.

Chapter 9

"You cannot find peace by avoiding life."
—VIRGINIA WOOLF

My new normal has become a tranquil reverie I am rather enjoying.

I spend a quiet Thanksgiving with the Chandlers at Clarice's insistence. Once she heard I had no plans to return home for the holiday, the decision was made for me. Of course Maysie's pleading to please, please, please say yes made it a little easier. And I hadn't really wanted to be alone anyway.

I spoke with Zoe, happily ensconced at her boyfriend's family home in Chicago, and tried to reach Adam on his cell, but no answer. Kevin asked if he could pick up Adam from his ski trip and take him back to school. I think Adam would have preferred to go back on the bus with the other kids, but he said yes anyway.

I'm half reading, half dozing on the couch Sunday night after Thanksgiving when my cell phone buzzes. I had it set to vibrate and have to search the house for it because, as usual, I have no idea where I put the thing. Eventually I retrieve it from under a pillow back in the living room. I don't bother to look at the screen. It has to

be Zoe at this late hour. So when I hear my husband say my name, I jump a little.

"Figured you'd find it sooner or later." He's
making a joke.

Why is he making a joke?

"Has something happened?" I'm fully awake
now. He wouldn't be calling so late unless . . .

"No." Kevin sounds surprised. "Everything's
fine." Like it's perfectly normal for my estranged
husband to be calling me at eleven o'clock at
night. "I sent you a message earlier, but I'm
guessing you haven't seen it yet. So I just got
home and wanted to let you know Adam's safely
back at school. He dropped his cell and it's
busted. He didn't want you to worry when you
didn't hear from him. I'll get him a new one this
week."

"Oh." I sink onto the couch and breathe a sigh
of relief. Adam doesn't call me every day, but I
did think it strange I hadn't heard anything yet.
A few years back when I was a helicopter mom,
I probably would've been on the phone to the
police in a panic. These days I'm attempting a
more relaxed method of parenting. "How is he?
How was the skiing?"

"Good, I think. No broken bones this time."
Kevin chuckles. Two years ago we had to drive
through a blizzard to get to Adam after the school
called to let us know he'd taken a tumble and
broken his leg. This year the trip happened to

coincide with the holiday and the majority of parents seemed okay with it. I guess it was better for Adam anyway. Thanksgiving up here would have been boring.

"We had a good talk," Kevin tells me. "He understands I'm trying to figure things out."

"Oh?" I swallow my next question.

Oh, what the heck. "What exactly are you trying to figure out, Kevin? When to introduce our children to Alison?"

There is a long, uncomfortable pause. I hear glass clinking. "I guess I deserved that."

"You think?" My eyes smart, and I silently curse him for ruining my perfectly peaceful evening.

"Zoe called me. On Thanksgiving." Kevin's voice is quiet. I nod and stare into the fireplace. A few embers spark as their glow fades, and the room is growing cold. She has not told me this, but knowing Zoe, I suspect she's probably still processing. Good for her.

"I thought she would at some point."

"We're going to meet. I'll go there, maybe next weekend."

"Okay. That's good." I'm out of words.

When did I forget how to talk to my husband?

Years ago, I think. And maybe he just got used to the silence.

"How was . . . Did you . . . have a good Thanksgiving?" he asks, swearing under his breath. Kevin is not good at small talk. Maybe he's also thinking what an odd thing it is to have to ask me.

Our first Thanksgiving apart in . . . how many years? I've given up answering those kinds of questions because it's too depressing. But I can't seem to stop asking them.

I try to put some enthusiasm in my voice. "It was nice. Quite pleasant, actually. I went next door to the Chandlers'. They've been very good to me since I arrived. I don't think you ever met them. Joe used to look after the house here, but he passed away. Brock cooked and Clarice—"

"Brock?" A hint of interest sneaks into his tone and I roll my eyes. Seriously?

"Yes. Brock Chandler. He's B. J. Chandler, actually. You know, the author? He lives next door. With his great-aunt and six-year-old daughter." And no wife. I still haven't given in to the temptation to google him. Somehow I feel that would be violating his privacy. Whatever Brock's story is, I hope someday he'll tell me himself.

"B. J. Chandler? Next door? No way." He's impressed, I can tell. I'm sorely tempted to make some comment on how good-looking the man is.

"Way. I was surprised too." More surprised that he also cooks like Emeril. A perfectly plump and tender turkey, honey-glazed ham, homemade rolls, sweet potato pie, baby beets, green bean casserole, and I can't remember what else.

Clarice barely had to lift a finger. Brock even did the dishes. Although he did let me help with those.

The day after Thanksgiving I went on the hunt for Mom's workout videos. I am determined to get back in shape.

"What's he like? You know he's really reclusive. Is he working on a new novel?"

"I have no idea. I haven't asked." In the few weeks I have been coming and going from the Chandler house, apart from brief conversations about the puppies—Hope will be ready to come home with me around Christmas—Brock doesn't seem to have much to say.

"I just finished his newest. *Simeon's Secret*," Kevin tells me. There's a hint of awe to his tone. "Have you read it yet?"

What are we, a book club?

I don't know why Kevin is still on the phone. Still attempting to have a civilized conversation with me. I picture Alison lurking somewhere nearby, glaring at him. The vision produces a grin. "Yes, I read it." Brock gave me a signed copy last week and I devoured it in one day. "Well. I'm glad you had a good time with Adam. And I'm glad you're going to see Zoe. But I should . . ." What? Get off the phone and throw my clothes in the dryer? Put the dishes away?

"You don't want to talk to me. I get it." Now he's using the "poor me" tone. Give me a break.

"Kevin, what? You can't just pick up the phone and expect things to be normal between us." Are you a total idiot? Oh, wait . . .

"I'm going to meet John," he blurts, startling me. "For coffee. This week."

I almost drop my phone. I can't stifle the long exhale that slides from my chest.

John Williams is Beth's husband, Kevin's former best friend. They haven't spoken in months, maybe a year. John knew what was going on long before Beth or I did, and he called Kevin out on it. Kevin didn't like that. John is also one of the counselors at our church.

Anger coils like a snake about to strike, overrides surprise and sorrow. Why is he doing this now?

"Savannah?"

"Have you signed the papers, Kevin? I haven't heard back from Walter yet." I need to countermand the unexpected attack he's launched on my emotions. My voice is shaky and I don't want to talk to him a minute longer.

"Uh . . ." I imagine him frowning, raking his fingers through his hair. "I guess I'll get on it."

"You do that. The sooner the better. Good night, Kevin." I click off, lean over my knees, and take deep breaths, willing my heart to slow down. My phone buzzes. I don't want to pick it up. But I have to. My hand snatches it up before my brain can say no. A text. From Kevin.

"It's no use going back to yesterday, because I was a different person then."

An Alice quote. We collected them, he and I, over the years. I have a tattered notebook filled with my favorites. Kevin stores them on his phone, on paper napkins, on receipts. That was one of the things we lost after Shelby died, along with the book. We stopped saying silly things to each other.

"There's no use trying," I text back. "One can't believe impossible things."

Ah, good one, Kevin responds.

Well played. Good night, Kevin.

Good night, Savannah. Watch the stars. ☺

I have no idea what just happened. What that conversation was about. I want to throw the phone across the room. But I curl up on the couch and clutch it to my chest instead. And I'm wearing a stupid grin, because I remember . . .

Paul tells us he's bringing a friend up to the lake house for a couple of weeks. They've been working together at a summer camp and plan to relax before heading back to their respective colleges. I've just turned seventeen and I'm not altogether thrilled with the news. While I'm pleased Paul is coming, I rather hoped to have my brother to myself.

We're all sitting on the front porch when they pull up: me, Peg, Mom, and Daddy. It's late

Sunday afternoon and Mom has been cooking all day. The beat-up red Mustang shudders to a stop, blaring music dies along with the engine, and Paul jumps out with a wave and a holler. His hair is almost to his shoulders, and I'm pretty sure Mom will be chasing him around the kitchen with a pair of scissors before the sun goes down. While they're all making a fuss over him, I watch his friend unfold himself from the passenger side.

He's tall. Like six feet or thereabouts. He stretches, pulls his arms behind his neck, muscles flexing under a white T-shirt. I'd say he was showing off, but he's not looking in my direction. He's studying the lake. And then he turns toward the house.

I've never seen a smile like that.

It lights up his whole face, says he's truly glad to be here. It's soul-deep, and it reaches right through me and takes my breath away. His dark hair is windblown, and I swear his eyes are a shade of blue that nobody has ever named.

"Hey, kid!" Paul wraps me in a hug and lifts me off the ground and I squeal. He drags me down the steps toward his friend. "Yo, Kevin, this is my baby sister, Savannah. She's a stargazer too."

"Yeah?" He grins and ambles over to us. He doesn't try to shake my hand, and I'm glad because my palms are sweating. "Must be beautiful out here at night, huh?"

113

"It is. We have the best view around." I indicate the widow's walk at the top of the house. "There's a pretty good telescope up there."

"Cool. Maybe you can show me tonight." His eyes lock with mine, and my entire being sizzles with sensations I wasn't even aware existed until this moment.

I know what this is.

I've read about it, secretly hoped for it, but never truly imagined it was possible.

Now I know it is.

Love at first sight.

⋙⋘

The sun is warm and I've spent most of the morning in the greenhouse.

Throwing things.

We set out pots that can be used again, and Brock hired a kid to haul in huge bags of potting soil. That rich, peaty scent permeates the air. Yesterday Clarice and I placed bulbs deep into soil in various-size pots. We'll leave the beds to warm a bit. She's determined we will see the fruit of our labors. I'm not so sure, but I've thrown myself into it anyway, pruning branches from trees that still show green beneath old wood, pulling weeds, and clearing debris from the flower beds, and I wonder if miracles still happen. Can things long dead really be brought back to life?

I thought putting myself to work today would

help, but I keep replaying last night's ridiculous conversation with Kevin.

And I just want to throw things.

I've lined up a few cracked pots on a crooked bench, found some small stones, and I'm just hurling. Missing, of course. I don't see Brock until he's in my line of vision, sidestepping another poorly aimed shot. The stone hits the ground and bounces against a pile of broken terra-cotta.

He frowns, pulls the zipper on his navy sweater, and comes a little closer. "Permission to enter the firing zone?"

My cheeks burn and I drop the stone I was about to throw. "Oh, gosh. I didn't think anyone was home."

Brock shrugs, gives a shadow of a smile. "Clarice and Maysie are out shopping. I was trying to work." He steps closer. "If you break any of those new panes of glass I just put in, I shall not be amused."

I'm mortified. Truly embarrassed. And it's all Kevin's fault. I want to pick up another stone, but I don't. I take off my gardening gloves and retie my hair in a messy ponytail. "I'm so sorry, really. I'll . . . uh . . . just go home. I'm not making much progress today."

"I've got a better idea. Come with me." He grins and heads inside through the back door. I follow him, not sure what else to do. In the kitchen he grabs his coat, keys, and chucks me

115

one of Clarice's woolly hats. "You'll need that."

A few moments later I'm sitting in Brock Chandler's truck, country music blaring, and we're driving down a snow-covered road to who knows where. The man might be a bestselling author, but he could also be an axe murderer for all I know. What the heck am I doing?

He pulls up beside a white field, slips down his shades, and sends me a wink that does nothing to soothe my suspicions. "Let's go."

In the middle of the field I spy a long bench strewn with cans and bottles. I get out of the truck and watch Brock forage around a lockbox in the back, then he pulls out a rifle.

"Oh, heaven help me." My laughter lands a little on the hysterical side. "I knew you were psycho."

"No, ma'am." He laughs too. "Just southern."

"You've got to be kidding me." But apparently he's not.

I follow him out to the middle of the field, boots crunching over snow. It's colder up here. The wind's picked up. I stand back after he sets a few targets, watch him nestle the wooden butt of the rifle into his shoulder, pull back the safety, and squeeze the trigger. Like he's been doing it his whole life. Which he probably has.

He's a good shot.

And I'm still a little scared.

"Your turn, Savannah." He turns, holding the rifle toward me with that half smile. I'm pretty

116

sure I look like I'm about to pass out. Because I am.

"I've never held a gun in my life."

"First time for everything, darlin'."

Oh good gracious.

I have no choice apparently. He swivels me around to face the bench and guides my hands into the proper position on the rifle. His arms are around me and I breathe in the slight woodsy scent of his cologne. Being in another man's arms, or close enough, is freaking me out, but I'm holding a gun, which freaks me out even more.

"Um, Brock . . ."

"Breathe, Savannah. Focus on the target and picture . . . oh, I don't know . . . your ex's face maybe?" His breath is warm in my ear and I giggle. Like a teenage girl.

That makes me angry again and I do picture Kevin's face, but he's looking at me in such sheer surprise that I can't imagine doing him any harm. And that makes me mad too, so I single out a medium-size can, pull back, and fire.

The can goes flying and I let out a squeal.

"Easy, Rambo." Brock's delicious laughter winds around me as he holds me still. "Set the safety if you're planning on doing the two-step."

Eventually Brock says it's too cold and I'm enjoying the sport a tad too much. He turns the truck back down the hill and sends me a sidelong glance. "Feel like getting a coffee? There's a new shop in town and they make the best melt-in-your-mouth chocolate chip cookies. I've been dreaming about them all morning."

"Sure. I guess." I don't know if he's asking because he wants to take me out or if he really just wants a cookie. I'm pretty sure it's the cookie. Because if it's not . . . then I'm going out for coffee with Brock Chandler. A single, very attractive man. And I haven't been out for coffee with a man since before I was married. And I'm still married. Kevin is technically not my ex. Not yet.

Now I'm freaked out all over again.

Brock insists on paying and leads us to a back booth in the cozy coffee shop where hipster couples and ladies' book clubs hang out. I see people looking, nodding his way. They know who he is and I am so in trouble. I envision my picture splashed across the pages of *People* magazine and Kevin calling, demanding to know what's going on. Oh, wait . . . I sigh and remember that it doesn't matter what I do now. My husband is living with another woman.

But I still don't want to be in *People*.

"Have a cookie." He's bought six and shoves the brown paper bag in my direction.

A groan slips from me. "I'm still full from Thanksgiving. On a major diet now." But my hand sneaks inside the bag anyway. They're warm. And the sweet, sugary smell is just about to do me in.

"You look fine to me." Brock stirs three sugars into black coffee. I open a packet of sweetener. Just one. "You're not one of those fitness freaks, are you?"

"Hardly. I should probably exercise more." I cursed a blue streak at Jillian Michaels this morning after all the muscles in my left thigh ganged up on me, pulled into a tight knot, and refused to stop throbbing for a good hour. That probably doesn't count as exercise. "You get to my age and the mirrors start to seem distorted."

He rolls his eyes and laughs at me. "Please. You're what, thirty-five?"

I think I love this man. "Forty. But thank you."

"Well, I'm forty-two and I couldn't give a rat's tail what the scale says. You only get one life, right? May as well enjoy it."

"Easy for you to say. You're a guy." One who does not appear to have an extra pound anywhere on him. I point at the bag of cookies. "Get those away from me, you devil."

He grins, takes another delectable cookie, and stares at me while he chomps. His cobalt gaze is mesmerizing. A bit of melted chocolate sticks to the corner of his mouth. I'm thinking about . . . Oh no. No, I'm not. Am. Not. I give myself a mental shake and study my coffee instead.

"Have you visited the bookstore down the street yet?" Brock asks.

I nod, managing to look at him again. "A few

times. It's fantastic. The place could use a face-lift, though. The floorboards are a bit scary, huh? But he's got some great books." I haven't bought any yet. I keep hoping one day I'll stumble across our same copy of *Alice's Adventures in Wonderland* and replace the one we lost. But as the years pass, I wonder if it's better that I don't. Some things aren't replaceable.

"It's for sale."

"What, the store?" I'm not surprised. The owner looked old and ready to retire.

Brock shrugs. "I hope he finds the right buyer. I'd hate to see it close." He fixes his gaze on me and smiles. "So, Savannah Barrington. Since you seem to have infiltrated my life without invitation, have both my aunt and daughter absolutely besotted with you within weeks, I figure I have the right to ask. What's your story?"

Chapter 10

"The grieved are many, I am told—"
—EMILY DICKINSON
("I MEASURE EVERY GRIEF I MEET")

Living dangerously, bucko.

Brock took a swig of coffee and watched surprise scoot across Savannah's face. She hadn't expected an interrogation, no doubt. He hadn't figured on asking the question either, but it kind of just popped out. Well, he'd never been one to beat around the bush. Wasn't about to start now.

She pushed an ash-blond curl behind her ear and stared back at him through eyes he hadn't quite figured out the color of yet. Hazel was too cliché. And over the last few weeks, Brock had come to the conclusion that there was nothing remotely cliché about Savannah Barrington.

"Direct, aren't you?" She faced him head-on, a slight hint of anger flashing his way, accentuating the gold flecks in her widened eyes.

He shrugged. "Everybody has a story. I'd like to know yours."

Her contemplative smile made him sad. It wasn't anything Brock could put his finger on, but ever since that first day on the porch, when she'd seen Maysie and dropped that coffee mug,

121

he sensed a heaviness around her, like she was carrying some burden she never intended to and didn't know how to put down.

"My story is rather depressing, Brock. Nothing you'd want to use in one of your books, that's for sure." She took a sip from her mug, her eyes a million miles away. "I met my husband when I was seventeen. He was friends with my brother, a couple of years older than me. We started dating eventually. I got pregnant a few years later, in my sophomore year of college. So we got married. I chose to stay home and raise our kids. And life was pretty good. Until he decided it wasn't. Now we're getting a divorce. Hardly the happy ending I dreamed about when I was a girl."

The busy room that buzzed with energy a moment ago seemed to still. Brock watched her fumble with the oversize mug, her hand trembling. "That's the abridged version, I assume?"

She sat back and folded her arms. "I figured you knew the rest." Her eyes narrowed in question.

Brock shook his head. "Clarice doesn't tend to gossip. And I don't tend to ask. All I know is that you're planning on holing up here awhile because you're going through some tough times. And for some reason you find it difficult to handle a cup of coffee."

Her cheeks flushed a pretty pink and Brock's heart lurched a little. She was really quite stunning when she smiled. Once again, he cursed God's timing.

"When I saw Maysie that day . . . it was a shock." She fiddled with the rings on her left hand. The raw anguish in her eyes almost made him stop her from saying any more. But curiosity kept him quiet. "Our first child, Shelby . . . died. Maysie bears a striking resemblance to her." She took a deep breath and looked away a moment. When she faced him again, her eyes were wet. "She was ten. Out riding her bike. I went inside to answer the phone, came straight back out, but . . . the car had already struck her."

"Oh, Savannah. I'm so sorry." Brock drew in a stunned, shaky breath. He knew that kind of pain. That searing forest-fire heat that eventually fizzles to dormant embers but remains a threat, a slow burn, never fully extinguished and easily flammable.

It was the same for him. Years later. Whenever anyone asked and he chose to tell his story, which he rarely did, the flames sparked and flared and burned twice as bad.

"She was in the ICU for a week." Savannah shrugged and wiped her cheeks. "We thought . . . well, there were moments when it looked like she was going to make it. She didn't."

He nodded. There were no words that would make the slightest bit of difference.

"That was ten years ago." Her almost apologetic smile didn't go far. "I don't suppose it'll ever get easier to talk about. We tried to go on after that.

I was busy with Adam and Zoe, Kevin threw himself into work, but I think the grief was just too much, you know? Eventually we turned into strangers living in the same house. I blamed myself for Shelby's death. Kevin kept trying to talk around it, saying it wasn't my fault, but I didn't want to hear that. So I shut him out. I . . ." Her eyes flickered again, then she blinked and drew in a sharp, beleaguered breath. "Why am I telling you all this?"

"Because I asked." Brock watched a certain awareness settle over her features. "You thought it was easier not to talk about it, right? Then pretty soon you can't talk about anything at all."

"Walking on eggshells." A shadow of a smile lifted her lips. "That's what it's been like the past few years. Constantly wondering what's going to set things off, where the landmines are buried and how to step around them. I wasn't the easiest person in the world to live with. I guess Kevin could only put up with it so long, so he stopped trying."

"Did he . . ." Brock cleared his throat. This was none of his business. But he'd already pegged Kevin Barrington for a first-class idiot. And the look on Savannah's face confirmed his suspicions.

"He did." She sniffed and waved a hand, a brave smile lifting her cheeks. "Of course he was the last man on earth I thought would ever cheat. I suppose every wife feels that way. When I began to suspect something was going on, he stepped up the game. Started coming back to church. Taking me out for dinners." She balled up a paper napkin and let it fall from her fist. "But I knew something wasn't right. When I began to question him, he denied it. What's that saying . . . those who shout the loudest have the most to hide?"

"Something like that." Brock smiled and shoved down a smart remark. It wouldn't help to agree with her. "How are your kids doing with everything? My parents divorced when Mitch and I were still in elementary school. I know how hard it can be."

"Oh." She pulled a Kleenex from her coat pocket and blew her nose. "Adam's doing okay, I think. He's busy with school and sports. I think he feels torn, though. He doesn't want to hate his father, but he can't condone what he's done either. Zoe has been vehemently opposed to having anything to do with Kevin since she found out. Kevin just told me last night that she's finally agreed to see him. They're going to talk."

Brock nodded. She wore a neutral expression he couldn't decipher. "And you're okay with that?"

"He's still their father. I don't want this to destroy their relationship. I guess I just never planned on being in this position. And, to be honest, I'm still furious with him."

"So that's why you were in the greenhouse doing a little creative redecorating?"

She raised her eyes to the ceiling and laughed. "Guilty. I mean, he just called out of the blue, like everything was normal between us, and wanted to talk about stupid stuff. Like your books."

"Really?" Brock cleared his throat and tried to look put out. "My books have been called a lot of things, but—"

"No, no, no." She waved a hand, looking a little mortified. "I didn't mean . . . I meant . . . Shoot." Her face flushed again and Brock almost sucked in a breath. He couldn't remember the last time he'd been this attracted to anyone. And suddenly the air seemed a little dangerous.

He tried not to enjoy her expression of horror, but it was too difficult. "Savannah. I'm teasing."

"Oh. Okay." Savannah smiled her relief. "Well. That's my sob story." She fixed him with those golden-flecked eyes. "So what's yours?"

⁂

Okay, that was stupid. But I can't take it back now. And it's only fair to ask, right? I pretty much opened a vein in front of him.

The mix of surprise and chagrin Brock wears says I probably won't get to hear it.

"You don't have to tell me." Wow. I really am a pushover. It's a good thing I never went into journalism.

Brock smiles, sits back, and gives a slow nod. "Maybe I will someday."

"But you don't want to." I try not to sound hurt or overly curious. "I mean, it's fine if you don't. I've just spilled my guts to you and . . ." His quiet laughter stops my rambling and I put a hand over my mouth. "You know what, never mind. I'm really not this annoying."

"I don't think you're annoying at all." Brock's eyes sparkle under the colorful glass light that hangs above our table. "It's refreshing to have a conversation with someone over six and under eighty."

"Well, I didn't mean to pry." I'm feeling tongue-tied now and so ready to leave. But he stays in his chair, looking quite comfortable.

"My wife died when Maysie was a baby. Let's just say the past few years haven't exactly been a Sunday barbecue. When Uncle Joe passed, I came up here to visit Clarice, and she invited us to live with her. I've always loved it here, and Atlanta was getting a little too loud for my liking. That was, oh, about two years ago now."

"Clarice is a wise woman." I fiddle with the small silver cross around my neck. "You ever notice how she . . . I don't know . . . seems to know things without asking?"

Brock chuckles and leans forward a little. "Between you and me, I think she's a bit of a clairvoyant. Not in the secular sense, you understand. But I do think sometimes she hears God louder than the rest of us."

"Must be nice." My smile surprises me. "I feel like he has to hit me over the head to get my attention most of the time."

"Yeah, I get that." His face takes on a serious expression I wonder about. "I don't know what I would have done without her these past few years. She's a huge help with Maysie. She has more energy at her age than I do most days."

I have to agree with that. "I don't know about her plans for the greenhouse, though. We've been at it for weeks now and I'm still not convinced the place is salvageable."

"It looks a sight better than when you first started."

"True. But . . . do you really think it'll ever be beautiful again? It's still seems so . . . desolate."

He ponders that, tips his head, and gives a smile. "You have a nice way with words. The day you first came to tea, you mentioned writing. I'm curious. What do you write?"

Oh no. No way can I possibly go there. I shake off the question. "Nothing, really. It's just a bit of a hobby."

"Poetry? Short stories? Romance? Haiku?" He's grinning, and I'm tempted to throw something at him.

"It's a blog. Okay? Nothing exciting."

He leans back with a satisfied smile. "I'd like to read it."

"No, you wouldn't." I don't want anybody

reading it, actually. I don't like the direction it's taken, the hostility, the anger, and the outrage coming from my followers as they share their own tales of woe. Many of my original readers have moved on. I've received more than one email expressing concern over what's happening. It no longer feels like the safe community it was. And I'm no longer okay with that.

"Hmm." He gives me that skewed look I have no idea how to interpret. "Well. Back to the greenhouse, then. Maybe you're looking at it from the wrong angle."

"How so?" Relief floods me. I'd much rather talk about the greenhouse.

Brock tips his head and gives a slight smile. "You can't change everything overnight, Savannah. Figure out what you want. What's worth saving, what can be saved, and what can't. Categorize. When I'm working on a new book, that's what I do. I have three sections. Crap ideas. Workable ideas. And really good who-in-the-world-would-ever-believe-that ideas."

"How do you decide which ones to use?"

"I don't. They usually tell me. But I'll let you in on a little secret . . ." His wink makes my heart stop. "My last three bestsellers? Crap ideas."

"No." I can't help laughing, but I don't think he's joking. He's collecting our trash and I guess it's time to go. "What are you working on now?" I push back my chair and he's already behind me, pulling it out and helping me with my coat.

Brock leans in a little, his hands on my shoulders. "My last book."

Something in the way he says it, the sadness in his voice, the finality of those three words, makes me shiver.

⚜

Two weeks after Thanksgiving I realize I should probably confirm my plans for Christmas. Go home. But the thought makes me feel a little ill. My mother has phoned several times insisting we all go down to them in Florida or they come back to Boston and she'll have everyone over this year. My mother doesn't cook. I imagine a gourmet meal being ordered from one of her expensive catering companies. The kids would hate that. So I find the courage to call and ask Adam and Zoe what they want to do this year. And whether they want to see their father. They both ask to come up here to the Berkshires. And they don't really want to see Kevin.

My brother calls midafternoon, so I seek his advice. Because I'm at a total loss here and I hate the feeling.

"Zoe says she wants a white Christmas. Wants to 'commune with nature.' What do I tell Kevin?"

"I suppose . . . maybe you compromise. Say the kids will be there with you for Christmas, but tell Kevin he's welcome to invite them to stay with him for New Year's. Do you think they'd do that?"

"I don't know." I stand at the long picture window and watch snow swirl around the trees. The season is turning into a skier's dream. "Zoe finally agreed to talk to Kevin, but I know she's still angry. Adam would probably go. It's just so . . ." An awful knot twists in my stomach. I can't imagine us split into two families. It doesn't feel right. It's not right.

"Hey." Paul interrupts my thoughts. "I was thinking we could fly out. Spend Christmas there with you. I'd do Christmas Eve service and then leave here as soon as possible on Christmas Day. We'd get there late, probably, but—"

"Really?" Excitement builds in me. I haven't seen my brother in two years. "Have you been talking to Mom?" Paul's laugh is all the answer I need and I groan. Loudly. "She's convinced everyone to come here, hasn't she? Peg too?"

"Peg will call you later. Listen, before you freak out, when's the last time we were all together? Think about it. We'll all pitch in. The house is plenty big, and Mom thinks it'd be better for you to stay put. Says you sound much more at peace since you moved up there."

Moved. Like I've left my old life behind completely.

Well, maybe I have.

"All right. I guess the kids will enjoy seeing their

cousins." I'm making it sound like torture, having to spend time with my family.

Paul's chuckle tells me I'm exactly right. "Try to find a little enthusiasm, Savannah. We wouldn't want to add to your misery by showing up and giving you a hug or anything."

"I know. I'm being horrible, aren't I?" I slump into a chair and pull my knees up. "I'm dreading discussing this with Kevin. He's acting really weird, Paul."

"Weird how?"

"Like friendly. Like he thinks we can actually be friends. He keeps calling . . . He makes up excuses, but I know it's to check up on me."

"Well." My brother lapses into momentary silence, and I hear his fingers tapping against his phone. "That's understandable."

I draw a deep breath and frown at the family portrait over the mantel. My mother has filled the house with framed photographs of all of us taken over the years. Kevin is in so many of them. "I'm not suicidal, Paul. I'd tell someone if I was. Seriously."

"Good. Okay." His intake of breath is unsteady. I'll never forget the look on his face when he walked into that hospital room six years ago. I don't think he believed I'd actually done it. Actually tried to end my life. I didn't either. But the bandages around my wrists told the real story.

"Is this what happens when people get

divorced? They just become sort-of friends who talk to each other about the kids and the weather and who gets to see the children when?"

"Sometimes. Sometimes they don't talk at all. That's worse, don't you think?"

"I don't know." I'm being honest. "Talking to Kevin right now hurts. Hurts a lot."

"Oh, sweetheart." My brother sighs again. "I know. Truthfully, I've been praying something would happen to change things."

Huh. "I've been praying too," I admit. "Trying to. But I don't know what to ask for anymore. I've given up trying to figure it out. God knows what I mean and what will happen, even if I don't. So I just pray for Kevin to be okay. And that I'll be okay. I don't want to hate him. I want him to be happy. And if he can't be happy with me . . . then I hope he finds happiness elsewhere."

"Sounds like you're doing better than I am. I still want to kill the man."

"Paul. You guys were best friends. Don't forget that."

"You're my sister." His groan is long, sad. "What he's done . . . I can't fathom it. I've heard pretty much everything since entering the ministry, stories that keep me up nights. But this hits too close to home. This has damaged my family."

"I think we were damaged long before Kevin decided to sleep with someone else." I know we were. I just haven't wanted to admit it before now.

"I'm glad you're not bitter, Savannah. It's best to try to love, no matter how hard it is." He gives a harsh laugh. "Guess I should try taking my own advice, huh?"

"Oh, some days I'm still bitter. Sometimes I don't want to love, Paul. I don't want to still love him." I lean back in the chair and close my eyes. Love. I thought I knew all about that once.

We talk a bit longer, until I run out of words. Paul asks if he can pray, and I listen, tears warming my cheeks.

After I hang up I think about what he said. Think about Clarice and how she keeps intimating that prayer changes things. If that were true I'd have to acknowledge God still listens, still cares about this tragedy that has become my life.

I need air. I can't sit cooped up inside thinking about things I don't understand. I pull on my winter gear and head out for a nice long walk.

The woods are snowy and silent and have that ominous feel about them, like I'm being watched, but the sensation doesn't scare me. I spent most summers here from a young age—this was my playground. I know these trails like the back of my hand. I don't worry about what might be out there wanting to do me harm. As my father would say, don't spend your time borrowing trouble. It'll catch you eventually.

Trouble really can't begin to describe the kind of trauma we began to endure on a daily basis after the accident. Thinking back now, I see the exact moment I began to retreat. Shelby's funeral . . .

Somehow I stand, half stand, half slump against Kevin, and watch as they lower that small shining casket into the dark cavernous hole beneath the ground. Ashes to ashes. Dust to dust. I've always wondered why they say that at funerals. Because we get it. God, we so get it. My little girl, full of life and energy and excitement for the future, here one day and gone the next.

"I'm just going to Caisey's, Mom!" she yells at me from the driveway, but the phone is ringing and I'm halfway through the front door.

"Put on your helmet!" It's the last thing I said to my daughter.

Shelby always wore her helmet. But in the end, it didn't matter. It didn't save her.

It's Kevin on the phone, calling to tell me he got tickets to that play I've been wanting to see. For our anniversary. I head back outside to the sickening sound of screeching brakes. Someone is screaming. It might be me.

"Savannah? What was that?" Kevin is yelling now. "Savannah? Savannah!"

I'm running down the street before I realize I'm still holding the phone.

Tears freeze on my face and my nose burns.

Five deer graze on the right-hand side of the path, and I slow my steps. They're standing together, nosing through the white stuff for shoots, I suppose. I wonder what they'll find this time of year. I stand and watch them. They're majestic creatures, really. Gentle and unassuming. A nuisance in the summer, though. Mom is forever chasing them out of her hostas. I half wonder if Brock might be out here with his rifle. I hope not.

Every now and then the tall pines around me throw down a light shower of snow. Real winter has come early here and decided to stay. The sun pokes through green branches in flashes as a soft breeze blows through the trees. I lock eyes with a doe and smile. Her ears flick and for a second I think she'll bolt, but she chooses to ignore me and resumes her foraging.

There is movement beyond the clearing. Laughter, I think. Or perhaps it was a bird. But I hear it again, the sudden high-pitched laughter of a child. I take a step forward. I don't want to startle the deer, but I wonder if that's Maysie, running around alone out here. I worry they give that child too much freedom when she is not in school. Come to think of it, I don't know for sure that she attends school. She's always been at the house when I've been there. It could be possible Brock homeschools her, but when would he have the time with all the writing he does?

A glimpse of red and a snatch of blond catch my eye and I pick up my pace. I'm sure I saw a child running across the path up ahead. "Maysie!" The deer scatter and leap away through the forest and I break into a run. She's too far from home. She could get lost. Hurt. Anything could happen to her.

"Maysie, wait! It's me, Savannah!" Looking to the left and then the right, I see no sign of her. I double back and head south, toward the Chandlers'.

Chapter 11

"Everything you can imagine is real."
—PABLO PICASSO

Someone is playing tricks on me.

By the time I reach the front steps and ring the bell, I'm out of breath and my heart is pounding so hard I'm sure I'll have a heart attack right here on the stoop.

Clarice swings open the heavy door and smiles. "Savannah, dear. Do come in. We weren't expecting you, were we?" She frowns as though she may have forgotten.

"No, but I . . . Maysie was out in the woods and I . . ." It's still hard to breathe, but what little air I have left leaves my lungs as soon as I enter the living room.

Maysie is sitting at the gaming table with Brock. Playing checkers. And they look as though they've been there for some time.

"Sh-she was just outside," I stammer. Of course she wasn't. I know it, deep down, but if it wasn't Maysie, then who was that out there? We are the only two homes on this stretch of land at the end of the lake.

Brock meets my gaze over the top of his

daughter's head. His brow furrows, and the way he half rises out of his chair tells me I look exactly how I feel, like I'm about to pass out. Maysie swivels to face me and smiles.

"Hi, Miss Sabannah. I hab a cold." Her red nose confirms it. A sneeze shakes her tiny frame and Brock hands her a Kleenex from the box beside them.

"I'm keeping her inside today." He gives me that quizzical look he wears so well, and I wish I knew what he was thinking. Well, maybe I don't.

"Oh. I guess it was . . ." What?

"You probably saw my angel." Maysie's eyes light with the notion.

Brock smiles and lifts a brow. "Mays . . ." Maysie shrugs, turns back to their game, and jumps three spaces for the win. Brock thumps against the back of his chair, says a word he's not supposed to, and covers it with a cough.

"Brock, dear." Clarice's admonishment makes him grin.

"Chess. I'll teach you to play chess. You won't win at that."

"Bet I will." Maysie giggles and I startle at the sound. That's not the same laughter I heard a few minutes ago.

"Sorry to have disturbed you," I manage to say. "I'm glad it wasn't Maysie out there. I was worried."

"I wouldn't get lost," Maysie pipes up.

Brock concentrates his gaze on me. "Thanks for checking on her."

"Well, since I'm here, could I see the puppies?" I feel like I've stepped into an old episode of *The Twilight Zone*. Puppies are soft and warm and real. I need a dose of reality right about now.

"Of course you can." Clarice smiles and leads the way. "I was just about to put the kettle on." In the kitchen she stops midway and puts a hand on my arm. "Why don't you sit down first? Catch your breath."

She fixes tea and I take off my coat and gloves and unwrap my scarf. The warmth of the room calms me and I settle at the long kitchen table. My eyes land on the big black Bible that sits near the fruit bowl. Clarice soon pushes a steaming mug of hot tea toward me and sits down with her own.

"Don't let those thoughts have their way, Savannah."

Thoughts that I'm slipping back toward the brink of insanity, she means. How she knows . . . I can't comprehend Clarice's freaky mind-reading tactics. I gave up trying weeks ago.

"I just want to be well." Tears burn and slip over my cheeks.

"Oh, my dear." She breathes out a long, sad sigh, rounds the table in a flash, and pulls me into her firm embrace. She smells like roses and tea and old books, and as she gently rubs my shoulder, I feel strangely at peace.

140

Being up here has had that effect on me. The last time I really felt completely peaceful or content was probably over ten years ago. Before Shelby died. But now there are moments I believe I might be able to overcome the turmoil inside that still takes hold every so often.

"I don't understand. Out in the woods today . . ."

I can't admit the truth. That for a moment, when I saw Maysie sitting safely inside, my mind suggested that the child I thought I saw was Shelby. "And the greenhouse . . . Normal people don't see and hear things that aren't there."

Clarice's laughter is soft as she sits back down. "How do you know that?" She sips her tea and studies me through luminous eyes I'm half afraid to look into. "Perhaps they do and they just don't discuss it."

"Do you think it's possible to see things we want to? Things we're so desperate for that our mind simply conjures them up?" It's the only explanation that makes sense.

She stirs a bit of sugar into her tea with a silver spoon. Her wrinkled cheeks lift ever so slightly. "When our dear Mark died, I would go into his room, into the nursery. I'd wait until Joseph was asleep, but then I'd tiptoe down the hall. That room was always warm, even in the dead of winter. I'd stand over his empty crib and ask God why. Why did he take our precious boy from us? Some nights I'd just sit in the rocker, clutching

141

his baby blankets, and cry. Sometimes I would hear him crying too."

I bite my lip and nod. I don't need to imagine that scene. I've lived it. I stopped going into Shelby's room after the first few weeks. I couldn't do it anymore. Her presence was still too real. Too absent. Neither of us could bring ourselves to pack up that room. Eventually, a year later, with Beth and John's help, we did. "Did it help? Going in there?"

"It allowed me to let go." Clarice pulls a red shawl around her shoulders and smiles. "Everyone grieves in their own way, Savannah. That was mine. But Joe . . . I don't know how he grieved. He shut down completely. And all I could do was hold on and wait."

"How long? How do you hold on when there's nothing left to hold on to?" Frankly, I don't know that I have the right to ask for things to be resolved. I've made too many mistakes, and I can't go back and change the past.

"How much faith do you have, Savannah?"

"You've asked me that before."

She places an arthritic hand on top of her Bible and nods. "That's what I asked my Joe too. He rejected my faith, you see. His own. Told me to stop praying for him because it wouldn't do any good. God wasn't listening. God didn't care about us. About him. Oh, he was so angry." Her sigh fills the kitchen with memories that could be mine.

142

"Kevin stopped coming to church with me about three years ago," I tell her. "He walked into our bedroom one Saturday night and said he couldn't do it. Couldn't go on pretending he still believed in a loving God when all he could see was Shelby in a casket. 'What's loving about that?' he asked. 'What kind of God takes children from their parents?' And I couldn't answer him." The heaviness burrows deep again. There isn't any point in fighting it. Sooner or later it will win.

"Savannah." Clarice's tone is surprisingly sharp, and I jerk my head up and meet her eyes. But they're not angry. They glow with tears of compassion, years of wisdom, and they shine with truth. "The moment you stop trusting is the moment you give up. Do you want to give up?"

I rest my head in my hands and close my eyes.

Do I want to give up?

I thought I did. Six years ago I was ready to give it all up. Ready to be done with the pain, the heartache, and the ever-present shroud of darkness that covered me day in and day out. But for whatever reason, Kevin came home from work early that day.

If he hadn't . . .

"Some days I still do." It's the truth. "Some days I don't know why I'm still here."

Clarice sniffs and gives that knowing nod. "You are here, dear girl, because you are loved. And you have much love to give. You simply need to find your way back to believing that."

"You don't think God's given up on me by now?"

"God doesn't give up, dear. People do."

Clarice finishes her tea and leaves me alone in her warm kitchen. Maysie's drawings cover the refrigerator. Everything is neat and tidy and seems to have a place. Small clay pots of fragrant basil, lavender, and thyme line the windowsill above the sink. Old photographs and Thomas Kinkade images hang on light-blue walls. Yellow checked curtains frame the windows that let in the light and keep out the cold. A sudden yearning for my mother tugs at my heart and I am glad she's coming soon.

In the dim light of the laundry room, things don't seem so bad. I watch the puppies roll around each other, nipping and making little growly noises. I'd forgotten how fast they grow. Willow pads over to me, flops down, and rests her soft head on my lap, as if to comfort me and remind me of Clarice's words. *God doesn't give up. People do.*

I don't know how long I've been sitting there thinking about that when Brock comes in. He doesn't say a word. Just sits against the wall opposite me, takes a pup into his lap, and stretches out his legs. After a while he knocks the side of my socked foot with his. "Maysie wants to know if you'll stay for dinner. I'm making pizza."

I do love pizza. "I don't want to impose." Hope is squirming so I set her down and push my hair behind my ears.

"I'll take that as a yes." Laughter rumbles in his chest and I glance up. It's hard to meet his eyes because I don't like the questions in them. "What did you see out there, Savannah? In the woods? . . . When you walked in the room you were spooked."

"I'm not sure." I can't tell him the truth. But the look on his face tells me I don't need to. "Do you . . . see things?"

His smile is more than charming. "No. But that doesn't mean you shouldn't." He lines his big feet up against mine and applies a gentle pressure that sends a flagrant flood of feeling through me and sets fire to my face. Thankfully the light is dim in here. "There's nothing wrong with seeing what you want to see. Maybe it's real, maybe it's not, but if God's in all of this, like Aunt Clarice keeps telling me, then it's nothing to be afraid of, right?"

"I suppose so." Does he really understand me? It's been so long since anybody has. "But I am afraid . . . I've been down that road before. Crazy Town is no fun."

Brock puts the puppy back on the floor and leans forward, his eyes shining into mine. Before

I can stop him, he's reached for my hand. He pushes up the sleeve of my sweater to reveal a story I don't want to tell.

"Don't." I tug my arm back, but he holds tight.

"The other day in the coffee shop, you had your sleeves rolled up." He traces the ugly scar with his finger and the sensation sends a shiver through me. His touch is too familiar. Almost as though I've known it before. Of course, I haven't. But it's easy to forget that when his gaze locks with mine. "Want to talk about it?" The base of his thumb rubs along my wrist, over the scar Kevin could never stand to see.

I press my lips together, my heart hammering. "It's nothing. I'm fine. I'm fine now." How many times have I said this over the years? To Kevin. To my parents. To myself. And the worry in Brock's eyes confirms the ludicrousness of it.

He exhales with a slow nod. "I think you want to be. But I'm not sure you are. Not yet."

Breath leaves my chest and I lower my head, then meet his eyes again. "Do you have things in your life you wish you could do over?"

Gentle laughter gets caught in his throat. "Don't we all? But we don't always get the opportunity. Sometimes we have to make the best of what we're given."

"Why is it so hard?" He's still holding my hand and I'm letting him. Because this kind of contact, the warmth and comfort of another hand in mine,

146

feels good. Sitting here, knowing that somebody in the world understands me, somebody cares. I hadn't realized how much I'd missed that until this moment.

"Who ever said it would be easy?"

I smile a little and shrug. "You're right. I guess I need more of that faith Clarice clings to."

He looks at me long and hard, then his serious expression splits into a smile. "You need to see something." He pulls me up with him, and before I can protest, he's escorted me out to the greenhouse.

"I really don't feel like doing any digging right now." In fact, I'm not sure I want to do any more work in here at all. I'm so tired of trying. Today all my effort feels futile.

Brock places his hands on my shoulders and maneuvers me to the edge of a flower bed. "Look there." He points toward the mound of rich dark soil.

A frustrated sigh slips out of me. "I don't see anything."

His chuckle wraps around me, along with his arm. "Look again, Savannah."

I blink and lean forward. "You're kidding me." It can't be. But there they are. A cluster of green shoots sticking up out of the brown dirt. "Did you put those in there to tease me, Brock Chandler?"

He laughs and shakes his head. "I promise you I did not."

A lump in my throat makes further speech impossible.

"You know what that is, don't you, darlin'?"

I turn and meet his eyes, still disbelieving. "What?"

"Hope." His smile warms me through. "A reminder to hold on, to keep going. You've got kids that need you, Savannah. Your family loves you very much, don't they? Isn't that enough?"

I step out from the cradle of his arm and wipe my eyes. "It should be."

Dear God, it should be. But some days it's not.

Chapter 12

"Experience is one thing you
can't get for nothing."
—OSCAR WILDE

"Don't put yourself in compromising situations."
Zoe Barrington arched her back in a catlike stretch, shivered at the feel of Tim's hands around her face, and ignored her mother's voice inside her head. Tim was the first guy she'd let get this close. They started dating over the summer. Tim had been working in Boston and they met through mutual friends, discovered they were both heading to Princeton in the fall, and next thing she knew, she thought she might be in love.

Ever since watching *Cinderella* as a little girl, Zoe dreamed of romance, love at first sight, and a fairy-tale wedding. And her faith made her want to save herself for marriage. Most of her friends had given up those ideals in high school, but Tim shared her convictions and her faith. They were the kind of kids parents dreamed of having. Good kids, respectful of the rules and the reasons for them. Lately, though, since her roommate had been spending more weekends at home, things were heating up a little more than they should.

"You're so beautiful." Tim kissed her neck as

his hands slipped under her untucked shirt. Zoe ran her fingers through his thick hair and kept her eyes closed. Listened to the music on the stereo and lost herself in a whirlwind of feeling. She wouldn't think about what a bad idea this was. Because right now it didn't feel that way. Right now it felt amazing and right and she didn't want him to stop.

His lips found hers again and he took possession of her mouth in a way that rendered her helpless to do anything other than surrender to the fiery sensations his kisses ignited. When his hands moved down, toward the top of her jeans, common sense kicked in. "Okay. Tim . . ." Zoe sighed, pulled his hands back, and prayed for strength. "We need to stop."

He groaned but rolled away, smoothing her hair off her forehead. "I know. Sorry."

She watched his brown eyes dance in the dim light, smiled, and propped her elbow, resting her head on her hand. "We should probably start meeting in the library."

"That would be safer." His grin widened as he leaned in again to kiss her. "But you're right. I'm going."

Zoe found his jacket for him and caught sight of her digital clock. "Crap, it's 2:00 a.m.!" She'd look like a complete wreck when Dad showed up in the morning.

Tim pulled on the leather jacket and took her in

his arms again. "Time flies when you're having fun."

How was she supposed to argue with a guy who looked that good? Zoe laughed and pushed him toward the door. "Out."

"Okay, okay. I'll come over around nine thirty, right? What time is your dad arriving?"

"He said ten. You don't have to come."

"I will. I want to make sure you're comfortable. Then if you want me to leave I will."

"I'll be fine." She managed a smile. "He's a jerk, but he's still my dad. You can come say hi, but I don't want him to feel like . . . I don't know . . . like I don't want to be alone with him."

"You didn't as of yesterday," he reminded her carefully. "You were the one who asked me to be there, remember?"

"True." She couldn't deny it. But she'd been thinking it over and it didn't seem fair to her father to have Tim there. They wouldn't really be able to talk. As much as she dreaded it, she knew she had to see him alone. "See you in the morning then."

"I love you." Tim pulled her closer and kissed her again. "Dream of me."

"I always do." Zoe closed the door behind him. She took a few deep breaths and frowned. She and Tim were walking a fine line. One of these days she was afraid she wouldn't be able to say no. Some days she wanted nothing more than to experience all he might offer her if she agreed.

151

But with both of them wanting to get into law school, she wasn't about to mess up her life with an unwanted pregnancy. That's what happened with her parents, and look how things ended up for them.

She pulled on the old Bruins T-shirt she slept in, brushed her hair, and glared at her reflection in the mirror. Every time she thought about the divorce she wanted to cry. Why did Dad have to be so stupid? Why couldn't they just work things out? Why couldn't life go back to the way it was before, when things had been normal and her family perfect?

As she crawled under the covers and flicked off the light, Zoe shook her head. They'd never been perfect. Things had never been normal.

Not really.

Not since the day Shelby died.

≫≪

When Zoe and Tim walked in, Dad was already there, seated at a table at the far end of Starbucks. It didn't surprise her; Kevin Barrington was always exactly on time, if not early, for everything. Which was why it hadn't been too hard to figure out something was up when he started forgetting dinners and family functions. Zoe suspected he was having an affair long before she could ever admit it. She might have even known before her mother.

She pulled warm, coffee-scented air into her lungs, gripped Tim's hand a little tighter, and pasted on a smile as her father saw them and stood.

"Hi, Zo." He gave her a hesitant peck on the cheek. She stood stiffly, not knowing whether to hug him. Part of her wanted to, more than anything. But if she did, she'd probably burst into tears. Not happening. The moment passed and Dad and Tim shook hands. Tim went to get their coffee and Zoe shrugged out of her coat and sat.

"He's not staying. He just wanted to say hi."

Dad nodded. Was that relief she saw on his face? Probably. She sat opposite him and studied the lines around his eyes. He looked completely exhausted. Like he hadn't slept in weeks. Zoe had always thought her father was the best-looking man on earth. Until she met Tim, of course. But for a guy in his forties, she'd still call her dad handsome. Maybe that's what got him in trouble in the first place. But she wouldn't go there. Didn't want to go there. "You don't look so hot."

He flashed a familiar smile that hit her right in the gut. "You have your mother's knack for being slightly less than subtle."

"Sorry."

"Oh, don't apologize. It'll come in handy in the courtroom."

"If I get in."

"Why wouldn't you get in? You're brilliant."

"Right." Last time she checked her GPA, she'd beg to differ. Law school seemed more out of reach than ever now, but the thought of not making it terrified her, pushed her to stay up later, study harder. Pushed her beyond the brink of terminal exhaustion. But she would do it. She had to. Their family could not afford another failure.

Zoe tapped her fingers on the worn table. Conversation buzzed at the tables around them, yet it seemed the two of them had nothing to say. She'd never found it hard to talk to her father. Today there was too much between them, too much pain and heartbreak to wade through before she could find words that wouldn't sound hollow.

Tim came back, and they drank coffee and made small talk for ten minutes before he got up to leave. And then they were alone again.

"How's your mom?" Dad sat back in his chair, feigning a relaxed look, but she knew better.

"Mom's good. Not exactly sure what she's doing up there all day. Sounds like she's spending a lot of time with that old lady next door. She said something about a gardening project."

"At this time of year?" His brow crinkled in his classic frown and Zoe couldn't stop a grin.

"I think there's some greenhouse. Remember that glass thing? You see it from the road. I guess it's heated."

"Okay." He shrugged and took another sip of

his espresso. "She tell you Brock Chandler lives next door?"

"Brock who?" Zoe rubbed her chin. Mom hadn't mentioned a man.

"Chandler. He's an author we both like. Really popular, but he rarely gives interviews. It's kind of weird that he's living up there. She says he's related to the old lady, her nephew or something. Anyway . . ." He put his mug down and pushed his fingers through his hair. "Zoe, look, I wanted to tell you . . . I'm sorry for everything. I know this has been really hard on you and your brother. I really screwed things up, didn't I?"

"You think?" She crossed her arms and blinked back tears. Dad sighed and pressed his palms down on the table. He looked like he wanted to cry too. That would be awesome, the two of them sitting here like blubbering fools where any one of her friends could walk by. "We're all going up there for Christmas, you know, to the lake house. Me and Adam, Grandma and Gramps and everyone."

"Oh." The surprise on his face said he didn't know. "Well. This is news to me."

Now what? She couldn't backpedal, pretend she hadn't said it.

"I thought Mom would have told you already."

He glanced away. "I'm sure she's planning on it. We haven't talked recently. I thought it best to give her some space."

"Sorry." The dejected look he wore pulled the

apology from her. "Maybe Adam and I can come home for New Year's to spend some time with you. We could stay at the house. Unless you have plans with what's-her-face."

Zoe clamped her mouth shut and studied the dark liquid in her cup. "You know what, never mind. I think that would be too awkward." Hot tears crested her cheeks. Maybe she could leave now. Get up without another word and pretend they'd never attempted to get past this.

"Sweetheart." Dad reached for her hand and held tight. "Zoe, look at me, please."

She forced her gaze up and sniffed. "What? What can you possibly say to me that will make this any better? I don't know why you wanted to meet in the first place."

Unless . . . The horrible thought twisted her stomach. She'd tried not to think about it. Not to let her mind go there. Because it was incomprehensible, and every time she imagined it, she wanted to throw up. "Are you going to marry her?"

"What?" Dad pulled back his hand, his eyes wide. Like she'd asked for his permission to go off and live in a Middle Eastern war zone. Indefinitely. "Marry Alison?"

"It's a logical conclusion to draw, don't you think?"

"Uh. I guess." His cheeks lost a little color as he brought his hands together, rubbed the spot on his left hand where his wedding band used to sit. "Alison is moving to California."

His quiet words fell into her soul and she took a minute to process their meaning. Tears came again. That's why he'd wanted to meet. It wasn't to make things better at all.

He wanted to say good-bye.

She gauged the haunted look on his face and wondered when it became so easy to hate her father. "Awesome. When do you leave?"

Dad stared back at her for a long moment filled with awful silence. Then he shook his head. "I'm staying. In Boston."

Relief zinged through her but she pushed it back, still too bitter. "Long-distance relationships are difficult."

"Zoe, give me a break, huh?"

"Are you kidding me right now?" She gave a harsh laugh and shook her head. "Give you a break? I should be telling you where to go!"

"Okay." He held up a hand and scanned the room. "I know how you feel, and believe me, I deserve it. I acted like a scum. I won't deny it, and I wish to God I could change it, but I can't. All I can do is try to figure out why it happened and how to move on from here."

He scratched his jaw and hesitated. "Zo, I ended things with Alison. I'm trying to get my life back, what's left of it. I don't know what that looks like right now, but I know I don't want to go on hurting you, Adam, or your mom. I don't want to be that person."

Zoe leaned forward and put her head in her hands. If she said one word, she'd totally lose it. So she stayed quiet, breathed deeply, and prayed. Wasn't this what she'd been asking for all along? For things to be made right again?

"Does Mom know?" She ran a finger under her eye, lifted her shoulders, and let them drop in a long exhale.

"No." Dad pinched the bridge of his nose and sniffed too. She could count the times she'd seen him cry on one hand. "Don't . . . mention it to her. I'll tell her. Look . . . I didn't figure this out very well, Zo. And now . . . I just want to do what's right."

"Maybe you should have thought about 'what's right' before you jumped in bed with another woman." The words shot out before she could stop them.

Dad's eyes flashed, but then a beleaguered smile slipped across his mouth. "You're right. I should have, but I didn't. And now we're all paying the price."

No kidding. Zoe sat silent a moment and measured her words. "If you want me to forgive you right now, I don't think I can. And honestly? I don't think Mom will. Ever."

He gave a slow nod. "I know I've got a long road ahead to even begin to make up for what

I've done, but I'm going to try, Zo. And I swear to you, I won't let you down again."

"I wish you'd never let me down at all, Dad." Unvoiced emotion burned in her throat. "But you did. And I don't know what to do with that or how to get over it. I just want my dad back. I want things the way they used to be, but I look at you and . . . I don't know you anymore." She stood and pulled on her coat. "I need to get out of here."

"Zoe, wait!" He followed her outside, through the courtyard, and into the parking lot before she stopped walking and turned to face him, anger merging with sorrow, creating surging, stifling feelings she didn't know what to do with.

"What?"

"All I'm asking is that you give me a chance. Let me make things right."

She shrugged, breathed in cold air, and tried to calm her frenzied thoughts. "I need some time, okay?"

"Okay." His eyes filled again but he moved forward. "Can I at least give my little girl a hug?"

The question hung in the frosty air.

Zoe trembled, tried to fight the longing to simply rest her head against his shoulder and have him tell her everything would work out. Just like he always had. His support and reassurance had always been the one constant in her life. But today she knew that even if he said the words, she wouldn't believe him.

"Daddy . . ." She gave up the fight and let him hug her anyway. And all the hurt and heartbreak of the past few months poured out of her in a violent explosion of emotion she wasn't prepared for and didn't have a clue how to deal with.

"Baby, I'm so sorry . . . so, so sorry," he whispered, smoothing her hair down like he used to when she was little. Then he just held her, wrapped her up tight in the safety of his embrace, and let her cry.

Chapter 13

"Love is but the discovery of ourselves in others,
and the delight in the recognition."
—ALEXANDER SMITH

I have settled into a strange contentment.

It's a few days before Christmas, and while I
can't say I'm ecstatic about the upcoming holiday, I am oddly comfortable. Tomorrow Zoe and
Adam will drive up. The day after that, my parents
will be here. Peg and her family will arrive on
Christmas Eve, and Paul with Janice and the girls
the next day.

My grocery list is long. I invited Clarice, Brock,
and Maysie to join us for Christmas Day dinner.
They've been so good to me. I want to return the
favor. In the morning, before the kids arrive, I'll
drive into town and start stocking up.

It's a snowy Sunday afternoon and I'm wrapping
presents in the living room when my cell phone
rings. I think it's in the bedroom. Sure enough, I
find it hiding under a pillow.

It's Beth. I haven't talked to her in a few days.
"Hey, stranger."

"Savannah, how are you?"

Something in the way she asks the question
makes me a little nervous. "Good, I think.

Wrapping presents at the moment." I sit on the edge of the bed and watch snow fall on the already white front lawn. "Are you okay? Everything all right at home?"

"Ye-ah. I guess. It's a beautiful day here. Sunny, not too cold at all. No snow yet. I'm just looking out the window at your house . . ." She's hedging. Something is definitely wrong.

"Beth? What? What's wrong with the house?"

"Um, nothing's wrong with the house. It's just that, well . . . Kevin's there."

"What do you mean he's there? Is *she* there? I swear if—"

"I mean he's up a ladder fixing your broken shutters, and no, she's not here. He arrived about an hour ago. Alone."

"Oh." I blow air through my lips. Unpleasant thoughts launch an attack. "Why is he doing that now? Those shutters have been off their hinges for over a year. Do you think he wants to put the house on the market? Oh great. That's all I need. Maybe I'll have to get a condo or something. Maybe he . . . Beth? What are you doing?" I hear her heels clicking on her wood floor and the squeak and slam of the screen door on her front porch.

"I'm standing here watching him. He's beating the crap out of that nail." She laughs. "He's met with John a few times. Did you know that?"

"I heard."

"Oh, he saw me. Hi, Kevin!" I can just picture

162

her waving enthusiastically. "Whoops. He's coming down."

"Beth!" I do not like where this is going. Not. One. Bit. I roll my eyes and squash the urge to hang up. I want to know what he's doing there first.

"Hey, Beth. Is that Savannah?"

"Yes, but I don't think—"

"Give me the phone."

"No."

"Beth. Come on."

There's a bit of a struggle and I shake my head. They're children, really.

"Savannah? Hey." Kevin's deep voice thrums in my ear, heads straight for my heart, and settles over it like a favorite forgotten blanket, found again after a long absence.

I stomp over that thought and strengthen my resolve. "What are you doing at the house, Kevin?"

"Fixing stuff. I had some time and I started thinking about all the things you'd been asking me to do and so I figured I—"

He's rambling like he always does when he's nervous. "Kevin . . . Kev. Stop. Why are you doing this now? Are you . . ." I don't want to ask but I have to. "Are you thinking about putting the house on the market?"

"What?" He sounds as confused as I feel. "No. Of course not. I'm just . . . fixing stuff. You don't mind, do you?"

163

Do I? "No, I don't mind. As long as you stick to our agreement. I don't want her over there."

"What?"

"Alison. Remember? I told you before I left that I—"

"I know what you said." He lapses into silence. "She's not . . . uh . . . Have you talked to Zoe?"

"I talk to her every day. Why?"

"Um, okay. Well, I guess I did ask her not to . . ." He exhales and my mind is mulling over the million and one things he could possibly be thinking. "Hey, do you know where my good hammer is?" That was not one of them.

A giggle gets stuck in my throat. It isn't funny, really, and I'm half embarrassed to tell him. "Under the bed."

"Where?"

"In our . . . my bedroom. Under the bed. So is your baseball bat."

"You're not kidding."

"No. You know I hate being alone in that house. It's scary at night sometimes."

"So you're gonna attack somebody with my hammer?" Kevin lets out a long whistle, followed by low laughter that winds around me and pulls moisture from my eyes.

Oh, I miss my husband. I can see his face so clearly, it's as though he's standing right in front of me.

"I'd probably try the bat first." Come to think of

it, now that I know how to use a rifle . . . maybe I should get a gun. "I know how to shoot now." I can't help it. I'm proud of the accomplishment.

"Shoot what?"

"A gun. Brock taught me. Well, it was a rifle, I guess. But he says I'm a fast learner and a very good shot."

Kevin makes a noise that sort of sounds like a growl. "Brock Chandler taught you how to shoot a rifle?" He doesn't sound impressed. Or happy.

"Yes. He's southern, remember?"

"Maybe you should get a dog."

"I did."

"What?"

"Well, she's just a baby, but she'll be big enough to come home with me soon. Brock's dog, Willow, had puppies just after I got here. So I took one."

"You took one. I see." He sobers, clears his throat, and I imagine the look he gives Beth. I also imagine her face and know she's going half-crazy standing there listening to only one side of the conversation. "You certainly seem to be spending a lot of time with Brock Chandler."

"Do I?" My grin is without a doubt wicked but I don't care. "Who I spend time with is none of your business anymore, Kevin."

"Savannah."

"You should probably give Beth her phone back. And don't forget to set the alarm again when you leave the house."

"I'm going to call you later."

"I'd rather you didn't. I might be out." I hesitate. "With Brock." I can't resist the jab.

"Seriously?" There is definite panic in that question, and I have absolutely no idea why it is there. But part of me takes pleasure in knowing it is. In the same moment I'm regretting my words.

"Bye, Kevin."

"Oh. My. Gosh." Beth is back on the phone, laughing her head off. "Sweetie, what did you say to that poor man? He's stomping back across the road like he wants to strangle the devil himself."

Oops. "I told him I might be going on a date with Brock Chandler."

"What?" Beth practically screams in my ear. "Why do you not tell me these things?"

"Because I'm not." I sigh and flop backward onto the bed. "I just . . . I don't know, Beth, it just popped out."

"Girl, that's just mean."

"I know. I feel bad." And I have no clue why. "Well, it's not like Kevin wants me. Why shouldn't I go out with Brock Chandler? Not that he's asked, but if he did . . ." If he did I'd probably run for the hills. Maybe.

"You . . . don't know, do you?" Beth's voice gets quiet all of a sudden and I'm a little scared.

"Know what?"

"When did you last talk to Kevin, hon? I mean, other than just now."

166

"It's been a while, a few weeks. I don't remember. Why?"

"Ah, John just pulled up. We're going to the mall to get last-minute Christmas gifts. I'll call you later, okay?"

"Sure." She's gone and I groan. Loudly. I can't let myself think about what she meant. I have too much to do.

Okay, back to wrapping. But of course all I can do is sit there and think about Kevin and the way things were . . .

"Close your eyes." I jump as Kevin comes up behind me. He covers my eyes with his hands anyway so I don't have a choice. It's Christmas Eve, the kids are in bed, and I have no idea what time it is. I just finished placing the last present under the tree. Kevin has been down in the basement putting the final touches on the dollhouse for Zoe and Shelby he's been working on for weeks.

He propels me forward, stops, grabs something . . . a blanket? . . . He wraps it around my shoulders and I hear the back door opening. "Where are we going?"

"You'll see." He wraps his arms around me and presses his cheek against mine. "Okay. Open."

Our back patio has been transformed into something magical. Twinkling white lights hang from new cedar planks above a gazebo where a brand-new hot tub sits, bubbling in merry invitation. A bottle of champagne and two glasses sit on the wooden deck, along with a plate of chocolate-covered strawberries and a vase filled with long-stemmed red roses.

"You've got to be kidding me." I'm speechless. "When . . . How?"

"This afternoon. While you and the kids were at the mall. John and Beth came to help. You didn't notice the blinds in the kitchen were closed when you got home?"

"Kevin, it's Christmas Eve and we have three overly excited children. I'm not noticing much."

"Well, they're in bed now." He growls low in my ear and slides his hands beneath my sweater. "So why don't we try this baby out, Mrs. Barrington?" He spins me around to face him, his grin more than sexy. Sometimes I don't know how I got so lucky.

"I don't have a bathing suit on."

His grin broadens as he puts his lips over mine. "Sweetheart, you don't need one. In fact, the only thing you need to wear"—he steps back and forages in the pocket of his jeans—"is this." He's holding the most exquisite diamond ring I've ever seen. "Merry Christmas."

I clap a hand to my mouth. "Oh my gosh, Kevin! What did you do?"

"When we got married I promised I'd get you a proper ring one day, remember?"

I do. We were so young back then, we could barely afford to pay rent, let alone worry about

168

an engagement ring. Our parents loaned us the money for wedding bands, and we'd always said those were more important anyway.

"It's stunning. I don't know what to say."

He smiles and slips it onto my finger, in front of my plain gold band. The brilliant cut glows under the sparkling lights above us. "Say you'll love me forever, Savannah."

I wrap my arms around his neck, meet his shimmering eyes, and nod. "I will."

My phone rings again and startles me. It had better not be Kevin because I'm not ready to talk to him. Not yet.

"Savannah? Walter Kline."

"Oh. Hi, Walter." I go into the kitchen and flick on the kettle.

"Sorry to bother you on a Sunday, hon, but I'm flying out to Aspen for the holidays and I'm wondering what's going on."

"With?" I have to stand on tiptoe to reach the mugs. My mother is shorter than me and I have no clue why she insists on arranging her cupboards like she's six feet tall.

"We haven't received anything from Kevin's lawyer. I called him on Friday and he says he's gone over the agreement, but Kevin hasn't signed the papers. Says Kevin told him the two of you might reconcile?"

"We might *what?* Reconcile? Kevin said that?"

I just shrieked at Walter Kline. And broke another of my mother's favorite mugs. At least now I know what to get her for Christmas. "Walter, I have no idea what you're talking about."

"So I gathered." He chuckles, then sighs deeply. "Look, Savannah . . . sometimes a couple needs a break. Time to work things through. If Kevin hasn't moved on this, I suggest you talk to him and find out why."

"Yes. That's probably a good idea." Uh, no, it's not. It's the most terrifying idea anyone has ever suggested, and I want nothing to do with it.

The clock on the wall reads 4:00 p.m. Close enough to five. I open the fridge and pull out a bottle of chardonnay.

"Get back to me after the holidays. Okay, Savannah? And have a good one."

"Thanks, Walter. You too." My hands are trembling so badly I'll probably break something else any minute. Like the wineglass I'm filling. To the brim.

My mind is swirling with a thousand unexpected thoughts, making me slightly dizzy. What in the world is going on?

Kevin must be having some kind of mental breakdown or midlife crisis. Well, that much is already abundantly clear. But it's possible he's crazier than I am. Which, right about now, would be pretty darn crazy.

I'm just about to sink onto the couch in front of

the fire with my glass of wine when the doorbell rings. I'm so flustered I don't even bother to put down the glass, just yank open the front door and stare into Brock Chandler's dancing eyes.

His large frame fills my doorway and he looks every inch the southern gentleman in a sheepskin jacket and Atlanta Braves baseball cap. A light dusting of snow covers the black rim. He's holding a tray laden with four small white ceramic pots each containing a red amaryllis in full bloom. His lips part in a lazy smile as his gaze rests on my glass and then on me.

"Well, I reckon it's five o'clock somewhere." His wink renders me speechless. Somehow I manage to move backward and allow him in.

"This looks bad, doesn't it?" Not that I care right now. I take a long sip and give a sigh of satisfaction. "Those are beautiful."

Brock strolls through my house and sets the cardboard tray on the kitchen table. "Clarice said they all bloomed this morning. I guess the heat's working the way it should in there."

"I had no idea they'd bloom so quickly. We only planted those bulbs a few weeks ago."

"I suspect Clarice waved her magic wand over them when you weren't looking." He turns to face me and shoves his hands in the pockets of his jacket. His grin is wide.

"Right. But still." I study the plants. "Weird."

"It's something. I have to admit, what goes on

171

in that greenhouse is beyond the scope of even my imagination, darlin'."

"Even yours?" I widen my eyes in mock surprise. "Now that's saying something."

"You haven't been by the past few days."

"No. Christmas kind of snuck up on me. I realized how much I had left to do."

"Oh. Well. I missed you."

He what? "Would you like a glass of wine? I probably shouldn't drink alone." I move past him in a hurry, off to find another glass, and I'm pouring him one before he's even said yes.

"Why not." Brock chuckles, hangs his coat and cap over a chair, and takes the glass with a grin. "I'm more of a beer guy, but when in Rome . . ."

"Precisely." I raise my glass in salute. He follows me into the living room, and I'm strangely aware that my nerves have jacked up more than a notch.

He nods toward the vast array of colorful tubes of wrapping paper and the pile of presents sitting by the fake tree I hauled down from the attic yesterday. "Ah, the dreaded wrapping wars. No wonder you're drinking." He makes himself comfortable in a leather chair near the fire and kicks up the footrest. "Look at these paper cuts." He holds up a hand. "I'm betting those elves don't get paid near enough."

"Slave labor. Speaking of elves, where's Maysie?"

"On a secret mission with Aunt Clarice. And then they're having dinner together in town. I wasn't allowed to accompany them." He doesn't look at all upset about it.

"Should she really be driving at her age?"

Brock shrugs in that nonchalant way of his, his mouth curling in that grin I've decided should be illegal. "I put a few pillows on the front seat and rig the brake pedal. She does pretty good for a six-year-old."

Wine fizzes up my nose as I choke on laughter.

He takes a sip from his glass, then sets it down on the coffee table and rests his hands behind his head. "I like watching you laugh."

Okay then. I'm wondering if I can blame my flushed face on the fire and the wine. I blow out a breath and steady my gaze. This is Brock. We're friends. What on earth am I nervous about?

We talk for a good hour, finish off the bottle of white, forage the fridge for cheese and crackers and some fruit. He's not much for sitting around apparently, because pretty soon he's rebuilt the fire and we're stationed on the floor in front of it and he's teaching me how to play poker.

"That's a flush, darlin'. Aces high. Which means you win." His hand brushes over mine as he retrieves the cards I've just laid down. A tingle of electricity starts at the spot he just touched and shoots all the way up my arm and back down the other side, and my mouth suddenly feels like the Sahara.

"Another round?" He shuffles the cards like he's working tables in Las Vegas, his dimple flashing far too dangerously. "Maybe we should raise the stakes. What do you think?"

There is no way he's getting an answer to that question. "I'll just . . . get some water." I scramble out of there and take a couple of deep breaths. This is okay. Nothing is happening. We're just . . . breathe . . . friends.

And, yes, I am fully aware how overused and ludicrous that statement is.

In the safety of the kitchen I fumble with a bottle of Perrier and wonder why I let Brock Chandler in here in the first place.

On my way out of the kitchen, I find him standing in the dining room over my open laptop. "Uh. Please don't read that."

The side grin he gives says it's too late. I put the bottle and two tumblers on the table and slide my fingers through my hair. Brock gives a low whistle and sits.

"This is your blog? You're Jane, right?"

"Original, I know." *Jane's Journal*. It was all I could come up with at the time, but it stuck. I sigh and sit beside him. No use hiding it now. I pour fizzy water, slide a glass his way, and take a long sip.

I watch him scroll through the various posts in

silence. "You write well." Finally, he pushes the laptop away and sets serious eyes on me. "Your last post was three weeks ago."

I nod. "When I first started blogging, it was more about Shelby. About dealing with the loss of a child. It was a good thing. Maybe even a healing thing. But now . . . all I seem to do is vent. And my anger spreads faster than the flu." I run my hands down my face with a groan. "I don't think this is helping anyone. Least of all me."

Brock drums his fingers on the table, thoughtful. "Remember when we talked about prioritizing, figuring out what you want? Putting the rest aside?"

"Sure."

"Maybe, and I could be wrong, but maybe you might want to set this aside now. It seems to have served its original purpose. Don't you think?"

"I guess. It's just . . ." It's been a part of me so long, a refuge of sorts, that it's hard to let go.

"Nothing says you have to quit writing if you don't want to. But start fresh. This isn't you, Savannah."

"What makes you think you know me so well?" I try to sound annoyed. But he's right. The angry, bitter, and sometimes spiteful woman I turned into after Kevin's desertion doesn't suit my current demeanor or my present-day sur-roundings.

"I'm not sure." He nails me with that half grin again and it's impossible to look away. "I've been trying to figure that out myself. But somehow I feel I do. Know you."

I try not to exhale too loudly. He's getting awfully close to giving Clarice a run for her money with her mind-reading abilities. Because I feel the same about him and I'm pretty sure he knows it.

"Well. You have a point." I smile, feeling more hopeful than I have in weeks. "Maybe it is time to let it go. I think I'm ready to move on."

"Good." The way his eyes search my face sets my heart racing again.

Food. We need food. And I need to get out from under the heat of that stare. "Um. I have leftover pasta. We should eat."

"Shall I open more wine?" He follows me into the kitchen.

I turn, back up against the granite counter, and shake my head. "I think I'll stick to water."

Brock nods and raises the glass of water he's holding. "Probably wise." He takes a few sips, his eyes fixed on me. A light shadow of stubble outlines his jaw and I wonder what he'd do if I ran my finger over it.

The insane thought almost chases me from the room.

I must be drunk.

Except I don't think I am.

176

Which means I'm actually attracted to him. Like I didn't know that already.

But seriously contemplating doing something about it? That thought terrifies me.

"So." Brock puts his glass down next to mine. "Do you have any other secrets you'd like to share with me, Savannah?"

Oh boy. I hoist myself upward and sit on the counter, swinging my feet like I used to as a kid. My mother would not approve. Of any of this. "Not right now."

"Pity." He plants his palms on the counter on either side of me. For a long, mesmerizing moment, he just stands there and stares. "I think there must be at least ten different colors in your eyes. They're kind of fascinating."

"My eyes are fascinating?" I tap him on the chest, laughter building. "That's the best line you can come up with, Mr. *New York Times* bestseller man?" Okay, I'm flirting now. Shamelessly.

"All right. Give me a minute." Brock smiles and tips his head. His thick hair is mussed, a wave curling the wrong way.

My hand moves of its own accord and brushes it back into place. The moment it's done, I inhale and close my eyes against the truth of it. Because I know I've just crossed the line.

"Savannah." The way he breathes my name confirms it. I don't dare think about what might come next. Not until he moves forward, slides his arms around me, and holds my gaze, seeking some kind of affirmation. He shakes his head, his lips mere inches from mine. "You don't want this."

"Yes, I do." My husky whisper echoes around the kitchen and startles me. I let my fingers finally touch his face. "You have no idea how much."

"You are very wrong about that, darlin'." He angles his head slightly and presses his lips to mine in one exquisite moment that is both beautiful and unbearable. A low moan gets stuck in his throat as he pulls me close until I'm crushed against him, his hands warm on my back, then tangling through my hair while his kiss becomes more demanding.

My arms lock around his neck and he lifts me in one easy motion, still searching, seeking, and finding my answer in the way I'm responding to him. It's only once we're on the couch and he's trailing hot kisses down my neck and reaching for the first button on my shirt that I realize exactly what we're doing and where this is headed.

And just how far I have fallen in less than five minutes.

"I can't. Brock . . . stop." I push him off me and struggle to sit up. My breath hitches in my throat and my pulse is pounding like I've just run ten miles. "Oh, Lord, help me." I bury my head in my hands and loud, aching sobs wrangle their way from my chest.

Because I know now.

It happens that fast.

Attraction. Desire. Longing.

It's that instantaneous.

That dangerous.

And that easy to act on.

"Savannah." Brock sits beside me and puts an arm around my shaking shoulders. "I'm sorry. I shouldn't have. That was way out of line."

"Yes. No. I wanted . . . Oh, Brock. I wanted it to happen." I did. I absolutely did.

I flash him a look and the sadness on his face sears me. I think I'm hysterical, but he doesn't seem to care. He just sits there, lets me burrow into his wool sweater and weep. For everything I've lost, everything I almost gave away, and maybe everything I still want but don't really believe I'll get.

By the time he pulls on his coat, it's been dark a long time.

It feels like we've talked for days, yet it's only been a few hours. I've told him everything about Kevin. His betrayal. My utter devastation and continued confusion. I've confessed my guilt over Shelby's death, shared my feelings of inadequacy—everything. Things I didn't even realize I was still holding on to. And somehow he seems to understand.

Like that first moment we met, when he looked at me as if he already knew my deepest secrets.

I stand with him at the front door, our fingers laced together. "Why do I feel like I've known you forever?"

He blinks, gives a beleaguered shrug and a sad smile that threatens to do more damage to my already broken heart. "Maybe you have. You just didn't know my name." His warm hands cradle my face while a million regrets move through his eyes. "Another place, another time, things would be different."

"I think so." Tears wet my lashes and cheeks and he wipes them away with the base of his thumbs. "But right now I'm not so sure I'll ever learn to love again."

"Don't say that." He tips my chin and studies me for an achingly long moment. "You will, Savannah. I know it."

"Are we . . . What do we do now?" I don't even know how to say it. "Can we still see each other?"

Brock's laughter warms me, makes me believe we'll actually get through this moment. "Shoot, darlin', you're not getting rid of me that easy. Besides, I need all the friends I can get."

"That sounds familiar." I step back and let him go with a sigh that says more than it should. "And you still haven't told me your story. Not all of it."

"No, I haven't." Brock pulls on his cap and yanks up the zipper on his coat. "You're not ready for it. Not yet."

I have no idea what that means and I can't ask

him because he's already heading down the steps and jogging into the dark night. Away from me.

A sob rises in my throat as I shut the front door and lean against it. And then my cellphone starts singing, "All You Need Is Love."

Kevin.

I have no idea why he's calling me again. And at this hour.

And I refuse to find out.

Chapter 14

"If you are not too long, I will
wait here for you all my life."
—OSCAR WILDE

Brock stared at that one particular quote, one of the
hundreds of quotes he'd amassed over the years,
handwritten in his leather-bound journal, for
quite some time before he finally fell asleep after
returning from Savannah's.

He didn't know what time he'd pushed out
of bed after hours of tossing and turning, solid
slumber proving impossible. He sat in the laundry
room awhile, watching the puppies. Willow gave
him the once-over as if to say, *"What's your problem now?"* He stroked her soft head and waited
for his heart to quit pounding so hard, but it
hadn't yet. And every time he thought about the
moment he'd taken Savannah Barrington into his
arms, it thumped harder.

He wasn't sure there'd ever been a time in his
life when he'd reacted on pure physical instinct
like that. The worst of it was, he didn't regret
it. The only thing he did regret was the look on
Savannah's face when she realized what she'd
done. What they'd almost done.

Would he have?

He shook off the thought. He wouldn't let his mind go there. The answer, the truth, was too damning.

Eventually he left the warm laundry room for the kitchen and made some attempts at fixing breakfast. Now he stood at the kitchen counter and chopped and diced until his eyes began to water. The sun crested over the trees some time ago and he was on his third cup of coffee.

"Good morning, dear." Clarice shuffled into the kitchen promptly at seven, already dressed and wearing those abominable pink slippers Maysie insisted on purchasing for her on her last birthday.

"Coffee's hot. I'm making pancakes and omelets." Brock poured milk into the pancake mix and smashed an egg open. Yellow yolk slid into the white batter and he began to beat it mercilessly with a wooden spoon.

"Lovely." His aunt fixed herself a cup and sidled up beside him as he reached for the chopping board. She gave a little sniff. "Brock?"

"What?"

"Does Maysie like onions in her pancakes?"

Brock's hand stilled as he watched a few chopped onions slide into the bowl. Crap. "No, I don't reckon she does." He shook his head and marched across the kitchen to the garbage can.

"Mmm." Clarice sat and watched him as he moved around, cleaning up the mess he'd made, and started over. "You were out late last night."

"Was I?"

"After midnight. I looked at my clock when the hall light went out."

"Was Maysie okay?" A pinch of guilt pricked him. He probably should have called.

"She was fine. She likes Savannah. I assume that's where you were."

Brock reached for an apple. Apples were safe. And highly choppable.

Clarice made a little singsong noise in her throat. "I imagine, given the way you're decimating that unfortunate piece of fruit, you're thinking the same thing I am."

"Which would be?" He kept his back to her. His chest tightened and he knew what he was in for. Knew he deserved it too, but that didn't make it any easier to hear.

"This can't happen."

"Why?" He spun around and glared, ignoring her astonishment. "Why can't it? What is so wrong with me wanting a little happiness? Tell me that, Aunt Clarice. Then tell me how I'm supposed to do this—deal with this—because I'm all out of answers here!"

"You might want to keep your voice down." Clarice's quiet but pointed words singed him.

Brock exhaled, picked up his mug, and joined her at the table. He sat for a long time with his head in his hands. Neither of them spoke. Birds sang their morning song like any other day. The

184

clock in the hall chimed on the half hour. Martin squawked his annoyance at not having breakfast.

Everything happened in sequence the way it always did every morning. But today his heart was in turmoil. Entirely his own doing; he let himself get sucked in, let his fascination with the beautiful woman next door go too far, but he didn't know how to rectify the problem. Couldn't write his way out of this one.

"Brock." The way his aunt said his name made him snap his head up. He knew what she was about to ask, but let her anyway. "Did you . . . sleep with her?"

"No." He breathed out a curse and closed his eyes. "But God help me, I wanted to."

"God will help you," she replied in that soft-spoken tone he loved so well. "I suspect he's the only one who can at this point." Her poignant sigh simmered and burned a hole through his conscience. "Is Savannah all right?"

Brock drummed his fingers on the table and met her inquiring eyes. "She's confused. Which makes two of us. On top of it, her lawyer told her that her husband hasn't signed the divorce papers. That he might want to reconcile."

"Yes." Clarice took off her spectacles and wiped them with a paper napkin. "Yes, I suspect he does."

This was getting tiresome.

Brock gave a low growl of frustration. "Don't

you ever get tired of looking in that crystal ball of yours, Aunt Clarice?"

She stared straight at him and raised both eyebrows, her mouth pinched. "My dear boy, I have no crystal ball. I simply pay attention to what I see and hear and feel. It might serve you well to do the same."

"This isn't fair." His eyes burned, but he didn't care. There was too much emotion in him. It had been begging to be let out for so long, and now he couldn't stop it. "None of this is fair. Not to me. Not to Maysie. Not to—"

"Since when do you get to make the rules, Brock Chandler? And since when is life fair? It isn't, and you of all people know that. But we must accept the lot we are given, no matter how much it hurts."

"What if I don't want to accept it?" He leaned forward, paid no attention to the tears in her eyes, and barreled on. "What if there's another way? What if I . . ." He flinched and put a hand to his head. After a year, he figured he'd be used to the white-hot pain, but it still took him by surprise and sent him sailing. "There has to be another way."

"No. There does not have to be." Clarice shook her head. "I pray there is, but . . . how many doctors do you have to see before you'll accept the truth?"

"I'll see them all until I find one who tells me

something different." He sank against the back of his chair and raked his fingers through his hair. "I have an appointment in New York next week. After New Year's. A specialist at Sloan Kettering. He's new."

"I see. And you'll leave Maysie with me, I gather."

"If you don't mind."

"Have you told Savannah?"

"No." Brock pushed back, the legs of his chair scraping against tile. "I think she has enough to deal with, don't you?" He steadied his breathing, returned to the counter, and began to fix a fresh batter. Maysie would be up soon and she'd be hungry. Martin squawked again. "Your bird wants his breakfast."

Clarice placed her empty mug in the sink, came to stand beside him, and put a hand on his arm. "Brock. You mean the world to me, and I'd do anything to take your pain away. But I don't think we can. Go to New York if you must. But you won't be able to hide the truth much longer. And you shouldn't want to."

"I know." He could barely speak. Clarice nodded.

"Please be careful, Brock, for both your sakes. Remember you're not the only one in this world with feelings. Attraction is a heady thing. And sometimes it can be dangerous. Don't fall in love with her."

Brock blew air through his mouth and winced as more white fire shot across his forehead.

Too late, Aunt Clarice. Too late.

≫≪

Christmas Day gaiety reverberates through the entire house and bounces off the walls. Peg's four kids and Maysie are charging around. I'd shoo them outside but the temperature has dropped and Maysie's still got a bit of a cough. Graham, Peg's seven-year-old, screeches like a banshee as he runs through the kitchen, a blur of denim and blond hair. I love my sister, but her parenting skills leave much to be desired.

From high school on, Peg spent a lot of years on the riding circuit, a hopeful Olympian equestrian at one point. She married later in life, and she and Hugh turned having babies into a recreational activity. I think they're done now. I hope they're done.

Dad and Adam are watching football, Zoe's around somewhere, on her phone with Tim, and Peg, Mom, and I are scrambling to get dinner on the table. Much to my surprise, Clarice is having a rather lively discussion about racehorses with Peg's husband. Paul and his family should be here any moment. And Brock is hanging out with us in the kitchen.

"Is it cooking? Shouldn't it be darker than that?" I peer into the oven. Brock puts a hand

188

on my shoulder and looks in. I try not to move. The longer I stand there staring at the turkey, his touch searing through my cashmere sweater, the easier it'll be to pretend like this is okay. We've been sidestepping each other since they arrived two hours ago. Every time I look at him, all I can think about is . . . what I'm not supposed to think about.

I let the man kiss me.

I kissed him back.

And . . . if I must be honest, I enjoyed it.

The memory has kept me up nights, guilt gaining the upper hand over the self-righteous side of me that says I have every right to act on my feelings. Kevin did. Why shouldn't I? But it's not that simple. It will never be that simple. Not for me.

The kids make another noisy pass through and I jump.

Brock squeezes my shoulder. "I don't suppose we can muzzle them?"

"I wish." His expression makes me smile, so I turn back to the bird. "What do you think?"

"Where's the bourbon?" He steps back and Peg hands him the bottle. Her eyes are positively gleeful as she sends me a knowing look.

"Oh, I do like you, Mr. Chandler. Savannah, can you keep him?"

My mother looks up from where she's putting together the biggest salad I've ever seen. Salads are her forte. "Land sakes, Peg. He's not a stray animal!" She laughs. Like this is actually funny. Nothing about this strange and sad situation is funny. I glare at both of them and hope and pray they get the message and keep their mouths closed.

"I'd give it another hour." Brock snaps the oven shut and swishes what's left in the bottle, looks at me with a wicked grin, and slugs it back.

"You did not just do that." I grab the bottle from him and shake my head. Good thing there's none left because I'm tempted to do the same. "I thought southerners were supposed to be all refined and genteel like. Isn't that what you're always telling me, Mother?"

"Well, now, that depends, sug-ah." She folds a dishtowel and slips an arm through Brock's. "There are those refined southern gentlemen who have much to offer, to be sure, but then there are the bad boys . . . and I suspect you're a little bit of both, aren't you, Mr. Chandler?"

"I reckon so, ma'am." And he actually winks at her.

"Yeah, he's a regular Rhett Butler." I roll my eyes and pitch the empty bottle into the trash. I knew they'd get along the minute my mother laid eyes on him. She knew who he was at once, of course. She's also a fan. Unfortunately, she took one look at me and in less than ten minutes had pieced together the entire scenario without me saying a word. I am so not looking

190

forward to the moment she hustles me off alone.

"Tim says hi." Zoe wanders into the kitchen and resumes work on the vegetable platter. Maysie skips in and throws her arms around her daddy's legs.

"I just love Christmas!" she declares with all the enthusiasm a child her age should have this time of year.

"Me too." Zoe's smile warms my heart. I can't remember when I've last seen her so happy. She remembers Shelby, of course, and stared slack-jawed when I introduced Maysie to her earlier the afternoon she and Adam arrived. But I simply shrugged and she recovered, and I think she's found a new best friend for life.

"Can I stay in here with you? Those boys are *loud!*" Maysie sticks her fingers in her ears.

Zoe laughs, pushes her dark curls over her shoulder, and nods. "Sure. Sit up here beside me and you can help me make this look pretty."

Brock plops Maysie on a stool next to Zoe, and they're soon busy setting out tomatoes and cucumbers, carrots and red and green peppers, and singing along to "Jingle Bells." Brock pokes his finger in the dip to taste it before putting it in the middle of the platter.

"Ew." Zoe rolls her eyes but smiles anyway. Brock Chandler has that effect on women. She's watching me too carefully, though, and I do my best to avoid eye contact with him. I'm not sure if it's just me or if everyone has picked up on the energy that seems to sizzle between us. If I could get rid of it, I would, but for now I've decided the best course of action is to pretend it's not there.

"Want to check the potatoes, Brock?" Oops. I looked at him. Big mistake.

"Sure thing." He's staring back at me, and for a moment I can't remember what I asked. His grin says he can't either. "Um . . . what was that?"

"Check. Potatoes." I think.

"Now?"

"If you wouldn't mind." I want to get lost in those eyes. Seriously lost.

"You're kind of in the way, darlin'." I'm standing in front of the stove. He clears his throat and moves me aside.

"Mercy, it's warm in here!" Peg crows.

Sometimes I really do not like my sister.

Time to set the table. I reach for the plates and do another mental head count. My mother is a big believer in owning more china and silverware than she will ever use, so we're good to go.

"Can I help, Miss Savannah?" Maysie is done with the vegetables and jumps off her stool, sticks the landing, and throws her arms up like the professional gymnast she's recently decided she wants to be.

"Sure." There's a commotion in the living room and I go to see what's happening. Adam and the kids are at the long window, their noses pressed to the glass. "Is it Paul?"

"Sug-ah." Mom comes up beside me, waves her cell phone in my face. "Paul's flight was delayed. He says he's sorry, but there's a snowstorm and they won't get in until tomorrow."

"Oh." I squint and try to make out the shadowy car coming up the drive. "Then who—"

"Ma." Adam walks toward me, confusion stamped across his face. He scratches his chin and gives his lanky shoulders a shrug. "I don't know what he's doing here, but that's Dad."

Chapter 15

"Things do not change; we change."
—HENRY DAVID THOREAU

Always expect the unexpected.

Except I never do.

Oh, this is so not happening.

"Seriously?" I press my face against the cold glass and stare through the snow. My chest tightens and I think I might throw up. What is he doing here? "Did you or Zoe ask him to come?"

"Not me." Adam shrugs again and folds his arms.

"Did you just say Dad's here?" Zoe is aghast. Clearly she didn't invite him. My parents would not have extended an invitation. Peg definitely wouldn't have. I'm floundering. I don't know what to say or who to look at or what to do next. I walk slowly toward the front door. My mother wisely ushers Peg back into the kitchen while Brock saunters past us to the living room with Maysie trailing him.

"The plot thickens . . . ," he says in a low voice that is way too sexy, amusement simmering under raised brows. If he were close enough to pummel, I would.

"Do you want me to talk to him, tell him to

leave?" Zoe's offer is kind, but the tremor in her voice begs me to decline.

"No, of course not. You guys just . . . go wait in the living room. Let me talk to him first, okay?" Talk, scream, punch his lights out. Not sure what I'll do, really.

The kids skulk off and I stand at the front door, watching my husband make his way up the slippery walk. That final scene in *Jerry Maguire* flips through my mind. My favorite movie of all time. We've both seen it probably ten times.

If Kevin dares to walk into this house and announce that he's looking for his wife, I really will hit him. Hard.

I take a deep breath and open the door just as he lands on the front step. He's holding a large shopping bag, presents poking out the top.

"Kevin. What a surprise." My voice is trembling. My entire body is trembling.

"Yeah." He exhales, cold air swirling around us. His eyes meet mine, and he's searching my face for I don't even know what. Permission, acknowledgment, absolution, and a thousand other things he probably wants from me, none of which I feel capable of giving at this particular moment.

"Do you have a death wish?" I have to ask. A sane man in his predicament would not dare show his face within firing range of my father.

"Ellie . . . is my old hunting rifle still in the attic?" Dad yells to prove my point.

"There's one in the back of my truck," Brock drawls.

Kevin rakes a hand through his hair and almost smiles. "They're all here, aren't they?"

"Yep. Well, not Paul. Their flight was delayed." My sigh sounds impatient, but I'm not heartless. "You'd better come in. We're letting all the heat out."

He stamps his boots on the rug in the foyer and I shut the door behind him. Snow falls from his hair onto his leather jacket. He's got jeans on. Weird. Kevin usually prefers cords or smart trousers with a button-down shirt, doesn't matter where he's going.

"Merry Christmas." He shoots me a tentative smile and I back up.

Is he kidding me?

"What are you doing here?" My throat is too tight. I take a deep breath and let it out. Slowly. "You could have called."

"I did. Left you a few messages. You're not returning my calls."

Well, that's true.

He has called about five times since the afternoon I spoke to him on Beth's phone. Since the afternoon I let Brock Chandler into this house. And possibly into my heart. But what does my heart know? It has been broken, stomped on, and shattered into a million splintered pieces. By the man now standing in front of me.

196

"Look, Savannah. I'm sorry. But I wanted to see the kids. It's Christmas." He holds up the bag of presents as if that explains everything. Like he thinks he still has the right.

"You can't stay here." My voice is frosty but I don't care.

"No. I know." He sighs and places a hand at the back of his neck. "I've got a hotel room. I just . . . well, I didn't want to be alone today."

"And why would you be—" I can't finish the question because Maysie suddenly appears beside me. Kevin takes one look at her and almost stumbles, color draining from his face. I quickly move to place a hand on his back. "Kevin . . . this is Maysie. Brock's daughter. From next door."

His eyes dart my way, then land on her again. "Maysie."

"Hi." She bounces on her toes, smooths down the front of her crisp red velvet dress. Clarice dressed her, no doubt, but the Christmas dress with its white lace collar is perfect.

She is perfect.

Emotion pools in his eyes, his jaw working as he tries to recover from the shock. "She looks so much like . . ." He can't say it, but I know what he's thinking, feeling. That same visceral, gut-churning reaction I had. The one that reminds us Shelby was once so young, so beautiful, and so full of life. And is no longer with us.

Kevin crouches a little and stares at Maysie. She

glances up at me but she doesn't seem bothered by his reaction.

"Hi, Maysie. I'm Kevin."

"You're Zoe and Adam's daddy."

"That's right."

"I'm very pleased to meet you, Mr. Kevin." She offers a tiny hand and her manners make me smile. After giving her hand a small shake, Kevin straightens, runs a hand down his face, and looks toward the living room, then back at me. It's awfully quiet in there.

"Maysie, come back here." Brock steps out of the shadows, hovering at a safe distance. I'm keenly aware of his eyes on me, and Kevin's on him. "Sorry," Brock apologizes. "She skipped out on me." He moves forward, placing his hands on his daughter's shoulders. He looks Kevin up and down, his smile tight. "Hi. Brock Chandler."

"Yes. You are." Kevin actually grins. "I'm a big fan." They shake hands, and I'm caught in what is possibly the most awkward moment of my life.

"Well, since you're here, Kevin, you'd better stay for dinner." Speaking of manners. I can't escape them even when I want to push him back out the front door into the pile of snow on the side of the walkway. I send Brock a despairing glance and make good my escape.

"Zoe, Adam!" I rush past the two men and wave the kids out of the living room. "Your father is here to see you." The kitchen seems safe at this point. And the last thing I need is for the turkey to burn.

"Did you know he was coming?" Peg thunks the bottles of salad dressing on the counter, her cheeks flushed with anger and the heat of the kitchen, but mostly, I think, anger. I inspect the bird, turn off the oven, and face her. And finally let out my breath.

"No. Of course I didn't." Does she actually think I would have invited him? Should I have? The thought was so far from my mind the last few days that I almost feel guilty about it. But why would I have bothered to ask Kevin what his plans for Christmas were? "Don't start anything, Peg. Please."

"Well, what's he doing here? He's got some nerve, showing up like this. If I—"

"Peg! I can't do this right now." Can't think about why Kevin is here and not in Boston with Alison. I have most of my family congregated in the next room and need to get dinner on the table. But I feel sick. Totally nauseated. How do I deal with what the rest of today might bring? And how will we get through this meal without World War III breaking out?

"Peg, leave Savannah alone. Put the salad on the table and get the kids to wash up." My mother takes command the way only she can. She never shouts but simply speaks with an authoritative tone none of us have ever dared defy. Peg leaves the kitchen in a huff and I stand at the sink, trying to calm down and trying not to cry. "Honey." Mom places an arm around my shoulders and holds tight.

"I don't want him here." It's an awful thought, an awful thing to say, but right now it's the truth. "I can't believe he'd just show up like this. It's not acceptable."

"Well, he is here and we've got to get dinner served, so I suggest you buck up, do your best to be polite and get through the meal, then deal with him."

"I can't even think." My heart is racing and my brain won't work properly.

"Savannah?" Brock's deep voice sends my heart rate skyrocketing again. This is not helping. Why did I invite him? The minute this day is over I'm going to join a convent. I'm not Catholic, but perhaps they'll make an exception.

I wipe my eyes, turn to face him, and shoot my mother a desperate look. She smiles and gives a slight nod. "I'll get your father in here to carve."

Brock waits until my mother is out of earshot. "Are you all right?"

"Do I look like I'm all right?"

His brief smile answers that quite nicely. "Should I leave?"

"No. That would make things worse." I push my fingers through my hair and meet his worried gaze. "Heck of a plot twist, huh?"

"Didn't see it coming." He gives my shoulder a light squeeze as he moves past me to the wine bottles I set out earlier and begins to open them. "Kind of ruined my appetite, actually."

"Ha. Mine too. I'm about to puke." I force myself to function, get things done so we can eat. Gravy. I need to make gravy. "I can't kick him out, can I?"

He chuckles and shakes his head. "You could, but it wouldn't be pretty. You need to talk to him anyway."

"Do I?" I do. He knows it. I know it. I just don't want to accept it. Or do it. "I think he'd rather talk to you. He's probably got all your books in the back of his car, waiting to be signed."

Brock looks up and meets my gaze. Whatever he intended to say, he thinks better of it and resumes the task at hand. "We'll stay for dinner, but we'll leave right after. I think that's best."

I can't answer him because my parents come into the kitchen and I have to pretend Christmas Day hasn't been entirely destroyed.

※※※

Eventually the evening draws to a close. True to his word, Brock hustled Clarice and Maysie home shortly after dessert. Clarice assisted by admitting to being overcome with exhaustion after such an exciting day, but I caught the worry in her eyes as she kissed me good-bye.

Peg and Hugh round up their brood and head upstairs. My parents are already up in their room, and Zoe and Adam are in the living room with Kevin. I don't know if they're talking. Zoe's eyes were red earlier and she had to excuse herself from the table twice. Adam barely touched his meal. My son not eating everything on his plate and then asking for seconds is a foreign concept.

Kevin didn't eat much either. He did manage to hold a fairly intelligent conversation with Brock, who played along and answered every question with more civility than I would have. Apart from complimenting me on the meal, Kevin and I haven't spoken. I wish he'd leave. I've been hiding out in the kitchen, putting dishes away and avoiding him.

"Need help?" Kevin appears behind me, reaches for a dish towel.

Perfect timing.

"No." Except there are still about twenty glasses in the dish rack and I'm on the verge of losing my mind. He sidesteps me in silence and reaches for a glass to dry.

I go to the fridge and attempt to make room for the leftovers.

"That was a great meal. Thanks for letting me stay." He is apparently determined to talk. I shut the fridge and face him, fuming.

"Did I have a choice? What were you thinking, showing up here out of the blue, no warning, nothing! You can't do this, Kevin. It's not fair."

"It's not fair? I don't get to see my kids on Christmas Day and you want to talk about fair?"

"Don't." I point a finger in his direction and think how lucky he is I'm not holding a glass. Or a knife. "Don't you dare talk to me about what's fair! *You* did this. You made this choice for us. Okay? The sooner you man up and take responsibility for that, the better off we'll all be."

In the background I hear the front door open and close, but I can't think about that now. All I can think about is how to prevent my hand from making contact with my husband's face.

"I didn't come here to fight."

"Then why did you come? Did you honestly think you could waltz in here and pretend the past year never happened? Pretend we're not getting a divorce because you couldn't . . ." I don't bother finishing the sentence. It's not worth it.

Kevin puts a couple of glasses away, braces himself against the counter, and sighs before he turns around. He blinks at me through eyes loaded with hurt and remorse. And maybe a bit of leftover anger, which he doesn't have the right to own.

"No, I don't think that. I'm not going to pretend it didn't happen. I never said what I did was right, Savannah. I know I made a choice, a wrong one, a stupid one . . . but I refuse to take all the blame here. Our marriage was in trouble long before that. You made choices too. You chose to shut me out of your life. To shut us all out. And when you hurt so bad you couldn't take it anymore, you tried to take the easy way out." He breathes out a curse and slams a palm on the counter.

"What? What did you just say?" I run trembling hands through my hair, my throat dry. I can't believe what I'm hearing. "You're actually going to use my suicide attempt to excuse your having an affair?"

"I didn't mean it like that." He gives that toss of his head that hints at his own frustration. "I'm just trying to sort through things. To figure out why our marriage failed. To maybe figure out where our relationship went so wrong that all I could do was walk out."

"Well, good luck. You have no idea what that did to me, Kevin. That level of betrayal? Yes, I knew things were bad between us, but I never imagined you'd cheat. And back then, when I wanted to die, I was an emotional mess. You know that. I was so unstable I thought it was my only option. You don't understand what . . ." I put a hand to my mouth. Our years of counseling clearly taught me nothing. Never start a sentence with an accusation. You'd think I'd have learned that by now.

"You're right, Savannah. I don't understand. God knows, I tried." Kevin's eyes grow stormy. "But I don't think you understand either. Did you ever think about what it was like for me? Coming home that day, finding you in the bathroom, blood everywhere? Have you ever thought about what I went through, having to explain to our kids why you were in the hospital, why you weren't coming home? Keeping the truth from them? You want to know what it still feels like, every single time I look at you, knowing I let you down, knowing I wasn't enough for you? Don't stand there and talk to me about choices! Yes, I am fully aware you have suffered. But so have I. You have no idea what I've dealt with all these years. Because you never asked."

I fold my arms against his harsh words, grip my elbows tight, and bite back tears.

He's right.

I never asked.

I stopped asking when he stopped answering.

"We both made mistakes." I'll give him that much. "But why bring it all up now? I don't see the point."

Kevin shrugs. "The point is that we never did talk about it. Not really. We gave up on counseling. You said it hurt too much to relive it all. At the time, I had to agree. So I never talked about Shelby because I figured that was how you wanted it. I thought it was easier on you." Kevin swipes the back of his hand across his face. "Maybe if we'd tried to talk things through instead of ignoring each other all these years, our relationship might have grown stronger, not fallen apart."

"And maybe if you'd kept your . . ." I swallow the sarcasm and slide my hands up to grip the back of my neck. "I really don't want to do this now. It's Christmas." And I'm in tears. I let out a long breath and stare at him. "I still don't understand what you're doing here." My voice is barely above a whisper, but I have to know. "Where is she?"

Chapter 16

"Children begin by loving their parents;
after a time they judge them; rarely,
if ever, do they forgive them."
—OSCAR WILDE

The tension in the house was suffocating. Zoe needed air.

She shut the front door behind her, zipped up her coat, and trudged around the back of the house to the lake. The moon lit her way, and as she rounded the corner toward the dock, she spied Adam in one of the Adirondack chairs, huddled under a thick plaid blanket.

"Hey." She slid into the chair beside him, pulled the chenille throw she'd brought out with her around her shoulders, and stared at the frozen body of water.

"I hate it when they yell." Adam slugged from a large bottle. Tequila.

"Where'd you get that?" Zoe worked to keep judgment out of her voice. In the silver light, her brother's eyes shone with sorrows she was all too familiar with.

"Gramps's liquor cabinet. Way in back. He won't notice."

"You'd better hope not."

He took another swig and held the bottle toward her.

Oh, why not? "Sheesh." She took the bottle, took a small sip, and felt the liquid fire burn all the way down her throat. It sent her into a fit of coughing.

Adam took back the bottle and laughed. "Wuss."

"Adam, don't drink any more of that. You'll be sick, honestly."

"Whatever. I can sleep all day. Mom's too busy yelling at Dad to worry about me." But he set the bottle down in the snow. There wasn't much left, and Zoe wondered how full it'd been to begin with.

"You didn't call Dad, did you, Adam? Ask him to come?" She was pretty sure her brother had been as surprised as she was to see Dad drive up, but still, it was bizarre.

"No way. I still can't really stand to be in the same room with him, Zo. I don't know what to say. It's awkward as heck."

"I know." She sighed and leaned over her knees. "I told you he came out to Princeton to see me."

"Yeah. And when he picked me up after my ski trip, he said he was working stuff out. Told me he wasn't with Alison anymore. Do you think that's true?"

"If he says it is . . ."

"Dad's a liar, Zoe. He cheated on Mom with that bimbo for how long? Seriously, he's an a—"

"Adam. Don't." Zoe's eyes smarted. For some strange reason, she felt the need to defend her father. It was still so hard to talk about. She'd tried not to think about it but couldn't help replaying that conversation in the coffee shop. Couldn't help holding on to a little hope. And there wasn't much of that going around lately. "What if it is true? What if he wants to work things out with Mom? What if that's why he's here?"

"Good luck to him, then," Adam growled. "Did you hear them in there? That didn't sound like anything's getting worked out to me."

"Maybe not." She leaned her head back and looked up at the stars. Thousands of tiny bright lights dotted the dark sky. Every summer, before they stopped coming a few years back, she and Dad would come down here or sit up in the widow's walk with the telescope, name the stars, and talk. Discuss all sorts of things from the big bang theory and the existence of God to boys. She missed that. The last time she'd really talked to Dad without watching every word had been well over a year ago. "But if they do want to try to get past this, we have to support them."

"I don't think it'll happen." Adam kicked at the snow. "How do you get past the fact that your husband cheated on you? Every time I look at him I want to barf. What kind of man does that to his wife?"

Zoe clenched her gloved hands and inhaled. "I don't know what made him do it, but he did and it's done. And he's still our dad."

Adam picked up the bottle again. "I'm pretty sure I flunked most of my finals. I'll be put on probation if I did."

"Oh, Adam." She gave his shoulder a squeeze. "I'm not doing so hot either. I'm going to have to work like crazy this semester if I want to keep my 4.0."

"You'll do fine." He shot her a sidelong glance and a grin. "You were always the smart one."

"Not always." She shook her head and huddled under the blanket. "Shelby would have been the star of the family."

"You think she isn't?" Sudden unbridled anger laced his tone and his eyes flashed under the moon's glow. "She's been dead ten years but I feel like she's still here, still with us. Everything we do, Zo, every birthday, every first, everything gets measured against their precious Shelby."

"Adam, come on . . ."

"No. You've lived your whole life trying to be as good as you think she would have been, and don't tell me that's not the truth because I'm not stupid."

Slow tears slipped down Zoe's cheeks. Her brother's words rang in her ears, twisted her heart, and piled on another layer of guilt. Because, no matter how much she wanted to, she couldn't disagree with him. "You've had too much to drink."

"Probably." Adam let out a shuddering sigh and a cough that came pretty close to sounding like a muffled sob. "The thing is, I hardly remember her. And I feel guilty because I think I should. I think I should miss her like they do. Mourn for her like they do. But I don't. And . . . sometimes I wish to God they could just get over it."

She didn't know how long they sat in silence.

"When do you think it all went so wrong?" Zoe frowned at him, thinking back. "Do you think it was because she died? Or was it after that? Was it when Mom—"

She caught herself. As far as she knew, Adam had never learned the truth about that summer.

She'd been fourteen, Adam ten. They were both away at summer camp, which was probably why it happened when it did. Zoe had never really been sure what went on. Why Mom wasn't there when they came home from camp. Dad told them she was sick, needed some time away, that she'd had some kind of breakdown and needed to be cared for in a safe place. A place that wouldn't remind her of Shelby every time she turned around. But Zoe always suspected there was more to it. A few years later she sat with Dad and begged him to tell her the truth.

When he did, she wished she'd never asked.

"When Mom what?" Adam yawned and leaned against the back of the chair.

211

Zoe bit her lip, retied her ponytail, and shook her head. "Nothing."

Across the lake, a few flickering lights could just be seen through the trees. Zoe tilted her head toward the sky again. A bright light burst from the darkness, arced a thin line, then disappeared into blackness.

"Shooting star," Adam whispered and pulled the hood of his coat over his head. Zoe smiled and nodded and watched her brother watch the stars.

"Remember how we used to do this with Dad?"

"Yeah." Adam sniffed and rubbed his nose. A few minutes later he spoke again. "Do you still believe, Zo?"

"Believe? In what? Santa Claus? The tooth fairy?"

Adam snorted and nudged her elbow. "C'mon. You know what I mean. Do you believe we're all here for a reason? That there's some higher purpose, some big dude in the sky watching over us, looking out for us?"

Did she? Zoe pressed her back against the wooden slats, tempted to take another swig of tequila. "I used to. I mean, I still believe in God intrinsically . . ."

"English, please."

She laughed and dug the tip of her boot in the snow. "I believe because I've been taught to. And on some level, it's basic instinct. Everyone needs to believe in something. Even atheists. They believe in their unbelief, I suppose. So, I believe God exists and I believe he created us, but . . ."

"But you don't believe he has some grand plan, that he's plotting our every move and just waiting for us to screw up?"

"Plotting?" A shiver of warning slipped down her spine and she shifted to look at him. "No, I don't believe that. God gives us free will. He doesn't make us do anything; we get to choose. The choices we make can either please him or not. If we're lucky enough, we'll make good ones. You know what they say, life is what you make it."

"My life pretty much sucks then." He pushed his fingers through his hair and let out a curse. "Nothing makes sense anymore. If God is there, if he is good and he loves us so much, then why is this so hard? Why are Mom and Dad getting a divorce? Why did Shelby get hit by a car and die? Why do we have to live with that overshadowing our every move?" He took a breath and rubbed his hands over his face. "That doesn't sound like a wonderful plan to me, Zo. That plan sucks. Every time I see Mom I'm reminded of that. She's just so . . . so broken up. You know?"

"You can't take care of her, Adam. You can't fix this."

"Then who can? God?"

Zoe swiped a hand across her face. "I guess. I don't know. I hope so. And we don't know

213

everything. Things could change. Things might get better."

"But you're not convinced."

"No," she whispered, hating the truth of it. "No, I'm not convinced."

"I don't know what I'm gonna do, Zo. What if I get kicked out?"

"Are you really flunking that bad?" Fear pricked her as she stared at her brother through the darkness.

"Probably. And there's other stuff too. I'm just not good, Zo."

"What do you mean you're not good? What are you doing?" Zoe pulled in a long breath of cold air as her pulse kicked up a notch. "Please don't tell me you're doing drugs."

"Nah." He laughed, picked up a handful of snow, rounded it into a ball, and hurled it across the lawn. "I mean, I smoked a joint once . . . it made me puke. But . . . me and some of the guys sneak out on weekends, get pretty trashed, and—"

"Drinking? You'll get expelled, Adam. You know your school has zero tolerance."

"I'm not telling you for the lecture."

"Then why are you telling me?"

"I don't know." He crossed his arms, and Zoe caught his scowl as the moon inched out again. Clouds moved toward the west and she shivered.

"Okay, listen. I know you're upset about Mom and Dad. I get that. But you're only sixteen. It's a

214

big risk, Adam. If you get caught drinking, even if you're at a friend's . . . I'm not stupid, I know everyone breaks the rules. All I'm saying is use your brain. Mom doesn't need any more stress. Please be careful. Don't do anything stupid, okay?"

"Whatever." His sullen look returned. Zoe's heart ached for him. Adam was the oversensitive one in the family. Probably got it from Mom. And she didn't know what else to say or how to make it better.

"We should go in. It's getting too cold out here."

"You won't tell them? About my grades?" He shuffled out of his seat, tripped over the blanket, and fell face-first in the snow. "Aw, crap."

Zoe got up and helped him to his feet, slipped an arm around her brother's shoulders. She'd have to get him inside and into bed, and hope Mom and Dad were still in the kitchen and wouldn't notice.

"I won't tell them." She smiled, but his expression was more serious than she'd ever seen it. "Just try not to take all this on yourself, okay, bro? We can't change it."

Adam looked at her for a long moment before his handsome face crumpled. "I don't want it to be like this, Zo," he said hoarsely. "I want it to end. I want things to be like they were before. I'm so tired of hurting."

"I know. Me too." She pulled him into her arms, held him, and let her own tears come. "Me too."

Chapter 17

"When angry, count to four;
when very angry, swear."
—MARK TWAIN

Time seems to stop with the question I asked.

The question Kevin still has not answered.

"Maybe you didn't hear me." My voice is ice cold. "Where. Is. She?"

Kevin takes a backward step and shoves his hands in his pockets. Gives a shrug that tells me nothing. I grip the back of a chair at the kitchen table and train my gaze on him.

"Kevin. Answer me. What are you doing up here on Christmas Day by yourself? Why aren't you with Alison?" Do I really want to know? Do I want to hear him tell me she's visiting her family and he's going to meet up with her tomorrow?

"I ended it."

Three words. They fly around the kitchen like swallows circling, looking for a safe place to land. When? Why? Why now? My unspoken questions hover over his words like vultures, waiting for the opportune moment to clutch them up in sharp talons and carry them off before I can accept them.

I don't understand. Why start something so

destructive in the first place if you're only going to end it? And what does he want from me?

Multiple answers and possible scenarios scramble in my brain until I cannot think or speak. So I sit.

Kevin sits too, and we stare at each other through painful silence, set like a rusty trap open on the table between us, ready to catch us in a viselike grip of cutting words and condemnation.

"Say something, Savannah."

"Oh . . ." I let the word out in a long, shaky breath, lean forward, and pull my fingers through my hair. At last I look into his searching eyes. And honestly, I don't know what I feel. "What do you want me to say? Congratulations?"

"You're not going to make this easy, are you?"

He seriously said that.

"Wow." I shoot out of my chair, grab a glass and one of the bottles of wine we didn't finish at dinner, pour, and drink quickly. My chest heaves as I blink back sharp, hot tears that tell me I am still not strong enough. Not strong enough to deal with the complexities that have crowded into my life, tied up clarity, and banished reason for the interim. "Walter says you haven't signed the papers." Unable to sit so close to him right now, I stand against the counter about five feet away. And I'm still too close.

"No. I haven't. I wanted to talk to you." Kevin spreads his palms on the table, and I watch his

217

chest rise and fall. His chest is solid, broad, warm, and safe. The place I would rest my head, listen to the steady beating of his heart, close my eyes, and cry silent tears through long, lonely nights. And all he could do was hold me.

"So talk. I'm listening." This ought to be good.

Kevin takes a deep breath. "The past few weeks I've been doing a lot of thinking. A lot of soul-searching. And praying, believe it or not. I don't have any clear answers yet. I'm not sure what to do, Savannah. I don't know what you want. I don't know if we can get past this or if you even want to, but I'm willing to do what it takes to find out. So, I guess the question is, are you?"

Am I?

I can only stare mutely at him. Words won't come. The last several days weigh heavy on me. Press in like the stifling heat of a sauna somebody has set too high. I finish the wine I poured and grip the crystal stem a little too tightly.

"Please don't throw that at me." His grin comes and goes in a flash of hope, a brief glimmer of light through this oppressive darkness that swells around us. I make a feeble attempt to reach for that hope, grab hold, and hang on tight. But it's gone before I can.

"I kissed Brock." The confession wrenches free from the confines of my conscience and catches both of us off guard. I put down the glass and breathe deeply.

"You what?" He pushes his chair back a bit, eyes wide, unbelieving.

I shrug. There's nothing else to say. It's out there and he has to deal with it. I've never lied to my husband, and I'm not about to start now.

"Brock Chandler? You've having an affair with Brock Chandler?"

"I'm not having an affair with anyone." Indignation flares. "I didn't sleep with him, Kevin. We kissed. Once. That's all. It happened, it's over, I didn't plan it, but there it is."

Kevin's eyes narrow and his jaw begins to shift the way it does when he's upset. "Is this your way of getting back at me?"

I lean over my knees and cover my face, exhale, and emit a laugh that chokes me. I shake my head and stare at him again. "No. Actually, I wasn't thinking about you at all when it happened. I'm sure you can relate to that."

I may as well have thrown the glass. He recoils and pierces me with a look that says more than any words could. "Do you want to keep seeing him?" Kevin is full of loaded questions tonight.

"Brock has become a friend. And, last time I checked, I'm still married. It shouldn't have happened but it did, and I don't really know why I told you. Maybe it was to hurt you. Maybe . . ." My thoughts run wild like the deer in the surrounding woods and I can't catch up with them. "Maybe I don't know what I want either."

Not right now. Not in this moment. "You've blind-sided me, coming here today. Telling me you broke things off with Alison. I don't know what to say, Kevin. I don't want to feel like I'm your second choice."

He sits in silence. His dark hair, just starting to curl around his ears, is longer than when I last saw him. His eyes shimmer with seriousness under the kitchen lights. I don't really want to know what he's thinking.

"Well, I wasn't expecting this." He's trying to assimilate the information. Line it all up, put it into neat, prioritized boxes, each of which he will deal with when he feels the time is right.

I slash my arm through the air like I'm knocking all those invisible boxes off the table. "You don't have the right to judge me."

"Uh. Okay."

He props his elbows and puts his head in his hands, taking me back in time . . .

"You're what? Savannah, are you sure?"

My stomach has been churning like an angry sea for days. Between the nausea and that sinking feeling that as soon as I tell him our relationship will be over, his questions are too much.

"Do you want to see the pregnancy test, Kevin? Why would I make this up? Look at me!" Tremors shake my entire body and I suck in a sob as he raises hooded eyes, catches my gaze, and shakes

his head in what I can only assume is utter dis-belief.

"Oh. Wow." He puts his head in his hands and utters a low moan.

The sun dips low behind the massive oak at the bottom of my parents' garden. They're out for the evening. Kevin and I were supposed to be going out too. There have been a lot of nights like this one. Nights when we said one thing and did another.

"When?" He leans back in his chair, curses, and slides his hand slowly down his face. "I mean . . . how far along are you?"

"Two months, I think. It was probably sometime over the summer."

"At the lake house."

"Probably." I reach for a paper napkin and blow my nose. We're suddenly like strangers, sitting across the table, discussing dates and times while the new life inside me cares not for either. Or decorum, apparently.

In the two years since we became an official couple, we did our best to take it slow. But last summer something shifted between us. I felt Kevin drifting . . . little changes at first, like not calling every night. Not coming back to Boston so often. We knew a long-distance relationship would be difficult, but so far we'd made it work. So when Kevin told me he'd secured a job at a resort near our place in the Berkshires, I decided to do everything I could to hold on to him.

It's interminably hot. Everyone is out for the day on the boat. I wasn't feeling well so I stayed home, finding refuge in the cool basement. It's the place Mom puts the boys, stores old boxes of memorabilia, art easels, and who knows what else. For us kids, it is our playground.

I spend the morning lounging on the old four-poster bed—how they got it down the rickety steps is a mystery—reading Danielle Steel and listening to my favorite CDs over and over again.

Humidity clings to my skin and makes everything damp. There's a slight breeze through the small open windows, but my eyes are slowly closing.

"I didn't think anyone was home."

I bolt upright, staring at the figure standing on the bottom step. "Kevin?"

He grins, jumps off the step, and enters my space. "Surprise."

I'm in his arms before I can ask what he's doing here. He was supposed to work this entire long weekend. Somebody got sick or something. But now he's here, staring at me with those dark-blue eyes that I dream about every night.

"You're here."

"So are you." His grin sends sparks of light into his eyes. His fingers brush hair out of my eyes as he raises a brow. "Alone, I gather." His

gaze wanders over my face and downward to the string bikini top I'm wearing with a pair of cutoffs I'd never wear in public.

"Completely. They're all out on the boat. I couldn't stand the thought."

"No, you wouldn't survive the day." He's witnessed my seasickness firsthand. "I've missed you, Savannah." His hands slide around the sides of my face as he brings his lips closer to mine. "Kiss me."

He doesn't have to ask. I would kiss him all day . . . and we have hours to spend right now, doing just that.

❧❦

"You're pregnant. I can't believe this . . ." Kevin finally speaks, his eyes wide and filled with fear. "I . . . I don't know what to do."

"Well, that makes two of us." We're both still in college. Kevin will graduate this summer; I'm a sophomore in my first semester. We haven't even talked about marriage, although I dream about it. But I don't know if Kevin does.

Fear pushes me out of my chair and I escape the stifling kitchen and the look of horror on his face. I can't bear it. I haven't cried so much in all my life but I can't seem to stop. A few minutes later the back door squeaks and Kevin's arms wrap around me. He sighs into my neck, holds me tight, and just stands there for the longest time.

Then he slowly turns me to face him, brushes away my tears with his thumbs as he caresses my face.

"Marry me," he whispers . . .

The past takes a final bow as I blink away the memories, and the kitchen is deathly quiet.

Kevin just sits there, staring at me.

Somehow I find words and force them out. "If you expect me to apologize, I'm not going to." The look of betrayal in his eyes makes me angry. Defiant. And sorry I told him.

He gets to his feet and gives a slow nod. "What ever." He's shut down again. I recognize the look. The one that says, *"You've hurt me and I don't want to talk about it."* And part of me is glad he's hurt. Glad I have been the one to inflict pain this time. Another part of me wants to take back my words and pretend the past ten minutes never happened.

"You're leaving?" The question doesn't need an answer and he doesn't give one. There's so much I could say now. Point out his flaws. How he's so good at walking out when he can't take anymore, but what good would it do? Instead, I follow him into the living room and watch as he pulls on his jacket. The fire has long since died and the room is cold.

"Do you know where the kids are?" He raises a hand to brush his hair back and I see the tremor, recognize he's holding it together by a thread. But all I can do is shake my head.

Kevin clears his throat. "I'll call tomorrow. Tell Zo to leave her cell on. We talked about lunch."

"I'll tell her." Cold air slices through me when he opens the door. "Kevin . . ."

He turns to face me. "Don't say anything else, Savannah. Not right now." He shakes his head, his haunted expression like long fingers that stretch through me and squeeze compassion from my heart. I want to tell him I'm sorry, but I don't know if I really am.

"Paul should be here tomorrow. When are you going home?" Home. I'm not sure where that is anymore or what it means.

"Probably sometime in the afternoon or the next day. I haven't decided." He puts a hand against the doorframe and shoots me a sidelong glance. His blue eyes shimmer with moisture. He doesn't speak for a few moments. "Are we really done? Did I destroy us for good?"

"I don't know." My whisper seems more like a wail, a prayer perhaps, one neither of us truly believes will be answered. "I know we can't go back, but I don't know how to go forward."

"Neither do I." He zips his jacket, faces me, and takes a few steps forward until he's bridged the gap between us. His eyes move over my face in a way that makes me tremble and ache with sorrow, and when his hand brushes my cheek, it's almost more than I can bear.

"Oh, Kev." I clutch his hand and press it against my face. My pulse picks up in a fast rhythm, pounding faster still when I meet his questioning eyes, frantic to find something I'm not sure even exists anymore. But as he pulls me against him and releases a shuddering sigh, I think it might.

"I'm not giving up." His hoarse whisper infiltrates the hardest part of my heart. "Not this time. Not until you tell me there is no hope."

Just a few words, but they rock the foundation of this new normal I've worked so hard to construct. How alarmingly easy it would be now to give him what I think he wants. What he might even need. Right now I want back what we had. So badly I think I could wind my arms around his neck and let him kiss me. Let him take me upstairs if he wanted and make love to me the way he used to, back when there was more love than anger and hurt between us.

But there is no going back. I can't bring myself to absolve him. So I step out of his embrace and retreat to my own space. "We had a sacred trust, Kevin. You broke it. I don't know how to get past that." And I don't know for sure, right now, whether I want to. If I can. But I don't tell him that, because there is already too much heartbreak here tonight.

"I know. I understand." He nods and pulls on a

slim gold chain around his neck. It's been hiding under his sweater and I haven't noticed it before now. He takes it off and reaches for my hand. Then he places the chain that holds his wedding band into my palm and presses my fingers over thick, warm gold. "I never should have broken our vows, Savannah. I never should have taken this off. But since I did . . . maybe you can hold on to it until we figure this out."

He turns and walks away, down the steps and into the cold, dark night.

Instead of returning to the warmth of the house, I stand on the threshold and watch him go. Icy air stings my nose and freezes the tears on my cheeks. For a moment I'm drawn back to the day he left. The day I stood at the edge of the patio and looked beyond the fields, beyond the horizon, and wondered. Wondered if there was a way to get things back, a way to return to that sacred space we once shared. Tonight I still wonder. I have more questions now than I did then. I know less about my heart and mind and soul, and I can't claw my way through this confusion.

It's in this moment, as I stand here utterly bereft and broken, that I feel it—a tiny flicker of a solitary, soul-deep flame—warmth that somehow seeps through to the hidden parts of me, floods every unseen inch, and asks me to hold on. Asks me not to give up. To keep talking, keep praying.

Because somehow I have to believe there is still a chance for us. That I have not been abandoned. Not completely.

A small cry leaves my throat and I drag my eyes upward.

And I watch the stars.

Chapter 18

"I gave in, and admitted that God was God."
—C. S. LEWIS

"We're all mad here."
I sip coffee and stare at the plaque on the wall of the kitchen, a Christmas present from Kevin to my mother years ago. I find the Alice quote rather appropriate this morning.

It's still early and the house is silent. I barely slept; my thoughts raced all night long, ping-ponging between anger and sorrow and stupefaction. As I ponder what to do with Kevin's questions, I catch a glimpse of the amaryllis on the windowsill above the sink. I rub sleep from my eyes and look again. The vibrant red flower, in proud full bloom yesterday, has withered into drooping brown, about to fall off its shriveled stem.

How did that happen? I know they usually last for weeks. I stick my fingers in the dirt, but it's not too wet or too dry. I should check the others.

The three white pots are lined up along the red-checkered table runner on the dining room table where we enjoyed our feast last night. These flowers are also dead, the green leaves and stems shriveled.

I ignore the urge to blog, finish my coffee, force down half a bagel, then bundle up, pull on my boots, and trudge through the snow toward the greenhouse.

The old door creaks in welcome as I push it open and step inside. Clarice is already there, huddled under her brown fur coat, examining the other pots we put the amaryllis bulbs into a few weeks ago.

Hers are dead too.

"What's wrong with them? Why did they die?" I don't even bother to say good morning. Clarice sighs and puts down the one she's holding. She moves along the newly erected shelf and touches each sickly plant in turn.

"Yours also, Savannah?"

"Dead. All of them." I grab a broom that sits in the corner, wrap my gloved hands around the wooden handle, and start to sweep. I smack at fallen leaves and leftover debris in furious motion, pushing the deadness away into corners, scanning the room for any signs of life.

We've planted bulbs and seedlings and created space for flowers and plants that we'll get going in warmer weather. Somehow my mind has convinced me I'll still be here. Maysie has an area mapped out for hydroponics. Apparently she's been learning about the practice and wants to try it out. "Do you think they had a bug or something?"

"I don't know." Clarice stands in front of what I believe to be a rosebush. She pulls a new green branch gently toward her, inspects it, then turns to me and smiles in that way that is both heartwarming and disturbing. "Did you talk with Kevin last night?"

"We talked." I kick at some stray gravel, study the newly repaired windows, and watch a flock of birds heading over the pines on the other side of the garden. "I'm sorry for that. The tension. Dinner was pretty awful. It wasn't how I'd planned Christmas this year."

"Oh, my dear." She laughs with the raspy good-natured sound I've grown used to. "Think nothing of it. At my age, a little drama is most welcome."

"At least I didn't throw anything at him."

"I suspect you wanted to." She moves to the other side of the shelves and starts stacking new pots. "Didn't you?"

At the far side of the greenhouse, there's a cherry tree. At least that's what Clarice tells me it is. The light-beige trunk is mottled and quite thick. She figures it's about twenty years old. Thin branches stretch long fingers toward the light. If I look closely, with enough faith to believe there will be blossoms in the spring, sometimes I see green shoots on the branches.

I don't understand the way things work in here, but I've come to accept it.

We've talked many times by now, Clarice and

231

I. She knows all my stories. Some days I wonder if she knew them before I got here. "Kevin told me he ended things with Alison."

"I see." She starts to whistle a haunting tune that is somehow familiar. Somewhere in the depths of my memory, I know that song. "And how do you feel about that?"

We turn to look at each other at the same time. Her steady eyes burn into me, and I clasp my hands behind my back, feeling very much like a child about to be reprimanded.

"It's too late." The words that kept me awake all night spill in welcome release.

"Too late?" Clarice's size 5 brown boots crunch over new white gravel as she comes toward me. She takes my hands and stares up at me, searching my face for God only knows what. The truth, perhaps. Truth I can't yet face. "Do you really believe that?"

My heart beats fast and it's difficult to catch a breath. Difficult to form words that might convey the vast depths of emotion I'm wrestling. "Sometimes." The whispered word bounces off frosted glass and floats back toward me. "I thought I was ready to move on. Move past all this."

Clarice tips her head, folds her arms against her thin frame, and takes one step back. "With Brock."

Cords of guilt tighten their hold again. "He told you?"

"Not in so many words." She smiles and shakes her head. I think there's a hint of sadness in her eyes. "I've lived a lot of years, Savannah. I see things. And as much as I adore my nephew . . ." Her chest rises and falls and she looks away for a moment. "He is not yours. You have no claim on him. To think you might . . . is neither fair to him or to you. Or to Kevin."

"Kevin left me! He's been sleeping with another woman." Anger surges and reminds me my heart still hurts. Still bleeds and pulses with voracious wounds that have not healed. Wounds that may have no intention of healing.

"Yes, he left you, Savannah. But it sounds to me like he's starting to regret his transgressions. And perhaps trying to make amends." She moves around me and runs a finger along the blotchy branch of the cherry tree. "May I ask you something?"

I almost laugh but sniff instead and shrug. "You will anyway."

"Well, that's true." She sets that knowing smile on me again. "Last night, when you and Kevin talked, did you show your husband grace, Savannah?"

"Grace?"

Her look says she doesn't need to explain what she means. She's right.

Did I?

Of course I didn't.

I was too angry.

Too hurt, too blindsided, and too eager to strike back.

Grace is no longer part of my vocabulary when it comes to Kevin.

"You don't have to answer. Just think about it." She coughs, the rattle in her chest alarming.

"Are you all right, Clarice?"

"Of course. Just a little bug I caught from Maysie." Her smile returns, but she moves away from me. "I'm going in. Come inside for some tea if you like. And I believe Hope may be ready to go home with you this week. If you still want her."

"Oh yes." That I do know. I want that bundle of fur more than anything. When she sets her deep golden eyes on me, I don't feel so sad. So vulnerable. I feel like I might actually get through this overwhelming season of my life. Brock was right. I did choose well.

Once Clarice disappears, I slide down, sit on the cold ground with my back against the cherry tree, and put my head in my hands. "Okay, I give up. Help me out here, God, because I don't know what to do."

I haven't voiced my thoughts, prayers, out loud in a long time. Not really. It's something I used to do a lot, to help me process. Back when my faith was stronger, I believed I'd get answers. Some, Brock perhaps, would write the words. I speak them. And sometimes I yell.

The heart-wrenching, aching, guttural groans that escape between fits and starts bring tears of sorrow and anger and, finally, a strange sense of joy. Even though I'm not altogether convinced I have any sort of solution, I feel it might be possible to release some of the bitterness I've been holding on to.

As I push up, my body stiff and sore and cold, a flash of pink catches my eye. I move closer to the tree, shake my head in wonder as a smile splits my face. There, on the lowest branch, sits one perfect pink bud, open and infusing the air with scent. I lean over, inhale, and stay in the moment. In five minutes it may not be there, but for now, inexplicably, it is. And I am simply thankful for the gift.

※

The following afternoon the house is quiet. Dad is snoring in front of the television, Hugh and Peg have taken the kids tobogganing, Zoe and Adam have gone to lunch with Kevin, and I'm puttering around in the kitchen. Paul and I talked for hours last night. I know he was tired when they arrived. Janice and the girls went upstairs shortly after supper, but my brother and I sat in the deserted dining room, drinking coffee and catching up. And I told him everything.

Paul challenged me to search my heart. To

seek wisdom and truth, not to rush headlong into a situation I might soon have no control over. I teased that he sounded just like Clarice. He laughed at that and said he hoped to meet her while he was here. I think he'd like to meet Brock as well, but I'm not sure I want him to.

"Anything I can give you a hand with?" Janice walks through the kitchen running a finger across the counter. She immediately grabs a cloth and wipes it down.

"Just putting a few dishes away." I try to smile but it's difficult. My sister-in-law and I have never gotten along.

"You're looking quite well, Savannah. Have you lost weight?" She reaches for a plate to dry. As usual, she's dressed perfectly. Today she's wearing crisp beige trousers with a striped sweater, her blond hair pulled back in a neat bun at the nape of her neck. And she is as slender as the day she married my brother. Janice is a few years older than me but I swear she looks younger. She homeschools their three girls, runs the women's ministry at their church, and does a million other things I could never begin to wrap my brain around, all with seemingly very little effort. She is the perfect pastor's wife.

I glance down at my plaid shirt, untucked over faded jeans. I am neither svelte nor stylish, and I'm not bringing sexy back anytime soon, but I have managed to shed a few unwanted pounds.

"I've started working out a bit. Of course the holidays . . ."

"Yes, well. You look good. Considering."

"Life goes on, Janice." I search the room for something else to wash, relieved when I spy a forgotten frying pan on the stove. I grab it and plunge it into the sudsy water.

"I was surprised to see Kevin up here," she starts up again, apparently determined to break through our usual stilted conversation. "That's good, don't you think?" She begins rearranging my mother's glassware, putting them in order of size. I grin, thinking of the battle that will ensue later, once Mom discovers Janice has been meddling with her stuff.

"Good for the kids, I suppose. How's the weather in Oregon this winter?" A lame switch of topic, but I'm desperate to get her to move on.

"Dreary. You know, Savannah . . ." She closes the cupboard and turns to me, her blue eyes giving the impression that she might be on the verge of tears. "Despite what Kevin has done, it's your duty to take him back. Surely you know that."

"My duty?" I back up against the counter and twist a dry dishcloth a little too tightly.

"You know what I mean. God hates divorce. The Bible says—"

"I know what the Bible says, Janice." I put up a hand and draw a deep breath. "Don't stand there and throw that at me. You have absolutely no idea what this has been like. You don't know how I feel or what I think or even what I pray for. The current state and future of my marriage is, quite frankly, none of your business."

"Savannah." She wears a pained look I'm tempted to slap off her face. "I was only trying to point out that—"

"You were judging me, Janice. And you have no right."

Her lips pinch together as if I've mortally wounded her. "I wouldn't say *judging*. That's a bit harsh, don't you think?"

"Sounds spot-on to me."

Kevin strolls into the kitchen, leather jacket open, his cheeks blistering from the cold. I know he's heard most of the conversation by the anger simmering in his eyes.

Janice backs up a little, her flawless face gaining some color. "Kevin. I didn't hear you come in."

"Clearly." He shoots me a cautious glance. "You okay?"

"Fine." I think I might actually be smiling. "I'm perfectly capable of defending myself."

"So I heard." I think he might be smiling, too, but Janice is still in the room so I look away.

"Well, I guess we're all done here." Janice attempts to scoot past him to the door but Kevin blocks her path.

"No, I don't think we are done, Janice." He

clears his throat and looms over her. He can be quite intimidating when he wants to be. "I'm well aware of your opinion of me, but leave Savannah out of it. This isn't her fault. If you must unleash your holy wrath on somebody, I'm right here. I'm more than happy to throw it back in your face and tell you exactly what to do with it."

"I . . ." Janice just stands there gaping.

But Kevin isn't finished.

"You know, the problem with you perfect people is that you actually believe the things you say are justified. You force your opinions on others and sleep soundly at night, secure in your small little minds that you've done right. And you don't think twice about calling someone out when you think they've gone astray, but you don't do it to help them, even though you say you do. You do it because it makes you feel better about yourself. Maybe it's a way to cover up your own shortcomings. You believe you have some divinely inspired, indisputable right to cast judgment, and you wield it like a weapon, never thinking you might be doing more harm than good. Well, let me tell you something, lady, you don't have that right."

He pauses, pushes his fingers through his hair, and glares at her.

The kitchen is supremely silent. The ticking of the clock on the wall is almost too loud. I don't hear the television anymore. Since Kevin's here,

I assume the kids are back. I imagine the entire family huddled in the living room, holding their breath.

My chest is so tight I'm ready to scream. The urge to grab my sister-in-law and push her out of the room before she does more damage is overwhelming. I study Kevin's face, his tight jaw, hardened features, and tired eyes. He's holding back. Actually showing great restraint in his silence. He's not overly confrontational by nature, but when it comes to defending his family . . . oh, can he bring it . . .

Days after Shelby's accident, curious onlookers, concerned neighbors, and a handful of local reporters still shadow us. We try to leave for the hospital as early as possible. I hadn't wanted to come home at all, but Kevin insisted. I've showered, changed, but not slept. Beth and John are here, their kids asleep upstairs with Adam and Zoe.

We don't speak. Kevin has the car keys in hand and we head out the front door before we see them.

Three, maybe four people coming toward us with cameras and microphones.

"Mrs. Barrington, can you tell us how your daughter is?"

"Is it true she wasn't wearing a helmet?"

"Where were you at the time of the accident,

Mrs. Barrington? A neighbor tells us you were inside. Not watching her."

Kevin swears, grabs my wrist, hauls me behind him, and thunders down the front steps. He lunges for the first camera he can get his hands on and hurls it to the redbrick path.

"Get off my property!" Before I can move, his fist plows into the startled reporter's face. My scream brings Beth and John outside and John manages to break up the fight.

The police arrive, Kevin is charged with aggravated assault, but thanks to Walter's quick intervention, the charges are later dropped.

"You shouldn't have hit him." I huddle into Kevin's chest later that day as we hover over Shelby's bed. She still hasn't moved, but her vitals are stable. For now. He puts an arm around me and kisses the top of my head.

"I'd do it again in a heartbeat. He deserved it. Nobody talks to my wife that way. Not as long as I'm around."

The enormity of it, what he's just done, standing up to Janice like that, defending me, floods through me, and it's all I can do not to crumple to the ground and weep.

But Janice doesn't back down easily. She's rooted to the spot, staring at him like he's the scum of the earth. "You have truly lost your way."

Kevin draws a long breath, then lets it out

slowly. "You're right, Janice. I have lost my way. What I did was wrong. Abhorrent. But you know, the faith I hold on to, the God I still believe in, who I believe somehow still loves me, he's all about forgiveness, not judgment. And I believe those who follow him are asked to extend grace and mercy. Even toward someone as vile as me. Shocking, isn't it?"

Janice stalks past him and disappears. It's only once she's gone and I'm breathing normally again that I realize I'm trembling. I meet Kevin's eyes and somehow manage a smile.

"Well, crap. I never did like that woman." He slides a hand over the lower half of his face and gives a low groan. "But maybe I shouldn't have said all that."

Unspoken questions bounce between us like live wire. I can't pick them up because I'm too afraid of the shock. So I cross my arms and nod. "You said what needed to be said. What I was thinking. And you probably said it better than I would have."

"I think I'd like a drink." He takes a few steps toward the refrigerator, then stops midway, looks my way with a wary glance. "You mind?"

"Whatever you want. And make mine a double."

He grins and some of the tension etched across his forehead disappears. "Shall I ask Janice if she wants a beer?"

"Don't you dare." Laughter creeps up and spills from me. Next thing I know, he's taken off his jacket and we're sitting at the kitchen table drinking beer at three in the afternoon. Not really talking, but that's okay. I think he's said enough today.

Chapter 19

"Do not judge, and you will not be judged.
Do not condemn, and you will not becondemned.
Forgive, and you will be forgiven."
—LUKE 6:37

"Curiouser and curiouser."
I underline the words in my book of Alice quotes.

I can't shake yesterday's scene with Janice from my mind. I didn't sleep well, again, for thinking about it. Kevin went back to his hotel before dinner last night. He didn't say much to anyone. The kids stood outside with him for a bit, watched him drive off, and returned to the living room with half-happy smiles. It seems they're working things out with their father, and I'm pleased about that. But since Kevin showed up, I'm feeling more conflicted than ever.

After my shower, I dress, blow-dry my hair, and pull back the curtains in my room. Kevin's car is in the driveway. I step back in a hurry and peek around the curtains. My brother appears and hops in, and off they go. My breath fogs the cold glass as I watch the car disappear out of sight. O-kay . . . now he's apparently going out for breakfast with Paul. I take a moment to pray for that meeting. For both of them. But mostly for Paul. He'd feel so bad if he actually hit my husband.

Just as I'm about to leave the room, I see a thick black book placed on the bookshelf. I know it wasn't there yesterday. It's a scrapbook. And it's heavy.

I sit on the edge of the bed with the book in my lap. And all I can do is stare at it.

My mother's handiwork.

Mom has been scrapbooking for a few years now. None of us thought the hobby would stick because they rarely do. Watercolors, pottery, crochet and knitting . . . she's tried everything. It became a running joke within the family—what weird gift would we get from Mom this year. I half expected some kind of framed collage this Christmas, but my present was a lovely cashmere sweater and a spa day at a nearby hotel. Which I'm grateful for. But this . . . I finally open the book and a handwritten note slips out.

Merry Christmas, Savannah, darling.

I wanted you to have this when you were alone. Take your time—look at it when you can, when you're ready to really appreciate it.

I love you, sugar.
Mama

It begins with pictures of us in our teens, here at the lake house. Paul, Peg, and me, and Kevin. She's catalogued everything in chronological order. My high school graduation. Our wedding . . . Once our parents got past the initial shock, arrangements were made as quickly as possible and we held a small ceremony that December with only family and close friends invited. I try not to laugh as I stare at the two starry-eyed youngsters standing on the front steps of my parents' home, me with my just slightly rounded belly. We had no idea what we were getting ourselves into. But we didn't care. Despite everything, we were happy.

Next is an assortment of photos of me at various stages of pregnancy. Shelby's birth. Her first year. Me, pregnant again, with Zoe. She was a surprise—we hadn't intended to add to our new family so soon, but by that time we'd settled into the routine of marriage and parenthood and we were quite excited. Then came Adam, planned and perfect, the boy to round out our clan. Pages and pages of memories . . .

I can't absorb it all now, so I put the book away and head down for breakfast.

Later that morning I take a walk with Mom and we pop in to say hello to Clarice and introduce Mom to the puppies. Hope is ready to come home with me, but I've decided to wait until everyone leaves, when the house will be quiet again. Brock is nowhere in sight and I don't ask for him. Part of me is relieved.

I show her the work we've done in the greenhouse, and Mom nods and smiles and tries to look impressed. Her idea of gardening is buying a flower arrangement from Whole Foods, putting it on the table, and waiting for it to die. Fortunately, she's always hired extremely talented landscapers; her gardens never tell the true story.

We're on our way back home, so I take advantage of the opportunity. "Thanks for the book."

Mom pauses by the lake, turns to face me, her eyes worried. "Was it okay? Daddy thought it might be too much, too hard."

"No." I smile and shake my head. "It's perfect. Really."

"Savannah . . ."

I nod. I know what she's going to say. I've known it since Christmas Day. "We don't have to have this conversation." I laugh it off, but she frowns and folds her arms against her forest-green down jacket.

"You know you've never been terribly good at hiding your feelings, darling."

"I must get that from you." I sigh, look away, and watch my breath curl in the cold air.

"I won't ask if there's something between you and Brock Chandler because I think that much is obvious. But I will ask if you're positive you're making the right choice."

I turn back to face the questions in her eyes. "Mom." I don't like the worried creases on her brow because I know I put them there. And I know she's right. "It's all so confusing." The sun parts the clouds and shimmers across the snow. I tip my face toward it and bask in the warmth. "It's not something I went looking for."

"How far has it gone?"

"Far enough." I shove my hands in my pockets and find the courage to tell her what happened, and didn't happen, that afternoon before Christmas. "And before you ask, I told Kevin on Christmas Day. Of course he thinks I'm trying to get back at him."

"Are you?"

I shrug and kick at the snow. "Maybe. I don't know. I don't think so. Maybe it's more that I . . . that I like being with someone who makes me feel special again."

"Well." Mom slips her arm through mine and we start walking again. "You're all grown up now, perfectly capable of making your own decisions, but this worries me. You've been hurt enough."

"By Kevin."

"Yes. Which is why it's not a good idea to barrel headlong into a relationship with a man you barely know. Because that's what this is, Savannah. And it's dangerous."

"I know." She's not telling me anything I haven't told myself. "I don't intend to continue it, Mom. Believe me, it caught me completely by surprise. But I'm not stupid. I know I'm not in a position to be in a relationship with anyone."

Mom nods, stops, and stares at me for a long moment. "I don't know if I should tell you this. I wasn't planning on it. But . . . yesterday, before Kevin left, he asked your daddy and me into the study. You were still in the kitchen." She runs a gloved hand over her face with a shaky sigh. "At first I didn't think Michael would agree. You know how angry he's been with Kevin over all this. But he heard him out. All I can tell you, sweetheart, is that that man is filled with regret. He's sorry and—"

"Mom, don't." I don't want to hear it. An awful lump sticks in my throat. "What if he was just telling you what he thought you wanted to hear?"

"And what possible reason would he have for doing that?" Contrite anger inches into her tone. My mother has always had a soft spot for Kevin. "Savannah, if the man still intended to divorce you, do you think he'd be up here? Do you think he'd bother giving any of us the time of day? I don't condone what he's done, not in the least, but I believe he's trying to make amends. And I also believe he still loves you."

I yank my arm from hers and take a step back.

I can't look at her. Because I don't want to believe what she's just said. I don't want to hope, because before I allow myself to do that, I need to deal with what's happened.

All of it.

"I don't know how to forgive him, Mom." And there it is.

The very idea of forgiving Kevin resembles something the size of the Hubbard Glacier in my mind. A few years ago we took an Alaskan cruise. I'll never forget the feeling of standing on deck, staring at that massive stretch of blue ice, cold sea swirling around it. Every now and again blocks of frozen water would break away with a horrendous crack, the splash shaking the huge ship I stood on. And I remember feeling incredibly small, and in complete awe of God's creation.

"Janice says I have to take him back. That it's my duty."

"Janice has some overzealous ideas." Mom laughs, then gets serious again. "The choice is completely yours, darling. You don't have to take him back, but I do believe, at some point, you need to forgive him. For both your sakes."

"He hasn't asked for my forgiveness."

"No." My mother's eyes fill with sudden tears. "Perhaps he hasn't. But that doesn't mean you shouldn't offer it."

❧❦

Paul returns just before lunch, a myriad of Christmas leftovers Mom, Janice, and I throw together. Kevin takes off without coming in and I'm okay with that. My brother picks at his meal in silence, not eating much, then disappears upstairs and stays there for most of the afternoon. Paul and Janice are leaving early tomorrow morning, and I want the chance to talk to him again before that. I hope he's all right. Knowing how close he and Kevin were, I know he's had a hard time with all this.

Haven't we all?

Paul finds me in the kitchen later that night, nursing a cup of tea at the table.

His smile apologizes without words. He joins me at the table, bringing two glasses and a bottle of brandy with him.

I smile back and raise a brow. "Rough day?"

"You could say that." Paul's smile is his best feature. He's always been more of the bookish type. He could pass for a college professor instead of a preacher. But he's also a champion wrestler, something only a few people know. As far as I'm aware, he hasn't put those skills to use since entering the ministry. I hope he didn't try any of his old moves on Kevin this morning.

"Want to talk?" I ask, because I know he's going to anyway, and he's probably not sure I want to hear what he has to say.

"Don't look at me like that. He asked me to meet him. I couldn't say no. Didn't want to say no." He corrects himself and slides a generously filled glass toward me, and we offer a silent toast.

"Is Kevin okay?"

Paul shrugs, his eyes shimmering under the overhead lights. "I think he will be."

"Are you okay?" My heart aches for him, for what their conversation must have cost him. Cost them both.

"I'm better than I was yesterday. Kevin and I have needed to talk for a long time. I thought about hopping on a plane a ton of times, you know, after you first called to tell me what was going on. But I was too angry. I didn't trust myself not to plow him into the ground."

"You didn't . . ." For half a second I can still imagine that scenario.

Paul laughs and shakes his head. "No. We just talked."

"Tell me what to do." It's a pointless request, but I make it anyway.

Paul's amused laughter fills the warm kitchen. "Not a chance. I learned that lesson a long time ago."

"Right." When I was around nine, I got so sick and tired of my brother bossing me around that one day, after he commanded I turn off the television and go put the dishes away like I was supposed to be doing, I punched him in the stomach. He stopped telling me what to do after that. "If I promise not to punch you?"

"Savannah." He rolls his eyes, drinks, and

puts down the glass. "This is something you and Kevin have to work out. I can't tell you what I'd do or what I think you should do. All I can do is be here for you, and trust that as you pray and think more on your situation, you will find the right answers."

"Is that what you told Kevin?"

"Yes. Among other things." He looks away, but I see his eyes mist over.

"Sometimes I think walking away would be easier." I swirl my glass and watch amber liquid spin in circles, the way my thoughts have been doing all day. "If he'd just stayed with Alison, I could have started over. But now I don't know which end is up. I don't know what he wants."

"I think you do know that." Paul locks his gaze on me, smiles in that gentle way of his, and I can't look away.

"He wants to reconcile." It's what I wanted weeks ago. But now . . . "What if I don't?"

Paul's gaze stays steady. "It's your choice to make, Savannah. But if you both decide your marriage is worth saving, there will be work."

"We'd have to go back, wouldn't we? Rehash it all . . . talk about . . . about Shelby." My hands begin to tremble and I slide them onto my lap.

"Grief manifests in many forms, Savannah. Sometimes it pushes people together. In other instances, especially in the death of a child, it can drive them apart."

"Exhibit A." I press my teeth into my bottom lip. Anger won't do any good. I know that. But the moment I think I've conquered it, it charges back for another round. "Do you think our marriage is fixable? Have you seen couples go through this?"

"More times than I care to remember." He splays his hands on the table, his eyes full of compassion.

"Do they stay together?"

"Some."

"How?"

My brother pushes his fingers through his hair and shrugs. "Counseling. A lot of hard work from both parties. Patience and the willingness to rebuild the relationship, gain back the trust. I'm not going to sit here and tell you it's easy. It's not. And sometimes, no matter how hard a couple tries, it doesn't work. Sometimes what they're dealing with is too self-destructive, too damaging, and too dangerous. In some cases, they are better off apart."

"You advise people to get divorced?" I wonder if Janice knows this.

"No. But I don't condemn them if that's the choice they eventually make. Yes, in a perfect world, happily ever after might exist. But we don't live in that perfect world yet. Do I believe miracles can happen? Sure. But we have to step aside and let them. The answers aren't always obvious. And sometimes things don't happen the way we want or intend them to."

"Tell me about it." I finish my drink and rub a hand over my eyes. "It's hard to look at him and not see her. Not think about what he did. I want to move past that, but I'm not sure how. I don't know when or if that will happen." Exhaustion is getting the better of me. But maybe I'll sleep better tonight. Talking with Paul always helps.

He nods, his face grave. "I imagine that will be one of the biggest obstacles for you to overcome. For Kevin too. He's going to have memories that won't go away. He's going to hate himself for a long time, Savannah."

"He should."

Paul props his elbows on the table, rests his chin over his clasped hands, and studies me through tired eyes. "I need to ask you something. I don't want to hurt you, but I believe it's something you need to think about, and work through. If you want to save your marriage, if you're willing to fight for it, this must be dealt with."

"Okay." I give a shaky sigh, sit back, and grip my elbows. Then I remember what one of my therapists said about body language and how it can be perceived and make a tense situation even worse, so I let my arms go limp, breathe deeply, and fold my hands in my lap instead. "Go ahead. Ask."

"Do you believe Kevin holds you responsible for Shelby's death?"

"What?" The question shoots from my mouth like a gunshot, my blood pressure shooting right along with it.

"I said—"

"I heard what you said! What I want to know is why you said it. Did *he* say it? This morning . . . did he tell you . . . No, never mind. I don't want to know." This was the last thing I expected to hear. Not from Paul. I have to calm down or I'll lose it. But I don't want to calm down. I don't want to sit here a minute longer. I don't want to have this conversation.

"Savannah, breathe." Paul is annoyingly calm while I am frantic.

I study my shaking hands, twist the rings on my finger, and think about the gold wedding band on the chain that sits on the dresser upstairs. And suddenly it's all too much.

"I can't do this. Not now." I push my chair back and rush from the room. If there had been a door to slam I would have slammed it. Hard.

Chapter 20

"The truth is rarely pure and never simple."
—OSCAR WILDE

Perhaps it was time he accepted his fate.

Brock folded another shirt and placed it in his suitcase. Clarice had caught Maysie's cold but was feeling better, despite the lingering cough, and insisted he not postpone his trip. And if he were honest with himself, he couldn't wait to get out of here. This past week, since Christmas Day really, life had been unbearable.

Lady Antebellum belted out a tune from the iPod dock across the room and he reached for the remote to turn the music down. Everything was too loud today. Too bright. He hadn't bothered to open the curtains. The sun on snow was glaring. Even taking a shower hurt.

Brock hadn't felt this much pain in months.

And it flat-out terrified him.

He planned to leave first thing tomorrow morning. He didn't know yet when he was coming back or what answers he'd bring with him. He reached for a sweater and jumped at the sound of someone knocking on his bedroom door.

"Brock?" Savannah poked her head in and his pulse slowed. "Oh. You are here. Sorry. I let myself in. No one answered the doorbell."

"Didn't hear it." Brock drank in the sight of her as she walked into the room. If he could commit that face to memory, freeze time and make like none of this was happening, he'd do it in an instant. He cleared his throat and avoided her questioning eyes. "Clarice and Maysie went to the store."

"And you're . . ." She rounded the bed, indicated the suitcase, and widened her eyes. ". . . going somewhere?"

"Business trip."

"Tomorrow is New Year's Eve. Odd time to go on a business trip."

"It is what it is." Man, he could be a real jerk.

"O-kay." He watched her try to hide her surprise. "Well, then I guess I won't invite you for dinner tomorrow night."

"Guess you won't. I'm sure Clarice and Maysie are free, though." Self-loathing curled in his stomach and he forced himself to face her and her confusion. "So. What are you doing here?"

Savannah leaned against his dresser, her coat unzipped. She wore that pink sweater he liked, her hair falling around her face in soft waves. But her eyes were sad; he'd chased away her smile the minute he opened his mouth.

She let out a breath and shoved her hands in the pockets of her coat. "I came for Hope. Everybody's gone now."

"Oh. Right. Did I know you were coming?"

Clarice probably told him, but his memory wasn't working the way it should. Nothing was working the way it should this week. Even walking was a chore.

Shooting pain sliced up his neck and wrapped around his head like barbed wire. Brock inhaled and took slow, measured steps toward the chair by the window. The room began to spin. He swore, slumped into the chair, and leaned over his knees.

She was at his side at once. "What is it? Brock, what's wrong?" Panic flared in her eyes. If only he could capture it and box it up, put it well out of reach with all the other nightmares he'd tried to kidnap over the years. Savannah crouched beside him, her hands on his arm. "What can I do?"

"Nothing." He leaned back and offered a brief smile. He rested his other hand on hers, grateful for the contact. Nights and days of living alone through the screaming pain were getting to be almost unbearable. "It'll pass."

"Is it a migraine?"

"I wish." He winced again, closed his eyes, and felt her hand against his forehead. "And it's not the flu, so don't go there." He pointed to the dresser where an array of orange prescription bottles sat alongside the fresh jug of water Clarice set out for him twice daily, no matter how many times he told her it wasn't necessary. "Grab me that first bottle, would you? The one with the red label, please." Every word was excruciating.

Not only because of the pain, but because of the other kind of pain he knew was coming. But he didn't have a choice now.

He had to let her in.

She did as he asked but took a long look at the label after she'd handed him a pill and a glass of water.

Savannah crossed the faded rug to put the bottle back where she found it. Brock steadied his breathing as he waited for the meds to kick in and watched her stand at the dresser for a long time, her back to him.

At last she turned, still huddled inside her coat, tears shimmering in her eyes. "You're sick, aren't you?"

Brock clenched his fists and shut his eyes for a second.

He didn't want to do this. Not here. Not now.

Not when he couldn't trust himself to stand.

When he couldn't even hold her.

"Go downstairs. I'll be down soon."

She shook her head, took off her coat, and hung it on the doorknob. She scanned the room and grabbed a footstool, sat in front of him, and nailed him with that stubborn look he was getting rather used to. "I'm not leaving this room until you tell me what's going on."

"I'm fine." He almost grinned at her annoyed expression but didn't have the energy.

"Brock."

"Okay." He sighed, held her gaze, and said it. "Brain tumor."

Her scowl deepened. "Very funny."

Brock lifted his shoulders and let them sag. The thumping was beginning to lessen, but he'd probably have to puke in the next hour. "You asked."

Her eyes puddled with fresh tears, and she clapped a hand to her mouth. "No." Savannah shook her head, took his hands in hers and held tight. "Brock, come on," she whispered. "Please tell me you're joking."

"It's just a little one. About half the size of a golf ball right now." He mustered a smile. "Only . . . they can't touch it because the operation might kill me."

She still didn't look convinced. "If you're making this up, Brock Chandler, you have a very warped sense of humor. And I will never forgive you."

"Darlin', I wish I were making it up. I can give you the number for my oncologist if you like."

Silence surrounded them and made an admirable attempt at suffocating him. He forced his eyes to stay open until he saw the truth register in hers.

"You're not kidding. Oh, Brock." Tears slipped down her cheeks. "How long have you known?"

"Almost a year. We've done everything, oral chemo, radiation. It's not shrinking. I'm going to see a new doc in New York this week, but I don't think he's going to tell me anything I don't already know." He leaned forward and brushed her tears away with his thumbs. "The timing kind of sucks, I have to admit."

"Does Maysie know?" She blinked, pulled his hands down, and clasped them in hers.

Brock sighed deep. He could happily sit here staring into her lovely face forever. Being with Savannah made him forget everything else. Even the one thing he dreaded most. Telling Maysie he probably wouldn't be around to celebrate her next birthday.

Or for the rest of her life.

"Not yet. She knows I get a lot of headaches. That I don't feel good sometimes. But I was waiting to see . . ." He let out a shaky sigh. "I was hoping for a better outcome."

"I don't know what to say." Her whisper reached right through him and squeezed his heart.

Unwanted tears stung and he swallowed the rock in his throat. "I should have kept my distance from you. I knew that the first day I laid eyes on you."

She studied her shoes, her long hair falling forward. He sat there and watched her shoulders shaking, heard her stifled sob, and wished for the thousandth time since they'd met that things could be different.

"Hey." He slid one hand from hers and tipped her chin so he could see her. "I'm not dead yet."

"Shut up." Laughter hiccupped from her. "There must be something they can do. They can't just tell you game over."

"Oh . . ." He smiled and traced a finger down the side of her face. "Yes, they can."

"But you were fine!" Anger flashed in her eyes, and he loved her all the more for it. "All this time, you—"

"I have good days and bad days. You just haven't seen the bad ones."

Savannah pushed her shoulders back and frowned. "Were you planning on telling me or did you think it'd be easier if I just stumbled across your obituary?"

"I would have told you. I was just being selfish. I wanted to enjoy being with you, without this hanging over us. But I guess that was wishful thinking on my part. Obviously it's not something I can hide." The searing pain returned for another round. Brock shuddered and clamped his jaw.

Fear flickered across her face. "What do you need me to do?"

"Think you can help me over to the bed?"

She nodded and somehow got him to his feet. He tried not to lean on her with his full weight, but it was difficult. Once they made it, she helped him swing his legs up, fluffed his pillows, pulled up the blankets, and sat on the edge, still teary-eyed.

Brock coughed, then tried a grin. "Thought we'd finish what we started before Christmas. You up for that?"

Her eyes flew wide; she opened her mouth, shut

it, and then dissolved into laughter. "I'm glad to see you haven't lost your sense of humor."

"No chance. And I'm sorry to say that if you're intending to take me up on that offer, tempting as it is, I'm probably going to have to decline."

"Just as well." She smiled but fell silent. When she looked away, her eyes landed on the pictures on his bedside table. "Is this your wife?" Savannah reached for the framed photo, studying it with interest.

"Yeah." Brock turned his head. "You can see Maysie just starting to show. Gabby was about five months along when I took that."

"She was beautiful."

"She was." He breathed a ragged sigh and closed his eyes.

"You miss her."

A little less every day. And that scared him.

"Gabrielle was everything to me. Yeah, I miss her. But part of me is glad she's not around for this."

He heard her put the picture back. "Will you tell me about her sometime?"

"Sometime." Brock closed his eyes under another wave of pain. "Savannah?"

"Yes?"

"Talk to me." He opened his eyes again and patted the empty spot on the other side of him. "Come here and tell me a story. Tell me something good."

"Okay." She rounded the bed, gingerly lay

beside him, and stared at the ceiling. "Once upon a time . . ."

Laughter shook him and he flinched with the effort it took. "Good grief, lady. You can't start a story with 'once upon a time.' Too cliché."

She flipped onto her side and gave him the look. "You did. What book was it? Oh, *The Midnight Call*. It definitely started with 'once upon a time' because I remember saying to Kevin how weird it was."

"Good memory. But what was the next line?"

"Um . . . I don't remember."

" 'Maxwell Carter hit the Delete button with more force than necessary. He wouldn't resort to clichés, no matter how desperate he was to meet this deadline.' "

"Ah." She grinned. "I suppose that's acceptable then." She propped her elbow and hummed a wistful tune. "I'm not very good at telling stories."

"Everybody's good at telling stories. They just don't know they are." Brock smiled at her look of chagrin. "Tell me about your life. Tell me what it was like back when your kids were young. What kind of stuff did y'all do?"

"Oh, gosh." Her eyes sparkled in a way that made him feel lighter. "It was like a circus most days at our house. Kevin worked long hours a lot of the time. But he'd make up for it on weekends. He always came up with the most outrageous ideas. Like driving north for four hours to find an orchard he'd read about that had the best apple cider. Or going to some llama farm out in the middle of nowhere because Shelby had never seen a llama. I swear he would have brought one home for her if I'd have let him. Oh—there was one year he decided to build an igloo in the backyard."

"An igloo?" Brock chuckled. "For real?"

"For real." Savannah rolled her eyes and laughed. "The kids thought it was going to be amazing. They used empty milk cartons to freeze the water, drew out elaborate plans and everything. I think it would have actually worked. They had two rows done and then the next day the weather warmed and the whole thing melted."

"Ah. That sucks."

"We took them to a movie and the ice rink. They forgot about it pretty quickly."

"Sounds like he was a good dad." The kind of dad Brock had wanted to be.

"He was. Is." She lay back down and laced her hands together. "He and Adam have gone skiing for New Year's. Zoe and her boyfriend are meeting up with them."

"You didn't want to go?"

"I don't ski. Besides, I didn't want the kids to think . . ." She trailed off and released a reflective sigh.

"Your kids are great. I enjoyed meeting them." Even in spite of the curious glances both of them sent his way most of the afternoon. Brock would have found it funny had he not been so ticked with their father for showing up and sending Savannah into conniptions. He had to hand it to her, though; she managed the entire fiasco with remarkable finesse.

"They are great. Although I think they'll be glad when this whole thing is over, one way or the other. They're both still pretty angry with Kevin. And Adam . . . he's not himself. I think he's really struggling with all this. I tried to talk to him, but he said he was fine and didn't want to talk."

They lay silent for a while, listening to the music. Brock's headache was bad, but it didn't compare to what was going on in his heart. "What are you going to do, Savannah?"

"Why does everyone keep asking me that?"

Her sigh of frustration coaxed a smile. Brock shifted slightly so he could see her. She moved at the same time, and he caught the hesitation in her eyes. "Do you want to know what I think?"

"No."

He grinned and somehow managed to prop himself up on one elbow. "I think you'll know exactly what you want when you least expect it. And when you do, you'll know you made the right decision."

"You've been hanging out with Clarice too long."

"Probably." His smile didn't quite make it. "But I'll tell you something else, darlin'. Second chances don't come around too often in this life. If you get yourself one, grab it good and don't let go for anything."

"Brock . . ."

"Promise me."

"Why?" She wore a pained look that he wanted to kiss away, but he wouldn't go there. Instead, he shook his head and lay on his back again.

"Because it would please me to no end to know you're happy, Savannah."

"And you think taking Kevin back will make me happy?"

"I don't know. But I think y'all had something pretty special until he screwed it up. And maybe that can't be fixed. But the way he looked at you Christmas Day?" Brock flung one arm across his eyes and wrestled with the truth. "I'd say you owe it to yourself to find out."

Chapter 21

"All the art of living lies in a fine mingling of
letting go and holding on."
—HAVELOCK ELLIS

Not quite what he'd wanted to hear, but perhaps
there was hope. If he allowed it.

Brock exited the hospital, eager to be rid of
its stifling air and smothering, life-altering
prognoses, stepped out into the winter sun, and
headed for the bar where Mitch was waiting.

Mitchell sat in a booth near the back of the dimly
lit establishment, eyes glued to his iPhone.

He'd flown in from Zurich yesterday, at Brock's
request. Dressed in skinny jeans, brown Oxfords,
and a white button-down, with a discarded leather
jacket beside him, Mitch could easily pass for a
twenty-five-year-old hipster rather than a high-
powered international lawyer.

At thirty-seven, his brother had been to more
countries than Brock could count. His ridiculously
high-paying job took him all over the world into
some of the most well-known boardrooms—and,
often, bedrooms. Sadly, Mitch's reputation among
the crowd of rich and famous friends he seemed
to attract like bees to honey was not exaggerated.

Brock had hoped to see his brother settled down

by now. Still, when he called Mitch a few days ago to ask if he would meet him in New York, that it was important, he hadn't hesitated.

Now Brock almost regretted asking him to come. He'd kept his diagnosis from Mitchell because he wasn't sure how his brother would handle the news. So, for the past year, he'd made Clarice promise not to say a word and had kept things to himself, hoping the situation might improve. But last night he came clean. And Mitch had been furious. Understandably so. But his brother never stayed angry long.

Mitch hated hospitals. Refused to go anywhere near them since the day their mother died. Brock counted himself lucky that Mitch had agreed to be with him today. Still, Brock gave him an out and suggested meeting after his appointments.

"Hey." He took off his jacket and lowered himself into the booth opposite his brother.

Mitchell pocketed his phone and looked up through worried eyes. "Well?"

Brock sighed, laced his fingers together. "Well. I could use a drink, and you're gonna need one."

❧❦

Mitch needed more than one. He was on his second double Scotch before he finally spoke. "That's it? This is the only option?"

"I guess." Brock glared into his bourbon, tempted to chug it.

270

Mitch swore, his eyes glistening. "No. This is crap."

Brock shrugged. "I sort of expected it. At this point I'm not sure it's wise to hold out much hope."

"You gonna do the operation?" Mitch's eyes narrowed. "Brock. You have to have the operation."

"Why? So I can be dead a few months earlier?" He finished his drink and signaled for another. The waitress brought menus with the next round. Brock wasn't hungry but knew he needed food.

The crazy thing was, weeks ago he would have jumped at this option. A chance to live. But now he wasn't so sure. It was a long shot at best. The specialist was honest at least. They'd only done the operation three or four times with a fifty-fifty success rate. Fifty-fifty. Only slightly better than his current odds.

"And what if it works?" Mitch drummed his fingers on the table, agitated. "What if—"

"That's a heck of a big what-if, little brother. You're the gambler in the family. Not me."

Mitch gave a slow grin. He mussed his blond hair and trained his gaze on Brock. "Well, excuse me for pointing out the obvious, Captain Doom, but at this juncture it's not like you have anything to lose."

"Ooh. So true. Glad to see that law degree isn't going to waste." Brock scowled and flipped open the menu. "Think I'll have a burger. Haven't had a good cheeseburger in a long while."

"Great." Mitch's grin faded. "You've just been told you've got six months, give or take, unless you have an operation that may or may not kill you, and you want to talk about food."

"May as well go out fat and happy." Brock tried to smile, but the sudden anguish on his brother's face stopped him. "Look, I would have told you before now, but . . ." He didn't really have a good excuse. He hadn't told Mitchell for a few reasons, but mostly because he didn't want to face the look he was seeing now. Didn't want to have to tell his brother he was going to need to plan yet another funeral.

The waitress stopped by and took their lunch order.

"Yeah. You should have told me. But I know why you didn't. And to be honest, part of me appreciates that." Mitch shook his head and gulped from his glass. "Clarice knows, I gather."

Brock nodded.

"And your agent? Your publisher?" Brock nodded again.

"Maysie?"

"No." Brock shook his head. "Not yet."

"Well. This sucks." Mitch swore, peeled a bit of skin off his sunburned nose, and blew air through his lips. "Have the operation. At least leave it open for discussion. You have a daughter to consider."

"You think I don't know that?" Brock sat back, hoping the food would hurry up. The booze was giving him a buzz that wasn't making him feel any better. "What do you think keeps me up at night? It's not the thought of dying, Mitchell."

"What will happen if . . . I mean, Clarice is pretty old. And I'm . . ." He looked away and blinked hard. "You're not going to ask me to take her, are you?"

Brock couldn't stop a chuckle. He'd thought about it. Once. At the beginning. Thought maybe Mitch might clean up his act. Might actually sort out his life and come through for his niece if push came to shove. But he'd quickly moved on.

"Don't worry, you're off the hook. There's a plan. It's pretty wacked and I don't fully understand it yet, but Aunt Clarice has been trying to convince me it's what needs to be done."

"I'm not sure I like the sound of that. What plan?" Mitch looked back at him, doubt marring his face. "I thought Gabby didn't have any family."

"She doesn't. Didn't."

Gabrielle's mother died when she was only ten. Her father couldn't cope with the grief and turned to alcohol, practically ignoring his young daughter. She'd learned to fend for herself at an early age, but Brock suspected the pain of her father's rejection had never quite dissipated. It had been what connected them, he supposed. He knew what it was like, having gone through his

273

folks splitting up, missing a parent. Feeling like you got the short end of the stick somehow.

"There may be one or two cousins someplace, but no immediate family. After her dad died, she was pretty much on her own."

Mitch scowled. "Well, whatever this plan is, it better be good. I love Clarice, but you know . . ." Mitch hummed *Twilight Zone* music and Brock grinned. If his brother only knew the half of it.

The food arrived and they got busy. After a few bites, nausea got the better of him and Brock pushed his plate to one side. His cell buzzed in his pocket and he fished it out.

Savannah. A smile moved across his face, unbidden. He glanced up to find Mitch watching him with interest. "You mind if I take this?"

"By all means." Mitch continued to eat but kept one eye on him.

Brock swiveled in the booth, stretched out his legs, and put the phone to his ear. "City Morgue."

Savannah's giggle made him grin.

"Brock. Don't be an idiot. How'd it go?"

"It went." Brock arched a brow as Mitch leaned in a little closer, grinning like a kid. "I'm having lunch with my brother. Who is apparently dying to know all about the beautiful woman I'm talking to right now."

"Well, I'd like to know about her too." She laughed and his heart lurched. "So what happened? Are you okay? What did they say?"

"Um. I'll fill you in when I get home. How's Maysie?"

"She's good. She misses you. So does Clarice, although she'd never admit it. When are you flying back?"

Brock drummed his fingers on the rough-hewn table and watched Mitch down the rest of his drink. He didn't like the tremor in his brother's hands. Maybe he should spend some time with him. While he could. "Not sure yet. I'll let you know. Do you mind staying over there a few more nights?"

"Not at all." Her pause was longer than he liked. "You're not okay, are you?"

Brock pressed his lips together and stared at the floor. "I've had better days."

"I wish there was something I could do." She was tearful, and he knew he needed to let her go.

"You're doing it. Give Maysie a hug from me, and tell Clarice I'll call later, okay?"

"I will. Well, I just wanted to make sure you know . . ."

"I know." He closed his eyes a moment. "Thanks."

"You're taking care of yourself?"

"Three square meals a day and in bed by six."

"Liar. Brock, you promised you'd—"

"Darlin', I'm fine. Quit worrying. I'll call you back tonight and you can nag all you want."

"Oh, goody. I'll make a list." Savannah laughed

at his low growl. "All right. Ack, Hope just peed on the floor. I'd better go."

"Yeah, okay. Thanks for calling." Brock hung up and faced his brother's inquiring gaze. "Don't ask."

"Oh, no sir!" Mitch shook his head and let out a low whistle. "You're not getting away that easy. Spill it."

Brock groaned and took another bite of his burger. Mitch would only hound him until the truth came out. May as well get it over with. "Her name is Savannah. Her family owns the house next door to Clarice. We're friends. Just. Friends."

"Sav-an-nah." Mitch sat back, muscles flexing beneath his shirt. "Just friends, my rear. I've said that enough times to know what it means."

"She's married, Mitch."

His brother stared, slack-jawed. And then he erupted. Mitch's laughter rang around the room and caused several heads to turn in their direction. "I can't tell you how pleased I am to know I'm no longer the only nefarious Chandler."

Brock slunk a little lower in his chair and glared. "Would you keep your voice down? It's not like that. It's . . . I don't know what it is. And I refuse to discuss it here." Or anywhere, for that matter.

Mitch was still laughing. "Whatever you say, big guy. Well, I'll be a pig on a spit. After that revelation I need another drink."

"No." Brock pressed his hands onto the table and pinned his brother with a scathing look. "Mitchell. You do not need another drink. I've got things I need taken care of, and I need you to do that for me. I need your head in the game, man. Please."

"Don't get your blood pressure up." Mitch sobered and signaled the waitress for the check. "Okay. You're right. I'm sorry." He sighed, ran a hand down his face, and gave a sad smile. "I know I haven't always been there for you. Haven't been someone you could count on, and I'm sorry for that. But I'm here now. You have my word. Whatever you need, just ask."

Brock nodded, relief untying the knot in his stomach. For all his faults, Mitchell never went back on his word. "Thank you. So, if you're free the rest of the week, what do you think about flying to Atlanta? Spend a few days in our old stomping grounds. Go see Dad."

"Heaven help us." Mitch rolled his eyes and chuckled as he counted out a few bills and slipped them into the leather binder that held their check. "Figured that was coming. What's the point? He won't know we're there, Brock."

"Doesn't matter." Brock stood and pulled on his jacket. "I'll know."

Chapter 22

"The tragedy of it is that nobody sees
the look of desperation on my face."
—HENRY MILLER

She just had to get through today.

Zoe splashed cold water over her cheeks that Monday morning, breathed deeply, and glared at the small bottle in the medicine cabinet. Carly told her the pills would help. *"But just take one. And a Red Bull. You'll ace that exam."*

She didn't know about acing it, but she needed to stay awake for it. A two-hour test that would make or break her grade. And if she didn't pass this course . . . Oh, she was so not ready for this. How did it creep up on her so fast? Christmas and New Year's should have given her time to study. She thought she'd prepared. But it was now the end of January and she felt like she didn't know a thing.

If she could stop thinking about Mom and Dad for just a few minutes, perhaps her mind would be clearer. But the thought of her parents divorcing consumed her. It had become an obsession that kept her awake at night and dogged her waking hours, as she wondered what the future held for her family. When Dad showed up at Christmas,

Zoe hoped it was a new start. That her parents might take a few steps forward and try to work things out.

That hadn't happened.

Dad went back to Boston and Mom stayed in the Berkshires. With that Brock Chandler guy living next door. It was so obvious something was going on between them. Zoe couldn't blame her mother, not really. After the way Dad treated her, she deserved to find someone who could make her happy. And maybe Brock would.

But Zoe still wished it could be Dad.

She slipped into her boots, yanked on her jacket, and beat a path across campus. As she passed the window of the coffee shop, she thought she saw Tim. She backtracked, ready to wave, but then stopped in her tracks. A chill slithered through her. It was Tim, all right. Laughing. He leaned back in his chair the way he did when he was completely relaxed. His eyes held that sparkle she'd fallen in love with almost right away. He looked like he was having the best time in the world.

With a blond girl Zoe didn't recognize.

He looked up and caught her eyes through the foggy glass. Zoe pulled her scarf tight, turned into the wind, and walked away. Quickly.

"Zoe! Zo . . . wait!" Tim's voice made her walk faster. He ran up, jogging alongside her until she slowed and glared at his confused expression.

"I have my poli-sci test, Tim. I can't do this right now."

"Do what? Zo, stop!" He stepped in front of her and gave her no choice. "What's the matter with you? What's wrong?"

"What's wrong?" She practically spat the question back at him. "Who is that in there?"

"What? Who? Oh . . . come on. Seriously?" His eyes narrowed, but he kept a firm grip on her arms. "Her name is Caroline. She's my lab partner. We're meeting with our two other partners, Rich and Stan. Who haven't arrived yet. I don't know what you think . . ."

The pained look he wore said he knew exactly what she thought. Zoe blew out a breath, her heart racing. They'd never fought. Not really. And this was probably ridiculous. "Never mind. Tim, I have to go." She yanked herself free, shook her head, and brushed past him. She seriously didn't have time to deal with this. Or even think about it.

"Good luck, Zo! I'll call you later!" Tim's voice got lost in the wind and the surge of students around her. Zoe kept her eyes down and concentrated on putting one foot in front of the other. Tried to ignore the suspicions seeping into her subconscious.

Nothing. It was nothing. She was stressed and overreacted.

And if he wasn't telling the truth?

What had she expected?

All men cheat.

Her father was proof of that.

Her cell buzzed just as she was about to enter the building. If it was Tim, she wouldn't answer. She fished it out of her pocket, kept walking, and glanced at the number. "BRO."

Great. Zoe rolled her eyes. She didn't have time to help Adam with math or listen to his latest love problems. Not right now. But she picked up anyway.

"Hey, dude."

"Zo?"

"Hey, what's up? I'm about to go take a test."

"Oh." He sounded stuffy, like he had a cold. Come to think of it, he shouldn't be calling at this hour of the day.

"You sick today? You're at school, right?"

"Zo . . . I just . . ." Silence. "Do you know where Dad is?"

Zoe glanced at her watch and frowned. She had to get inside. "No. I haven't talked to him since last week. Why?"

"Because." Adam's voice sounded very far away, almost like he was slurring his words. "I called him Saturday, and some chick answered."

No, no, no.

"You called his cell?"

"He wasn't answering for the longest time. It was going straight to voice mail. I called a few times over the weekend. I don't know where he is. And then she picked up."

"Well, who was it?"

"I didn't ask. I hung up."

Zoe rolled her eyes. "Are you sure you had the right number?"

"Of course I have the right number."

"Did you try him again? Leave a message?"

"No. Zo, do you think he's—"

"Adam, stop." Zoe swore and shook off unwanted thoughts. She couldn't handle this now. She was on thin ice with this course, and if she missed this test . . . "Look, I really can't talk now. I'm gonna call you later, okay? Sorry, but I really have to go."

❧✦❧

Maysie stands in the middle of my living room on Monday afternoon, attempting to teach Hope to sit. We told her the puppy is probably a bit young still, but Maysie is stubborn. Like somebody else I know.

Brock is stretched on the La-Z-Boy by the fire, maybe sleeping, and Clarice is on the couch, reading. I've taken to inviting them for lunch instead of dinner. It's easier on Brock, and I don't think Clarice minds the earlier mealtime either.

He stayed in Atlanta two weeks. Now we're at the end of January and he still hasn't said much about his appointment in New York. I don't know what the doctors told him. Every time I ask, he says he's not ready to talk. Truthfully, I'm not that sure I want to know.

He spends most of his time writing and sleeping. I'm trying to be there for Maysie, to support Clarice, and to be a friend for him if he wants me to, but he doesn't always make it easy. Some days I think he's right. It might have been better if we'd never met.

The peaceful afternoon is suddenly shattered by the sound of Martin the parrot's obnoxious squawking. "Hello, Savannah! Hello, Savannah, SAVANNAH!"

"Goodness gracious!" Clarice jerks her head up. "Is Martin here?"

I'm wondering the same.

Maysie's uncontrollable giggles tell us she's hijacked my cell phone again. I pull her in close for a hug and a tickle and she laughs harder. "I thought you liked Martin, Miss Savannah. Aren't you going to answer it?"

Brock groans but doesn't bother to hide a grin. "Cute, Mays. Savannah, I don't suppose you know where that thing is?"

"I do!" Maysie skips across the room, Hope bounding after her, the puppy's little black tail wagging a mile a minute.

Brock has only eaten half of the ham and cheese baguette I made for lunch. I pick up the plate from the side table next to him. "You want anything else?" His color is okay, but his mood could use an upgrade.

"My rifle." He pulls up the plaid blanket that's covering his legs and grumbles out a yawn. His face is lined with exhaustion and worry, and dark circles shadow his eyes. I don't think he slept well last night. I don't think he's slept well in weeks.

Neither have I.

Clarice gets to her feet, hovers over him, checks his forehead, and ignores his protests. Maysie skips back with my phone, which is still squawking.

"I'll go make some tea, shall I?" Clarice places a hand on Maysie's shoulder. "Come along, dear. I suspect that puppy will need to go out for a piddle."

"A piddle!" Maysie is overtaken by another fit of giggles as they head in the direction of the kitchen. I take the call, surprised it hasn't gone to voice mail.

"Mrs. Barrington? Hi, this is Louise Eldridge . . . How are you?"

Adam's principal. I'm instantly on alert.

"I'm well, thank you. Is everything all right?" Please let everything be all right. I suppose it's a mother's prerogative to jump to dramatic conclusions almost at once.

"Well, I'm not sure. Mrs. Barrington, I wanted to schedule a meeting with you and your husband.

To talk about Adam. I realize your separation has been hard on him, understandably, but his grades have slipped terribly the past few months. As you saw by his report card, I'm sure you're aware that he's failing most of his classes."

His report card. I never saw Adam's report card over the holidays. Didn't even ask to see it. Guilt pounds me and I close my eyes for a moment. "Did you mail a copy to me?" I informed the school I'd be here in the Berkshires, but I don't recall giving them this mailing address.

"No, I'm afraid not. We emailed the online link to your husband's address and sent one copy to your home address. I assumed Mr. Barrington would discuss it with you. In any event, I think we should meet as soon as possible to talk and see how best to approach things, don't you?"

"Of course." My heart plummets. What else can possibly go wrong?

"Good. Now, that said, I wondered how Adam is feeling. I know he was with his father this weekend, but when Mr. Barrington called this morning to say Adam was sick and wouldn't be coming back to school today, I was a little concerned. He didn't sound himself either. Are they both ill?"

I lean back in my chair and stare at Brock. He's listening, concern etching a line between his eyes. My throat dries up. "What . . . When?" I can't even get words out. "Did Kevin pick Adam up? I'm sorry to say this is the first I've heard of it, Ms. Eldridge. I thought Adam was at school this weekend."

"Oh dear. No, he didn't pick Adam up. Mr. Barrington emailed us the permission slip and asked that we put Adam on the bus to Boston on Saturday morning. I just assumed . . . Mrs. Barrington, is there a problem?"

Um, yeah. There is a problem, all right. I have absolutely no idea where my son is.

"I'm sure everything is fine. I'll call you back, Ms. Eldridge." I end the call and stand, not sure my legs will hold me. "Adam's not at school." Brock struggles out of his chair. I'm already punching in Kevin's number. It goes straight to voice mail. So does the landline at his apartment in Boston. I try Adam's cell, but that goes to voice mail too. "I don't believe this."

"Where is he?" Brock doesn't bother telling me to calm down.

"She said Kevin emailed and apparently Adam's with him, but this doesn't feel right."

"Would Kevin make those arrangements without talking to you?" He's skeptical, and I'm inclined to follow that train of thought. Kevin wouldn't do that. He might not have been happy with me over Christmas, maybe he was expecting me to fall at his feet and just take him back, I don't know, but when it comes to the kids, he doesn't play games.

"No. He wouldn't." I press the button for his

cell again. "Kevin, it's me. Is Adam with you? Call me back right away. As soon as you get this." I put a hand to my mouth and shake my head. My stomach churns. "Something's wrong. I can feel it."

"Okay. Savannah, stop it." Brock runs his hands down my arms and forces me to look at him. "You don't know that. This could all be a mis-understanding. Don't go climbing a tree unless you know for sure you're being chased by a bear, darlin'."

I sigh and manage to nod. And grin. "That makes no sense. Bears can climb trees."

Brock grins back. "Lion, then."

I shake my head. "Could probably jump into the tree and eat me alive."

He laughs a little. "Rhino. That sucker ain't climbing anything."

"He'll push the tree over with his horn thing-amajig."

"I'm not going to win this one, am I?"

"Nope." He's distracted me, though, which was probably his intention. I glance at the clock on the mantel. "Maybe Kevin left a message I didn't get or something. You know I'm useless with this thing."

"Got that right." He gives me a hug and heads back to his chair.

I check all my messages and email and find nothing. I want to call Zoe but I know she's in class.

She's got that test she's been worrying about. Clarice and Maysie return with tea, but I'm too restless to drink mine. Another hour passes and I figure Zoe has to be done by now.

"Mom. Hey." She doesn't sound happy. At all.

"Zo? How did the test go?" We haven't talked all weekend because I wanted to let her study. My throat is tight. I concentrate on Maysie playing with Hope and try to smile.

"It went. I don't know. We'll see. What's up?"

"Zoe, have you talked to Adam lately?"

"Yeah. He called me just before I was going into my class. He sounded kind of weird."

"Oh no." I sink onto the couch and lean over my knees. "Did he say where he was? Zoe, is he with Dad?"

"With Dad? No. I thought he was at school." Her voice rises a notch. "Actually, he asked me if I knew where Dad was. He said—"

"He said what, Zo? Whatever it is, just tell me."

She's panicked now. I inhale and lean into Brock when he comes to sit beside me. "He said he called Dad's cell on Saturday and some woman answered. But I couldn't talk to him to find out more. I had to get to class for the test. I was just about to call him back. Mom, what's going on?"

"I'm not sure. Adam isn't at school. The principal just called. Apparently he was supposed to be spending the weekend with your father, which

288

I knew nothing about. And neither of them are answering their phones." My phone beeps and a shot of relief fires through me. "I have a call coming in. It's probably Dad. I'll call you back." I hang up with Zoe and answer the incoming call, fully expecting to hear Kevin's voice.

"Savannah?" But it's not Kevin.

It's Beth.

Crying.

And I know.

Chapter 23

"Courage is not simply one of the virtues, but the form of every virtue at the testing point."
—C. S. LEWIS

I can't think.

Can't form one coherent thought to tell my body what to do.

"You're not driving and that's the end of it." Brock already has his jacket on. Clarice has gathered our dishes, washed and put them away, organized Hope's things, and is ready to take the puppy and Maysie to her house. I'm upstairs randomly throwing things into a small suitcase.

All I know is I have to get to Boston. *Now.*

"What do you suggest I do, Brock? Sprout wings and fly?" Albany is closest and still an hour away, and I don't want to risk waiting around the airport. I yank the zipper around the overnight case and glare at him.

"Yeah. Fly. I can make a call and have a plane ready by the time we get to the airstrip. It's only twenty minutes from here."

"You can?" I rush through the room, check the bathroom, and grab a toothbrush. "You have a plane?"

"Well, no. But a buddy of mine does. Takes

tourists around. Flies businessmen back and forth from New York, Boston. It's just a prop plane but it'll get us there."

Unless we die first. "Fine . . . just . . ." I brush my hair into a messy bun, stare into the mirror, and lose focus. All I see is bright sparks. "Jesus, help me." I brace myself, palms down.

"Savannah." Brock has his arms around me before I can contemplate passing out. "Take a breath, darlin'. Okay?"

I let myself lean against him for a minute, nod, and turn to face him. "Are you sure about this? I can drive. I'll get there just fine."

"No." He places two fingers against my lips and nails me with that look I don't dare challenge. "We're doing this my way and I'm going with you and that's that."

"Brock. You can't. What about Maysie? And you're . . . you're—"

"Dying?" He lifts a brow. "Clarice can handle Maysie. And I am fine. You, on the other hand, don't look so hot. No offense." He tips my chin and gifts me with a smile that somehow calms my racing pulse. "And if we go down in a fiery crash, then all my problems will be over."

"If you're trying to convince me this is a good idea, you should try another approach." I manage a shaky laugh, but now I'm petrified. But I don't have the time to dwell on it. I have to get to Adam. "All right. We'll fly." I won't protest. I need to get out of here fast. And I need Brock. Because my husband is nowhere to be found.

❧❦

When we get to the airstrip I'm still making calls. Zoe is on her way to Boston. My parents are already in town, halfway to the hospital, stuck in traffic. Mom is on the phone. We're still trying to find Kevin.

"Where do you think he is?" Mom is trying not to cry because we both know if she starts, I'll lose it. "Honey, do you think . . . Do you want me to get your father to call . . . her?"

Alison.

I've been thinking it since I got off the phone with Zoe the first time.

We're all thinking it.

"If Dad can get her number, yeah." I wipe my eyes and feel Brock's hand squeeze mine. "I think he'd better. Kevin needs to get to Boston as soon as possible."

Mom calls back just as I'm about to board the plane. Dad has tracked down the tramp. "She claims she hasn't heard from Kevin since before Christmas." My mother sniffs. "I suppose that's the good news."

My breath comes out in a slow sigh of strange relief. "But the bad news is we still don't know where he is."

Brock sleeps on the flight and I scroll through

my messages, hoping to see something I missed from Kevin. The flight is short and relatively turbulent-free. I turn my phone back on as soon as we land. It buzzes immediately, and I somehow set it off silent mode and Martin starts to squawk.

I shoot a furtive glance in Brock's direction.

"Oh, shoot. I'm so sorry. Should I . . ."

Brock rolls his eyes. "Answer it or I will."

Considering it's Kevin calling, that's probably not a good idea.

⁂

It's after 11:00 p.m. by the time Kevin arrives at the hospital. He's been in Maryland all weekend, apparently. His father took a fall and broke his hip. Or so he says. I can easily confirm it, but right now I honestly don't care.

He strides down the hall, a duffel bag slung over his shoulder, black coat flying, hair mussed, and eyes screaming with worry.

This look I know.

I've seen it too many times. Times I can't bear to think about.

Times I've been dragged back to and forced to face since I first set foot in this hospital four hours ago.

"Kev! Kevin, over here." I rush to reach him and he stops midstride, frantically searching my face for answers I don't have.

All day I've held it together. I talked Zoe down

from her ledge of worst-case scenarios twice, maybe three times. Told my parents it would be okay more times than I can count. I even managed to hug Maysie before we left, when she held on tight and started to cry. I kissed her sweet face and said we'd be back soon and everything would be fine. I've talked to Adam's school. Talked to the attending physician. Talked to Beth and John and Paul, but I let my mother handle Peg. I'm even a little proud of myself for making it this far without morphing into a raving lunatic.

But right then, when Kevin's haunted gaze lands on me, I'm done.

"Savannah." He wraps me in his arms and breathes into my hair. And I hug him back and hang on with everything I've got left.

Then I take his hand and we walk toward Adam's room.

Past my parents, huddled together, concern aging their tanned faces. Past Zoe, looking desperate to shoot out of her chair and hug her daddy but still too angry with him to do it. Past Brock, who just sits there, stalwart, yet a silent presence I am grateful for.

I doubt Kevin even sees him.

Inside the darkened room, a nurse fiddles with the IV tube attached to my son's arm.

My son.

My handsome, talented, athletic son . . . who tried to take his own life today.

Kevin drops his bag, shrugs out of his wool coat, lets it slide to the floor, and steps over it. I pick it up from habit, fold it over a chair, and almost hold my breath as he stands over the bed and stares at our son in utter disbelief.

"Hey, kiddo. Dad's here." He reaches out to brush thick dark hair off Adam's forehead.

All I can do is stand at the end of the bed, trembling. Kevin rubs his jaw and takes a few quick, short breaths. He sniffs, turns, and looks at me. And I see it then. See it in his eyes. What he can't, won't say, because it would be his undoing.

He is completely, utterly terrified.

I clasp my hands, bring them up to my mouth, and pull air into my lungs. Let out a slow breath and hold on to the footboard of the bed for support. The nurse leaves us, quietly closing the door behind her.

"What has the doctor said?" Kevin rasps out.

Silence wages war with unspoken accusations and questions I cannot do battle with right now. "They pumped his stomach as soon as he got here. They've sedated him. He'll be groggy when he wakes up, but they wanted him to sleep tonight." I'm repeating what I've told everyone already. "Beth saw the lights on all weekend but figured it was probably you. They had a family function so she didn't go over until today. And she . . ."

I can't continue. Can't think about that scene. Beth found him. On the floor in his bedroom, music blaring. Pills everywhere. Pills from a bottle he could have bought over the counter or found in our medicine cabinet.

They don't know how many he took, but the doctor said it was a good thing Beth found him when she did. I figure it's better not to share that with Kevin.

"They're not sure how long he was unconscious. If there's brain damage."

"What?" His eyes widen. Tears slip down his ashen cheeks.

"They'll know more when . . . if . . . he wakes up."

"*When* he wakes up." He leans over the bed and looks into Adam's face. I don't know what Kevin is thinking, but I've got a pretty good idea what he's feeling. "He's breathing on his own, right? That's good, right?"

"Yes. And he came around in the ambulance. They said he was still pretty out of it. But yes, the doctor seems to think we can hope for the best."

He shifts, turns his head, and stares at me through wet eyes. "I can't do this again, Savannah."

God, help me.

Neither can I.

I can't respond so I manage a shrug. "I'll be out in the hall. My parents don't need to be here. I'll send them home. And Zoe." I sniff, not sure if he's listening. "There's nothing we can do right now except wait." And pray.

It's like he doesn't even hear me.

Outside, everyone wants news. I have none. "He's the same. Sleeping. The nurse said his vitals are good." Mom and Dad hug Zoe, and my father tips his head toward Adam's room.

"He okay?" He means Kevin. I'm surprised. I shouldn't be. My father is gracious.

"I don't know." I blow my nose and glance at Brock. "I think he's just . . . in shock, maybe?" Shock. It's the only word I can think of to describe the atmosphere of this day. The burst of heat that sliced through my soul with Beth's phone call has boiled down to simmering coals, creating a fog I cannot see through.

Brock stands and walks the few steps needed to join us. "You should eat. Let me go grab some food."

"No, I couldn't." The thought makes me nause-ated.

"He's right, honey. You need food." My mother rubs my back, trying to comfort. "At least some soup or a sandwich. And water. You need to hydrate."

"Don't tell me what I need!" Anger strikes without warning. "I need my son to wake up! I need this to not . . . to not be happening! I need . . . Mama . . . I can't do this!" I collapse into her arms with a wail that comes from some untapped place of grief inside and terrifies me.

"I know, sug. It'll be okay. Sweet Jesus, let it be

okay." She hugs me hard and I stay in the safety of her embrace until I hear the door of Adam's room open and close.

Kevin comes toward us, his eyes still wide and filled with disbelief. He's on the verge of breaking, too, and his shaky sigh betrays him. That's enough for Zoe.

"Daddy . . ." She launches herself at him and he folds her into his chest.

"Hey, baby." Kevin steadies himself, stands back, and cups her face. "He's going to be all right, Zo. Stay positive, okay? We need to stay strong."

She wipes her tears, nods, and hugs him again.

Brock clears his throat and sways on his feet a little. I place a hand on his arm and notice a few beads of sweat on his brow. He's not looking good.

Kevin lets Zoe go, shoves his fingers through his hair, and pins us with a scathing look that burns through me. "What is he doing here?"

"I . . ." Have no idea how to answer that.

Brock lifts a hand and shakes his head. "I'm here because Savannah needed someone. I didn't want her driving or coming alone. And you were nowhere to be found."

"Now you wait just a minute . . ." Kevin steps closer, eyes flashing dangerously.

"Calm down, son." My father puts a hand on Kevin's shoulder while Mom pulls Zoe away.

My stomach lurches and I shoot up a prayer for

intervention. If God doesn't send a sudden power outage or something, this is going to get ugly.

"Stop it, both of you." The words come out in a hiss and I glare at Kevin, then Brock. He's in no shape for this. He knows it as well as I do, but I can tell he's not about to back down. "This is a hospital! Adam is lying in that room, so don't you dare even think about starting anything, either of you."

"Wouldn't dream of it, darlin'," Brock drawls, folding his arms across his chest. He narrows his eyes and takes two steps closer to Kevin. "Do you have any idea how frantic Savannah was today, not knowing where you were? You can get ticked all you like, but you ever put her through that again and I will plow my fist into your face before you see it coming. Got it?"

"You son of a—" Kevin lifts his arm and pulls back.

"Don't!" I leap toward him and yank it back down with a sharp cry. "Stop it! Kevin, you can't hit him!"

"Give me one good reason why."

Brock sighs and steps away. "Because I have a tumor pressing on my brain. If you hit me, I'm likely to lose consciousness. I might even go into cardiac arrest. And quite frankly, I'd just as soon leave y'all the heck alone and go home. If that suits."

Kevin stands there gaping while Brock walks

away, picks up his jacket, and saunters toward the elevators. I run to catch him, the heels of my boots clicking against linoleum.

"Brock, wait."

"Leave it, Savannah." He pulls on his coat and gives a grim backward glance at my family. "I'm gonna head back to the airport. I want to be home when Maysie wakes up in the morning."

"Okay." There isn't any use in trying to change his mind. And I don't want to be worrying about the two of them lighting into each other every second. "Was that true, what you said, what would happen if he hit you?"

A grin slides across his face. "I have no idea, but it sounded good, huh?"

"Oh my gosh. You're terrible." My eyes fill again and I half laugh, half sob as he leans in and plants a kiss on my forehead.

"I acted like a jerk." His eyes cloud over. "His son is . . ."

"Brock." I shake my head. "Forget it. We're all stressed."

"Tell him I'm sorry anyway." His concerned expression makes me want to cry all the more.

"Okay. Thanks."

"Call us with an update. Anytime. I should be back home around three, if there are no delays."

"Go straight to bed. Don't write."

He rolls his eyes and zips up his leather jacket. "What are you, my mother?"

We share a smile and I'm all choked up. "Thank you. For getting me here. For . . ."

Brock nods, stares down at his beat-up cowboy boots, then lifts his head. "I'd do anything for you, lady. Just so you know."

All I can do is nod. I do know.

And right now, it's more than I can bear.

Chapter 24

"Hope begins in the dark, the stubborn
hope that if you just show up and try to
do the right thing, the dawn will come."
—ANNE LAMOTT

Nobody knows what to do next.

Kevin and I refuse to leave Adam's room. We know too well what might happen if we did. I doze on and off while Kevin paces. Eventually he slumps into a chair and puts his head in his hands. And just sits.

I think he's probably crying. I draw my knees to my chest, sink my teeth into my bottom lip, and watch his shoulders shaking. I've always envied his ability to hold in his emotions. To cry so quietly no one knows he's doing it. How many times over the years has this happened? How many times has he released such torment, anguish, pain, and sorrow, and I've never known?

God, help him.

Help us both.

I don't have energy for more than the brief prayers I keep repeating. Inside, my spirit is groaning. God knows, surely, what we need in this moment. Yet it is a challenge to trust and stand on faith. Tears trail a slow path down my cheeks as I sit in silence and wonder what the next few hours might bring. Wonder what to say to my son when he wakes. How to get him through this. How to get us all through it. And all I see when I close my eyes is Shelby's small casket being lowered into the ground.

I'm not doing this again, God.

Old anger surfaces. We prayed for Shelby. Prayed harder than we ever had in our lives. And still . . .

"Ma . . ." A low groan comes from the bed and I'm out of my chair at once.

"Adam! Oh, baby." I can barely speak through tears and relief, but I know I can't give freedom to the sobs that scream to be let out. His eyes are bleary and filled with fear, and I don't want to frighten him further. "It's okay, sweetie." I brush back his hair, feel his cool forehead, and lean in to kiss it. "You're okay."

"Am I in the hospital?"

"Yes. But we're here. Everyone's here."

Kevin huddles close, slips an arm around my waist, and rests a hand on Adam's head. "Hey, sport." He blinks back tears and smiles.

"Dad." Adam's eyes fill and his bottom lip begins to quiver. "I'm sorry." Once he starts crying,he can't stop. Huge, heartbreaking sobs rip from him, rip through me, and pummel me with guilt. Why didn't I know? Why didn't I do something?

What kind of mother doesn't know her son is on the verge of suicide?

What kind of mother . . .

Kevin maneuvers the side arm of the hospital bed down, sits, and scoops Adam into his embrace. Adam holds tight and cries harder.

It's the final push that sends my emotions hurtling over the cliff into deep waters.

I spin away and stumble toward the chair Kevin vacated moments ago. Hold on to the arms and hang on with all the strength I have left. I let one sob out in a quick breath, then gulp the next back down. It's hard to steady my breathing, to control the overwhelming need to give in to the tension I've bottled up since Beth's phone call, but I have to. I have to be strong.

Take a breath, darlin'.

I imagine Brock's voice. Imagine his arms around me in that moment as I fight for calm.

Okay.

I can do this.

※※

The doctor checks on Adam and lets Zoe come in, and the three of us huddle around the bed. He's looking better and we're told he's no longer in danger. He drifts in and out, but eventually opens his eyes again and asks Zoe to sing.

When they were little, every time Adam was scared, Zoe would go to his room, snuggle in bed with him, and sing. Usually songs from the latest Disney movie they'd seen. Sometimes she'd just make up her own.

Today, for some reason, she picks a hymn. "Amazing Grace."

And it is perfect.

My throat hurts and my eyes burn by the time she's done. Adam finally falls asleep and Kevin makes the hesitant suggestion that he drive us home.

Snow has turned to drizzle. Light drops dance in the glow of the headlights as we drive through darkened streets, the car splashing slowly through puddles. We are battle-weary warriors returning from the bloodstained field.

Kevin stares straight ahead, hands clenched around the wheel. He's got the radio tuned to light jazz and keeps it low. Zoe huddles in the back-seat, and I gaze out the window at the dark neighborhoods I know so well. Past the park where I pushed my kids on swings and watched them play. Houses where my friends sleep. Past the elementary school, yellow buses lined up in the parking lot. Past the church we attended as a family.

Before we stopped being one.

The car slides effortlessly into the driveway I haven't seen in so long. We enter through the front door because the garage is too full of junk we haven't decided what to do with. Inside, I inhale the familiar: wood polish and pine scents. Somebody has cleaned.

Kevin carries in my bag and his duffel, turns on the lights, and I look around. Nothing seems out of place, everything neat and tidy, just as I left it. My home. The place I loved so much for so long, and then couldn't wait to get away from. I'm not so sure I want to be here now, now that I know what has happened. Now that I know the disturbing depths of my son's emotions. Emotions he hid so well from us all.

"I'm going to my room." Zoe hangs up her coat, swings her backpack over her shoulder, wipes her eyes, and hugs us both. I hug her tighter than I normally would.

"Try to sleep, sweetheart." Kevin's voice is hoarse as he folds her against him. She starts crying again, which sets me off. Him too.

"Wake me if . . ."

Kevin shakes his head and somehow smiles. "None of that. He's going to be fine. You heard the doctor." Zoe's wide eyes lose their fear almost at once. "We'll wake you when we hear something. They said to check in around nine. You need to rest. We all do."

"I know." She sniffs and smiles. "Are you going to stay here?" she asks him, then throws me a cautious glance.

He clears his throat and looks my way.

"Of course he is." It seems the logical response,

but the minute I say it, I have second thoughts. "I mean, if you want. You don't have to."

Kevin almost rolls his eyes, then takes off his coat. I shrug out of mine and reach for his. Zoe trudges upstairs, her door closing softly.

And I lose what little control I had left.

My knees buckle, but Kevin has his arms around me before I hit the ground.

"Okay, take it easy. You're okay." He picks me up and releases his breath against the side of my face as he carries me through the living room. Gently he places me on the couch, wipes my tears, and stares at me through sad eyes. "Savannah." Then he finally says what he's thinking. "Do you want me to call Dr. Clarke?"

"For me or Adam?" It's a loaded question, I suppose, but for some reason it makes him smile.

"I think Adam's in good hands right now. It's you I'm worried about."

"I'm fine." I'm not. Not yet. But I will be. And I have to believe that for my son as well. A million scary thoughts race through my head, pushing and pulling and trying to find their way out, but none of them make the slightest bit of sense. "I thought . . . he . . . might . . ." I can't say it.

"I know." Kevin gives a shuddering sigh, his eyes glimmering. "But he's okay, thank God. We didn't lose him, Savannah. We'll get him through this."

"How?"

He moves down the couch away from me. Turns on the lamp on the side table and leans back into the deep cushions. "I don't know."

I don't even remember what the doctor said now. It's all a jumble of words and feelings and total helplessness. Today, as long as Adam remains stable, they'll move him to a psychiatric ward. He'll be evaluated and treated appropriately. He'll probably have to stay for a week, maybe more. But I just want him to come home.

"They'll call us if—"

"They will. But you saw him, Savannah. Sound asleep. He won't know we're gone."

I take a few deep breaths and lace my fingers together. It's then I realize I'm not wearing my rings. I took them off a few days ago when I was cleaning. Slowly I lift my head and lock eyes with my husband. He's also staring at my hand.

Kevin blows out his breath and looks away. "Do you want tea? I don't know if there's any food, but I can look. And you should try to sleep a bit."

"Tea. Okay. I can make it." I start to move but he turns to face me with a frown.

"I may not have ever cooked a turkey, but I do know how to boil a kettle."

"Kevin . . ."

He shakes his head and leaves the room before I can say another word.

"Wonderful." I lean over my knees and breathe deeply. My thoughts won't settle. No way will I be able to sleep. I wander back through the hall and find my purse, fish out my phone, and check my messages. It's going on five in the morning. I tap out a brief message to Brock, letting him know Adam's okay. As I enter the kitchen my phone buzzes. It's Brock, texting me back. Figures he wouldn't be asleep. He's probably been in front of his computer since the minute he got home.

I look at the message, make sure my cell is set to vibrate, and shove it in the pocket of my jeans. Kevin has set out tea, found an unopened box of melba toast and a jar of strawberry jam.

"I'll have to go to the store." I'm thinking out loud.

"I can go later. Make a list." He sits at the table, scanning his iPhone. Slowly he looks up, staring at me through eyes that hold a hundred questions. "Did you call Alison?" His voice is shaky.

"Alison?" I pull my fingers through my hair and sit. "Why the—" And then I remember. "Yes. We were looking for you." I pull the teapot toward me and pour out two cups with an unsteady hand.

He's still staring, incredulous. "Why would you call her?"

"I didn't. My father did." Bitterness balls in my throat. "You can tell her everything's fine and we won't be bothering her again."

Kevin puts down his phone, mutters a low curse, and runs a hand down his face. "I wasn't with her, Savannah. I haven't talked to her since she left town. She sent me a message to say you were looking for me, that there was some emergency. She wanted to know what was going on, that's all."

"Kevin, I don't care." I sip my tea and settle into this feeling of indifference that seems to have moved into my heart.

He dumps a spoonful of sugar into his tea and stirs. He never takes sugar. I doubt he even realizes he's done it, but I'm not about to point it out.

"I left you three messages on the house phone up there, Savannah. I figured you might not hear your cell, so that way at least you'd know where I was. Then I was stuck at the hospital with my dad, first in emergency, then getting him settled in the ward. I left as soon as I got your message."

"Sorry." I shrug, not sure what to say. Things can't get any worse, really, so I suppose it doesn't matter what my response is at this point. "I never check that answering machine. You should have called my cell or sent me a text. I'm getting better with it." Thanks to Maysie. "How's your father?" My in-laws are older than my parents and their health has not been good the past few years. Since Kevin and I separated, I haven't kept in touch. But neither have they.

"Grumpy. But not in as much pain when I left." His fingers scratch the stubble on his jaw. "I don't think I'll tell them about Adam yet. If I tell them at all."

"I don't know if he'd want anyone to . . ." The reality of the past twenty-four hours slams into me like an out-of-control tractor trailer. "This is an absolute nightmare."

"Yeah." He reaches for a piece of melba toast, snaps it in half, and lets it fall onto the white plate in front of him. My phone buzzes. Probably Brock, but I don't want to answer it.

Kevin holds my gaze for a long moment. "Aren't you going to get that? It could be the hospital."

Could be, but I doubt it. Reluctantly I reach for my cell and scan the screen. "It's not the hospital."

Kevin sits back with a grunt. Musses his hair and swings his gaze across the room. "Answer it."

My chest is too tight for words, but I manage to hold a brief, albeit strained conversation with Brock while my husband sits across the table, watching me. We don't say much and I hang up quickly.

"He was worried." I put the phone down and cradle my mug of tea. I'm so tired it's all I can do to keep my eyes open, but I'm still running on adrenaline. Still not sure I could sleep.

Kevin nods slowly, slides a little lower in his chair, his expression dark. "Is it true? What he said at the hospital. The brain tumor?"

Tears fill my eyes again and I dab my cheeks with a Kleenex. "Yes."

Silence smothers the room like early-morning fog. The sky grows a little lighter. Kevin opened a window earlier, just a crack to let in some fresh air, and dawn songs from the birds I used to feed filter through into the kitchen. I wonder if there's any birdseed left in the cupboard.

"Savannah? Is he going to be okay?"

I look back at Kevin, the worry creasing his forehead, the haunted look in his eyes, and the dark shadows under them that make me wonder when he last slept well. I have no clue what he's thinking, and I'm not so sure I want to.

I shrug and spin my phone in a circle. "He's been told it's terminal. I don't think there's anything more they can do."

Kevin sucks in a breath and scratches his head. "I'm sorry."

I stare at him in surprise. He seems sincere. "Yeah. Me too." I don't want to talk to him about Brock. "He asked me to apologize for what he said to you at the hospital. He wasn't thinking straight."

Kevin massages his jaw. "Neither was I."

My thoughts drift to Adam again as I look at all the photographs pinned on the door of the fridge, held in place by an array of colorful magnets the kids collected from our many family road trips. "Adam told Zoe he called your cell on Saturday. That a woman answered."

"What?" Kevin narrows his eyes. "What woman?"

"I don't know, I thought you might. Apparently

he didn't stay on long enough to find out."

He moves his plate around and shakes his head. "Since I was at my parents' house, I'd say it was either my mother or my sister. Which Adam would have found out if he'd asked who he was talking to." He props his elbows, presses his hands against his forehead, and groans. "So he thought . . ."

"Don't go there. This isn't your fault." I say it quietly, not sure I really mean it. Not sure I'm ready to support him in this. Not yet.

Kevin doesn't speak. Just sits back and settles his gaze on me. "Easy for you to say. You're not the one who has a hundred mistakes to make up for."

"Don't I?"

"Savannah . . ."

"I don't want to do this now." It's all I can say without tears. We sit in silence for a while. Then I have to ask. "Why didn't you tell me Adam was failing his classes? I assume you knew by the time you came up to the Berkshires on Christmas Day."

Kevin closes his eyes and emits another low groan. "I wasn't keeping it from you intentionally. I planned to talk to you. But then things got crazy up there. I thought when I got Adam on his own, when we went skiing, he and I could talk and figure it out."

"Did you?" I pinch the bridge of my nose, my throat dry. "Did you figure it all out, Kevin?

Because clearly, Adam didn't get the memo."

"You *are* putting this on me."

"No. I'm not. I'm just . . ." He's right. I am directing my frustration at him. "That wasn't fair. I'm sorry."

"I wasn't angry with him, Savannah." His eyes flash a little dangerously. "We had a good conversation and he promised to try to do better. He seemed happy enough. I never imagined—"

"No, why would you? Neither did I." It's more than I can contemplate, more than I can take right now. "What have we done?"

"Not we. Me." Kevin pushes up the sleeves of his sweater and gives me a grim look. "Maybe you're right. Maybe this is my fault."

I wave off the comment but can't come up with words. He reaches for his mug and takes a gulp, then screws up his nose in disgust, and unbidden laughter bursts out of my mouth.

Kevin stares. "I put sugar in that."

"You did." My shoulders shake with the effort it takes to control sudden giggles.

"You saw me." He tries to look angry but a grin escapes.

"I did. I'm sorry."

"Sorry not sorry." His smile feels like aloe on blistering sunburned skin and I soak it in. Kevin holds my eyes for a long moment. "If I could go back and change it all, I would." His grin is gone and my laughter fades.

"Really?" I break his gaze and study the pictures on the wall instead.

Why can't I just give the man a break?

When I look back at him, I see he's thinking the same thing. "You'll never forgive me, will you?"

I lean over the table and put my head in my hands. "Let's not do this now, Kevin. We're stressed and exhausted and we probably shouldn't be attempting conversation."

"Right." He glances at his watch, then back at me. His expression is stony, like I've hurt him somehow. "I'll dump my stuff in the guest room and take a shower. You really should rest. I can wake you in a couple of hours."

"Okay. I'll try." I slide my chair back and get to my feet. It's hard to think. Hard to formulate words that make sense. Because nothing about this does.

Suddenly the gong of the grandfather clock in the hall echoes through the house.

Crisp and clear.

The sound reverberates through me and wakes something akin to hope. I meet Kevin's eyes again. "You fixed my clock?"

The antique mahogany clock was a gift from my grandmother a few years after we were first married. She knew how much I'd always loved it. We had a heck of a time getting it up here from Georgia. I had to convince Kevin to put out the money for transportation, but he finally did.

Eventually it stopped keeping time properly and never sounded quite the way I remembered it in my grandmother's home.

"I found a guy to come here to the house." Kevin gives a small smile. "Polished it up real nice too."

I asked him so many times to look into getting it fixed.

"Savannah, if you ask me about that stupid clock one more time . . ."

I suppose I could have found someone to fix it myself, but it was the principle of the thing.

Stupid, insignificant issues I was too stubborn to let go of.

So many of them.

"Thank you." Two quiet words spoken in a moment that somehow holds more meaning than I think either of us knows what to do with. Hesitation hovers over his face, but then Kevin reaches for my hand, holds it tight, and nods.

I doze for maybe an hour and then wake with a start. The room I once shared with my husband seems strangely foreign, the bed a little unfamiliar. Memories hang heavy. Good ones. Bad ones. I wipe sleep from my eyes and widen them as things come into focus.

Kevin is curled in the lounge chair by the window. Watching me. Or he has been. Now his eyes are closed and he's breathing deeply. He's changed into sweats and a T-shirt, his dark hair damp. It's longer than I've ever seen him wear it. A lock curls over his forehead.

It's been so long since we have shared this room that his presence startles me. The realization makes me sad.

After Shelby died, we slept sporadically. I'd wake at all hours, pace the house, clean, read, watch TV. Kevin would get out of bed and sit in that chair. Sometimes he'd stare out the window. Sometimes he'd pick up a book. Sometimes he'd watch me sleep. I asked him once why he did that.

"Because knowing you're there, knowing you're okay, somehow makes me believe we'll get through this."

And suddenly the sight of him sitting there this morning makes me smile.

I slip out of bed, grab a blanket, and tuck it around him.

My hand hovers over that errant lock of hair. I study the face I know so well, have loved so long, and wonder whether forgiveness is truly possible. Wonder whether I'll ever trust him enough to let him take me in his arms again, kiss me, and love me like he used to when things were good. When things were the way they're supposed to be between a husband and wife.

Memories play with my mind and stir old feelings. An inexplicable longing surges through me.

Kevin shifts in the chair and my heart jumps.

His eyes flutter open, land on me for just a moment before they close again, but a smile slides across his mouth. "Thanks, Savannah," he mumbles, pulling the blanket up around his shoulders.

I let out my breath and find myself smiling too. This man.

What he's put me through.

But I know right now in this minute that despite it all, he still owns my heart.

Whether I want him to or not.

And I must choose what to do with that.

※※

I huddle back under the covers and hope for another hour of sleep. When I wake again, Kevin is gone.

After my shower, I check the time and wonder if it's too early to call the hospital. I do it anyway. The nurse is kind. Adam's had a good sleep—is still sleeping, in fact. I ask her to tell him that if he wakes we'll be there later this morning.

In the hallway, everything is silent. Zoe's door is closed and I assume she's still asleep. As I pass Adam's room, I stop. And stare.

"Oh no."

To say Adam had trashed the place would be a massive understatement. Drawers are tipped out. His mattress flipped on its side. Things thrown all over—clothes, books, trophies, a lamp, picture frames—Kevin crouches in the middle of the mess, tossing broken items into a black garbage bag.

"Don't come in. There's glass everywhere." His eyes are bloodshot. I have no idea how long he's been in here, when he started, or what it looked like before. He chucks an empty pill bottle in the bag and swipes a hand across his eyes. I'm wearing slippers so I venture forward, take a deep breath, and wonder when it will be easy to breathe again.

"I want to help." I move across the room and start folding clothes. Putting things back in their place. "We can't bring him back to this."

"You know he might have to stay in the hospital awhile. When you . . ." Kevin clamps his mouth shut and shoves a ripped-up notebook in the bag. "Never mind."

He's remembering the weeks I was hospitalized after I tried to kill myself. I never really thought about what he must have gone through that day and the weeks and months that followed. I was too caught up in myself. Trapped by my own grief and turbulent soul that refused to calm. By the time I got tired of my misery and decided to live again, it was already too late to fix what was long broken.

I push my hair over my shoulders, stare at the floor for a long moment, and measure my words. "Kevin." He snaps his head up and locks eyes with me. "It's okay to talk about it. About what I did. If you want to. I'm not that person anymore. I'm stronger than you think I am."

His blue eyes shimmer and he looks away. "Okay." He braces his hands on his knees and lowers his head. "We can talk about it. But not today."

We move around the room in silence. Picking up, throwing out, trying to fix things that can't be fixed. I make up the bed and my foot hits something sticking out from underneath.

A shoe box.

I pick it up and set it down on the bed and stare at it. Kevin stands behind me and puts a hand on my shoulder. Maybe we're violating Adam's privacy, but I lift the lid.

Pictures of Shelby. A drawing. A pink ribbon. A few cards.

The order of service from her funeral.

"I didn't know he had this," I whisper. It's so similar to Kevin's, the box he retrieved that night so many weeks ago. "Did you?"

Kevin takes the box, closes the lid, and places it back under the bed. "Yeah."

He did. I can imagine him helping a young Adam, selecting the pictures, watching him put things into that box. *"Don't tell Mom, we don't want to upset her."* And I imagine Zoe has one too.

"We did it all wrong, didn't we?" I whisper. "I shut everyone out. I wouldn't talk about her.

About Shelby. Wouldn't let you in . . . the kids . . . Oh, Kev, what have I done?" The truth hits me with the force of a raging waterfall, waking me from a deep sleep. "I did this. *I did this!*"

The room starts to close in and I fold my arms against the pain that threatens to take me down again. Breathe. I have to force myself to breathe. Deep, calming breaths. In and out. But harrowing sobs have the upper hand.

Kevin stands behind me and pulls me backward into his embrace. He doesn't speak, just holds me while I cry. His own tears wet my neck.

Eventually he turns me around to face him. "We've got to stop this. This incessant blame game. My fault, your fault. It's not helping. You did not do this, Savannah. You hear me? We're not going down that road again. We're moving forward."

"This is too hard. Too much." I search Kevin's anxious eyes. "Isn't it?"

He takes my hands in his and pulls me close. Close enough for his lips to brush mine if he wanted. "I don't know . . ." He trails a finger across my forehead and down the side of my face, and his eyes light in a way I haven't seen for a very long time. "Maybe it's just enough."

Chapter 25

"Of the blessings set before you,
make your choice, and be content."
—SAMUEL JOHNSON

Life is never simple. I know this now.

Perhaps it is not meant to be.

"How's Adam?" Beth and I sit in front of the fire in my living room Saturday morning, drinking coffee, catching up, and trying not to cry.

It's February now. Almost three weeks have passed since that awful moment when my world stopped spinning again.

"He's doing better. Seeing his doctor three times a week, and we've been having family sessions. Zoe has no Friday classes this semester, so she drives home on Thursday nights. She's committed to coming."

"Good for her. I've been praying those meetings would go well."

"It's hard." Adam also sees a counselor one-on-one. "We've decided to keep him home from school for now. They'll send work and he can set his own pace." The flames flicker and dance and I reach for another blueberry muffin. I wish I could bake like Beth.

"And how are things with you and Kevin?" She

hesitates, then smiles a little sadly. "It's still weird for me to have to ask that."

"Yeah." I'm not sure how to answer her question, so I shrug.

"You haven't blogged recently," Beth says, cau-tious. "I still check from time to time. It's been weeks."

"I know. It's . . ." I bite my lower lip, meet her eyes, and admit the truth. "I don't think I want to do it anymore."

She sends me a relieved smile. "Good. That's good. Isn't it?"

She sounds too hopeful.

"I guess so. Brock says I'm a good writer, if you can believe that. I do enjoy it, writing. But blogging might not be the way to go. You know?"

"You could write a book."

I give a half laugh. "I've certainly got enough material." I splay my bare fingers across my jeans and catch her curious glance. "My rings are at the house in the Berkshires. I left in a hurry. I'll get them when I go back."

"Are you sure about that?" Beth asks quietly.

"Maybe. I don't know." It's the truth. I don't know now whether, when I took them off, I intended to put them back on again. "I'm trying, Beth. Trying to do the right thing, say the right words, trying to be there for Adam and Zoe. But part of me doesn't want to be here. Part of me just wants to go back."

"To Brock?"

"In a way." He's been on my mind. Constantly. But when I dream, it's always Kevin who shows up. I thread my fingers through my hair and wish this wasn't so hard. "I'm so confused. When I left here I knew what was happening. Kevin had moved out and we were getting a divorce. He didn't want me. I'd accepted it. And after a while I felt like I was starting to heal. Like I was moving on. Being back here feels stifling. I can't think. Can't breathe."

"Kevin's still here at the house?"

I nod. "In the guest room. Said he'd rather be here than at his apartment in the city. He asked if it was okay and I couldn't tell him no. He's driving almost two hours to get to work and back, but he wants to be here for Adam."

"And for you?"

"I don't know." Part of me thinks I do know. I'm just not sure what to do about it or whether I want it to be true. "Kevin said . . . he said he thinks I'll never forgive him. And I think he might be right. Even if I get to the point of for-giving him, truthfully, I don't know if I could start over with him."

"Because you've met someone else?" She's hesitant and I see a hint of disapproval in her eyes, even though she's trying her best to be sup-portive. I don't blame her.

"Beth, no." I reach for her hand and watch

her expression change. I let out a sigh and acknowledge the truth. "Brock's dying. He has an inoperable brain tumor. I have no future with him even if I wanted one."

"Oh goodness." Her tears come quickly and she squeezes my hand tight. "Honey, that's . . ."

"Awful. I know." I sit back against the couch and stare at the photographs on the mantel. "I do have feelings for him, and I know that even despite what Kevin did, it's wrong. I'm still married. But I didn't plan this. To meet him, to feel this way. I had no idea it was coming. And I got sucked in."

"Oh, hon. You've been hurt. You were vulnerable."

Sad laughter catches in my throat. "I've tried to justify it more nights than I care to count. And maybe if I'd never met him, this wouldn't be so complicated. The worst of it is, I really think if things with Brock were different, I might . . ." I can't voice that thought. The reality is too raw, too startling. Too wrong.

"I can't tell you what to do, you know that." Beth smiles, dabs at her eyes with a tissue. "But you have to figure out your feelings, figure out what you want. If you don't want to reconcile with Kevin, he needs to know that sooner rather than later."

"Do you think it's possible? To get past this kind of pain? That kind of betrayal?"

"Anything is possible if it's what you want. If you're willing to work at it." Beth smiles and I know what she's thinking. But she won't spout Scripture. I know the verses anyway.

"I wish somebody would just whack me over the head with some sign, you know?" I smile with a halfhearted shrug. "I'm trying to pray and listen . . . but sometimes I doubt I'll ever get the answers I'm waiting for."

I startle when the grandfather clock in the hall starts to chime, and we burst out laughing.

"Is that you, God?" Beth jokes, but I get the point.

"Remember how long I asked Kevin to get that clock fixed?" I recall the satisfied expression on Kevin's face the first day we were home and I realized it was working.

"He made us come over and check it out the moment the guy left." Beth laughs softly. "Said he wished he'd had it fixed years ago."

"It sounds good. Good as new." Sadness curls around my heart. "Too bad you can't fix a marriage just as easily."

"Sweetie, he's trying. I really believe he is."

"I know." I'm starting to believe it too. I've seen changes in his behavior. Things that tell me he's doing his best to put me and the kids first. It wasn't always that way. But I don't know what comes next. We're at a stalemate. Pieces on a chessboard, hovering, waiting to see who will make the next move.

And I don't like playing games.

Another weekend creeps up on me. I've been back home a month now. I miss the life I created up north. I miss talking with Clarice. Miss the sound of Maysie's giggle. Going into the greenhouse, that strange, fragrant aroma and the feel of my fingers in the dirt as I attempt to coax new life into being, and imagine what miracles might happen in my life if I'd let them. And Brock. No matter how hard I try to put him out of my mind, he's there.

But it's been surprisingly easy to step back into my old life as well.

I've visited the elderly ladies I used to take library books to, given them new books I discovered during my time away. I've met up with friends I haven't connected with in so many months and found them willing to begin again, willing to let me back into their lives. And I want them in mine. I walk each morning, along trails I'd forgotten, grateful for the fresh air and exercise and a chance to escape the static tension in the house.

It's Saturday and Adam is downstairs in the basement family room with some friends, watching football, and Zoe is out. I make coffee, sit in the kitchen, and stare at all the photographs and magnets on the fridge. Kevin always stuck a couple of Alice ones in my stocking each Christmas.

"Would you tell me, please, which way I ought to go from here?"

"That depends a good deal on where you want to go," said the Cat.

"I don't much care where—" said Alice.

"Then it doesn't matter which way you go," said the Cat.

"—so long as I get somewhere," Alice added as an explanation.

"Oh, you're sure to do that," said the Cat, "if you only walk long enough."

Which way, indeed.

I reach for my laptop, open the page to my blog, and pause, run my fingers over the keys. I remember what Kevin said to me in Adam's room, about how we need to stop blaming each other. That it's time to move forward. I don't know much, but I do know that angry venting about my husband, even anonymously, is not the way forward.

Dear friends, I type, *this will be my last post. Today, after much thought and deliberation, I've decided to shut down the blog.*

And so I begin.

When I'm done I pour another cup of coffee for myself, hesitate, and then reach for a clean mug. Kevin's been bringing work home on the weekends. He's been holed up in the study for most of the day.

I wander through the quiet house, mugs in hand.

The door to the study is open and Kevin sits at the desk, his dark head bent over paperwork. We've been sidestepping each other for days. Not sure what to say or how to react to being in the same house again. The kids watch us with wary eyes, waiting for some hint of which way the wind will blow.

He looks up and sees me standing there. "Hi."

"Sorry. I didn't mean to disturb you. I made coffee and thought you might want a cup." I approach the desk and place the steaming mug on a coaster. "No sugar."

He puts down his pen, stretches his arms above his head, and flashes a smile. "Thanks."

"No problem." I survey the study, Kevin's domain. The dark-green walls and built-in bookshelves filled to overflowing, the old basketball that still sits pride of place on a shelf, signed by all the members of the varsity team he captained. They won the championships that year. Framed photos of the players surround the ball. I wonder what some of those guys are doing now. Whether they are husbands, fathers; happy with their lives; or if they too have marriages that have somehow fallen apart despite their best intentions.

Photos of Zoe and Adam sit on his desk, ones he didn't take when he left. I thought he would have gotten rid of the pictures of me. But they're still here. Our wedding day, me with each of our children the day they were born. Vacation shots taken the year we took the kids to London. The trip was my parents' idea. Mom was into family vacations for a few years. I focus on one picture in particular—Kevin and me on a riverboat cruise along the Thames. Mom and Dad had ferried the kids off to the zoo that day, and I'm relaxed, leaning back into Kevin's arms, looking up at him with such innocence, joy, and adoration. Little did I know in a few short years our world would implode.

For some reason, seeing Kevin here, back in the room he spent so much time in throughout our marriage, puts an unwanted lump in my throat. Because I always told myself he worked too hard, that he was obsessed with his job, never made time for the family, which wasn't really true, but I never saw it from his perspective. Never understood that he was only doing what he felt he had to. That he only wanted to give us a good life. To allow me to stay home and raise our children like I wanted. To give the kids extracurricular activities like soccer and tennis and ice hockey. Summer camps, piano, and riding lessons. Maybe to some extent, for him that came with a cost, but I'm not sure I ever thanked him for the sacrifice.

I'm overwhelmed with emotion and I head for the door, not wanting him to see my tears.

"Savannah?"

"Yeah." I don't turn around.

330

"Want to sit?" I hear him push his chair back.

"Okay." I exhale and find a space on the old leather couch by the fireplace.

Kevin puts his mug on the long table in front of me, throws a couple more logs on the fire, brushes his hands on his jeans, and flops down at the other end of the couch. "Nice that Adam's buddies came over, huh?"

"Yes." I swallow hot liquid and try to smile. "He's had a good week, I think."

"I think so too. He's more talkative at least. Don't you think?"

"He is. How do you feel about him going back to school?" Adam broached the idea last night. Said he was getting too bored and wanted to be somewhere that would take his mind off things. Wanted to get back to normal.

"I think if the school agrees, it's probably a good idea." Kevin runs a finger over the face of his watch. "We can schedule a call with Ms. Eldridge. He'd be able to continue counseling there too."

"Okay. Let's talk to her." I take a breath and just put it out there. "What about us? Our family sessions? Have you had enough already?"

He rolls his eyes. Neither one of us was a fan of pouring our heart out to a complete stranger. The doctor we've been seeing is nice enough, but . . .

"I'd rather talk with John," Kevin says. "I have been. But he . . . he's offered to see you as well.

The two of us together, I mean. If you . . ." His voice trails off and he looks away.

"Oh." I wasn't expecting that. My pulse picks up as I struggle for the right words. But I have no idea what they are. Or what I want. All the times I've asked him, begged him to come back to counseling with me, and he adamantly refused. Of course now I know why. Even then, in the years following Shelby's death, when it got too hard, I suspect he had thoughts of leaving. "Is that what you'd like to do? You want us to go back to counseling?"

Kevin meets my eyes and nods. "Yes. I do." Then he shrugs. "But it's totally up to you. If you're not ready, I won't push it."

"Can I think about it?"

"Of course." He rubs the scruff on his chin and pulls his fingers through his hair. "Meant to get a haircut today. Guess time got away from me." He gives a sheepish smile that somehow makes my stomach flip.

"It's not horrible," I offer. "Gives you that sexy, movie star kind of look." Um, what did I just say?

"Yeah?" He doesn't hide his surprise, grins a little too widely, and lifts a dark eyebrow, which does another number on my insides. Whoa. I can't remember the last time I felt this attracted to my husband.

The moment feels so awkward it's stupid. "Well.

I was wondering if Zoe said anything to you about Tim?" Changing the subject. Safety first.

"Tim? No."

I curl my legs under me. "I think they might have broken up. It's weird that he hasn't been around, especially when Adam was in the hospital. And she hasn't talked about him. With everything going on, I haven't wanted to ask."

Kevin drinks his coffee and studies the flames. "That would be a shame. I like Tim."

"Me too." I pick at a few dog hairs on my red sweater. Poor Hope. By the time she finally comes home with me, she'll be so confused. "I'll bring it up when I feel the time is right. So . . ." I glance his way again. It's hard to think of things to say. Hard to imagine we used to talk so easily. "Thanks for . . . coming back. I mean, for being here. For Adam. I think it means a lot to him."

He shoots me a sidelong glance. "I should probably be thanking you. For letting me stay."

How did we get to this? Stilted conversation, worrying about what to say next.

A shaky sigh leaves my lips. "How do you like your new job? Looks like you're working hard as usual."

"It's a job. It pays the bills." He leans back against the couch and studies me through serious eyes the color of a stormy sky. "Truthfully? I hate it. I really hate what I do."

"You do?" Confusion sneaks up on me. "Really?

Even when you were working for my dad?"

"Yes, even then. I only went into it because your father said there would be great opportunities. And there were. I'm not ungrateful or anything, it's just not really what I want anymore." He shrugs and his lips curl in a sad smile. "I'm looking down the road at fifty and suddenly I don't know what I've done with my life."

"Well." Surprise shakes me as I ponder my response. Because I feel exactly the same way. And that scares me. "I think that too. I mean, we've got two amazing kids, but they're pretty much out of the house. Adam will be off to college in a few years. They'll get married eventually and have families of their own. And I . . ." The truth is too daunting but I can't look away. "I don't know where I'll be."

"Where do you want to be?" He asks the question quietly, like he's almost afraid to hear the answer.

"Right now, I'm not sure." We used to talk of traveling. We said as soon as Kevin hit retirement, we'd start on our bucket list. We dreamed about exploring Italy, Greece, maybe Australia. I probably still have that list somewhere. But now? I don't know what my future holds. So I'm being honest, and I think that's okay. "Things aren't exactly going according to plan, are they?"

"I guess not." He nods slow and thoughtful. "You know what I'd really like to do?" His grin comes back, boyish and full of mischief. I shrug and smile, sad in a way, because I have absolutely no idea.

"Tell me."

He sits forward, new light shining in his eyes. "I'd like to run a bookstore." A chuckle rumbles from his chest.

"A bookstore?"

"You know, one of those delightfully old buildings with shelves and shelves of books to browse through. And a reading area with comfy couches and a coffee counter."

It's so easy to catch the vision that I'm right there with him. "I can see that. And you could feature local authors too, have readings, poetry nights. Remember that place we used to go when we started dating, what was it called . . ."

"Bill's Books." He tips his head, smiling. "Wonder if old Bill is still around."

I grin at the memories. "You know that old bookshop in the Berkshires is for sale."

"No kidding?" His smile slips and he sits back with a sigh, rests his foot over his knee. "Ah, well. I guess we all have our dreams."

"I never knew you were unhappy, Kev." It's not until the words are spoken that I realize the deeper meaning to them. But it's true. I didn't. And I should have.

He doesn't speak for a few moments. The pain of the past mars his face and he's having trouble keeping his emotions in check. "You know . . . after Shelby died, I thought you coped so well. You seemed to carry on, with Adam and Zo, church, our friends. You gave our life this air of normalcy, and, well, I envied you that. Then after a while I hated you for it. Because you were moving through the days like things were actually going to be okay. And I was dying a little inside each day."

"So was I." I lower my head and watch tears splash onto my hands. Kevin reaches over and grasps one of them. Our fingers lace together from habit.

"I know that now. But I didn't know it then. And I'm sorry for that, Savannah. I'm sorry I didn't see through your brave front. I'm sorry I didn't sit you down and ask how you were really doing. You might think you shut me out, but I did the same to you. I didn't want you to know how I really felt. And until that day I came home and found you . . . I had no idea how much pain you were in."

"I didn't want you to know," I manage to whisper. "How could I burden you with that on top of everything? And it wasn't your fault. It wasn't anything you did or didn't do, Kevin. I just got to the point where I couldn't cope. Couldn't see another way."

"I get that now. Still. I wish . . ." He sighs and swallows the words. "I miss her too. Shelby." His voice trembles and he blinks back tears. "Some days it still hurts so bad I don't know what to do with it." His voice catches and he clears his throat. "John says it's to be expected, even after so long. That it won't ever fully go away. But we will heal. If we work at it. I think that's what I didn't understand, you know? I thought not talking would be better. That one day we'd wake up and everything would somehow magically be okay."

My chest shudders as I process his words. I have yet to figure out how to be strong about this. Slowly I push off the couch and move to stand in front of the fire. "Is that why you found Alison so appealing? Because she didn't remind you of the past? Didn't remind you of Shelby? Or was it just about the sex?" I swivel to face him and catch the shock and shame in his eyes.

Kevin puts both feet on the ground and leans over his knees, breathing deeply. Then he looks up and meets my gaze. "I was somebody else when I was with her. Yes, I used her to escape what was going on here at home. What was going on with us. And maybe in a way I was punishing myself."

I snort. I probably shouldn't have, but it's so ludicrous, really. "Having sex with a beautiful younger woman, yeah, that's punishment all right."

"You don't know, Savannah," he says hoarsely. "You don't know what it was like, coming home to you. Having to look at you, knowing what

I'd done. Knowing how deeply I'd hurt you. Betrayed you. How far I'd fled from everything I ever believed in . . . the guilt I felt. When you found out what was going on, I was actually relieved. But it didn't help. I thought leaving was the right thing, for me, for you. Part of me even thought it would be easy. I convinced myself I could start over. But walking away was the hardest thing I ever did. The stupidest. And for me, it only made things worse."

In a way, I do understand. Because when I look at Brock sometimes, even knowing he could be gone in a month, a year, I do think about leaving Kevin, leaving this life we've built, as imperfect and dysfunctional as it is, signing on the dotted line and just being done with it. But the thought, the reality of that final decision, twists my stomach, makes it so I have to catch my breath, and I can't believe I'm actually considering it.

"Did you love her?" I thread my fingers through my hair and recoil at the anguish in my voice. It's the last thing I ever intended to ask him, ever wanted to know. But now I need to hear the answer.

"No." One word. Final. Authoritative.

And somehow strangely freeing.

Kevin sniffs, pushes to his feet, and positions himself a foot away from me. His eyes pin me in an intense gaze that I cannot escape. "No." He shakes his head and folds his arms. "She told me

I'd never once said those words to her, and then she said I never would, because the only woman I could ever love was you. And she was right. You will always be the only one for me, Savannah."

Oh, how many times I longed to hear those words. But now they fall flat and I struggle to accept the sincerity in them. "I wish that was enough," I say, my voice hoarse. "You walked away, Kevin. You broke our vows. You gave yourself to someone else. Tell me how I'm supposed to live with that. How do I live with you again, knowing . . ." I put a fist to my mouth. "What if I'd had the affair? What if I came home one night and told you I'd been sleeping with another man? What if I'd slept with Brock?"

He stares in stunned silence. "I don't know." Lifts his hands and lets them fall. "Is that what you want? Do you want to be with Brock? Do you . . . love him?" Fear widens his eyes as reality steals home. We're at an impasse. And I don't know what to say next.

Had he asked me this a few weeks ago, I might have hesitated. But now I know for sure. It's something I've realized over the past few days, watching Kevin move around the house, coming home with groceries unasked, offering to make dinner even after working a full day or insisting on doing the dishes so I can rest.

I watch the way he interacts with the kids—the easy way he's always had with them is slowly returning and the walls of distrust and hurt seem to be crumbling before my eyes. I know, even now, despite the pain, the rejection, and his final abandonment, that I will never love anyone like I love Kevin. Not even Brock Chandler.

"I'm not in love with Brock."

"You're not?" He sounds a little unsure, so I shake my head. And then, because the way he's looking at me says more than he probably wants to, I manage a smile.

"No. I care about him. We've grown close, I won't deny that, but I guess I must be a bit of a masochist, Kev, because in spite of everything, apparently I still love my husband."

His smile almost makes it to the edge of his mouth. "Is Brock in love with you?"

"Does it matter?"

He lets out his breath in a low exhale and runs a hand over his face. "Savannah. Do you think . . . do you think you might give me, us, another chance?" He moves closer and takes both my hands in his. "Do you think you can forgive me?"

It sounds so easy in theory. All I have to do is say yes. "Is that what you want, Kevin? For me to say I forgive you? To say we can start over? Like it never happened?"

"No. Not like it never happened. It did, and we both have to deal with that in our own way. But yes, Savannah, I am asking for your forgiveness. Not just the words. God knows I don't deserve it, and I don't have the right to ask for it, and which-ever way this goes . . . I need you to know that I am truly, truly sorry. I don't know that I can ever forgive myself. So I don't blame you if you don't think you can take me back. But I don't think either of us can ever move on if you can't forgive me."

"I know." Weariness cloaks me. I'm so tired of fighting this. Tired of the bitterness, the stale anger that still sits within me. "I wish it were easier. I know I should forgive, but . . . right now . . ."

"You can't." He lets me go, like he expected as much. "So what now? Do you want to proceed with the divorce? Do you want to end our marriage, Savannah?"

"No." A small cry gets stuck in my throat. "Did you not hear me? I love you! I do, but I hate what you did. Some days I still hate you for it. I just need some more time, Kev. I'm not saying no. I'm saying not now. Not yet."

He pinches the bridge of his nose and shrugs, dejected. "Okay. I guess I can accept that."

My cell phone buzzes in the pocket of my jeans and I jump. The stillness of the room shatters and Kevin steps back, away from me. I pull out my phone and study the number. Time slows as dread slithers through me. "It's Clarice. I should take this."

"Yeah. You do that." He nods, shoots me a smile singed with sorrow, gives a shrug, and walks out, shutting the door behind him.

Chapter 26

"Let other pens dwell on guilt and misery."
—JANE AUSTEN

Some days Zoe found the idea of quitting school and running off to Africa totally appealing. Today was one of those days.

She so did not want to go back to school tomorrow.

A knock on her door made Zoe look up from her packing. "Enter at your own risk."

Mom poked her head in and grinned. "This doesn't look so bad."

"Well, I've only been home a few days. Haven't had enough time to mess it up." The state of Zoe's bedroom had always been a source of lively debate. Mom said that was the one good thing about Zoe being in college—she could actually see the rug in here.

Zoe zipped up her bag and heaved it off the bed. "I'm glad you guys talked me into waiting until tomorrow. It's supposed to snow tonight." She had planned to drive back this afternoon, but it got late and they decided with the unpredictable weather, it'd be better to drive in daylight. Mom and Dad were taking Adam back to school tomorrow, so they could all leave at the same time.

The memory of Adam in that hospital bed still kept her up nights. Other than losing Shelby, this had been one of the hardest things she'd gone through. She made a point of coming home as often as she could. She needed Adam to know she'd be there for him, and she needed to get past the guilt of not doing more when he'd called her that morning.

Zoe couldn't bear to think what might have happened if they'd lost him. Couldn't go there.

"I'm so thankful you've been able to be around on the weekends, Zo." Mom read her mind as usual. Zoe grinned as Mom sat on the edge of the bed.

"Me too." Zoe hated the weariness on her mother's face. She looked so tired since coming back from the Berkshires. Dad wore that same beaten expression. Since bringing Adam home from the hospital, it was like they were all tiptoeing around each other, nobody knowing what to say.

"So, you ready to go back tomorrow?" Mom ran a hand over the wrinkles on the patchwork quilt she'd found at some quaint store years ago. Zoe rolled her eyes and they shared a smile. A glimmer of happiness lit Mom's face, but it was gone too quickly.

When Zoe arrived home on Thursday night, she'd shrieked in delight at her mother's new stylish shoulder-length bob. She'd lost some weight over the last few months and looked more like the pretty young mom Zoe remembered from her youth. If it weren't for the shadows beneath her eyes . . .

"Zo . . . I wanted to ask you about Tim." And there it was.

Zoe sighed. She'd known it would come up eventually. She sat on the other side of the bed and met Mom's gaze. "We broke up."

"When?" Mom didn't look surprised. Zoe figured they'd known or at least assumed but hadn't wanted to ask. Not with everything going on. And that was fine by her because she hadn't wanted to talk about it.

Early-evening light flickered through the curtains. Everything in the room was exactly how she left it the summer she went off to Princeton. At some point she supposed they'd begin to clear things out, put everything into boxes and pack up her life. That day might come sooner than expected if Mom and Dad went through with the divorce.

Zoe pushed her hair behind her ears. "About a month ago." She got off the bed and paced her spacious bedroom. She loved this room with its dormer windows and view of the garden and the fields beyond. Some days she missed being home with an aching loneliness. Other days, when she'd been home too long, she couldn't wait to get back to school. Tonight she wasn't sure how she felt. "I saw him with a girl and I overreacted.

After that, I realized I didn't really trust him. And I didn't know what to do with that. Neither did he."

"Oh, Zo." Mom's sigh wound around the room and sadness settled in her eyes.

Zoe's tears warmed her cheeks. "He said it was nothing, that they were in a group, lab partners. Mom, the whole thing was so ridiculous . . . but all I could think was . . ." She sank her teeth into her bottom lip and hesitated. Voicing her thoughts might be like throwing gasoline on an already burning fire.

"You thought he would turn out like your father." Mom's words were quiet, heavy with sorrow that made Zoe cry harder. She dropped to the bed again and Mom moved to sit beside her and took her in her arms.

"He said that. 'I'm not your father, Zo . . .' Yelled it at me, like I just didn't get it. And maybe I didn't. Maybe I wanted us to break up because somehow, deep down, I know I'm only going to get hurt anyway."

"Zo. Don't do that." Mom smoothed Zoe's hair and kissed her forehead. "You can't spend your life being afraid that every man you meet will let you down. At some point you have to learn to trust again."

"But he . . ." Words jammed together in her throat. "Mom, Daddy cheated on you. He broke your marriage vows. Will you ever get over that?

Will you ever be able to trust him again? I don't want to go through that with anyone. I'd rather stay single the rest of my life."

"Oh, sweetie. You won't always feel this way." Mom gave a half smile, but her eyes still held the pain of what they'd been through. "People will let you down. Even the ones who aren't supposed to."

"And what do you do with that?" Zoe whispered.

"You love them anyway. And you pray that at some point you find the grace to forgive." Mom sat back and took a breath. "I've learned something these past few months. We were made for relationships. You know that? Marriages and families are what hold us together, give life real meaning. And even when it all goes wrong or things happen that we just don't know how to deal with, that doesn't mean we shouldn't try again. Even when it's hard and it still hurts."

Zoe sniffed back more tears. "Dad ruined everything. Some days I still hate him for that."

"But things weren't perfect, Zo. Things weren't good between us." Mom's voice got quiet, trembled a little. "Hadn't been for a long time. I had a lot of issues I needed to deal with. You know that. Don't you?"

The past skittered across the room, and for a moment Zoe almost heard her sister's laughter. She wished she could remember more about

Shelby, but she did remember her laugh. Memories pulled her back to that summer four years after Shelby died, the summer she came home from camp and Mom wasn't there.

She slid off the bed and fiddled with the framed photos on her dresser. The truth had marched into the room uninvited and demanded to be acknowledged.

"A couple of years ago I asked Daddy what happened that summer you were sick." Zoe found the courage to face Mom again. "Things didn't make a whole lot of sense in my mind. Why you weren't here when we got home. Why you stayed away so long."

"He told you." Mom inhaled, a painful expression freezing her face.

"Why did you do it?" The question came out more like a wail. "Were we not enough for you? Not good enough?"

Silence followed. She had finally unwrapped years of unspoken thoughts. Unspeakable subjects Zoe always thought were best left alone.

Mom lowered her head and covered her face with her hands for a long moment. "I was in a bad place back then, Zo. Nothing made sense for me anymore. I wasn't thinking rationally. I don't know why I did it now. How I thought it would solve anything. How I could have ever imagined leaving you, putting you through that pain."

"Adam doesn't know." Zoe met her mother's

347

anguished expression. "When you called to tell me what happened, that's the first thing I thought of. You. All those years ago. How desperate you must have been. How desperate he was. I knew he was unhappy. I knew he wasn't doing well at school. I should have said something to you and Dad. Maybe if I'd—"

"No!" Mom was beside her in an instant, her eyes flashing with an intensity that was almost frightening. "Do not blame yourself." She ran a hand down Zoe's wet cheek. "My darling, no. We've got to stop this. We're all carrying around enough guilt to fill an entire container ship."

Mom shook her head, her hair shining under the glow of the bedroom light. "What I did, what Adam did, what happened to Shelby, none of that was your fault, Zoe. Or Dad's. We made our own choices. That's all it is: bad choices and circumstances beyond our control."

"Why is it so hard to move on?" Zoe held her elbows and hugged her arms tight. "I wish I could forget everything that's happened the past year, but I can't. This thing with Adam seems like the last straw. Why does our family have to be so messed up?"

A sound pulled her gaze away from Mom.

Dad stood in the doorway, looking like somebody had punched him in the stomach.

Zoe's heart sank. Mom stared at him, too, and nobody spoke.

"I filled up your car." He tossed her car keys from one hand to the other. "Checked the tires. You should be all set in the morning." He placed the keys on the dresser and hesitated. Zoe had never seen him look so sad, so broken. It was like all the life had suddenly been sucked from him. He looked from her to Mom, let out his breath, and turned and left the room.

"Oh my gosh, he heard everything! I know he did." Zoe stared at her mother in horror. "Should I go talk to him?"

Mom shook her head, pulled Zoe against her in a brief hug, and stood. "No. Let him be. When he's ready to talk, he will. Why don't you go find Adam and order a couple of pizzas for dinner?"

"Okay." She pushed trembling hands into the pockets of her jeans. "I didn't mean to hurt him, Mom. I wouldn't do that."

"Sweetheart, I know. And he knows that too. Part of facing up to the consequences of our choices is dealing with the fallout. I think Daddy is slowly starting to realize that."

Mom shut the door and Zoe sank onto her bed, chest heaving.

Finally, her tears spent, she reached for her cell. And punched in Tim's number.

≫※≪

We eat a quiet dinner. Poor Zoe. As if things weren't bad enough. She has no idea what to say

349

to Kevin. Neither do I. It's been two weeks since we last talked about reconciling. I think he's afraid to bring it up again. Or maybe he's waiting for me to. And part of me is still afraid.

Tonight it's Adam who keeps conversation going. He cracks corny jokes and talks about the trips we used to take and the time the new tent Kevin bought—he was so proud of the purchase—came crashing down on us in the middle of the night, startling campers and wildlife for miles as we all shrieked and hollered, tangled up in sleeping bags and canvas and laughter.

Zoe asks if Tim can come stay next weekend and we share a smile. Before Kevin and Adam came in to eat, she told me they'd talked, that she and Tim wanted to work things out. I'm happy for her.

Later, once I shove paper plates in the trash, wash cutlery and the salad bowl, I go in search of Kevin.

I know exactly where he'll be.

I grab my coat and gloves, pull on my boots, and head out to the patio. The night is cold, starlit, and snowy. In typical New England fashion, Mother Nature has decided to give one last nod to winter, and there's even talk of a blizzard heading our way this week.

Down the concrete steps, careful not to slip, I follow the path past the covered pool into the garden toward the methodical sound of metal making violent contact with wood.

He's by the toolshed, the outside light illuminating the pile he's created and the anguish on his face. He grips the handle of the axe, jaw set, eyes fixed on the task he's determined to complete. Snow falls softly, landing on his windblown hair and blue wool sweater. On the other side of the shed, out of sight, there are piles and piles of wood.

Meticulously stacked monuments that pay homage to years of pain and anger and sorrow so deeply embedded in our souls but never shared.

I know this now.

I've learned more about Kevin in these months of being apart than I knew in a lifetime of living together.

Some people face their trials with drink. Others medicate with drugs or food or maxing out their credit cards or they gamble away the pain.

My husband chops wood.

I find an old abandoned lawn chair, wipe the snow off, sink into it, shove my hands deep into the pockets of my coat, and wait.

Chapter 27

"And now these three remain: faith, hope and
love. But the greatest of these is love."
—1 CORINTHIANS 13:13

Kevin is not a talker. Never has been. But perhaps
this needs to change.

"Go back inside, Savannah." He brings the axe
down hard, catching my eyes with his. "You don't
need to be out here."

I wait until there's a break in the chopping to
reply. "No. I don't *need* to be."

Kevin stills the axe, lowers it to the ground,
and leans on the handle, breathing hard.

I shrug at the questions sitting silent in his eyes
and wonder how best to answer them.

"Do you remember the verse we read at our
wedding?" I came across it quite by accident this
morning. I was sorting through drawers in an old
dresser in the basement. I don't know why really,
whether I was looking for something in particular
or just needed something to do, but I found the
old piece of paper with the handwritten words on
it and stared at them a long time.

Kevin sets the axe aside and sits on the sawdust-
covered stump. His breath curls around him in
the cold air. "Corinthians something or other."

He scratches his head and tosses me a grin. "I was never very good at memory verses."

"Neither was I." We didn't have a church wedding. My mother didn't think it would be appropriate under the circumstances. But I know God was there anyway. " 'Love never gives up,' " I begin, almost afraid he'll shoot to his feet and walk away like he would have not so long ago. But he doesn't. He sits in silence as I speak again. " 'It never stops trusting. Never loses hope and—' "

" 'Never quits.' " He lets out a shaky breath and stands. Turns his back to me and bends over his knees a little. When he finally stands and walks toward me, the light catches the tears in his eyes. "Savannah . . ."

I meet him halfway.

Kevin threads his fingers through my hair and holds my gaze. For a long moment, all I can do is stare at him. Then I find the courage to ask him what I must.

"I need to know something. And I need you to answer honestly. Okay?"

"Okay."

"Do you blame me for Shelby's death? Do you think it was my fault, Kev? Because I went inside, I wasn't watching her, I—"

"Don't." He presses two fingers against my lips and stops the rush of words that wring out my soul and lay it bare before him. His hands move slowly upward, over my hair, lifting a strand off my face, brushing tears and snowflakes from my cheeks. "If it had been me, would it have been any different?" he says softly. "Would I have gotten distracted by something, forgotten she was out there for a moment? What if your mom had been watching her? I don't know, Savannah. Maybe it would have happened anyway. But second-guessing doesn't do any good. And no, I never blamed you for it."

"But . . . I thought . . ." Years of confusion and guilt barrel toward me in a tidal wave of grief ready to suck me under.

"I know what you thought." He pulls me against him and I fit neatly into his embrace the way I always have. The comforting smell of his cologne, wood, and wool wrap around me in welcome and make me wonder why I fought this so long.

"I'm sorry, Kevin." If I don't say it now, nothing will ever change. "I wasn't willing to take any blame for what went wrong with our marriage. I was too angry with you. Too hurt. But now I understand how I made you feel. I'm willing to own that now. And I'm truly, deeply sorry. More than you'll ever know."

"It wasn't just you." Kevin presses his lips to my forehead and groans in frustration. "You thought I blamed you for Shelby's death, and that infuriated me." He leans back a little to look at me. "But I never really told you I didn't. I figured you were hell-bent on blaming yourself anyway, might as well take me along for the ride. I couldn't get past my own grief to see what it was doing to you. And in the end it seemed easier to walk away."

"And I thought it would be easier to let you." My gloved fingers grip his arms. "I got tired of trying to make you stay. Trying to make you love me." The arguments come flooding back, us yelling so loud that the kids would go running for their rooms.

Nights I'd lie awake and wonder how two people in the same bed could be so far apart. Nights when all I could do was cry and listen to him out here. All the times we could barely look at each other. The last few years, after my attempted suicide, conversations were sparse, stilted, and of very little significance. "In the back of my mind I always wondered . . . if I hadn't gotten pregnant with Shelby, whether we'd have stayed together."

"What?" Astonishment widens his eyes. "You think I wouldn't have married you anyway, Savannah?"

I've asked him to be honest. I'll do the same. "I never knew for sure. I always felt like I trapped you somehow. That you thought marrying me was just the right thing to do. So maybe part of me wasn't all that surprised when you finally found someone else." Words I've never been able to say suddenly tumble out like clothes from

355

a dryer opened too soon. They scatter around us and fill the air with truths that cannot be ignored.

Kevin lets me go and makes a slow circle in the snow. He kicks at it with the top of his boot and sends a white shower of flakes upward. I catch my breath and watch them dance in golden-yellow light. After a moment he walks back to me, shakes his head, and shivers slightly.

"You were my best friend." His eyes glisten intently, filled with feelings he's never expressed. "I loved you more than I ever thought possible to love anyone. You were my life. I never could have walked away from you. Didn't you know that?"

Maybe I did then. I'm not so sure I know it now. Not so sure it's still true.

"So what changed?" The hollow ache in my chest reminds me again how far removed we are from those early giddy days of our relationship.

"Me, I guess. You. Circumstances." He exhales and swipes a hand across his face. "We stopped talking to each other. Stopped listening."

"I guess we forgot about the 'love never gives up' part."

"I guess we did." He closes the space between us and wraps me in his arms again. "I forgot a lot of things."

I rest my head against his chest and stay in the moment. I'm afraid that when I step back, when I walk away, this closeness I feel will be gone. He was my best friend too. And I never thought I'd lose him.

"What are we going to do, Kev?" Since making the decision that Adam will return to school, neither of us has brought up the question of what will happen once both kids are gone. But now I have to know.

"Can we . . . start over?" He lets the question fall into the surrounding darkness. His piercing eyes beg me to give him another chance. To give us one more shot.

"Kevin. I . . ." What? I actually have no argument. No good reason to refuse. "I've got to close up the house up north. I need to see how . . ." I can't finish. It doesn't seem right somehow, to say his name. To try to explain what I still don't understand.

Clarice has called almost daily the past week. Brock isn't doing well. He seems to have accepted his fate. Given up.

And he's refusing to talk to me.

"I know." He nods, brushes my hair back. "I know what you need to do. But after that, when you're ready, will you come home? To me?"

The overwhelming urge to put my arms around him is more than I can bear. So I hold him close and listen to him breathe as he waits for whatever I'll say next. Silently pleading with me to agree.

"It won't be easy." I meet his searching eyes

again. "I don't know how long it will be before I can fully trust you again. You know that, right?" I break his gaze and study the snow around my feet. I don't want to make promises. Don't want to give false hope. It wouldn't be fair.

"Yes." Kevin's hands are cold as they cup my face and force my eyes up to meet his. "I know. But I'll do whatever it takes to get us there. Whatever you need me to do. Don't give up on me, Savannah. On us. I promise I won't let you down this time."

And I nod, because, somehow, with everything in me, I believe him. "Maybe we can start by being friends again."

"Friends, huh?" His breath warms my face and I laugh a little. A delicate tingling like tiny butterflies in flight stirs within and takes me by surprise. The fluttering hints that despite my cautious heart, there is hope here. Because I know what I'm feeling—that familiar tug, the wanting, the need—the very obvious signals that tell me I still desire my husband.

If I'm not mistaken, he's feeling the same. And there's a look about him that says the whole friends thing is so not going to fly.

"If that's what you want." He raises a brow, eyes glinting a little dangerously. "For us to be friends."

Well then.

I don't remember his voice ever sounding that

sexy. Don't remember ever feeling this kind of anxious anticipation. "I suppose we have to start somewhere." It's a lame response, and nerves rain like hail against the wall of my stomach.

"We do. Have to . . ." Kevin angles his head slightly and his lips part in a scandalous smile that slays me. "Start somewhere." His mouth is mere inches away. Then he brushes his soft lips over mine in tentative exploration, flirting a little, not quite sure what I'll do.

When I don't protest, his hands thread through my hair and he pulls me closer into a smoldering, heart-shattering kiss. One that steps over decorum and stakes its claim quite clearly. The things he's doing with his mouth send rivers of molten fire into every part of my trembling body.

We pull back just a bit and stare at each other.

The shiver that rips through me has nothing to do with the cold.

He's never kissed me like that before. With such desperate, deliberate intent.

There's a smidge of hesitation in his eyes, like he might have crossed the line. But I meet his lips this time and chase it away. His mouth is warm, familiar, and unyielding as he crushes me against him, groans into me, and draws me even further into that soul-deep connection I believed we'd never share again.

Kevin breaks the kiss with a guttural moan that implies his need for so much more. "Whoa,

Savannah." He rests his forehead against mine and lets out a shuddering breath. "Sorry."

"Really?"

"Not in the slightest."

I giggle like I've had one too many glasses of champagne, still trying to steady my breathing. "Well, that was quite a start."

"Yes, yes, it was." His satisfied smile reaches right through me, pushes aside the hopelessness I've clung to for so long and replaces it with something new. "And, uh, I don't kiss any of my friends like that. In case you were wondering."

"Good to know." I breathe a happy sigh. "Just your wife, huh?"

"Only my wife." He kisses me again, this time with a little more determination, a little more promise, and a sure hope unfurls in my heart and unleashes a fierce, passionate response that almost brings me to my knees.

"Okay . . . time out." I break away this time, exhale, and smile at the laughter in his eyes. It's like we're suddenly seeing each other for the first time. "We should probably go inside." My mouth is still tingling, but my heart is singing an old familiar tune.

"That sounds like a plan." Kevin's smile suggests things I'm not yet prepared to investigate.

I roll my eyes and give him a little push, then pull him to me again. "Slow. Okay?"

"You call the shots." He runs a finger down my

nose, still smiling. "Whatever you want." Kevin shuts off the light above the shed, puts an arm around me, and holds me close as we walk toward the house in step. It's a practiced rhythm we've forgotten somehow, but it has not forgotten us.

"Zoe will be okay. She doesn't really hate you." It's the reason I came out here in the first place, I remember, to tell him that.

"I know." He sighs and rubs the back of my neck with cold fingers. "I'll talk to her tonight."

"Good."

We talk as we walk. He tells me about the lady who lives in the apartment beside the one he's been renting in the city, an elderly black woman who's quite convinced Kevin is her long-lost son. Easy laughter passes between us and I suddenly feel lighter than I have in years. We head up the steps and I stop, seeing two pairs of eyes peering out the window at us.

Our children.

I can't imagine what they're thinking, but if the surprise smacked across their faces is anything to go by, I'd say they weren't expecting this.

They weren't the only ones.

The thought makes me smile again.

A chuckle rumbles from his chest as Kevin shoots me a sidelong glance. "We could really give them something to talk about." His grin edges on evil and I clear my throat.

"Oh, no you don't. I think we've all had enough surprises for one night."

"Spoilsport." He laughs, but doesn't try to kiss me in front of them.

For which I am eternally grateful.

I think.

But I'm also a little mystified. Because the truth is, I really wanted him to.

Chapter 28

"Forgiveness is the fragrance that the violet sheds on the heel that has crushed it."
—MARK TWAIN

Out-of-the-blue surprises are the best kind.

The kids make no comment as we enter the kitchen, but they grin and share looks that tell me they're jumping to all sorts of conclusions. Part of me wants to run for the car and hightail it out of here as fast as I can. To run back up north where things are safe. Because, what if this doesn't work out? What if we fail again?

How will we survive that?

Zoe suggests a game and we sit around the kitchen table playing Scrabble, eating popcorn, and enjoying the hilarity in the air. When the clock chimes eleven, my daughter declares herself the winner and says it's bedtime. I tell her good-bye because I always do the night before she leaves. It's a ritual we have, the hugging and noisy kisses on the cheek and hugging again until she laughs and tells me to suck it up, Buttercup.

Kevin follows her upstairs and I shoot up a prayer for that conversation.

Adam helps me clear the table and put the last

of the supper dishes away. Then he leans against the counter, sighs, and sends me a heart-melting smile.

"I love you, Mom."

I blink through the myriad of emotions those words stir up. He doesn't say it often. He's always been that way. Like Kevin. Just a little too reserved with his feelings.

"Adam." I draw him into a long hug. "I love you too."

"I know." He grins, sidles away, and shoves his hands in the pockets of his jeans. "So you're going to give the old man another chance, huh?"

My smile falters but I nod anyway. "I think so. We're going to try."

"Figured you would." He paces the kitchen with slow steps. "That's good. Good." Then he faces me with a brave smile. "I wanted to tell you, before I go back to school. I'm sorry. Sorry for what I did. It was a lousy thing for me to do to you and Dad."

"Oh, honey. I understand." I breathe it out, afraid to take the next step, but knowing I must. It's time to face the past for what it was, and time to let it go. Release the claim those wounds and stark memories have on me once and for all.

"Adam, there's something you need to know." I head for the table and smile at my son. "Come sit a minute."

For some reason I can't really sleep.

The events of the evening replay in my mind over and over, and truthfully, I'm still a little giddy. And sad at the same time. Because although nobody wants to say it, we all know we're like Alice, at a crossroads, wondering which way to go. Wondering whether there will truly be a happily ever after at the end of it.

Adam listened to my story, nodding, both of us crying a little, but I'm glad I told him. Glad he knows now. There are no more secrets between us. In a way, it's like we're all starting over, not just Kevin and me.

I stare at the ceiling and pray the weather will be good in the morning. I ask for Zoe to get back to Princeton safely. I'm pleased she and Tim seem to be working things out. I mentally prepare myself to drive Adam back to school and say good-bye. My mind wanders to Brock. I hate the thought of him in pain and I wonder if it'd be all right to pray for a miracle, because the thought of Maysie growing up without him breaks my heart.

The floorboards creak outside in the hall.

It's after 2:00 a.m. Apparently Kevin can't sleep either.

I know the pattern of his pacing. He'll stop, adjust the pictures on the wall, pick up his pace again, and walk back and forth until he gets sleepy. I shiver slightly and pull the covers up tight. I listen for more movement and there is none. Maybe he went back to bed. But then I hear a sound coming from the room next to ours.

Shelby's room.

Oh, God, help him.

My fingers clench the blankets and I close my eyes in one last prayer.

He hasn't set foot in that room in years.

Not since we packed up the last box, put away her furniture, and repainted. I've used the room sporadically for crafts and wrapping presents, but I'm still reminded of her when I go in there, and it's too overwhelming.

I lie very still, bite my lip, and wrestle with my conscience.

Maybe he needs this. Time to be in there alone. Time to deal with what that means for him. What it means for us.

Or maybe he needs you . . .

I don't know where the thought comes from, but it's as clear as if someone leaned in close and spoke into my ear.

My heart taps a reluctant beat, but I get up, pull on my robe, and pad down the hall.

There's not much left in the room that once belonged to our eldest child.

The old rocker where I nursed her, where we held her through fevers and ear infections and stomach bugs, her pink princess blanket draped over it.

A writing desk with a few framed photos on it, the table lamp turned on low, and a beat-up couch from Kevin's college days. He and John dragged it up from the basement one year, thinking it might help him, might make it easier to be in this room. It didn't.

Kevin stands by the window, his back to me. He's only wearing sweatpants, and I wonder how he's not freezing in here. But as I step farther into the room, my bare feet sinking into soft carpet, I realize it's actually quite warm. Warmer than it should be. Perhaps he adjusted the thermostat, but somehow I don't think so.

"Kevin?"

He jumps a little and turns, surprise widening his eyes.

He stands in silence, the shadow of a man so bound by grief and remorse that I wonder how it hasn't killed him.

But perhaps it has.

Oh, Kev.

Kevin lets out his breath and drags a hand down his damp face. "I didn't mean to wake you."

"You didn't." I get a little closer, almost afraid to interrupt this outpouring of sorrow. But I want to share it. I need to share it.

"We have to let her go, don't we?" The question

is ragged, yet resolute. There is so much pain here I almost can't bear the weight of it.

"We do." I nod and take the last few steps until I'm close enough to reach for his trembling hands.

And I think, at last, I am ready.

Kevin clears his throat. "I keep thinking about what Adam said the other day, about how we haven't moved on. How he thinks everything he and Zoe do must measure up to Shelby somehow . . . and . . . he's right."

Last week, in one of our final counseling sessions together as a family before Adam goes back to school, we talked about Shelby. I never knew how Adam and Zoe really felt. Never knew the extent of their own grief and loss. Or how they believed we never really got over their sister's death. Talking all that through was probably one of the most difficult things any of us have ever done. But sometimes the honest truth just hurts and there's no getting around it.

"I know. I get that now." A gentle breeze stirs the air and makes me smile. I don't know where it comes from, but I don't suppose it matters. "She'd hate to see us like this. Broken. Too stubborn to heal, to let her go. She'd hate what we've done to each other. The pain we've caused."

He nods in silence as tears slip down his cheeks. "You're right."

"I told Adam." I swallow fear and level my gaze on him. "While you were upstairs talking to Zoe, I told him what happened that summer. How I tried to take my life too . . . so now he knows."

Kevin lets out his breath and shuts his eyes a moment. "Why is it all so horrendously hard?" He presses his forehead to mine and I slide my arms around him with a shaky sigh.

And then I realize what's happening.

I don't see the past when I look at him.

I don't see his sins. Or mine.

I only see a brokenhearted man struggling to free himself from the chains that dragged him down, dredged his soul, and took him into dark places he never dreamed of going.

My man.

My husband. The one I chose to live my life with.

The one I promised to love forever.

And God help me, I will fight for that.

I will fight for this marriage.

I will do battle with him, for him, but never again against him.

"I think the things worth having are the ones we have to fight the hardest for." My fingers brush across his face, move through his hair and back down to pass over the stubble that shadows his jawline. "Shelby will always be with us, Kev. In our hearts, in our memories. But she's been gone a long time. And we need to start living again."

He sniffs, nods, and grazes the pads of his thumbs over my wet cheeks. "Have you always been this smart?"

"I don't think so." I smile a little and try to be brave. "I've just had more time to think lately."

"I guess you have." He smiles back at me through bleary eyes, but there's a different light in them now. That palpable energy rises between us again and I press my hands against his warm bare skin, watching him watch me.

"Hey, Kev?" His heart beats hard against my palm. I lower my head a bit, my hair falling forward as I wait out the moment. Wait for the courage to speak the final words that will truly free us.

He places his thumb under my chin and tips my face up. "What?"

My breathing is shaky, but I reach for his hands and slip my fingers between his and bring them to my lips. "I forgive you."

We stand there in the quiet of the dimly lit room, our eyes and hearts and souls connecting at last.

Kevin sniffs and takes a deep breath. "What you said up at the house, over Christmas, about not wanting to be my second choice?" Tears spill onto his cheeks, but he smiles through them, winds his arms around me, and pulls me against him. "You're not. You never could be. You're my only choice. Always, forever." He breathes into my hair and holds me until we both stop crying.

In that finite moment, I hear laughter.

It rings around the room in one quick spin and then it's gone.

I'm afraid to ask if he heard it, too, but the incredulous look on his face tells me I don't need to. He shakes his head, gives a shrug and a lopsided smile. And then we're back to staring at each other.

"You're stunning." His eyes move over me, over every curve, slowly, sensuously. "My beautiful Savannah."

I don't want to cry again but I can't help it. It's been so long since we've shared anything close to this kind of intimacy.

"No more tears." He presses soft kisses all over my face. "I love you," he whispers, running his hands over the silky fabric of my robe. "I will always love you."

"I love you. So much." I hesitate, but only for a moment. Then I place my hands on his broad shoulders, slowly slide them over his biceps and up again. I relish the groan that gets stuck in his throat as I trace my fingers across his chest in slow motion, watch him drink me in and allow myself the luxury of feeling completely and unabashedly desired by my husband.

"You call the shots, remember?" His low voice tickles my ear as his hands move across my back in a way that makes me tremble. "I don't want to rush you. Tell me what you want."

I shiver under the heat of his touch. "You. That's what I want."

Kevin moves my hair aside and presses his lips to that sensitive spot just above my collarbone. "What happened to slow?"

He's torturing me now and I'm suddenly impatient. "Slow is for sissies." I shove my fingers through his thick hair, pull his face up, and cover his wicked grin with my mouth. "Unless you'd rather go back to sleep."

"Uh, no." He captures my laughter with his lips and molds me against him in an exquisite kiss that should be outlawed. Then he lifts me off the floor, still working his magic over me.

My husband carries me back down the hall to our bedroom. We are heading toward a future that, until today, I was reluctant to claim. But I welcome it now, in that slow and silent moment as he takes me back into his arms and we give and receive a love renewed.

I welcome him back to the place he belongs.

Because I know now, this is life.

This is what it's all about. This is what we were made for.

Living through the pain, the heartache, facing fear and finally . . . finally . . . finding the courage to grab hold of grace and savor the chance to begin again.

꧁꧂

Sometime in the early hours of the morning Kevin shakes me awake. "Morning, gorgeous. Zoe's getting ready to go." We share a sleepy smile and head downstairs to see her off. I beat a hasty retreat back to the bedroom where it's warm. Kevin will wait at the door, watching her car drive down the road until it disappears, just like he's always done.

Sometime later he slips back into bed.

I let out a squeak as his cold feet brush the back of my leg. "You're freezing."

"Yup." His arms come around me and his low laughter warms the back of my neck. "We should do something about that, Mrs. Barrington."

And so we do.

꧁꧂

Somebody is yelling my name.

"SAVANNAH!"

I pull a pillow over my head and groan into the mattress. I didn't realize I still had my phone turned on. It's probably a telemarketer. Kevin startles as it rings again in Martin squawk and I peek over at him.

He moans and flings an arm across his face. "What . . . in . . . the . . . world . . . is that?"

"Um. My phone."

"Why does it sound like a parrot?"

"Long story."

"Where is it?"

"No idea." I cover my head again. I hear him fumbling around, cursing until he finds the thing.

"Who is Mitch Chandler?" His voice sounds gravelly, satiated, and still heavy with sleep and it makes me smile. But then I realize what he's said and open my eyes.

"Brock's brother." Crazy fear wraps cords around me. "Oh no."

Kevin holds the squawking phone toward me but I shake my head. I think I might actually be sick. "I can't. Please answer it, Kev."

He nods. "Hello? Uh-huh. No." He narrows his eyes a bit. "Yeah. This is Kevin . . . Who is this . . . Maysie?"

I sit up fast, pulling blankets with me as I lean against his shoulder.

"Slow down, sweetheart. Where are you?" He pushes his fingers through his disheveled hair and looks at me through worried eyes. "Hang on, honey. Savannah's right here." Somehow he knows exactly what button to press for speakerphone and Maysie's tearful voice trembles out.

"Mi . . . Miss . . . Savannah?" she hiccups. "Are you there?"

"Yes, I'm here. Mays? What's going on, sweetie?" My heart begins to thump in wild staccato and I take a breath. Kevin puts the phone between us and puts an arm around me.

374

"Daddy fell down. He's in the hospital and I . . . have to wait out here."

"Are you at the hospital, Mays?" I put a hand to my mouth as she lets out a sob. "Sweetie, are you by yourself? Where's Aunt Clarice?"

"I'm in the hospital, too, but I hafta stay out here in this room. Aunt Clarice is with my daddy. And so's Uncle Mitch. He . . . bought me . . . donuts and said I could play games on his phone." She gulps out the words. "I'm sc-scared."

I close my eyes and imagine her sitting in a hospital waiting room all by herself with a big box of donuts on her lap.

Kevin grabs the phone because I can't get words out. "Don't be scared, sweetheart. Everything's going to be okay."

I widen my eyes at that one.

"Okay." Maysie sniffles a little. "I 'membered your number with my picture memory. You know, like what Daddy has?"

A sob mingles with laughter. "That's good, sweetie. I'm so glad you did."

"Can you . . . come . . . back, Miss Savannah?"

Oh, Lord. Help.

I don't even have my car. I left the Escalade up north. I've been using one of my parents' cars while I've been home. How . . .

Kevin jogs my elbow to get my attention. "We can drive up right after we drop off Adam. If the weather holds we can be there this afternoon."

Oh, this man. "Are you sure?"

Kevin runs a thumb over my cheek and nods. "Maysie? We'll get there as soon as we can. I'll get Miss Savannah up there today, okay?"

"You promise?"

"I promise. Hey, Maysie?" Kevin gets out of bed, already searching for clothes. "Is there a nurse or someone there I can talk to?" He's taken charge, looks back at me over his shoulder, and jerks his head toward the bathroom. *Go,* he mouths, *I've got this.*

Before I can even think, we're packed and on the road, halfway to Adam's school. Our son is leaning forward between us, ignoring my pleas to sit back and put on his seat belt.

"Just let me get this straight." He shakes his head again. "You're going to drop me at school, then go back up to the Berkshires to see this Brock guy who's got the hots for Mom."

"He does not have the hots for me!" I gasp and ignore Adam's chuckle.

Kevin shoots me a sidelong grin and lowers his sunglasses a little. "He totally has the hots for you, *darlin'.*"

"But he's probably gonna die, so it's a moot point," Adam decides.

I slink lower in my seat and cross my arms. "Are you done with the interrogation, counselor?"

"I guess so." I hear the click of Adam's seat belt and let out my breath.

"What's the verdict?" Kevin wants to know, teasing in his tone.

Adam laughs a little too loudly. "That you guys are even weirder than I thought you were. Hey, lawyers make good money, right?"

"If they're good at what they do, yes." I roll my eyes. Just what we need. Another one in the family.

"Maybe I'll talk to Zo about that. We could open our own firm."

"Perfect." Kevin grins. "So you've given up the professional skateboarder dream?"

"Ha-ha. That was when I was, like, eleven." Adam leans forward again. "I might want to go to Harvard, though, if I can get my grades back up. Sorry, Dad."

Kevin gives a mock sob. "You're just angling for your grandfather's millions."

"Well, I didn't think of that, but . . ." He cackles when I turn around and give him the stink eye. We drive on a bit in silence.

"So . . ." Adam pipes up again when we settle at a stoplight. "You guys aren't getting a divorce?"

I lean back in my seat, smile, and look over at my husband.

Kevin reaches for my hand and brings it to his lips. "No. No divorce."

Chapter 29

" 'Tis better to have loved and lost
than never to have loved at all."
—ALFRED LORD TENNYSON

How do I do this?

We don't say anything on the ride up the hospital elevator. I have no idea what to expect and no idea what I'll say or do when I see Brock. So I try to think about Maysie instead. Our first task is to find her.

Kevin follows me down the busy hallway, past empty beds and monitors, nurses walking hurriedly and wandering visitors searching for the right rooms. Kevin has done the legwork for us and we find the waiting room easily enough.

Maysie is curled up on a red faux-leather couch, sound asleep, a brown teddy bear tucked under her arm. A man is sprawled in a chair, hands behind his head, with long denim-clad legs and cowboy boots.

I glance back at Kevin, who's looking a little uncomfortable, and I wonder if he's having second thoughts. But we're here now. I move in and study the sleeping man, hoping he's Mitch Chandler or I'm going to be sorely embarrassed. "Excuse me?"

He startles, sits forward with a grunt, and settles a pair of familiar blue eyes on me.

It would appear the Chandler brothers have the market completely cornered on the genes for good looks.

"Mr. Chandler? Mitch?"

He rubs his eyes and gives me a skewed look. "Yes?"

"I'm Savannah Barrington. A friend of Brock's."

I see Brock in the way he musses his blond hair and scratches the stubble on his jaw. His smile broadens as he gets to his feet. Clearly he knows who I am. "Savannah." He takes my hands in his. "Did Clarice call you?" He still looks a bit confused.

"No. Actually, Maysie did." Now the poor man is really confused.

Kevin moves in, clears his throat, and sticks out a hand.

"Kevin Barrington. Savannah's husband."

"Um. Okay." Mitch looks at me in some surprise and I know then exactly how much Brock has told him. But Mitch recovers quickly. "Great. Great to meet you both." They shake hands and Mitch glances from me to Kevin to Maysie. If the situation wasn't so stressful I might laugh.

I fill him in on Maysie's early-morning call. He shifts a little uncomfortably, then flashes a smile. "To be honest, I wasn't sure whether to call you, Savannah. Clarice was so upset I didn't want to ask." He's got the same southern drawl. "But I'm glad y'all are here."

"I'm here for Maysie." It's half true, though I know both men in the room see past the pretense.

"Of course." Mitch nods too seriously. He adjusts a loose-fitting polo shirt and flicks some fluff off his dark jeans.

"How is he?" I can see the stress on Mitch's face and wonder how bad things really are.

"Not fantastic. According to Clarice, he's spent the last few weeks holed up in that library of his, writing like the devil was after him. A few days ago he could barely get out of bed, but she couldn't get him to see a doctor. I flew in yesterday and he looked like hell. Then this morning he was up and making breakfast like always. I thought I was dreaming it. He turned around to say something and just passed out. I was pretty sure"—he shoots Maysie a look—"that this was it. But . . . he is miraculously still with us."

Suddenly Maysie stirs. She pushes herself up and lets out a shriek. "Miss Savannah!" The next minute she's thrown herself at me and I pick her up and wrap her up tight. "You're here!" She buries her face in my neck and I press back tears.

"Has she been here all day?" I train my gaze on Mitch. "Surely there was a better option than bringing her here?"

"I didn't know what to do with her," he explains, a little snappy now. "Like I said, Clarice was beside herself. I couldn't get two words out of her. I don't know anyone in this town. And the way he looked when he came around, I didn't know if . . ."

Maysie lifts her head and sticks out her bottom lip. "They won't let me see Daddy. Miss Savannah, can you make them?"

"Oh, Mays." I stroke her tangled hair and shoot a furtive glance at Kevin.

He shrugs out of his coat and tosses it onto the couch. Then he produces the take-out bag from McDonald's. His idea. "Hi, Maysie. Did you eat up all those donuts yet?"

"Forever ago." She sniffs dramatically and rubs one eye, checking out the bag he's holding. "Is Zoe here?"

"No." Kevin smiles. I put Maysie down and she joins him on the couch. "We can call her later if you want. But I'm kind of hungry. How about you?" Maysie nods and the two of them soon have their heads stuck in the bag, deciding what to eat first.

"There you go, Mays. The cavalry has arrived." Mitch gives a strained grin. "Don't suppose you stopped at a liquor store?"

Really? I ignore what I assume is some attempt at humor and take off my coat. Just as I'm about to ask what room they have his brother in, Clarice marches through the door.

"Oh my stars!" She rushes me with open arms

and I receive her warm hug with a smile. She dabs her cheeks with one of her embroidered handkerchiefs. "You're a sight for sore eyes, my dear." She turns her attention to Maysie and Kevin. "Mr. Barrington, how lovely to see you."

Kevin gets to his feet. "You as well, Mrs. Chandler. How is your nephew?"

"He's certainly been better." She proffers a cheek and Kevin leans in to kiss it. He's got a dab of mustard on his chin. Maysie is wolfing down her burger like she hasn't seen food in a week. Clarice looks over at her nephew. "He was asking for you. But perhaps since Savannah is here . . ."

"Go ahead." Mitch nods in my direction and his smile seems genuine. "It'll make his day."

I'm tempted to grab Clarice's walking stick and whack him one. If Kevin doesn't beat me to it.

"What about me?" Maysie's mouth is full, ketchup dripping from her chin. Kevin searches for napkins and cleans her up.

"Oh." Clarice lets out a shaky sigh. She is aging before my eyes. I help her into a chair and she works to catch her breath. "Maysie, dear. Remember what we talked about? Just as soon as the doctors say you can, we will let you see him. I promise."

"Okay." She slurps a chocolate milkshake and turns to Kevin with adoring eyes. "Didja know I have a guardian angel?"

"I didn't," Kevin replies in all seriousness.

Mitch shakes his head. "Not everyone believes in angels, Mays. Man, I need a drink."

"Mitchell, that's enough, dear." Clarice shakes her head and gives me a despairing look. "All right." Clarice pushes to her feet. "Come along, Savannah. And you"—she points her stick at Mitch again—"stay right here. Or we will have words."

"Yes, ma'am."

I'm a little flustered now and I fiddle with my hair. My throat is suddenly dry. What am I doing? Why did I think this was a good idea? I fumble in my purse for I don't even know what.

"Hey." Kevin's quiet voice shakes me from my distracted thoughts. I look his way and he holds out a hand. I grab it, hold tight, and concentrate on his steady eyes. "I love you," he says, and suddenly I'm calm again.

I sniff and nod because my throat is too tight for speech. I catch a glimpse of Clarice's triumphant smile and suspect she's not in the least bit surprised.

"Miss Savannah?" Maysie stares at me through wide, fearful eyes.

I crouch before her and put my hands on her shoulders. "What, sweetie?"

"Will you tell my daddy I love him? And that he needs to get better?" Her little face crumples and Kevin puts an arm around her.

"I will." *God, help me not to lose it.* I smile

and place a hand on her cheek. "When I get back, we'll go home. I'll bet the dogs need to be fed, huh?"

"Yes. Jimmy from church came to let them out. I told him what to do."

"Okay. That's good. Why don't you tell Kevin about the puppies while I'm gone?"

Maysie seems satisfied with that and settles back on the couch. "Well, first of all we had one dog. Named Willow. Then one night this nasty man dog came an' . . ."

I follow Clarice out of the room, the sound of Maysie's singsong voice and Kevin's laughter giving me courage.

⁂

Brock is in a private room. The curtains are drawn, the lights dimmed. He looks like he's sleeping. Even from my vantage point at the door I can see he's lost weight over the time I've been gone. His skin has an unhealthy gray pallor. Clarice hustles over to him, places a hand on his forehead, and leans close to whisper something in his ear.

His eyes flutter open and he turns his head and settles a weary gaze on me. "Well, crap. I guess I really am dying."

Clarice squeezes his arm, gives me a smile, and lets herself out before I can stop her. I step toward the bed, take a breath, and somehow find a smile. "Amazing what some people will do for attention."

He wheezes out a chuckle and pulls at the oxygen tube in his nose. "Stupid thing." He presses a button to raise the top half of his bed, even the slow movement making him groan.

"Put that back on." I point to the plastic tube, drag a chair toward the bed, and take a seat. "What happened?"

Brock sighs, adjusts the tube again, and rewards me with a grim smile. "You want the doc's version or the English translation?"

"English."

"I passed out."

"Ah. That's unfortunate." I lean forward slightly and refill the glass of water on the table beside him for something to do.

"Gave my head a good crack, but other than that, I should be fine until the tumor grows another inch, and then I'll pass out again. But that time I won't wake up. Win-win."

"Right. I think your brother was being kind when I asked him how you were doing and he said not fantastic. I'd put you somewhere around morose and miserable."

"You met Mitch."

"I did."

"He called you?"

"No. Maysie did." I retell the tale and he laughs a little.

"Your arrival must have surprised him."

"He did seem a little out of sorts."

Brock tugs the collar of his hospital gown and scratches his neck. "My brother has an aversion to hospitals. And stress."

"Didn't you say he was a lawyer? Perhaps he should consider changing professions."

Brock laughs again and winces. He reaches for the plastic cup and I help him with the straw. He drinks a bit, then leans back on the pillows with a sigh. "It's good to see you, Savannah."

"Shouldn't you be someplace else? This isn't exactly a cancer center."

He waves a hand. "The doc here's all right. They've been talking to my doctors. Nothing to worry about. I can probably go home tomorrow."

"Nothing to worry about." I shake my head at the crazy man. "So . . ." I exhale and wonder if this is the right time. I heard about his appointment in New York from Clarice. "The last time Clarice called, she said you still hadn't decided whether to have the operation. Brock—"

He groans and puts a hand over his eyes. "I'm not discussing it."

"But what if—"

"How's Adam?"

Fine. No sense in upsetting him. But at some point I will bring it up again. If there is an operation that could possibly save his life, he needs to have it. And none of us understand his hesitancy.

"Adam's good. He's made a lot of progress the

past few weeks. We dropped him off at school this morning. It was his idea to go back. He seemed really happy when we left."

Brock gives a slight nod and a small smile. "How'd you get up here?"

I settle in my chair again and stare at him a moment. "Kevin drove me."

His mouth forms a thin line and he studies the ceiling like the Holy Grail is hiding somewhere in the tiles. "He's here?"

"Outside. With Maysie." I didn't mean to sound like that was the best thing in the world, but somehow it came out that way.

"Okay." A sliver of a smile passes across his face as his eyes meet mine again. "You look happy."

I can't stop my smile this time. "I am."

"Well, wouldn't you know. There goes my reason for living."

"I was never your reason for living." My trembling tone tells me this is harder than I thought it would be.

He reaches for my hand and gives it a squeeze. "You could have been." Tears burn my eyes and he croaks out a low chuckle. "Shoot. I'm not gonna lie and say I'm overjoyed, but I am happy for you. Really."

"I know." There's too much I want to say. Too many things I never said and now I can't because it wouldn't be right. But I hold tight to his hand and lean on the rail of the hospital bed. "In case

I never told you, I'm really glad we met, Brock Chandler."

"Yeah?"

"You made me laugh again. You made me feel like I was worth something again, like I mattered. And I never thanked you for that."

"No need, darlin'." His eyes get a little brighter. "I probably shouldn't say it, but since I'm dying an' all . . . I want you to know something too."

"Brock." Everything in me knows I need to stop this. Because I'm not so sure my heart can take it. But he's shaking his head, serious, intent on telling me what he needs to.

"You . . . uh . . . you gave me some mighty sweet dreams." His wicked grin hints at an underlying meaning. A squeak of horror gets stuck in my throat. His shoulders start to shake and slow laughter tumbles from his lips. "Sorry. Couldn't resist."

"If you weren't in a hospital bed right now I'd probably hit you." But I can't help laughing at the smile he's now wearing. "Jerk."

"Oh, come on. It's true. Can't deny it."

"Whatever." I groan and press fingers against my eyes.

He sobers and lets out a breath. "So you really came back up here just to see me, huh?"

"Maysie was so upset. And I didn't really know what was going on. Kevin made the decision for me."

Brock gives a low whistle. "Sounds like our Mr. Barrington might be redeeming himself."

"He's trying. We're trying."

"And so it should be." It's the last line from *Charity's Box*, one of my favorites of his books. Yet somehow it seems appropriate. He smiles and looks toward the door. "Is Mays doing okay?"

"She'll be all right. It's been a long day for her. I'll take her home and get her cleaned up."

"Don't mind the mess. We've had a fun few days."

"She wants to see you."

"I know. But . . ." He clenches his hands. "I don't want her to see me like this, Savannah. I don't want to scare her."

"She's already scared. Why won't the doctor just let her see you?"

He looks away and my heart flounders as the truth settles in.

I close my eyes for a moment, blow out a breath, then focus on his face. "Come on, Brock. You've got a little girl out there who depends on you. She needs her daddy. Do you think she cares what you look like? Do you think not telling her what's going on will make it easier in the end, if things don't work out? And what makes you think you have the right to simply check out on her, when there's a chance you could actually be okay?"

"A small chance, Savannah."

"I don't care. It's still a chance worth taking, Brock. You have nothing to lose."

"Thank you for that succinct reminder."

"I'm going to get Maysie." My temper is sizzling now. As I move to stand up, he grabs my hand. I'm forced to face him again, and as soon as I do, my anger fades.

He stares at me through watery eyes, not saying anything for a long moment. And then he smiles. "I'm really glad we met, too, Savannah Barrington. In case I never told you."

Chapter 30

"Trust your instinct to the end,
though you can render no reason."
—RALPH WALDO EMERSON

I'm floating between leftover elation and strange desperation.

Sometime around 9:00 p.m., I finally slide the key into the lock of the lake house, and Kevin and I walk inside almost in slow motion.

I'm beyond exhausted. Brock hadn't been kidding about the mess. We left Mitch at the hospital, took Clarice and Maysie home, and I almost fainted when I saw the state of Clarice's normally pristine house.

We let the dogs out and fed them. I introduced Hope to Kevin and he actually seemed rather delighted with her. Only sneezed about six times. Then I took care of Maysie. Plopped her into a bubble bath, washed and combed and dried her hair, found clean pajamas, and put her to bed. She was tearful, but eventually drifted off to sleep.

Kevin was about halfway through the stack of dirty dishes by the time I went downstairs. He'd made tea for Clarice and forced her into an armchair in the living room. When I went to check on her, she was sound asleep. I picked up a little.

Newspapers, magazines, more dirty dishes. Even a few discarded shirts and socks and soda cans. When Mitch arrived he immediately went to work cleaning up. He got bored fast, though, and spent the rest of the time wandering through the house with a drink in one hand, his cell phone in the other.

While I didn't really want to leave Clarice, I'm awfully glad to be back in my own space.

"That was one unholy mess." Kevin takes off his coat and runs a hand over his hair. "Is it always like that?"

"Never. I expect Clarice has been too busy with Brock to worry about housekeeping."

I hang up our coats and glance around the living room. Everything is how I left it. The warm pine scent is welcoming and almost makes me smile. It's good to be home. Except it's not really my home. My home is back in Boston. I think. I'm so tired I can't formulate a proper sentence in my head.

"The brother wasn't much help."

"No. He's probably just under a lot of stress right now."

"Why are you defending him?"

I sigh and head for the kitchen. "I can take some leftovers out of the freezer. Are you hungry?"

"It's late. Not sure I could eat." Kevin wanders around, checking out photographs and fiddling with the magnets on the fridge. "It's weird not having everyone here, huh? Quiet."

"I like it. Christmas was crazy."

"Yeah, just a little." He grins when I look his way.

How far we've come in twenty-four hours.

"Um." I don't remember what I was doing. Food. Looking for food.

"How was he?" Kevin shoves his hands in the pockets of his jeans, serious now. It's the first time we've had time to talk since I saw Brock.

Suddenly I need to sit.

Kevin joins me at the table, arms crossed.

"He didn't look good." I pull my fingers through my hair and shake my head. "If he'd just have that stupid operation . . ."

"What operation?"

And then I remember he doesn't know. Of course he doesn't.

"It's a long shot, but there's a new procedure his doctor in New York wants to try. No guarantees, of course, but . . . there is a chance it could save his life."

"So why wouldn't he do it?"

"I don't know." I shrug, at a loss for words. "Maybe he's scared. Maybe he doesn't want to cling to false hope or give anybody else a reason to think he might be okay."

"What about Maysie? If he doesn't . . ."

"I know. Honestly, I don't know what he's thinking."

"And if he had it, if it worked? If he was okay?"

A pained look creeps across his face. "Would he think the two of you—"

"Stop it, Kevin. Don't even go there." I stare at him in disbelief. What is going on here? The conversation has become ridiculous, and I'm so tired and don't want to continue it. I push my chair back and return to the fridge to see what we can eat.

"I'm not hungry, Savannah."

When I turn around, Kevin's on his feet.

"Okay. I'm not either." Tears burn and I bite them back. "Why do I suddenly feel like we've taken ten steps backward? Like everything has changed?"

He walks to where I am and takes me in his arms, burying his face in my hair. "I'm sorry. I'm being a jerk."

"We're both tired. It's been a crazy day."

"Yeah. We should call Adam, see how he's doing." His brow furrows and he reaches for his phone.

I make tea while he punches in numbers, then listen to my son on speakerphone. I find some cookies in a tin and put those on the table. Everything's good. Not too much to catch up on. Then he says he has to go because they're about to watch a movie and, like, he just saw us this morning.

"He's going to be okay." I say it more for myself, but Kevin nods in agreement.

"Sure. He will. And I'll pick him up on Saturday morning for the weekend. You'll be back by then, right?"

"I . . . back?" What? I stare at him and fumble for words. "No. I thought . . ."

Understanding settles into his features and he frowns deep. "You want to stay. You're going to stay."

"Kevin, you saw the house. Clarice is over-wrought, and Maysie's just a little girl. And, like you said, Mitch is no help."

"So now you're agreeing with me." He sits back a bit and narrows his eyes.

"Did you think we'd drive all the way up here, say hello, turn around, and go home again?" Did he? Really?

"Well, yeah." He rubs his jaw and shrugs. "I guess I did. I have to be at work in the morning. I already took today off."

"Uh . . . wow." I sit forward and put my head in my hands. "I didn't think this through. I just heard Maysie's voice and you . . . you made the final decision." I lift my chin to meet his eyes. "I'm sorry, but I can't leave."

His shoulders sag and he looks away for a moment. "I knew that. I guess I was just hoping you'd choose me."

"That's not fair."

"Isn't it?"

I can't believe this is happening. I scoot back my chair and walk to the long window at the end of the kitchen and stare at the dark woods until I can form a coherent thought. Then I find the courage I need to face my husband. "I've already chosen you. Or did last night mean nothing to you?"

"Are you kidding me?" He widens his eyes, clamps his jaw, and looks away.

How is it that we've already forgotten how to talk to each other?

"Can't you bring Adam up here for the weekend?"

"I don't know. I'll have to check my schedule."

Anger creeps in and takes over. And suddenly I can't take a minute more.

I brush past him and head to the living room where I sink onto the couch, grab a soft cushion, and bury my head in it.

A few minutes later he's there beside me, brushing hair off my face, leaning in to kiss my forehead. "I'm sorry. Savannah? Sweetheart, sit up a minute."

A shuddering sigh escapes, but I push myself up and catch the sadness in his eyes. Kevin wipes my tears and pulls me in for a kiss.

"You didn't deserve any of that. Really. I'm so sorry."

"It's okay." I brush my hand across his cheek, worried by the harried look in his eyes. "What's really going on?"

He leans his head against the cushions and

exhales in a noisy groan. "I got an email earlier this afternoon. While you were in with Brock."

"From?" I don't like the sound of this. Don't like it one bit.

"My boss. Uh . . ." Kevin drags a hand down his face and swears. "It seems that Alison has applied for a position in the company. She'd be working in my division. And she put me down as a reference."

I blink through the silence and process this news. "I thought she was in California."

"I guess it hasn't worked out there."

What I really want to say probably wouldn't go over well, so I shove those words down and find a thin smile. "Well. That's. Interesting."

"Savannah."

I slap his hand away and jump to my feet. "No. Just. No."

Terrible thoughts swirl around my mind and drag me down. It's starting all over again and I can't stand it. And just when I thought it was safe to unlock the chains around my heart.

"I haven't responded," Kevin says quietly. "I wanted to talk to you."

"Well, that's big of you. I actually factor in this equation?" *Oh, God, help.* The biting sarcasm slips off my tongue without permission.

Kevin moves before I can leave the room. He stands in front of me, grabs hold of my arms, and locks his desperate gaze on mine. "Will you stop?

Savannah . . . stop! Look at what we're doing to each other already. We can't get sucked in again. Don't you see that? Don't you see what this is? We've come too far to turn back now."

"What are you going to do?" I can barely whisper the words. "You can't . . . She can't . . ."

"I know." He leans in, folds me into him, and hangs on. "I need this job, though. I—"

"I have money. It's always been there. You know—"

"Yes." Kevin sighs deep and steps back. "And you know how I feel about that. Working for your father was one thing. I had to earn that position and I worked hard for it. But I'm not touching your trust fund. That's for you. For the kids. Not me."

Desperation claws at me. I imagine the next few months like a bad soap opera, my husband coming home one dark, stormy night and telling me he's really still in love with his mistress. That we're truly not meant for each other and it's just not going to work.

"I'll figure it out. Savannah, this doesn't have to be a big deal."

"It what?" I take two steps backward and put a fist to my mouth. "You did not just say that." He gives me a blank stare that stirs my anger further. "Kevin. Get real. You can't work with her. You can't be around her. Not if you want this reconciliation to work. Not if you want our marriage back."

"And what if I said you can't be around Brock? What if he has that operation and he's fine? You can't stand there and tell me the man is not in love with you, because I'm not that stupid. So what then, Savannah?"

"I never slept with Brock. There's a big difference. You lived with that woman."

Suddenly the past is right there with us again.

Jeering, taunting, and unpacking its bags.

And I have no idea how to make it leave.

Kevin utters a low curse. "I know what I did. You don't need to keep throwing it in my face."

"That's not what I'm doing." I gasp for air and suddenly feel light-headed. "I'm trying to make you understand . . . Oh . . ." The truth dawns on me like somebody just flicked on the lights after an extended loss of electricity. "She wants you back. Doesn't she?"

"Whether she does or not is irrelevant. I don't want her." Kevin steps toward me, his face lined with stress, cheeks pinking and moisture shining in his eyes. "I swear to you, Savannah, I've had nothing to do with her since I ended things. This came out of left field. You can look through my cell phone, my computer, whatever you need to see." Kevin closes the gap between us and takes my face between his hands.

"Ever since Christmas all I've been able to think about is how empty my life was without you in it. I didn't count on us getting back together, but I prayed for it. Prayed for it like I've never prayed for anything, except Shelby. But this time I felt like God heard me, took pity on me. Like he forgave me and really does want the best for me, for us. I don't have all the answers, but I do know that we've been given a second chance. And I won't let anyone take that from us."

"Okay." I hear him. And I believe him. My vision blurs, but I smile anyway. "We're on the same page there. I'm not letting you go again, Kevin Barrington. Not without a fight. You've been warned."

"Yeah?" He grins and rubs his nose against mine.

"Yeah." I breathe out the stress of the last few hours and melt into his embrace. "I think I told you this wasn't going to be easy."

"You did." He tips my chin and brushes his lips with mine. Tenderly at first, but the kiss becomes suggestive in minutes. "So . . . I could stay the night. Leave early."

"You could." I wrap my arms around him and meet his lips with a long, lingering kiss that conveys how I feel about that idea. "You're going to wear me out, husband."

"Oh, I don't know. I thought we could just, you know, watch the stars. Or something."

"Or something?"

"Or something."

I grin wide and shriek when he scoops me up

into his arms and heads toward the stairs. If he keeps doing this, he's going to put his back out. But I'll let him this last time.

❧✦❧

It's before dawn when he leaves the bed. I stretch and yawn and try to force my brain awake. After he kisses me good-bye, I come to my senses, jump out of bed, stop at the dresser, and scurry down the stairs after him.

"Kev! Wait!"

He's pulling on his coat, turns and flashes the grin I know I'll never get enough of. "Good gravy, woman. Put some clothes on or I'll never get out of here."

I'm only wearing my thin nightgown, and it's cold down here, but I don't care. I fumble with the rings I'm holding in my hand and open my palm. "You forgot something."

He exhales, smiles, and stares at me awhile without words. "I did, didn't I?"

Silently I take my husband's hand and slip his wedding band back on his finger.

Back where it belongs.

And then I give him my rings.

And he's crying a little as he gingerly takes my trembling hand in his and puts them back in place.

I put my arms around him and hold tight. Like it might be for the last time.

401

"Hey." Kevin sniffs, moves hair out of my wet eyes, and smiles. "I know what I'm asking, but trust me, okay?"

"I do. I will." I nod, press my lips to his again, and wish he didn't have to go. "You do the same."

"I will."

"I love you." I brush his hair back, stretch up to kiss him once more, and then step back, shivering in the cold morning air.

"You are my world, Savannah. I'll never forget that again. And I'll make sure you know it every day for as long as I have breath." Kevin hesitates a moment, pulls me back into his warm embrace, and claims my lips again. When he's finally done, I'm not so cold.

"I'll call you later," he says as he reaches for his bag. "Charge your cell."

"I'll do that right now."

"See you on the weekend. I'll let you know what time."

"I'll be waiting."

I watch him drive off on that snowy Tuesday morning and I wonder whether we truly will survive this. Because I know now that nothing worth having comes easy. There will always be another obstacle. Another hurdle. One more road-block on the way to peace.

But perhaps this time will be different. This time we're in it together. And we're determined to fight for what we want.

To claim what was meant for us all along.

As Kevin's car disappears down the drive, I catch a glimpse of the small figure standing in the snow. My breath hitches, but I stay there in the moment, real or not. Our eyes meet for a split second and we share a smile. Then she lifts a hand, waves, and skips away.

And this time I know it is not Maysie.

Chapter 31

"There is an appointed time for everything. And there is a time for every event under heaven—a time to give birth and a time to die."
—ECCLESIASTES 3:1–2 NASB

So this was what dying felt like.

Brock leaned on Mitch and walked the four steps to the front door. Four steps that felt like fifty. He wanted to pass out right there on the stoop, but Mitch propped him up, casting a cautious glance his way, and Brock grimaced. "I'm not gonna drop dead in your arms, bro. Chill out."

Maysie skipped beside them while Clarice went ahead into the house and made sure there were no obstacles for him to fall over. Another crack on the head would probably do him in at this point. Although the way he felt today, the idea held some merit. Everything ached. He'd pop pills for the pain. But it was the hurt in his heart he didn't know what to do with. No quick fix for that.

Over the course of his hospital stay, they'd converted the living room into a makeshift bedroom for him, complete with hospital bed.

"Gimme a break," Brock muttered as soon as he saw it, then allowed Mitch to help him ease out of his coat. They should have settled in Florida. Then he could have passed away peacefully on a sunny beach, surrounded by beautiful bikini-clad women.

"Let's get you into that bed. Man, I could use a nap too." Mitch was trying his best. Trying to sound upbeat, like his only brother wasn't about to pop off at any given moment, but Brock heard the strain in his voice.

He waved a hand and moved toward the couch. "Grab me some pillows. I'll lie here for a bit."

"Hallo, Brock, hallo, Brock!" Martin squawked and Maysie giggled and ran for pillows. Soon he was tucked in, stuffed animals surrounding him, with Maysie on a stool by his side and Clarice and Mitch hovering like overeager servants waiting to do his bidding.

"I'm sure y'all have things to do," he growled.

"Yeah. I do." Mitch ran a hand over his hair. "I need to call your doctor again and make sure he's gonna be on that plane tomorrow."

Brock bit back a curse and glowered at his brother. But there was no arguing. Mitch had already made the arrangements. And Brock knew by the time Dr. Reece Radcliff left the Berkshires, one way or another he'd be scheduled to have his skull split open.

After the last week of horrendous pain that pretty much sucked the life out of him, he wasn't sure why he'd been so stubborn about it. But dying didn't scare him.

Not dying did.

What if something went wrong? What if he lived but he couldn't talk or walk or never emerged from the comatose state they'd put him in?

There were a million what-ifs.

Like the stars in the sky Savannah liked to watch.

Brock turned his head and locked his gaze on Maysie's worried face. She was just a kid. She didn't deserve this.

"Want to go get your puppy? What'd you name him again? I can't remember."

"Watson." Her eyes lit but veered toward Clarice. "Am I allowed?"

"You are allowed." Clarice held out a hand for Maysie. "But in a little while. Let Daddy rest and we'll come back in a bit." They left the room and Mitch pulled up a chair.

Brock picked up a teddy bear and stared into beady black eyes.

"HALLO!" Martin squawked again.

Brock startled, dropped the bear, and glared at the bird in the cage across the room. Then he looked at Mitch. "Will you get that thing out of here?"

Mitch snorted. "What do you want me to do with it?"

"I don't care. Open a window."

For some reason the very idea sent them both into hysterics.

It felt good to laugh.

Brock sobered quickly and shook his head. He wouldn't put that past Mitch. "I was kidding. But take the cage out of here when Clarice isn't looking. He can go in the kitchen until—"

"Until you're well enough to go back to your room," Mitch said quietly.

Brock shut his mouth and took a moment to study his brother's face. "You doing okay?"

Mitch blinked, his nose getting red. He blew air and pressed his thumb and forefinger to his eyes. "You're asking me if I'm doing okay?"

"Well, you're not exactly living the life these days, little brother. Figured you'd be beating a trail back to the big city by now."

"I won't lie and say I haven't thought about it." Mitch tapped the Rolex on his wrist. "Fortunately I've been able to handle most things online and through conference calls. Might have to fly out for a few days next week, though. But they're aware of the situation here, so if I can't, I can't."

"You make me proud, Mitchell." Brock meant it. Hadn't had cause to say it often, heaven knew, yet the past few days, Mitch had come through. "But I still don't think you're parent material."

"And thank God for that." Mitch gave a sudden grin. "I love your kid, but I think she'd agree with you."

Brock smiled and took a moment to catch his breath. "Have you done what I asked?"

His brother sighed, sat back, and stared at the

ceiling for a long, painful moment. "Are you absolutely sure there's nobody who will crawl out of the woodwork to contest this?"

"I'm sure. You saw the PI report. You talked to him. There's no one."

"What if they won't do it?"

"They will." Brock reached a trembling hand for a glass of water.

Mitch stood to help, stared down at him, and shook his head. "I don't suppose I have to tell you I'm not at all happy about this. And I'm hoping beyond hope that it won't be necessary. But I'm glad you've finally come to your senses and agreed to the operation."

"That makes one of us."

"You agreed to what?" Savannah stood in the doorway, a basket of laundry in her arms. Her eyes widened as her furtive gaze darted from him to Mitch.

Brock ground out a sigh. He'd forgotten she was in the house. Clarice told him Savannah had spent most of the last three days here, cleaning, cooking, and looking after Maysie. He was beyond grateful. His aunt needed rest. He'd been more than worried about her lately.

"Well, if it isn't Florence Nightingale." Mitch grinned and Savannah scowled.

Brock chuckled, the movement hurting his chest. "Knew you two would get along."

Savannah let out a soft laugh that made him feel

better. "That, my friend, is stretching the truth. You must be a writer." She put down the overflowing basket and walked toward him.

"It's the Chandler charm. She can't resist it." Mitch quirked a brow and put on his I'm-too-sexy-for-myself look. If Brock had the strength, he would have smacked him one.

Savannah shot his brother a venomous glare. "I'm getting a bit tired of you." Her cheeks flushed with exertion and she looked like she hadn't slept well for days. Suddenly all he wanted to do was sit her down, pour her a glass of wine, tell her silly stories, and make her laugh until she cried. But he couldn't even get off the couch.

"Brock? Have you agreed to have the operation?" Her eyes were on him again.

"Only if you'll agree to run away with him once it's all over," Mitch drawled.

Brock couldn't stop a grin at the scathing look Mitch earned with that remark.

Savannah pushed up the sleeves of her sweater and gave a low whistle. "You don't know when to quit, do you? Make yourself useful for a change, Mitchell, and take that basket to my car for me." Clarice's dryer was broken, he remembered. Mitch had supposedly ordered a new one, but it was anybody's guess when it would arrive.

Much to Brock's surprise, his brother obeyed, picked up the basket, and disappeared out the door. Savannah pulled a chair close to the couch and studied him through anxious eyes. "So?"

"I'll do it." Brock rolled his eyes at the squeak she let out. "You know it's a long shot. The odds are not good. In fact, they're pretty darn awful."

"I know. I heard the whole spiel from your brother. Optimism is not one of his strong suits."

"He's protecting himself." Brock pushed up a bit and pain shot down his neck. "Cured or dead. At this point I'm not sure which sounds better."

"I wish this wasn't happening." Tears shimmered in her eyes, but he couldn't look away. When he was lucid enough to pray, he actually asked God to take away the tumultuous feelings he had for this woman. Because if he lived . . . a wry smile jumped him without permission . . . well, Mitch hadn't been that far off the mark.

"You're tired, Savannah." He wanted to reach for her hand, but clasped his fingers together instead. She gave a watery smile and a shrug.

"Not sleeping very well."

"When's he coming back?" Brock hadn't wanted to ask. Mitch told him, with a glint of glee in his eyes, that Savannah's husband hightailed it out of here a few days ago. But the man did have a job to get back to. Brock couldn't believe he'd brought her up here in the first place.

"Hopefully on Saturday. With Adam."

"That's good. Day after tomorrow, right?"

"I know." She twisted her rings and frowned at the floor.

"What's going on?"

"It's nothing. Just . . ." She met his eyes again and he saw fear in them. "The woman Kevin had an affair with has applied for a job at his company. And put him down as a reference."

"She what?" Brock had to work to keep horrified laughter in check. "Well, that's gutsy."

"There are other words I can think of." She bit her lip, fiddled with her rings some more, and faced him again. "If she moves back to Boston, I don't think I could take it."

"Hey." Knowing it was so not a good idea, he reached for her hand anyway. "You know there's a long road ahead. A lot more healing to come. It's not going to happen overnight. You're going to have to trust him."

"It's her I don't trust. What if—"

"There you go climbing up that tree again." Brock grinned, gave her hand a squeeze, and let go. "Have a little faith, Savannah."

She nodded, put her hands on her knees, and nailed him with a stern look. "I will if you will."

"Touché, darlin'." They shared a smile and his eyes stung. That happened a lot lately. "Thanks for coming up here for Maysie."

Savannah smiled and wrapped a lock of hair around her finger. "I'll stay as long as they need me. As long as you need . . ." She shook her head and her gaze shifted to the window.

"Hey. In my bag over there." He pointed to the

411

small duffel Mitch had left in the corner of the room. "In the side pocket. Grab that journal, would you?"

Savannah did as he asked and sat down again, handing it to him. Brock tried to get rid of the lump in his throat, met her curious look, and pushed the book toward her.

"I want you to have this."

She narrowed her eyes, opened the leather-bound book, and turned a few pages. Then she stared up at him through tears. "I can't take this. All these quotes . . . so many years . . . Brock. This is practically your whole life right here in this book."

"Yeah. It is." He took in her incredulous expression and somehow found a smile. "So it has to go to someone who'll appreciate it. And I think that's you."

"No. No, Brock. You're going to be fine. You'll have the operation and—"

"And if I'm not, you'll take care of that for me. Give it to Maysie one day. When she's ready."

She clutched the book to her chest, stood, and paced the room, emitting a shaky sigh every now and then. Then she sat again, too much heartache in her eyes. "Okay. Fine. You win. Now can we talk about something else?"

"Sure." He sat back, content with the victory. "How's the greenhouse? I'm not sure Clarice has been in there much since you've been gone."

Her eyes widened a little. "You know, I haven't

even checked. But when I was in the kitchen just now, I'm sure I smelled jasmine."

"I don't know what we'll do when you head back to Boston," he said quietly. Assuming he was still alive.

Savannah shrugged. "Who knows if we'll stay there anyway. Kevin might have to find another job." Her tired smile broadened a bit. "He told me he's always dreamed about owning a bookstore."

"A bookstore? Really?" Funnily enough, though he didn't know the man well, that wasn't hard to imagine.

"All these years, I never knew." She let go a wistful sigh. "So much I never knew."

"You're getting your second chance, Savannah. Don't let go."

"I won't." She sat silent a moment, then met his gaze again. Opened her mouth, then closed it quickly.

"What are you thinking?"

Her cheeks flushed a little. "Well. I wanted to ask you . . . How did your wife die? You never did tell me the rest of your story."

"Ah." Brock smiled. "Well, she—"

"I have no idea why I asked you that." Savannah stared at him in sudden horror. "I'm so sorry. Just forget I said anything."

"No, it's fine. Really." He shifted onto his side and let out a long breath. "I think it was time you did."

She nodded. She understood.

And somehow he'd known she would.

"There will come a time when you will know. And you will understand. And believe." Clarice spoke those words to him months ago, during one of their heated arguments when he still couldn't bring himself to face the truth. Or accept the possibility that a greater force was at work here.

"Gabrielle was a few years younger than me. Worked at a bookstore I used to frequent. Anyway, we had sort of a whirlwind courtship, if you will. I married her after only six months of us knowing each other, and she wanted to get pregnant right away." Memories ran hard and fast and made his heart pound against his chest in an uncomfortable rhythm. "She didn't, though. It was about a year later, I guess. We had a good marriage. She got me, you know? I mean, we weren't without issues, it wasn't perfect, but it was close."

"She must have been some kind of saint to put up with you." Savannah's soft smile skewered him and he gave a low laugh.

"I reckon so. Well, anyway, Maysie was born and life went on. I don't think I'd ever been happier. More content. My books were starting to take off. I was making real money. And a few months after Maysie's birth, I hit the bestseller list for the first time. There was talk of a movie deal." His eyes began to burn but he went on, needing to finish it now.

"We bought a house in the country. Near the

Chattahoochee River. The road around it was steep, winding. One day there was a heck of a rainstorm. Maysie was about six months old. I needed to run some errands, and Gabby asked if I would go to the store. It wasn't a big deal, but I was on deadline, and I just wanted to get out and back, quick as I could. We had a stupid fight about it. Gabby said fine, she'd just take Maysie and go herself. Once I was on the road and saw how bad the weather was, I texted her to stay put. I'd get the groceries. She never answered and I figured she was still mad at me. I went to the store anyway. And on the way home . . . there was this accident up ahead." Brock let out a tremulous sigh and watched tears creep into Savannah's eyes. Like she knew what was coming.

"Gabby's car slid off the slick road and went through the guardrail. With Maysie in her car seat."

"No, Brock." Savannah gasped and grabbed hold of his hands. He pulled strength from her and somehow smiled through the blistering pain that still blindsided him from time to time. The physical pain he'd learned to live with over the last year was no match for the emotional trauma those memories still put him through.

"Gabby was killed instantly. At least, that's what they told me. I hope it's true. I hope she didn't suffer, wondering about Maysie."

"And Maysie? How . . . in a car seat?" A mix

of confused amazement furrowed her brow and made her eyes shine brighter.

"Yeah. I know." He liked this part of the story. Even though he didn't fully understand it and probably never would. "By the time I got there, she was on the riverbank with the cops and EMTs and a bunch of people . . . It was mass confusion. Afterward, they told me a young girl had pulled her from the water."

Savannah ran the back of her hand across her eyes. "I bet you hugged the life out of that kid, whoever she was."

Brock held her gaze, swallowed hard, and fought the urge to brush the tears from her cheeks. "I never found out who she was. Nobody did. There were no kids at the scene, Savannah. Just some couples in canoes, a few fishermen, and some people driving by who stopped to help. But no girl that matched the description five people gave the police. To this day, I don't know where she came from."

Silence fell around them, sheltering his sorrow and reminding him that even now, there was grace. Mercy. Second chances.

Miracles did happen.

Maysie was living, breathing, irrefutable proof of that.

"Her guardian angel." Savannah breathed deeply and presented him with the most beautiful, peaceful smile he'd ever seen.

And somehow he smiled back.

416

"So it would seem. They called her the miracle baby for the longest time. I guess over the years . . . well, she's heard the story enough times. So I don't pay that much attention to her angel sightings."

"Or she really has one."

"Or there's that."

She sat quietly for a bit, then drew a shaky breath. "You said Maysie was about six months old. When did the accident happen? What date?"

Brock hesitated, not sure why it mattered, but he told her anyway. Savannah gave a slow nod and swiped at fresh tears.

"Brock." That serene smile hit him again. "That was the day I tried to end my life."

A chill raced through him and he blinked tears. He let her words sink in and slowly shook his head. What she was suggesting seemed so improbable it made perfect sense. "So you think . . . that . . ." He struggled to piece it together. "You and Maysie both got a second chance that day. In some way, we've been connected all this time?"

"Doesn't that give you hope?" she whispered.

He sighed, desperately exhausted now. "Yeah, it does. It actually really does."

"You need to hold on to that, Brock. Whatever happens. We will be okay." Her smile lit the room and set fire to the renewed hope in his heart. "I knew Maysie was special the moment I laid eyes on her."

"Yeah?" He couldn't stop a chuckle. "That's kind of how I felt about you."

"Oh, Brock." She groaned and covered her face for a moment. Then those luminous eyes were staring back at him again. "I have to say something."

"I know you do. But say it anyway."

"After the operation, if things are okay . . . we . . . you and I . . ." She hesitated, sadness stamped across her face. "As much as you've come to mean to me, I don't think that we should still, I mean, Kevin knows that you . . . that we—"

"Okay, stop." Brock sighed and took pity on her. Wishing things were different wouldn't help. She'd made her choice. And it was the right one. "You don't have to explain. I get it. I know." He couldn't look at her now. "I'll leave you alone. I promise."

But he had a gut-deep feeling that he'd just made a promise he wasn't going to have to keep.

Chapter 32

"What we call the beginning is often the end. And to make an end is to make a beginning. The end is where we start from."
—T. S. ELIOT

It cannot end like this.

Friday morning I've been up for hours, sorting laundry and doing a final load before heading back over to the Chandlers'. It's hard to believe I've only been back here a week because it feels like so much longer. Brock's operation is scheduled and he will leave next weekend. Clarice is going with him and Mitch, of course. I've offered to look after Maysie. I'm not sure how much she knows yet, what Brock has told her.

I don't know how you do that. Tell your child that she might not see you again. I've cried over it all week. Losing Shelby—having to tell Adam and Zoe that she was gone—that was horrendously difficult. But this . . . my heart aches for that little girl.

I head to the living room with an armful of towels as there's a rapping on the front door. I hope it's not Mitch with more laundry. I'm hoping at some point the man will learn to be helpful. I struggle to unlock the door and open it.

"Kevin!"

My husband stands there on the front porch, the early-March sun bouncing off his dark hair, an even stranger light shining in his eyes. He has bags. A large suitcase and a black duffel slung over his shoulder. And at least a dozen red roses in his free hand.

Fresh, fragrant air fills my lungs as I step backward to let him in. "You're not supposed to be here until tomorrow," I manage to say, stretching to look past him at the car. "What about Adam?"

"I'm still going to get him tomorrow." He places the bags in one corner and the roses on a nearby side table, grabs the bunch of towels I'm holding and puts them on the couch, then reaches for my hands. He shakes his head and takes a moment to catch his breath. If I hadn't seen his car out front, I might believe he ran all the way from Boston.

"So, here's the thing." His grin flashes, then he sighs heavily and sniffs. "I lay awake all last night thinking about this. Thinking about why you're doing this, and I realized it's because you're you. Because you love people. You've always been that way. Always the first to jump in when there's a crisis. The first to do whatever needs to be done." He takes a breath. " 'She who saves a single soul, saves the universe.' "

"What?" I stare in utter confusion.

"It's an Alice quote."

"I know that. But what does it have to do with anything?"

"Because that's you, don't you see?" His eyes widen like I'm being a little stupid. "I've always loved that about you, how you just want to help people, and I had absolutely no right to make you feel like you were doing something wrong by staying here. So—"

"Kevin—"

"No." He puts a finger to my lips. "Let me finish." He lets out another breath, smiling. "So then I thought, while you're so busy up here cooking and cleaning and"—his sparkling eyes move toward the couch—"doing laundry, and looking after them . . ." Kevin gives my hands a squeeze. "I thought, who's going to look after you?"

I shrug. I don't know what to say. I am truly speechless.

He leans in and kisses me, a little laughter sticking in his throat. "I thought about our wedding day. About the promises I made you that day. And about how I broke them. But you took me back. You forgave me and offered me another chance to love you. I thought about how I told you I'd never let you down again. And letting you stay up here alone, that's not going to work. So this mission you have, it's mine too. We're in this together, Savannah. We do life together now, no matter what."

"What about your job?" My nose and eyes are burning, but he gathers me close and places his lips to my forehead.

"I quit." Kevin pulls back and a smile slides across his face. "Yesterday. I told my boss why."

"Oh, Kev." I push my fingers through his hair and think about what that must have cost him. "You're serious about this."

"Well, I'm currently unemployed, so yeah, I'd say I'm serious." His grin is back and I can't resist the overwhelming urge to kiss him.

And I'm suddenly reminded of that verse about God being able to do so much more than we even dare ask for.

This is so much more than I prayed for, hoped for, or even imagined.

So much more than I deserve.

But he's here.

For me. For us.

Forever.

"Want to fold some towels?"

Kevin laughs, and his gaze lingers as he traces the shape of my face, his fingers moving like feathers, creating that tingling sensation I never can resist. "Maybe later. Right now I think you could use a little TLC, my love. You're looking a little peaked."

I lean against him, hold on tight, and breathe him in. "How did I ever think I could live without you?"

"Ditto." He tips my face toward his and smiles. "Now . . . where were we?"

❧❦

The Chandler house gets quieter as each day goes by. It has been the longest week. We're moving toward the moment we have to say good-bye, and I'm dreading it.

Kevin jumped into life here with both feet, carrying laundry baskets for me, helping do the dishes and feed the dogs. He even brought toys for them and informs me he's started taking allergy meds.

Maysie was thrilled to see him and couldn't wait to show him all around. Clarice beamed as though she'd expected it, which of course she did. Mitch grunted affirmation and Brock . . . seems strangely accepting of my husband's sudden presence in his life.

He gets weaker each day, and it's hard for him to get around. They'll fly down to New York on Sunday, but Mitch has arranged for a doctor to be on the plane with them. The lawyer in him won't leave things to chance. At this point I don't think Brock cares too much, because he's not putting up a fuss about anything.

Friday evening we eat early. Brock and Kevin play a game of chess. Mitch has no idea how and doesn't want to learn. Adam is here for the weekend again. Zoe picked him up and they

423

arrived a couple of hours ago. I know they think this whole situation is strange, but they've been mature about it, and provide a good distraction for Maysie.

They've gone back over to the house now, said they'll watch a movie until we get home.

I read with Maysie for a bit, and then I notice that Brock and Kevin have disappeared. Mitch is sprawled in an armchair, playing some stupid war game on his iPad. I still can't believe the man is an outrageously highly paid attorney.

"Hey, Matlock."

He arches a brow and pins that scintillating gaze on me. "Yes, dear?"

"Where'd they go?" I nod toward the empty chairs.

"Uh . . . hmm." Mitch scratches his jaw. "Wonder where Brock put that rifle of his . . ."

Maysie sighs and pats my hand. "They went to Daddy's library. To talk. I heard Daddy say he had something he wanted to ask Mr. Kevin."

And I can't imagine for the life of me what that might be.

Clarice shuffles around watering her plants, talking to them, and humming that familiar tune. The walls fairly sing with it. The setting sun catches my eye and pulls my gaze toward the window. And I see her again, the same little girl with the blond curls, running across the lawn.

Dear Lord, this place is making me insane.

Maysie's breath hitches a little and I look back at her, and she smiles wide.

Words aren't needed.

⁂

Kevin appears some time later, somber yet oddly peaceful. He crouches before us, settles his gaze on Maysie, and smiles. I've seen that smile before. A lifetime ago.

It's the way he used to look at Shelby.

"Your daddy wants to talk to you, sweetheart." He glances up at me and arches a brow. His eyes are wet as he puts a hand over mine. "He asked for you to go too."

Maysie and I walk with quiet, reluctant steps toward the library. She holds tight to my hand and gives it a little squeeze every now and then. I think she knows what's coming. I wish I didn't.

Brock is stretched out on the couch at the far end of the room, but he struggles to sit as we approach. Maysie skips over to him and snuggles into the crook of his arm. He lifts his chin and gives me a weak smile. I back off but he shakes his head and indicates a nearby chair. "Stay."

It's the last thing I want to do.

But somehow I lower myself into the chair, let out my breath, and watch him pull his daughter onto his lap. He runs his hands over her hair, tweaks her nose, and leans in for a kiss.

"You know how much I love you, right, Mays?"

"To the moon and back?"

"More."

"To infinity and beyond?"

"More."

"Forever and ever and ever?" She gives a little giggle and his face cracks in a broken smile.

"And even more than that." Brock sighs and strokes her hair again. "You know Daddy's sick, Mays."

"Uh-huh. Your head's 'bout to esplode."

"Yeah. That's about how it feels." He sniffs back tears and I'm already done. "But there's this doctor, in New York . . . who thinks he might be able to fix me. So I'm going to go there and see if he can."

"Really?" I hear the hope in her voice and choke back a sob. "But . . ." She sniffs too and runs a finger down his face. "What if he can't?"

"If he can't . . ." Brock leans back against the cushions on the couch, then lifts his head and somehow smiles. "Then I get to go to heaven, Mays."

"Will you see my mama?"

"Sure."

"But you won't be able to come back home." She hiccups a bit. "Will you?"

"No. I won't be able to come back." His jaw clenches as he meets my eyes over the top of her little head. "Oh, Mays. I'm so sorry, baby." He exhales a hoarse cry and wraps her trembling frame up tight against him. Maysie's heartbroken sobs soak up all the air in the room.

I take a slow walk around in search of tissues, grab a handful, and then sit next to Brock on the couch.

When Maysie finally sits up, I wipe her eyes. Then she wipes mine.

And then she takes a fresh tissue and wipes her father's cheeks. "What are we supposta do without you, Daddy?"

"Well. You . . ." He rubs her back in slow motion, presses his forehead to hers. "You remember all the fun times we had. How we played and laughed and told silly stories. Remember when we went to Disney World. And the time you figured out it was really Uncle Mitch dressed up as Santa on Christmas Day, and you pulled off his beard and he was so startled, then we laughed and laughed. You'll have those memories forever, Miss Maysie. And so will I."

"But what if I don't want you to leave? What about me? Will I get another mommy and daddy?"

Brock turns his head until his eyes meet mine.

And in that moment, I know.

I raise a trembling hand to his cheek. He covers my hand with his, looks back at Maysie, and gives a slow nod. "God's taken care of that, sweet girl. You're going to be just fine."

Zoe and Adam leave early Sunday morning. She'll drop him back at school, then head to Princeton. I'm sorry to see them go, but I'm glad they were here. It did my heart good.

Brock, Mitch, and Clarice leave for New York later this afternoon.

It's surprisingly warm for early March, and after a lunch of roast beef with all the trimmings and Clarice's famous English sherry trifle, Brock says he wants to go to the greenhouse.

Mitch stares at me across the table and I know what he's thinking. His brother's brain has finally succumbed to the incredible pain he's been battling these last few weeks. I clench my fists in my lap and look away.

"What a wonderful idea!" Clarice cries, already on her feet.

Maysie is just as enthusiastic, but Kevin grabs my hand as we get up from the table and gives me a questioning look.

"Just go with it." I'm beyond the brink of normal exhaustion now, both longing for and dreading the hour they leave, the moment Kevin and I will take charge of Maysie.

We make a motley crew as we shuffle through the house, Kevin and Mitch on either side of Brock, supporting him, Clarice marching along with her walking stick, and Willow ambling beside her. Maysie skips around us like we're going to a Fourth of July parade and the two puppies tumble over one another with yips and tiny barks that make me smile despite the overwhelming sadness suffocating my heart.

Clarice pushes open the glass door that connects the kitchen to the greenhouse and hot, perfumed air hits my face. She steps inside and I hear her happy sigh.

Kevin and Mitch half carry Brock in and I follow after Maysie.

I knew it would be this way.

The long room is more beautiful than I have ever seen it, dripping with moisture and hope and promises in full bloom, bright flowers and lush green plants at every turn, just the way it was when I first stepped foot in here so many weeks ago.

"You guys did all this? In winter?" Mitch has his lawyer face on as he stares first at me, then at his aunt, his expression one of utter amazement and definite disbelief. Clarice and I exchange a knowing look. For all our efforts, somehow we sensed the task was beyond us. The real gift was the challenge of our faith. The challenge to see past the improbable likelihood of anything growing in here again.

To push aside what the world would deem impossible and hold out for the miracle.

"No, Matlock." I bend down and pluck a red hibiscus from an overcrowded bush. "We didn't do any of this."

Laughter tickles my throat and I share Brock's smile as they lower him onto a nearby bench.

"Butterflies!" Maysie gives a squeak of delight and goes chasing after them, her patent leather shoes crunching on pristine white gravel, colliding with her giggles.

Mitch sits next to Brock and drapes an arm around his shoulder. They wear identical grins that make my eyes water. Clarice nods her satisfaction, takes a seat on Brock's other side, and loops her arm through his.

Kevin stands behind me and pulls me against him. " 'Have I gone mad?' " he whispers.

I laugh quietly, grab hold of his hands, and finish the Alice quote. " 'I'm afraid so. You're entirely bonkers. But I'll tell you a secret. All the best people are.' "

"What am I seeing?" He's serious now. "How is this possible?" He's more astounded than I was that first day I walked in here and saw the beauty in the brokenness.

"Oh, Kev." I lean into him with a smile, inhale the heady scent of jasmine, watch the shiny blue butterflies, and let the tears trail down my cheeks. "You're seeing everything we don't deserve, but somehow get. It's the miracle of faith. Grace.

And hope." I tip my face toward his and catch the wonder in his eyes. "Isn't it glorious?"

"It is indeed." Kevin smiles and looks at me a long time. And then my husband nods, pulls me closer, and kisses me.

Epilogue

"Gratitude bestows reverence, allowing us
to encounter everyday epiphanies, those
transcendent moments of awe that change
forever how we experience life and the world."
—JOHN MILTON

CHRISTMAS EVE

Some days it's hard to believe my heart was in so much turmoil this time last year.

We have been greatly blessed.

The package arrives for Maysie on the exact day Mitch said it would. We don't see much of him, but he calls on Skype once a week, and the two of them talk for as long as I'll let them, which usually means Maysie stays up past bedtime. He always manages to have her in stitches of laughter before the conversation is finished.

Last time he visited he brought along a nice young woman. A state prosecutor, around his age, never married, no kids. I'm sure their dinner conversations are more than interesting. I wouldn't put money on it, but I have a feeling Mitchell Chandler might actually grow up one of these days.

Our new house in the Berkshires is modest

compared to the one we sold in Boston, seven months ago. But when I walk through the rambling rooms with their warm wood paneling and brightly colored walls and stacks of books in practically every corner, I've never felt more at home. Or more at peace.

We're not far from my parents' lake house, and Clarice trundles down the driveway in her clanking Chevrolet every day for tea, promptly at 4:00 p.m., laden with baked goods and flowers. Always flowers.

Maysie has settled in at the local school and is of course excelling in nearly every subject, but especially in English. Her teacher tells us she's going to make a fine writer one day.

I knew that already.

The adoption will be final next week, just before New Year's. And then we're all flying to Orlando, to Disney World, as a family. Maysie will legally be ours. We've asked her if she wants to keep Brock's surname, and in the end she decided she would like to be called Maysie Chandler-Barrington.

Because it sounds like poetry.

Kevin spends his days at the bookstore in town.

Hearing Brock had gone into cardiac arrest on the operating table wasn't the shock it should have been. In a way, I think he'd prepared me for it. I think he was prepared for it. And so, when Mitch sat down with us at some point during the devastating days that followed, I knew what was coming. Knew that Brock had asked Kevin if we would become Maysie's legal guardians, adopt her. What I wasn't expecting was the bookstore.

Brock bought the place before he left for New York and put the deed in our names. All we had to do was decide what improvements and changes to make, turn the key, and let the construction crew in to work their magic. We planned everything in great detail, down to the exact position of the coffee counter and Brock's portrait on the wall above it. Kevin calls it the dartboard, but he hasn't thrown anything at it yet.

Brock only asked that we use the name he picked. And he chose quite well, I think.

Second Chances.

We smile each time we walk beneath the sign.

"Halloo, anybody home?" Kevin gives his usual greeting and shakes snow off his hair as he enters the living room late that afternoon, brown paper parcel in hand. Maysie hops up from her position on the floor where she's been playing with Hope and Watson. Adam and Zoe are running last-minute errands, and she was miffed that she had to stay home. But she never stays mad for long.

She runs to Kevin, and he scoops her under one arm and spins her in a wide circle. "Well, if it isn't the most beautiful girl in the world!" He props her up and she smacks a kiss on his cheek.

Our two dogs, puppies no more, jump around them, eager for attention as well.

"Don't forget Mommy."

"Oh no, I would never do that." He sends me a wink and shrugs out of his coat while Maysie makes short work of opening the package.

A book and two envelopes slip out, one addressed to her and one for me.

And there's a DVD.

Maysie checks out the book, grins, and hands that to me as well.

She sits cross-legged on the floor and reads her letter in silence. "It's from my daddy," she whispers, looking up through wonder-filled, teary eyes.

Kevin crouches by the TV and fiddles with the DVD player for longer than he needs to, and I know he's giving me time. So I look down at the book and smile when I read the title.

Savannah's Gift
A NOVEL
by B.J. Chandler

With shaking hands, I slide open the envelope, take out one thin, crème-colored page, and blink down at Brock's loopy handwriting.

Hey, darlin' (just for old time's sake).
So . . . if you're reading this, I suppose it's the end of the road for me.
But I'll never forget the day it began.

Thank you for your light, your laughter, and your love.

You were a gift I never expected.

And I'll say it now, because you won't have to say it back.

I love you, Savannah.

Always,
Brock

"We must be willing to let go of the life we have planned, so as to have the life that is waiting for us."—Joseph Campbell

I nod, breathe deeply, fold the letter, place it in the pocket of my sweater, and smile at Kevin as he lowers himself beside me and we wait for Maysie to finish.

"We can watch it now." She pushes her blond hair back, then plops in between us. The screen flickers and then Brock's face is grinning at us. My heart clenches and Kevin tightens his grip on my shoulder.

"Hey, y'all." His smile is just as I remember it and I'm already crying.

"Hi, Daddy," Maysie breathes, then looks up at us with a little grin.

"Hey, Savannah." Brock sits back and smiles real slow. I shake my head and press back tears, joyous laughter inching up just the same. He quirks a brow and gives the camera a knowing look. "Kevin. I trust you're behaving yourself."

"Dude." Kevin sighs and chokes up a bit, and I catch him wiping the back of his hand across his face.

Brock talks for a few minutes, mainly to Maysie. Tells her how much he loves her, hopes everything is going great . . . I won't remember half of what he said, but that's okay because I know we'll watch it again. And again.

"Well, I guess that's it." Brock adjusts the Braves cap on his head and stares at us for a long, heartbreakingly silent moment. "I love you. And I'll see you when I see you."

"See you when I see you," Maysie says softly.

And the three of us sit there, unable to move, unwilling to give up this astounding gift we've been given too soon.

Then Kevin sits forward and squeezes my leg. "Savannah . . . do you . . . see . . ."

I blink tears and focus on the screen again. The room gets very warm. And then I see her. Sitting on the couch behind Brock, her nose in a book, as it so often was.

How I wish I could see the title of that book. But I don't really need to.

Whether what we're seeing is real or imagined is of little consequence.

In this moment, it is our gift.

She looks up, right before he says good-bye, and smiles.

The most beautiful smile I have ever seen.

One I thought I'd never see on this earth again.

The screen goes black and we both sit back. Kevin and I stare at each other in wonder. Chill bumps crawl up my arms and I steady my ragged breathing. Kevin takes my trembling hand in his and kisses it, his other hand resting on Maysie's head. "You okay, kiddo?"

"Uh-huh." She leans into his chest with a satisfied sigh. "Didja see my angel?"

Kevin and I lock eyes. But then he nods, smiling through tears. "I think we did."

Maysie gives another little sigh and reaches up to play with my hair the way she likes to do when she's sleepy.

"She doesn't come play with me anymore. She has to look after Daddy now. And she told me I have to look after you." Her smile says this is the coolest thing in the world.

And I have to agree.

A Note from the Author

Some final words . . .

Honestly? I didn't want to write this book.

In fact, I almost pushed the idea aside. Except I could see the story playing out like a movie, which doesn't usually happen until I have a few chapters written. So I figured I better pay attention. And I began to write.

I believe stories are God-breathed. I ask God to give me the words, to show me the story, and it's always a collaborative effort. But, as Savannah's story began to unfold, I had questions. Like, really? Adultery? You really want me to write about this? But even as I questioned, the words flowed. Never have I written a book so quickly and so easily, though I worried about the subject matter. Adultery. The loss of a child. Suicide.

You can see why I didn't want to write it, can't you?

I wrestled with this story on a soul-searching level, praying for the sensitivity needed to address such tough issues. As always, God was faithful. Unbeknownst to me, while I was writing, two dear friends were dealing with the unimaginable—learning they were no longer loved, no longer wanted, by the person who had promised to love them forever.

Maybe you know the pain that kind of betrayal brings. As we walked alongside our dear friends on this unexpected journey, I knew our lives would also be forever changed. Sometimes forgiveness seems out of reach, doesn't it? Impossible. We put up walls of protection. And it becomes harder to believe in happily ever after.

Here is where I struggled. What kind of ending would I give Savannah?

Eventually, I knew she would get the ending she deserved, the one we all deserve. But I am mindful that happy endings don't always happen. If you're reading this thinking, how nice for her, but that's not my reality, please know I hear you. And I mourn with you for that loss. But I also pray you find some hope here within these words.

I pray that you know you are still loved and cherished by the One who formed you in your mother's womb. The One who knew your name before you took your first breath. I pray you know that great love to the very depths of your soul, because it's the only thing that truly sustains us when we can't take one more step. I pray you know you are not alone.

Finally, thank you. Thank you for reading

Where Hope Begins. For trusting me with such a heavy topic, and allowing me to share this difficult, yet hope-filled story with you.

With Love,
Catherine

"Hope begins in the dark, the stubborn hope that if you just show up and try to do the right thing, the dawn will come. You wait and watch and work: you don't give up."

–Anne Lamott

Acknowledgments

The writing of a book does not happen overnight. And, while the writer may write alone, they are always in need of support from friends and family.

This one took so much. Each chapter presented a new challenge. I needed a place to go to laugh and vent and simply get away from the heavy thoughts for a while. Thank you to my wonderful friends who gather under the auspicious name of The Spice Girls—we may not sing together, but along with being incredibly talented authors in your own right, you are skilled in encouragement, hilarity, and prayer support, and I'm so thankful for each of you.

Rochelle and Lydia . . . it has been an honor and a blessing to watch you navigate the new roads you find yourselves on. You are brave, strong, and an example of everything a godly woman should be. You've both always been so encouraging to me, but these past few years, your courage has astounded me. I am honored to call you friends, and I thank you for sharing your heart with me on so many occasions. And for praying for this story, and for me.

My wonderful friend and agent, Rachelle Gardner—another dream becomes a reality, thanks to your perseverance and hard work and godly counsel. I will never forget the day I opened my email to find one from you entitled "WOW"—your first reaction after reading this book. You have no idea how much that encouraged me! Thank you for walking alongside me on this exciting journey. It definitely wouldn't be happening without you!

Thanks must go to all my dear friends near and far who make me smile and force me to go out for lunch or get on Skype and interact with humans! LeeAnne, I always treasure our times together and thank you for always being a phone call away. Cathy K., I miss singing with you and laughing with you, but I know you're always praying and I appreciate that more than you know! Beth Vogt, our Skype chats pour life and hope and encouragement into me. While I wish they were in person over coffee talks, I'm definitely looking forward to the next time we get to see each other. Thanks for all the advice, the laughter, the love, and the friendship! Jennifer M., your early reads as I was furiously writing chapter after chapter pushed me forward, made me laugh, and gave me hope that I really was onto something—thank you for the time!

And my wonderful readers for always providing support and encouragement with each book, I'm so grateful I get to share my words with you!

And thanks go to so many other supportive souls in my online writing communities, ACFW, and the Books & Such group—I would truly be lost without you.

A book cannot publish itself, and I am, as always, truly grateful to the amazing team at HarperCollins Christian Publishing for everything that happens behind the scenes before a story becomes a real book! Thanks to all who gave wonderful insight and helped shape the story into what it is today, Becky Monds, Erin Healy, and Jodi Hughes. I'm sorry (not sorry) I made you guys cry. Amanda, Kristen, Allison, and Paul, and countless others, thank you for all the work it takes to launch a book and make an author feel confident! And I have to say this cover blew me away!

To my truly incredible family—I would be miserable without you. To the Canadian clan, thanks for always being hilarious. I love it when we're all gathered in one place: so many kids, so much love and laughter. To my sister and family in the US, I'm so grateful for you and treasure each time we're together.

My kids—Sarah and Christopher—you are our greatest blessings and we thank you for the other blessings you have brought into our lives—Randy, and Deni, and of course precious Annabel, who lights up every day with her smiles and giggles and big baby hugs and smushy kisses.

I am awed by God's goodness in giving me each of you.

And of course, to my one and only love, Stephen. There really aren't words to express my heart. Thank you for the continual support, encouragement, and for telling everyone about your wife the author . . . even though it's embarrassing. Thank you for all the dinners in, the dinners out, and the margaritas. And for just being there, even when I'm in writer zone and not fit for human company. I love you beyond everything.

Thank you, Jesus, for the words, for the redemption, and for the promise of a thousand tomorrows with you.

DISCUSSION QUESTIONS

1. *Where Hope Begins* deals with some very difficult issues—adultery, suicide, loss of a child. Which situation in the novel impacted you most and how did it speak to you?

2. Tragic events can have a lasting impact on our lives. As Paul says to Savannah, tragedy can either draw a couple closer or drive them apart. How do you think Kevin and Savannah coped with the loss of Shelby, and what do you think they could have done differently?

3. The family's favorite book is *Alice's Adventures in Wonderland*. Do you have a favorite book or a "family book" that has been read so often you can quote from it?

4. Was there a particular character you were drawn to? What appealed to you most about them?

5. Which scene or chapter in the novel did you find most challenging?

6. Despite Kevin's unfaithfulness, Savannah feels guilt over her relationship with Brock and her growing feelings for him. Do you think she judged herself too harshly given the circumstances?

7. Savannah carries a huge burden, blaming herself for Shelby's death, and feels judged

by many—the church, her sister-in-law, even some friends. Why do you think it seems easier for people to judge and criticize, instead of offering grace?

8. Clarice's greenhouse becomes a refuge for Savannah: a place where anything can happen, if she has enough faith. Did you appreciate the symbolism of the greenhouse for what it was?

9. Like Savannah, have you been in a place where you didn't have the strength to pray anymore? What happened?

10. Readers will no doubt have different views on Maysie's guardian angel. Do you believe in angels?

11. Clarice has many wise words for Savannah, including "Sometimes God allows us to glimpse the beauty within the brokenness." Have you seen beauty even when hopes and dreams have been shattered?

12. Brock knows his condition is terminal. Did you empathize with him as he acted on his attraction to Savannah, or did you think he was being selfish?

13. When you turned the final page, what emotions did you experience?

About the Author

Catherine West writes stories of hope and healing from her island home in Bermuda. When she's not at the computer working on her next story, you can find her taking her Border collie for long walks on the beach or tending to her roses and orchids. She and her husband have two grown children. Visit her online at catherinejwest.com.

Facebook: CatherineJWest
Twitter: @cathwest

Center Point Large Print
600 Brooks Road / PO Box 1
Thorndike, ME 04986-0001 USA

(207) 568-3717

US & Canada:
1 800 929-9108
www.centerpointlargeprint.com